Praise for the
Home Repair Is Homicide mysteries
of Sarah Graves

"Readers won't be able to put this page-turner down—but it will certainly make them think twice about vacationing at that Maine lakeside cottage."
—LESLIE MEIER,
author of *Chocolate Covered Murder*

"Sarah Graves continues successfully reinventing her much beloved Home Repair Is Homicide series. *Dead Level* is a terrific thriller and an all-around treat, bearing Graves's trademarks: edgy traditional mysteries peppered liberally with humor, and sprinkled with layered, well-written characters. This series is better than ever!"
—JULIA SPENCER-FLEMING, *New York Times*
bestselling author of *One Was a Soldier*

"Memorable characters and helpful household tips enhance a dark cozy that will keep the reader turning the pages until the surprising and dramatic conclusion."
—*Publishers Weekly*

"Blends do-it-yourself home repair tips into a very suspenseful murder mystery, with well-depicted characters and plenty of action. . . . Always staying one suspenseful step ahead of the deductive reader, this scary story nails it."
—Fredericksburg *Free Lance-Star*

"Graves transcends the boundaries of the conventional mystery by allowing her protagonists to indulge in heroics that land them in the shark-infested waters of the thriller."
—*Library Journal* (starred review)

"Reigning master of the [cozy] genre."
—*Romantic Times*

"A fast-paced tale of hide-and-seek . . . exciting and entertaining . . . If you are a mystery fan, you will love it."
—*Galveston County Daily News*

"Relentless pacing, an appealing heroine and perfectly loathsome antagonists will more than satisfy series fans."
—*Publishers Weekly*

"This first-rate thriller features nail-biting suspense that ensnares the reader to the final page. . . . Full of courageous women and compelling action. Highly recommended."
—*Library Journal* (starred review)

"Laugh-out-loud funny and laid with enough false trails to delude a troop of Boy Scouts. But they shake it out to a terrifying finale."
—*Romantic Times*

"This Home Repair Is Homicide series is more fun than a soap."
—*Booknews* from The Poisoned Pen

"Sarah Graves has a vibrant and colorful way of creating memorable scenes and characters. Home improvement tips scattered throughout the book add a little extra charm in this cozy home improvement mystery."
—*Fresh Fiction*

"When it comes to mixing cozy suspense with do-it-yourself home repair, Sarah Graves . . . has the blueprint for success."
—*Quoddy Tides*

"Reliable entertainment for fans who enjoy nooks, crannies, subplots, and carpentry tips."
—*Kirkus Reviews*

"Home repair is Graves's gimmick, and she uses it very successfully. But it is her light, humorous tone and well-chosen cast of characters that grow and evolve from novel to novel; her obvious love for coastal Maine and its inhabitants; and her ability to marry all of those ingredients to serviceable plots that make this a series whose popularity will continue to grow."
—*Alfred Hitchcock Mystery Magazine*

"Entertaining . . . a nicely drawn cast of characters, both human and animal, plus humor built around domestic bliss and angst, personal foibles and outrageous situations, all make for plenty of cozy fun."
—*Publishers Weekly*

"Hours of cozy entertainment."
—*Kirkus Reviews*

BY SARAH GRAVES

The Dead Cat Bounce
Triple Witch
Wicked Fix
Repair to Her Grace
Wreck the Halls
Unhinged
Mallets Aforethought
Tool & Die
Nail Biter
Trap Door
The Book of Old Houses
A Face at the Window
Crawlspace
Knockdown
Dead Level
A Bat in the Belfry

A BAT IN THE BELFRY

A
Home Repair Is Homicide
Mystery

SARAH GRAVES

BANTAM BOOKS • NEW YORK

2014 Bantam Books Mass Market Edition

Copyright © 2013 by Sarah Graves
Excerpt from *Winter at the Door* copyright © 2014 by Sarah Graves

Published in the United States by Bantam Books, an imprint of Random House, a division of Random House LLC, a Penguin Random House Company, New York.

BANTAM BOOKS and the HOUSE colophon are registered trademarks of Random House LLC.

Originally published in hardcover in the United States by Bantam Books, an imprint of The Random House Publishing Group, a division of Random House LLC in 2013.

This book contains an excerpt from the forthcoming book *Winter at the Door* by Sarah Graves. This excerpt has been set for this edition only and may not reflect the final content of the forthcoming edition.

ISBN 978-0-345-53500-9
eBook ISBN 978-0-345-53858-1

Cover design: Jamie S. Warren
Cover images: VisionsofAmerica/Joe Sohm/Getty Images

Printed in the United States of America

www.bantamdell.com

9 8 7 6 5 4 3 2

Bantam Books mass market edition: April 2014

A BAT IN
THE BELFRY

URGENT WEATHER MESSAGE
WEATHER SERVICE CARIBOU MAINE

FOR INTERIOR HANCOCK-COASTAL HANCOCK-CENTRAL WASHINGTON-COASTAL WASHINGTON-
INCLUDING THE CITIES OF . . . EASTPORT . . . PERRY . . . PEMBROKE . . . CALAIS . . . LUBEC . . . MACHIAS

. . . WEATHER ADVISORY IN EFFECT UNTIL MIDNIGHT EDT TOMORROW NIGHT . . .

THE WEATHER SERVICE IN CARIBOU HAS ISSUED A WEATHER ADVISORY FOR HEAVY RAIN AND POSSIBLE GALE FORCE WINDS.

* PRECIPITATION TYPE . . . RAIN HEAVY AT TIMES. LOCALLY AS MUCH AS 1 INCH PER HOUR.
* ACCUMULATIONS . . . RAIN 3 TO 5 INCHES TOTAL EXCEPT WHERE DOWNPOURS FREQUENT.
* TIMING . . . TODAY INTO TOMORROW NIGHT.
* TEMPERATURES . . . IN THE LOWER 40S.
* WINDS . . . NORTHEAST 35-65 MPH. WITH POSSIBLE HIGHER GUSTS ESPECIALLY COASTAL.
* IMPACTS . . . EXPECT SOME TRAVEL DIFFICULTIES. WIND DAMAGE POSSIBLE. POWER OUTAGES POSSIBLE. LOCAL FLOODING LIKELY.

PRECAUTIONARY/PREPAREDNESS ACTIONS . . . TRAVEL DELAYS MAY OCCUR. PLAN EXTRA TIME TO REACH YOUR DESTINATION. SECURE LOOSE OBJECTS.

POSTPONE TRAVEL AT HEIGHT OF STORM IF POSSIBLE.
DO NOT DRIVE THROUGH FLOODED AREAS.
THIS IS PRIMARILY A COASTAL STORM. WIND EFFECTS
WILL BE STRONGEST ON ISLANDS AND ALONG THE
SHORE. INLAND AREAS NEAR TIDAL RIVERS AND
STREAMS MAY SEE FLOODING AT TIME OF HIGH TIDES.
HIGH WINDS MAY IMPACT COMMUNICATIONS
TOWERS. EXPECT OUTAGES.

Chapter 1

To fill a small plaster crack fast,
use a flour-and-water paste
packed in with
your wet index finger.
—Tiptree's Tips

"Carolyn, if you're going to lie to me, you could at least make it a good one," Chip Hahn said sorrowfully into the phone.

He sat by the window in the upstairs front guest room of the big old house on Key Street, looking out at a late-night view of Eastport, Maine. Through the wavery antique panes in the elderly wooden windows, the full moon seemed to wobble liquidly.

Or maybe that was because he was seeing it through tears. Angrily he swiped them away, then closed his hand reflexively on the rabbit's foot hanging from a thin chain on his belt loop.

Not, he realized miserably, that the talisman he'd carried around for years was going to give him any good luck tonight. How could it? After all, it wasn't as if he hadn't known what he was getting into, becoming involved with Carolyn.

In the blue-white moonlight downhill beyond the houses of town, Passamaquoddy Bay was a pewter-colored disk. Above, a plane's contrail streaked thinly northeast through the indigo night, the aircraft itself already racing out over the Atlantic.

"Carolyn?" Two miles distant across the bay on the Canadian island of Campobello, a car's headlights appeared, then vanished.

"Carolyn, are you still there?"

She said something in reply, but he couldn't make out what. He'd forgotten how poorly his cell phone worked here in remote downeast Maine; his city phone plan was wrong for the area. But he hadn't wanted to use the landline. Someone in the house might pick up an extension and overhear this conversation.

Its tone, especially: the ragged pain in his own voice, which he tried to hide, and the carelessness in hers, which she didn't. The CD player on his laptop played the Roche sisters' first album, nearly as old as he was but in its wry lyrics and harmonies the perfect background music for him now.

"I had dinner and then a few drinks with Siobhan," Carolyn went on unconvincingly. "It got late, she let me sleep on her couch. End of story, okay?"

Through the window, he watched clouds begin streaming in gauzy tatters over the moon. Something ugly was coming, according to the weather forecast he'd heard earlier. Something . . .

"Chip?" The leafless branches of the ancient maples lining Key Street were elongated fingers, reaching out for something they could never have. *Like me,* he thought miserably, still clutching the rabbit's foot.

"Yeah," he said. "End of story." But of course it wasn't.

Silence from Carolyn, who after two days of not answering her cell or responding to his messages had at last taken his call. Now he imagined her sitting cross-legged in the oversized leather easy chair he'd bought for their apartment in Manhattan, a year ago when they'd first moved in together.

Her slim frame clad in a black leotard and a smock dress—the purple corduroy one, maybe, now that it was November and getting chilly—and her glossy dark hair falling in waves over her shoulders, she would be tapping her long nails impatiently on the chair's soft leather arm. Her high-heeled boots would be on the thick Persian rug nearby, probably, flung where she'd shed them.

"Have you eaten lately? I mean today?" he asked. She wasn't lazy, and she could be very well organized. But Carolyn had never learned to take care of herself. She had him for that. "No," she said guiltily. "But

I will. Chicken and corn, maybe. And a baked potato."

Yeah, right. The idea of her cooking a meal for herself in his absence, let alone a decent one, was beyond far-fetched. More likely she was subsisting on takeout until he got back.

If she was even eating that. But he didn't press it. "Sounds good," he told her instead, not wanting to start a quarrel. "Drink some fruit juice with it," he advised, knowing she wouldn't do that, either. In her simple obduracy Carolyn was like a stone, impenetrable unless you wanted to crush it, or break it.

And he'd never wanted to. After nearly three years' working together, he as the researcher and she the writer of a string of bestselling true-crime books, they'd become a couple, and Chip had briefly thought his life was complete. Even before they began sharing the same address he'd imagined them curled together in the leather chair, large enough to hold them both comfortably.

Just how comfortably, he had also pictured in considerable detail. But once it was delivered, Carolyn had claimed the chair as her own, her pointy knees and sharply jutting elbows fencing it off from him silently but definitively.

"Chip? You believe me, right? About last night?"

His hand felt cramped. Tucking the phone awkwardly in the crook of his neck, he heard the signature opening fanfare of *The Tonight Show with Jay Leno* coming on in the background at her end.

Good old Carolyn, the original multitasker. "Sure," Chip said, absently worrying the cuticle on his right thumb. "Like you said, you were at Siobhan's."

This too was improbable, however. Siobhan was Carolyn's editor, and in that role had proven to be an honorable, reliable friend. But she was about as likely to have a writer sleeping on the sofa in her elegant apartment overlooking Gramercy Park as she was to have bedbugs infesting it.

"I believe you," he said, since what good would it do to say otherwise? Carolyn was in Manhattan, over five hundred miles away, and he was here visiting his old friend Sam Tiptree in a place so different from the city, it felt like some other planet.

"Good." He heard relief in Carolyn's voice. It was this faint whiff of her caring that he clung to, knowing she depended on him not to give up on her or forsake her. He'd never done that either, even when he'd known her only as his employer, the writer of crime literature.

Which it was: What she wrote was never just another hack job on yet another wife-murder, child disappearance, or greed-fueled parent-slaughter, turgid tomes mixing sex, cash, and subnormal IQs to predictably gory effect. Instead, word by word and sentence by carefully crafted sentence, she presented the human elements behind the headlines, delicately and in their subtlest colors.

It was what he'd loved first about her, this freakish genius she had for communicating the emotions and motives of others while—the tragic irony of this did not escape him—possessing almost no insight into her own. But there was more.

Much more. Even now, if he'd been there he'd have gathered her in his arms, brushing aside the jutting knees and the sharp little elbows, and that would've been the end of it. For a long time her mercurial side had seemed a small price to pay for the rest of it.

All the rest of it. "You should get some sleep," he told her gently. "You're okay? You're going to be able to?"

Sleep, he meant. She wasn't any better at that than she was at eating, when he was away.

He heard her put her drink down on the low marble table that had been her only contribution to the room's decor, the little click of the glass striking stone. Even that had been grudging; if he'd left it to her they'd still be using stacked milk crates.

"I'm okay." Then: "Chip?"

"Yeah," he exhaled. All the rest of it . . . which he'd adored, and still did. The trouble was, something was changing. And in the week since he'd been away from her it had gotten worse, this feeling of not being able to bear the few things he didn't adore.

A lot worse. "Chip, could you do me a favor? Call up Maury Cahill for me, ask if I could go in and see him for a minute?"

Chip felt his mental eyebrows rising; Cahill was a criminal lawyer specializing in the kinds of scandalously illegal antics rich people's kids got up to, keeping them out of Rikers and off the front pages of newspapers.

Maury's son had been Chip's classmate at prep school; they still got together for a beer once in a while. But why might Carolyn need his old school pal's dad?

"It's for a friend," she assured him hastily but unconvincingly. Still, if she or her "friend" needed a lawyer, she had picked a good one.

And a request from Chip would indeed produce the desired appointment. So he agreed to phone Maury Cahill in the morning, then made a mental note to check in with him again later in the day. The old attorney wouldn't violate any oaths, but if Carolyn was in real trouble he'd probably give Chip a general heads-up.

"Thanks," said Carolyn. "I'm sorry I didn't call you."

"Right." He knew she was sorry. That wasn't the point. "Get some rest. Just . . . go on to bed. You'll be all right tomorrow."

Would he be, though? The trouble was, he was beginning not to be sure how much longer he could take the situation before something bad happened. He drew his gaze from the moonlit rooftops, skeletal tree shapes, and the few warmly lit windows still visible in the village of Eastport at this late hour, and from the metallically gleaming bay. Here in this room the softly hissing radiator and the wallpaper's faded florals lent the sense that everything might still be fine, that he could get through this somehow.

His shirts and slacks hung on hangers in the tiny closet, but his socks and underwear were still in his suitcase, open on one of the plain pine twin beds. The room-size rug was a threadbare Persian long missing its fringes, indigo and red.

The bedspreads, white chenille, smelled of soap and bleach. "Listen," he told Carolyn. "Tomorrow you'll work, and you'll feel fine. And when I come home, we'll look at my new research together, all right?"

Across the room on a round wooden table were

heaped his open laptop, stacks of papers, and spiral notebooks, preliminary materials having to do with a series of killings in Milwaukee two years earlier. If all went well, the crimes were to be the subject of his and Carolyn's next book.

Atop the heap lay a photograph of a human torso, or what was left of it after someone got done with the acts he'd committed upon it. All told—if indeed all had been told; the perpetrator had died in jail of a heart attack before he finished confessing—there were a dozen photos like this. All were taken by the killer while committing the crimes, about one per month during the time he had been active.

Which was another thing nobody was sure of: *How long?* And its corollary, *How many?* The accused man had said a year, but his methods were sophisticated. His staging of tableaux, especially, was what the FBI analyst out of Madison had termed "fully developed."

"Yes, Chip, I'll sleep," Carolyn agreed, sounding subdued. "And work sounds good."

The victims in the dozen photographs had all been young women. These were the only known photographs in the series, but a new cache of them might yet turn up, Chip believed, because the police weren't the only ones who had seen the pictures. Long before his capture, the killer had also posted them on the Web, in private chat rooms Chip had found while following obscure links the way a hound sniffs scent.

He'd phoned and emailed the Wisconsin authorities in case they didn't already know about the websites, but hadn't heard back yet. He'd never have found the sites himself if his own research talents weren't as prodigious as Carolyn's writing chops.

But through long practice and stubborn persistence, Chip could click his way unerringly to a needle in an electronic haystack; thus he'd discovered the forums where the gruesome pictures had resided, and since then memories of what else he'd seen and read there clung dankly to the inside of his head. *Chat rooms for killers,* he thought, *what a concept.*

"Good night, Chip," Carolyn said. "I love you."

"I love you, too," he answered, because he did.

He truly did. "Good night," he added, and hung up.

Only then did he realize that while he and Carolyn were talking, he'd torn off the strip of cuticle he'd been worrying without even feeling it, and now the rabbit's foot he always carried was smeared with his own bright red blood.

Just across the hall in his own room, Chip's old friend Sam Tiptree was also having problems with women.

Two women, to be precise.

WHERE R U? W8TNG W8TNG W8TNG

The first one, pretty and fun-loving Carol Stedman, had been texting him all evening. She wouldn't take no for an answer, which under other circumstances he tended to find attractive.

He supposed he should have known that she was going to be a difficult girlfriend; from the start, she had not by any means been a safe bet. He'd met Carol while she and a guy she'd been traveling with were wreaking small-town havoc—no violence, and the money and stolen car were recovered, but still—in Eastport, and this had been an omen of things to come, relationship-wise.

I HV SMTHNG 4 U . . .

I'll bet, Sam thought. He'd never been convinced by the new leaf Carol had sworn she'd turned over.

Still, she was lively and irreverent and game for all kinds of delightful adventures. Tall and athletic, she'd even sampled new-to-her activities like kayaking and camping, things that involved getting dirty, wearing clunky boots, or carrying your toilet paper along with you into the woods (or all three), and she had ended up really liking the outdoorsy stuff.

Or at least she did as long as it was liberally diluted by weekends in downtown Portland, on tours of bars, clubs, films, concerts by bands he'd never heard of, and plenty of time in bed.

"Sam? Are you still there?" The voice, not Carol's, came from the phone he held to his ear, the land-line handset because his cell was being occupied by Carol's messages.

"Are you *texting* someone while I'm talking to you?"

This voice belonged to Maggie, the other young woman in Sam's life. A longtime friend, she had gradually turned into much more; for a while there'd been a clear, unspoken sense between them that they would marry, sooner or later.

That it was inevitable, which was what had spooked him, he guessed. "Uh, no," he managed while his thumbs moved deftly. "Why would you think that?"

TOLD U NOT COMING SORRY. He pressed Send.

"The way you breathe when you're texting. And I can hear it, the way your sleeves rustle a certain way or something. So stop it. What's she trying to do, anyway, get you to go out?"

Carol was at a party on the mainland, on the Golding Road near Boyden Lake in Perry. She'd been cajoling him to join her since nine-thirty. But he had early plans tomorrow, with Chip.

"She just wants somebody to drive her home," he told Maggie, thus leaving himself an out in case he changed his mind, decided he did want to go. After all, as a recovering alcoholic himself, he couldn't refuse a designated-driver request, could he?

"Uh-huh," said Maggie skeptically. "She wants somebody to do something, all right. You're just the handiest doer."

Sam laughed. "You're bad." But he liked it. No one else he knew talked that way. Maggie was smart, way smarter than he was, and so thoroughly down-to-earth, her sense of humor embarrassed even him sometimes.

"No, just accurate," she shot back. She took no guff, and she was talented, too, at the violin as well as at a number of other activities he very much enjoyed.

"Yeah, well," was all he could muster. He never could win a verbal jousting match with Maggie, which was relaxing, actually, once he'd gotten used to it. And on top of all that, she was no-kidding gorgeous, a big, red-cheeked, luscious-lipped brunette with so many curves, he still hadn't managed to find them all.

And he didn't want to stop trying. "You're not going to go, though, right?" she asked.

A tearful emoticon popped up in the text message box on his phone. R U COMING? MISS U. ♥ ♥ ♥ ♥ ☺

Unfortunately, this time Maggie heard the small *bloop* sound his cell made, notifying him of the new message.

"I thought you said you weren't texting." In the background at her place, a jazz violin CD was playing.

"But I can't stop people from sending texts, can I?" he asked, realizing too late what the answer to that was.

"You could shut your cell off." *Genius,* she didn't add. "But I have to go now, I've still got some practicing to do."

"Oh," he said. He'd been about to suggest that he come over to her place. Just talking to her had reminded him pleasantly of all those curves, whose mysteries he now felt inspired to have another go at solving. His own room, with its plaid-covered twin beds and clutter of electronic gadgets looked down on by posters of sports heroes, seemed all at once unbearably male.

Maggie's place was a lush cave of velvet upholstery, soft rugs, and the smell of Constant Comment tea. She kept apples in a bowl on her table, and a clean white terrycloth bathrobe in her bedroom closet especially for him.

R U COMING W8NG 4 U ??? NOT DOING GR8 PLZ

Also, as Carol's tipsy-sounding new text message reminded him, Maggie didn't drink. That wasn't a biggie for Sam, whose taste for alcohol nowadays was (*thankyouthankyou*) just about nonexistent.

"Sam?" Maggie's voice was gentle. "I'm hanging up now."

Refusing to drive him into Carol's arms by nagging him was what Maggie called this tactic—she was perfectly open with him about it—and he had to admit that so far tonight it had worked.

Unfortunately, it also meant that there was no chance of his getting to wear that white terrycloth bathrobe this evening, or pursuing activities that usually preceded his wearing of it, either. The sports heroes on his posters seemed to smirk down at him knowingly.

Chump, their looks seemed to say. *This Maggie, she's a line drive, right down the middle. So whatchoo want with a pop fly?*

Easy for you to say, he thought at the poster athletes for whom pop flies were no doubt a regular occurrence. "Okay," he said aloud, but once he'd hung up, he felt ridiculously lonely and unsettled. His phone blooped again; without looking at the text box, he shut the thing off.

The room was suddenly very quiet, and the big old house all around him was, also; in another hour, it would be midnight. Carol was still waiting, probably, but the idea of giving Maggie the idea that he was staying home, then going out to some party the minute he'd hung up, just didn't hit him right.

Which was how Maggie had planned it, of course, but that didn't change the fact: he was in for the evening. Idly snapping his penlight on and off—the blue plastic promotional item bore the name of his employer, Eastport Sailyard & Marina, Ltd.—as he leaned back in his office chair, propped his sneakered feet on the door-atop-two-filing-cabinets he used for a desk, and stared at the long crack in the plaster ceiling above him.

So. Here he was, all woken up and nowhere to go, or at any rate nowhere that he wanted to. In the bad old days, he could've solved this problem, toot sweet: fire up a joint, break out the Bushmills, and have himself a nice, companionable little party of one. But not anymore.

His landline phone jangled. He quickly shut the ringer off so it wouldn't wake up the rest of the house: his grandparents, his mother and his stepfather, Wade Sorenson, and Sam's houseguest, Chip, who'd gone to his room early and was by now probably sound asleep.

The caller was almost certainly Carol, wanting to try by her voice what she hadn't succeeded at accomplishing via text. Getting up, he snapped off the lamp on his desk, leaving on only the lava lamp that Carol had given him for a joke of the "look what the old folks used to like!" variety.

Now the lamp's tall glass cylinder seemed to smolder from within, its hypnotic swirlings of green, orange, and dark purple oddly pleasant in the dim room. *Maybe the old hippies were on to something,* he thought, but then the silence hit him again.

He didn't feel like watching TV or playing video games, and his chronic dyslexia made reading for pleasure an oxymoron. But he enjoyed being read to, and he had the audio version of Simon Winchester's *Atlantic* on his iPod. So he cued that up.

Fifteen minutes later, he'd washed and brushed his teeth. By some trick of light, the young man looking back at him from the bathroom mirror, with his curly dark hair and long lantern jaw, so much resembled his dead father that Sam had startled briefly, thinking he was seeing his dad's ghost.

But of course he wasn't. Now he padded downstairs; at this late hour, the big old kitchen with its tall bare windows and beadboard wainscoting was a shadowy, clean-smelling cave. Only a night-light burned by the soapstone sink.

The woodstove in the corner made faint crinkling sounds as Sam passed it carrying his snack of cookies and milk. The two dogs curled in their beds near the stove shifted, muttering, but didn't get up as Sam checked the door leading out to his stepfather's workshop, where guns were repaired and where a variety of other weapons were stored, too, to make sure that it was locked.

His guest, Chip Hahn, had been fascinated with the hunting knives in the workshop when he'd gotten the tour from Sam's stepdad this afternoon. Glancing out the kitchen window, Sam wondered idly if any of the knives or other implements his stepdad owned might make it into one of the books Chip researched and cowrote.

Or maybe Chip was just being polite as usual. Sam peered up at the sky where a full moon with a rainbow ring around it hung hazily, the ring promising rain though the sky was a moonlight-infused blue, the ragged clouds of earlier dissolved away.

But if the weather forecast held, that clear sky was only temporary, and the ring around the moon sealed the deal as far as Sam was concerned. *Rats,* he thought; he might have to postpone tomorrow's kay-aking trip with Chip, and he'd been hoping for at least a day away from both his unnervingly demand-ing girlfriends.

A week, actually, wouldn't be too much. The strong wish for radio silence on the romantic front, building in him quietly over the past month or so, suddenly felt huge as he headed back down the hall past the massive old cast-iron hot-water radiators and under the front foyer's antique chandelier, to the stairs.

Heaped near a metal stepladder leaning against the front hall radiator was a collection of patching and painting supplies that Sam's mother was using to repair the hallway's ornate acorn-and-grapeleaf-patterned tin ceiling: a roll of duct tape, a tin of white-tinted Kilz metal primer, the painting tray, and a new, still-in-the-wrapper extra-thick paint roller and roller handle.

There were other collections like this one all over the old house, as his mother—a fervent if not neces-sarily very expert home-repair enthusiast—got ready for a long winter of indoor projects. If only he had some massive project planned, too, Sam thought as his hand slid along the curved oaken banister, its sur-face smoothed by two hundred years of people going up to bed in this house. Some excuse not to see Carol *or* Maggie for a while. Something he had to do, im-portant and all-consuming . . .

But both young women knew his job schedule at the boatyard, and knew, too, that except for it, his time was his own. Or theirs, whichever one of them won the fight they seemed to be waging for it.

Flattering, he guessed, but also confusing; sighing,

he climbed the stairs, got into bed, and put the iPod's earbuds into his ears. As he settled back against heaped pillows, the audiobook began playing and the author's own voice began narrating a story of an ocean voyage that he himself had taken when he was only eighteen, and of a curious incident that had punctuated it.

Sam sighed with happy anticipation: a curious incident! But then he noticed that he'd left the window shades up and the lava lamp on, its colorfully smoky swirls roiling lazily like the crayon-hued eruption of some miniature underwater volcano.

Drat, he thought, and crossed the room once more to snap the lamp off. He tucked a penlight into the pocket of the pants he'd be wearing tomorrow so he'd have it with him at work; the thing was surprisingly handy. Then he turned to lower the window shade.

Which was how he noticed that Chip Hahn was not sound asleep in his room at all but obviously wide awake, slipping silently down the front walk and away down the street, toward downtown and the gleaming bay.

The rabbit's foot Chip had always carried ever since Sam had known him flashed whitely in the shimmering moonlight, the good-luck talisman dangling as it always did from the dully glinting chain clipped to his friend's belt loop.

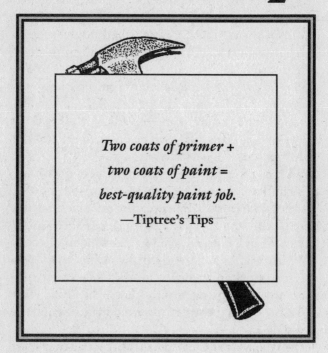

*Two coats of primer +
two coats of paint =
best-quality paint job.*

—Tiptree's Tips

If the huge bell hulking silently in the tower of the two-hundred-year-old All Faith Chapel in Eastport, Maine, had been working that night, none of the rest of it would have happened.

Or at any rate it wouldn't have happened there, or to her, because she wouldn't have been able to gain entry to the belfry at all and neither would the person who followed her in.

Decades earlier, when the bell still did ring out the hours and the half hours, the door to the enclosed stairs leading up to the slatted-in belfry was kept locked, because it was well known that the bell's monstrous peal could flat-out kill a man unlucky or careless enough to experience it at close range.

But not anymore. All Faith Chapel, built in 1824 a stone's throw from the larger and more respectable Hope Lutheran, was the second house of worship on the aptly named Two Church Lane. Meant as an alternative to the traditionally doctrined Hope, in its foursquare construction, white-clapboarded height, and towering spire, it resembled its huge neighbor so closely as to be almost a twin, right down (or up, in fact) to its massive (and massively troublesome, eventually) old bell.

Cast in 1819 and finally hung in the belfry at All Faith in 1825, the bell first malfunctioned while bonging out the news of World War II's end in Europe. The tidings, so welcome at first, grew calamitous when the bell didn't stop but instead clanged on deafeningly for hours, terrifying the horses and causing local farmers' pregnant pigs to abort. People swore later they'd heard it in Bangor, and that it scared schools of codfish right out of the icy salt water of Passamaquoddy Bay, local people gathering up the still-flopping silvery victims in baskets.

Once the din stopped, the church's custodian had scrambled up four flights and a rickety ladder to where the big bell still vibrated, the air inside the belfry humming, he said later, like a million maddened bees. He unhooked the flywheel from the clock-driven timing mechanism (praying all the while that the thing wouldn't start up again before he got done, and scramble his own mechanisms) and was forever afterwards regarded as a hero.

But even though he'd stopped any chance of the bell ringing uncontrollably—that is, by stopping it altogether—he was not able to fix it. Oh, he got it jiggered around so that when it ran it would strike the hour, all right, but not the *correct* hour. The bell wouldn't turn off for the night anymore, either, a problem for neighbors who wanted to sleep more than thirty minutes at a stretch.

Still, at first it was thought that the trouble might be simple. After all, the custodian wasn't a clock expert, just a fellow in blue overalls with a big bunch of keys on his belt. A real clock man, people believed, would do the job up elegantly.

But over the next thirty years, every one of the skilled clock technicians who could be found (and persuaded to make a long trip by rail and ferry to a remote downeast Maine island town) tried his hand at the repair. After a while the bell became a grail and the journey a sort of pilgrimage, as one timepiece genius or revered clockworks sage after another threw his hands up in defeat.

Finally, sometime in the 1970s—the exact date isn't known—the enormous white-faced clock on the outside of the tower was stopped, deliberately and for good. Afterwards, the huge Roman-numeraled face read perpetually 11:49 and the sound of the bell faded swiftly into Eastport's collective memory.

Sadly, said some. Criminally, said others, who

thought still more repair funds should have been found. But they were not, and subsequently the door leading to the bell tower, no longer a potentially fatal chamber, was left open or shut as the custodian (not the same one who had scrambled so bravely up the tower at the end of World War II) saw fit.

After a while, tattered hymnals and missals began to be stored on the narrow steps leading upward, as did lost scarves, umbrellas, and orphaned gloves whose owners might still come hunting. The way up and up to the tower became storage, then degenerated into a catchall area. One day a latch on the door to the stairway came loose, and then the key was lost, so it couldn't be locked or even closed very tightly at all. Not that there was any real reason to do so; there was nothing of value in the stairwell, and the old church's massive front door still did lock properly.

Or anyway it locked when people remembered to lock it, which on that particular day perhaps some-one hadn't.

All of which was why Karen Hansen, a local four-teen-year-old with big plans but few distinguishing qualities other than the fact that her father was the town drunk, had been able to get in. Then she made her way with the aid of a small flashlight to the nar-row enclosed stairway's first cramped wooden land-ing. But once she got that far, her courage deserted her suddenly and she sat, surrounded by lost gloves and hats and, inexplicably, a clutter of tools.

Claw hammer, pry bar, a retractable tape mea-sure . . . Squaring her thin shoulders under the long-sleeved plaid flannel shirt she wore, Karen idly fingered the items that lay on the steps while trying hard to feel as romantically tragic as the main character in the *Twilight* series, books about vampires and werewolves that she and her friends all loved.

But the only emotion she could summon up was loneliness. That, and a trickle of fear . . . *Oh, don't be a dumbass,* she scolded herself stoutly. Pulling a lighter and a pack of Marlboros out of her denim vest pocket, she lit up efficiently and sucked in a steadying drag. There, that was better . . .

But then she abruptly drew her blue-jeaned knees tightly to her chin and nearly busted out bawling. *Karen the crybaby,* her dad would've jeered, *just a damned useless crybaby.*

No good for anything. His harsh voice rasped in memory, its rough edges tearing at the already sore places in her heart. But the thought of the flat-handed slap that often followed his words got her moving again: *I'll show you. You'll be sorry.*

You'll be very sorry. She swiped her sleeve across her nose, had a final drag off the cigarette, then pinched it out the way she'd seen him do often, between a spit-moistened thumb and forefinger.

That was when she heard the sound from somewhere below in the stairwell's thick, musty darkness. A scuffing sound, like a shoe's sole sliding just the tiniest bit as it landed on the next stair's wooden tread. Not a loud sound.

But real. No question about it. And coming toward her. She stood up, listening, too frightened to shine her flashlight's fading beam down the steps. Suddenly the vampires and werewolves from *Twilight* weren't romantic at all, only hungry.

Hungry and mean. *Who's there?* she might have

ventured, but she couldn't make her throat move. A need to pee seized her, along with a wish, deep and piercingly hopeless, to be home in her own bed with the covers pulled up and her flashlight illuminating the pages of a library book; her dad said reading at night was just a waste of expensive electricity.

And reading in the daytime's a waste of eyesight, probably, she thought bitterly, since if it weren't for her father and his drinking and his meanness, she wouldn't be doing this at all, she wouldn't be here.

But she was, and so was whoever—or whatever— had made the sound, down there in the darkness of the old wooden stairwell of the All Faith Chapel on Two Church Lane in Eastport, Maine.

No further sound followed. Gradually, her heart slowed. Her breathing, which had felt like an iron band was tightening around her chest, came a little easier, and her urgent need to relieve herself was no longer quite so acute.

She still couldn't move, though. The sound didn't come again but neither could she un-hear it. It had been there.

Hadn't it? Gradually, she became less sure. *Crybaby,* one side of her mind jeered meanly at her. *Useless little crybaby, dumbass, scaredy-cat.* But the other side still knew . . . what?

Slowly, she turned. In the flashlight's weakening glow, the stairs vanished into the gloom above. Three more long flights to go, and then a ladder for the last part of the climb, or so she'd heard. She'd never even been in the church before, her dad being more of a regular worshipper at Murphy's Tap Room and her mother being dead.

Also, Karen was afraid of heights; luckily it was nearly midnight and pitch dark out, so at least once she got where she was going, she wouldn't be able to see very well just how high up she was. *Do it. Just do it and be done with it. And then . . .*

Then she could get out of this hick town. Far away, where nobody would ever find her, not her dad or anyone else. The idea sent her scrambling up the bare, dim-lit wooden steps to the next landing, and the next. Her job was not so hard, after all: climb to the top, stick the flashlight out between the slanted wooden slats in the belfry, then snap it on and off so Harvey Spratt and his creepy friends could see that she'd done it.

The boys were hanging out on the breakwater, downhill and only a few blocks away from the church, waiting for her signal. Laughing, Harvey had promised her fifty dollars, betting she couldn't accomplish the task he'd set her.

A thin, pimpled high school senior, Harvey had been selling pot and pints of Bushmills to his equally mangy buddies since he was in sixth grade. Now he was into the harder stuff, too, Oxys and other pills, and worse. Karen had learned this two nights earlier when sixteen-year-old Bogie Kopmeir, an awful little thief and Harvey's ever-present sidekick since the school year started, had shoved her hard just to show Harvey how eager a sidekick he really was, and she had stumbled right into Harvey.

As she clutched at him to keep from falling, nearly pulling the Saint Christopher medal on the chain from his neck, a baggie of foil packets had tumbled from his pocket onto the damp concrete breakwater. His murderous look at her as he grabbed them back up told her that he was selling them, even if she hadn't guessed.

So she knew he had money. And he would pay her, even though he wouldn't want to, because Karen might be poor, what the people around here called mackerel-eating poor, and get her clothes from the thrift shop and school supplies from teachers who took pity on her, knowing who her father was and that he would rather spend money on beer than on pens and notebook paper.

But Karen had a way about her, she wasn't sure what it was, exactly, but it made the other girls at school like her, and want to be friends. Harvey knew it, too, that if *he* wanted those girls to like *him*— which why any of them would, Karen had no idea, but if he *did*—well, then, he'd better not piss off Karen.

Reminding herself of this, she paused on the next landing for a deep, self-encouraging breath. The smells were different here: two centuries' worth of old candle smoke, and the sweetish scent of lead-paint dust. Here, too, were more tools: a T square, a screwdriver with bits of rotted wood stuck to the blade, a string with the nut from a big steel bolt tied onto one end of it.

Also on the landing lay a small spiral notebook with a lot of measurements written into it in pencil. And somehow, it was the definiteness of these that reenergized her, rejuvenating her courage. Two flights to go; not four, or six.

Specifically: two. And with that her whole future, started off by the fifty dollars that Harvey would have to pay her, rose up wonderfully before her. First a hitchhike to Perry Corners, a five-minute ride off the island over the Broad Cove causeway to the mainland. She'd have no trouble getting a lift; everyone knew her, yet another of the reasons she wanted so desperately to get away. Making up a reason for the trip would be easy, too.

A friend's mother was meeting her, she would say, or her father would be picking her up. The sweet, obedient girl that she was known to be wouldn't lie.

So no one would suspect. After that: the bus to Bangor and a room at the YWCA, and a job. Dishwashing, yard work, Karen didn't care. With winter coming soon, it could even be shoveling snow. All she needed was enough to get to New York and to a modeling agency, and then . . . well, she wasn't entirely clear on the details of what her life in the big city would be.

But it would be fabulous, she knew. After all, she was tall, thin, and young; that she wasn't quite pretty didn't matter, since neither were the girls whose pictures she saw in the glossy fashion magazines. Instead, they had a look she recognized:

Direct. Dead-eyed, as if they'd gone way inside somewhere, no visible remains of what they thought or felt left on their faces at all. When Karen saw these girls in the print ads she pored over at the public library on Water Street, she found no more feeling in their expressions than in the clothing they wore or the accessories they displayed.

It was the same look she saw every day in the mirror, so she knew she was the type wanted by the men—even at fourteen, she knew they would have to be men—who took the photographs and would pay her for them. Karen felt confident that she could do whatever those girls had done to get where they were. All she had to do was try.

How hard could it be? Like now, for instance. Above, the last flight of steps angled sharply upward. At the top, the wavering beam of her flashlight picked out the bottom rungs of a ladder. Sighing at the sight of this last challenge, she took one step up toward it.

But then she froze, hearing a sound again in the stairwell below and behind her. "Hello?"

Silly. There's no one here. But . . .

Not a scuffing sound, though that would've been bad enough. No, it sounded like someone *breathing*.

And then suddenly it didn't. Karen held her own breath and waited, but the dark mouth of the stairwell as it curved down and away remained silent. Even the fluttery skittering of mice in the walls ceased.

She poked the flashlight's faint beam one more time into the black maw yawning below, then turned sharply from it and climbed the rest of the steps. *Dumbass*. If she kept getting spooked like this, claiming her fifty dollars could take all night.

So let's get to it. Grimly she tucked the flashlight under her arm and put a foot on the ladder's bottom rung. Above her, the top rungs disappeared into the gloom inside the tower's bell chamber. But beyond that, a faint glimmer hovered, the pale, silvery moonlight from outside coming through the tower's wooden slats.

Up, up . . . she poked her head through the square, wood-framed trapdoor's aperture. Around her, moonlight fell in bars on the dusty old floor. The huge, hulking shapes of the clockworks set into the walls loomed enormously, notched iron wheels and angled ratchets and massive pulley lines like the rigging on ships.

Karen had a sudden, bad thought that the mechanisms might start moving all by themselves in a nightmare meshing of gears, one that might seize her and grind her up. Fright made her hands loosen on the ladder's rungs briefly, just for an instant.

But that was enough. The flashlight slipped from under her arm, its lens popping out and the bulb shattering as it smashed to the wooden landing below. It bounced clattering away down the stairs, leaving her in near darkness. Still clinging to the top rung of the ladder, she froze in horror, unable to believe what had just happened, trying to take it back, that careless moment.

Knowing she couldn't. All this way, she'd come all this way, only to . . . but then a new thought struck her: the lighter. Her cigarette lighter would work, wouldn't it?

Not in daylight. But now, in only the moonglow, its tiny flare was enough to be seen for two blocks, surely? Now, in the dead of night?

Well, it would have to be, was all. Just as she'd planned to do with the flashlight, she would creep over the dusty floor of the bell tower, stick the cigarette lighter out through the slats in the wall, and send a signal: SOS.

Get me out of here. Away, to a place where no one knew her as the charity case, poor drunk Hank Hansen's daughter. Then she would be mysterious, exotic . . . free.

Oh, it would be elegant . . . Abruptly, the ladder shook and rattled as, shockingly, someone unseen scuttled rapidly up it. A hand clamped roughly onto her shoulder. A breathy shriek came out of her mouth before another hand clapped over it, cruelly.

Then, before she could fully comprehend what was happening, somebody shoved her *upward*, through the trapdoor's small opening into the bell chamber. In darkness she staggered and fell, and her head hit the floor hard. Hands seized her legs and she heard the rich sound of thick tape ripping.

Swiftly, her ankles were shoved together and tied, tape was slapped over her mouth, and some rough, smelly cloth was tied over her eyes. Her hands were grabbed firmly and bound.

"Please . . ." It came out a gagging "mmmph." But she swallowed back even that as another sound, this one very familiar, began. A bright, metallic *ringing* sound, over and over . . .

Not the church bell, which Karen had never heard. She willed it to ring now, prayed for the iron clapper to smack the bell's massive side with a sound so explosive, it killed her on the spot and took her from the world this very instant.

Because one of the few things her father was good at, that he could do no matter how drunk he was, was game hunting. Moose, deer, bear, partridge, in or out of season, when he went hunting there was meat to eat. Steak, chops, stew in an iron pot . . .

But for all those animals to be turned into food, they first had to get dressed out: bled, skinned and gutted, then cut into pieces that got wrapped in butcher paper with labels written on in a black crayon kept specially for the purpose. Karen's dad knew how to do all that, too, commandeering the whole kitchen for his bloody work.

And before he began, he always sharpened his knife. *Zip, zop*, the blade slid ringingly down the specially roughened surface of the sharpening steel, until with a narrowed eye he examined the glinting edge he had produced and pronounced it good.

Zip, zop . . . The sound now was of a smaller steel, pocket-sized, and the blade it moved on was shorter, too, she could tell from the sound. But she still recognized it. And the sound scared her into remembering that even with her wrists bound, her fingers were still free. So she could get the cigarette lighter out of her vest pocket.

Seizing it between her thumbs, pulling it out, then letting it slide down between her shaking palms, she found the friction wheel. Tears leaked down her cheeks, her throat aching with suppressed weeping, but if she let herself sob she knew she would choke, so she didn't.

Instead, she waited for a hand to try to do something to her. When it did, she would thrust up the cigarette lighter, at the same time pulling her thumbs down over the friction wheel. The sudden flame would hurt someone, maybe even set them on fire, send them blazing down the stairs away from her . . .

Gulping back tears, she gripped the lighter with her thumbs poised tremblingly over the wheel. There would be a warning, some sound from her attacker, and she would be ready.

She held her breath, waiting until a tiny movement very near her face told her someone was there, right in front of her. Then, snapping the lighter and feeling the flare of heat as she thrust it up, she was rewarded by a yell of pain, followed by an angry curse.

Ha, she thought grimly, but then a sudden sharp blow to both her wrists knocked the lighter from her hands. As it clattered to the floor the rest of the attack came from behind, her hair gripped tightly and her head yanked painfully back to expose her throat.

After that there were more sounds, but they didn't last long, and for most of the time that they went on, fourteen-year-old Karen Hansen was not even fully aware that she was the one making them.

It was a chilly night in November, and all over Eastport windows were closed against a breeze with a salt-sharp edge on it. So not everyone heard the church bell at first. On most of Moose Island, where Eastport was located—at the north end, looking toward New Brunswick, Canada, or the south, with its view of the town of Lubec and the International Bridge that linked it to Campobello—the sound was merely a far-off tolling that could have been a bell buoy bobbing on the dark bay.

But Eastport police chief Bob Arnold's small two-story house on Clement Street stood only a few blocks from Two Church Lane. He had just put his head down on his pillow when the bell bonged for the first time, vibrating the glass in his closed bedroom window.

His wife, Clarissa, swung her feet out of bed; a

strange sound in the night—strange anything, night or day—was her husband's business until proven otherwise. "I'll make coffee," she said.

Bob sighed, contemplating his own bare feet, which he wanted very badly to tuck right back in under the toasty-warm covers. His little girl, Annie, had been up all the night before with an asthma attack, and both he and Clarissa were exhausted.

From Annie's room came the tinkling of a sweet, lively tune from her new favorite musician, an artist with the (to Bob) unlikely name of Caspar Babypants. It had taken him a while, but now Bob thought he was beginning to get Caspar's message, which boiled down to "Everything's okay."

He wished he could stay here and appreciate the music a bit longer. Perhaps the okay-ness had further levels, he thought; more to appreciate. But that ringing church bell needed investigating.

Also, it needed stopping. If he knew Eastport, half the town was on the phone with the other half by now, all mad about it. He pulled his pants on.

A few blocks away at the Eastport Boarding Hostel, Tiffany Whitmore put down the romance novel she was reading at a desk in the front hall. The Boarding Hostel was not a nursing home—Eastport already had one of those—but at night, the desk served as a nursing station because nighttime was when residents needed nursing.

Or some of them did, anyway. On a nearby mantel a portable radio tuned to the local station, WQDY, played what it called classic rock and Tiffany just called oldies; the tunes, after all, were from way back in the seventies, their artists now nearly as geriatric as Tiff's patients.

Meanwhile, in Tiffany's novel the heroine was learning that the hero was not a mild-mannered nursery school teacher as she had believed, but an international spy whose real name was Trace Savage. Trace had just swept the heroine, Maggie DeLorean, into his muscled arms and was preparing to ravish her in, Tiffany supposed, an appropriately savage way when the church bell's loud *bong* rattled the wheeled medications cart across from the desk. The vibration sent eight small fluted paper cups full of sleeping pills and antacid doses shivering to the cart's metal edge and over it, scattering the pills across the green linoleum floor.

As Tiffany, who was not a small person, bent heavily to try capturing the pills as they rolled away from her, the first loud cries of fear and consternation began emerging from residents' rooms. And soon, so did the residents, alarmed by the clangor of a bell they had last heard when they themselves were of an age to be ravished or ravishing, or possibly both.

Residents who were ambulatory came tottering on walkers or canes to find out what was happening. The ones who weren't ambulatory yelled for Tiffany.

Tiffany wanted to know what was going on, too. But when she straightened with an effort to peer out the hostel's bay window—at one time it had been a sea captain's mansion, its formal gardens now paved over for the employee parking lot—she saw only the twin churches of Two Church Lane.

Each enormous white clapboard building squatted

massively on no more than a quarter acre of grass, its tower and spire rising into the night sky, which had been clear but was now beginning to thicken with fog. From where she stood looking out, Tiff could only see the whole of the closest one, the All Faith Chapel. Near its lofty top was the square, slatted belfry with the clock just below, its huge face ghostly-appearing, and above the belfry a spire capped by an elaborate brass weathervane shaped like a fat, feathered arrow.

The big bell rang on, monstrously loud, as Tiffany squinted through the fog now beginning to gather in the streets. Nothing moved. No one had yet arrived to investigate the disturbance. In Eastport, with a population of only twelve hundred or so now that the summer folk had mostly gone home, there wasn't enough money in the city budget to keep a police officer on patrol all night.

And mostly, there wasn't a need. Except sometimes, like now.

"I'm coming," Tiffany called as the racket of demands from behind her rose in number and volume.

The bell's sound, by contrast, stayed the same, so loud she felt it vibrating through her, maybe even into the marrow of her bones. *Bong, bong* . . . Could a bell that loud cause brain damage? Even cancer?

Just then the only aide on the night shift, Jannalyn Rand, popped out of the staff room, blinking sleepily. "What's all the commotion?"

In Tiffany's opinion, Jannalyn was as dumb as a box of clamshells, and lazy to boot. Smelling of cigarette smoke, hairspray, and Juicy Fruit, she had a talent for vanishing into the staff room for a nap whenever she didn't have a specific task assigned.

But Jannalyn was strong enough to lift a person up off the floor and back into bed whether or not that person wanted to go, or to muscle a man who believed he was General Westmoreland down the hall and into his room for the umpteenth time in a night. And in the Boarding Hostel, that counted for something.

"Hey." Jannalyn joined Tiffany at the window. From the reek coming off her, it was clear she hadn't bothered to go outside for her smoke, as the rules required. But that wasn't important now. The important thing was the indistinct shape creeping stealthily out the back door of the church.

Jannalyn snorted knowingly. "Can you believe that? Some damn kid must've snuck in there and got that old bell ringing."

The shape slipped into the bushes and trees massed behind the church and vanished, just as a squad car pulled up out front. Bob Arnold, Tiffany realized as the driver got out. Hadn't taken him long, either.

Tiffany shivered. Back in the residents' rooms, somebody was banging a bedpan against a nightstand, *bang-bang-bang,* not quite in time with the bell's bonging. Someone else moaned monotonously: *helphelphelp.*

That would be Mrs. Brannigan, who in daylight was as sharp as a sewing needle. She read Shakespeare, played a mean game of bridge, managed an online stock portfolio profitably, and was the recording secretary for the Eastport chapter of the national Poetry Society.

"Yeah," said Tiffany, trying to agree with Jannalyn that what they'd glimpsed had been just a kid. But she couldn't quite shake off her chill. In *daylight,* she thought with a shiver of unease, a lot of people were as sane as anyone.

But now it was night. And that shape had been weird.

"Some kid," she repeated, hoping to convince herself.

Bob Arnold put on the hearing protectors that his wife, Clarissa, had insisted he bring along. The plastic earmuffs were unwieldy, bulky, and uncomfortable. But at least now the old bell wasn't slamming his eardrums halfway to his eyeballs every time it rang.

Why was it ringing? That was his big question. One hand resting on his gun, he pulled the heavy old church door open with the other and peered inside.

The door had not been locked. "Police! Anyone in here?"

Not that they'd be able to hear him. Entering with caution, he drew his flashlight from his duty belt. As the beam stabbed the darkness, the shapes of wooden pews jumped out of the gloom.

But nothing else did. He made out the stone baptismal font and a rack of church literature. A little farther in, he found the bank of light switches in the vestibule and snapped them all on. Overhead, the bell continued its horrendous tolling.

Everything in the vestibule and the sanctuary and on the pulpit were all as they should be. To the left of the pulpit was the sacristy; Bob peered in, found the vestments on their hangers just inside the door. A little office area held a desk, a small file cabinet, and a bulletin board with notes and phone numbers on bits of paper thumbtacked to it.

Bong, bong . . . Jesus Christ, Bob thought, *wouldn't somebody please turn off that fricking . . .* But then he stopped, because of course he shouldn't be taking that name in vain here.

Still, he had to get the thing silenced somehow. Though the sound was well muffled by his ear protectors, he could feel it in his teeth, loosening his fillings and shooting a rhythmic stab of anguish into the dental work he'd just had finished last week.

And even if he couldn't get it turned off, he had to go up and find out why it was ringing in the first place, because the bell hadn't started up all by itself, that was for sure.

No, somebody had started it: maybe by accident, more likely for a prank. And when Bob found out who it was, which he would because in Eastport there were a very limited number of possible suspects for anything, and Bob knew all of them—

Well, then. He would have the culprit's butt. And he would kick it, too, if the culprit gave him even the slightest excuse.

Kick it hard, Bob decided balefully, because his kid was sick, his wife was worried, he was so short of sleep he felt like a mad scientist's experiment, and there were things on his mind; life-changing things he didn't want to think about right now.

And on top of it all, that damned bell was trying to beat his brains out. *Shut up, shut up,* he thought, striding angrily down the center aisle of the old church. He'd have to get outside, call Jeb Harmon, the custodian, and ask Jeb to get down here as quickly as possible. Because this had to be, *needed* to be—

The thought cut itself off as he reached the stone baptismal font at the rear of the church. Because his ears might be plugged so no sounds but the bell's muffled thunder reached them, but his eyes still worked, and so did his nose.

And his gut worked. It told him now that more was wrong here than a screwed-up bell. Behind and to the left of the baptismal font, a door stood open. Beyond, he could see the first few steps of the stairway leading up to the bell tower.

And on the first one—yep, he thought, feeling his heart sink, that was a pool of blood, all right. As he stared at it, a fat, dark droplet plopped down into it from somewhere above, and then another.

"*Oh, Jesus.*" He said it aloud, not fearing any blasphemy this time, feeling his shoulders sag with sadness and the weight of a dead person up there somewhere; nobody lost that much blood and lived.

He drew out his duty weapon and, with its heft steadying his hand, approached the stairway's door. The narrow wooden steps led away up into the darkness. Groping, he found another switch and flipped it. A bare bulb lit up.

In its dim glow he could see dark smears on the old plaster wall, once painted cream but now a sad sort of brownish-yellow, and on the stair treads with the brittle shreds of rubberized material still clinging to them, held on by rusty carpet tacks.

The carpet tacks, some of them, had wet, red heads

and dark stains spreading around them in the aging gray wood. Someone had stepped in blood, gotten it on their hands, too, which meant that there might be a fingerprint or footprint. Bigger, indistinct brushlike marks on the wall might've come from someone's sleeve.

Bob kept his own arms close to his sides and his hands off the metal rail that was bolted as a banister through the stairwell's plaster and into the framing behind it, because, please God, there would indeed be prints. He'd have just gone straight outside, not risked confusing this scene with his own physical presence at all, if he'd been *sure* that the owner of all that blood was dead.

Medically sure, that is: cold and pulseless. But he wasn't, so he began climbing the stairs, being very careful where he put his feet. The blood kept leaking down the wall beside him, first on his right side for a flight of stairs, then on his left for the next flight, flowing freely in the light of the twenty-five-watt bulbs screwed into ceramic fixtures set head-high on each landing.

Just as he reached the top one and found the wooden ladder leading up through the tower's trapdoor, two things happened. First, the bell stopped ringing, a sudden silence opening up all around him, a vast, stunned-feeling void like a universe so empty it might just suck itself inside out.

And second, a woman's body half-fell down through the open trapdoor, first her long hair and then her shoulders, her flannel-sleeved arms flopping bonelessly and her bloodstained fingers dangling. Startled, he staggered back, one foot finding only the thin air of the stairwell before he righted himself.

Then, as he stood trying to catch his breath, the body began sliding the rest of the way down the old ladder. The skinny blue-jeaned thighs followed the upper body out of the hatchway, then the knees and at last two sneakered feet. The ladder's splintery rails caught the body's clothing, slowing its descent; the rungs pulled the jeans down slightly, exposing pale hipbones that looked bird-fragile; a girl's bones, he realized.

Not even a grown woman. A child. Filled with horror and pity, he reached out to slow her fall, not caring anymore about what he might do to any evidence. He just couldn't . . .

He couldn't let her fall. Seizing her thin shoulders, he eased her body over the rungs, its weight a mere nothing, like an infant's weight, or a leaf's, until at last it reached the floor and puddled there, pathetically limp. By the time he released her, he was shaking.

Jesus, he thought. Twenty years a cop, he'd seen everything, or he'd thought he had. Shootings and stabbings, beatings and car crashes, drownings and hangings and smotherings, carbon monoxide poisonings and wrist slittings.

Everything. But nothing like this. Gingerly, with an index finger that still trembled, he hooked her collar down a little. The wound was a meaty smile. He snatched his hand away, looked up through the trap-door.

Dark up there. "Police!" he yelled, then yanked his cell phone out, speed-dialed Jenny Margolin in the dispatcher's office. He didn't want this out on the radio.

"Washington County 911." The phone rang in Jenny's kitchen, on the Shore Road overlooking the Cherry Island lighthouse. By now it was one in the morning, but as always, Jenny sounded wide awake. "What is your emergency?"

"Jenny, this is Bob." He kept his weapon trained on the trapdoor opening. "I'm in the All Faith Chapel on Two Church Lane in Eastport. There's a girl's body here."

"Oh, Lord. Do you know who it is?"

Jenny's kitchen radio was tuned to the Eastport high school station, WSHD. Bob knew it because it was the only radio station in Maine where you could hear Tibetan throat singing at one in the morning— or at almost any other time, really—and that was what they were playing now.

Well, with the exception of WERU in Blue Hill, of course, but that signal didn't get all the way up here. Meanwhile, Jenny was a good woman and an excellent dispatcher, but she was related to practically everyone in the county.

Including this victim. "We'll deal with that later. Right now I want you to call the state boys, the M.E., and all my guys."

His Eastport officers, he meant. "Get them all here, please, as fast as they can, except Toby Farrell."

Stolid and unimaginative, Toby was as big as a bull moose and just as unstoppable when he needed to be. And there was only one way off the island by car.

"Tell Toby I want him to get out to the causeway in his squad car and just sit there, stop anyone trying to cross and get a good, solid ID and a story out of them unless they're in the middle of having a heart attack or a baby. Make sure he gets that, okay?"

"Yes, Bob, I understand."

At this hour of the night, there was hardly anyone driving around, anyway. He'd worry about complaints later.

"Call the Coast Guard," he went on. "No vessels leaving the harbor or the boat basin, not even a row-boat. And I want Bobby Roth to get out to the air-port."

Bobby was the city council member who headed up the airport committee. "Nothing takes off. Not until I say so. Oh, and get whoever's on call for Customs and Immigration on the phone. Say I might need en-forcement help if anyone at the port gets sniffy."

Freighters came in and out of the harbor all the time, from all over the world. For all Bob knew, one might be getting ready to cast off right this minute.

With, for all he knew as well, his perp aboard and thinking himself safe. Or the killer could be some local person, taking a shower at home by now, burn-ing up bloody clothes in a woodstove, with no one to see or know.

In short, it could be anyone. "Bob? That it?" Jenny asked.

He looked down at the dead girl, and the blood. Whoever had done this most likely believed he had gotten away with it. So *he* thought. "Yeah," Bob said. "For now."

He snapped the phone shut. Above, the trapdoor's opening gaped blackly. Bob didn't know why the bell had stopped ringing, but he had a bad idea about it, and before he could go back down all those stairs again, he would have to check it out.

The very idea of sticking his head into the darkness up there made his gut clench sourly. If she knew what he was about to do, his wife, Clarissa, would be up one side of him and down the other.

But she didn't know. And even if she did . . . Sighing, he put a foot on the ladder's first rung, hauled his weight—which was getting to be considerable lately, but that was another story—up to the second rung, and then quietly to the third.

Softly, softly . . . It was a line from one of the Kipling stories he'd been reading to his little girl, on the nights when he got home before she was asleep. And it seemed like a good idea now, too, not letting whoever else might still be up there know he was coming.

A good idea, just not very doable. The ladder creaked, and the things on his duty belt—Mace, whistle, handcuffs, baton, weapon holster (he still had the gun in one hand, too, which made climbing the ladder even harder)—it all clanked, rattled, and clunked as he made his way laboriously up the wooden rungs.

Nothing he could do about it, though, or about the wheezing of his own breath, either, like tiny high-pitched whistles inside his chest. Partly they were due to his extra poundage, but most of the internal sound effects were because he, too, had asthma.

Just like his daughter. He'd just never paid any attention to it before, figuring that everybody had some damn fool problem or another, and doctoring for it was a waste of time and money.

Lately he felt differently, wishing that over the years he'd stayed in better shape, that he was a better physical specimen as a husband and father, and—let's face it—as a cop, one who once in a while was required to climb a ladder, find out whether or not a girl-murdering scumbag was hiding up there in the dark.

Hell, there might even be *another* body lying up there, or—

Just as he was about to stick his head through the hole, the first Eastport squad car pulled up outside. Bob recognized the sound of the old Crown Vic's engine, the little *thweep-thweep* squeal of the fan belt keeping time with the knocking from either a valve or a rod.

Then came the solid thud of the Vic's door slamming, and a voice from the church vestibule. "Bob? You inside?"

"Yeah. Up here. Look around outside, Paulie, stop anyone you see looks iffy. And watch where you step and so on."

"Got it" came the reply, then the sound of Paulie Waters's boots heading out again. Waters was a young guy, in his twenties with not much cop experience, but a quick study and he read a lot. He'd know how to proceed. Bob aimed the flashlight up, then followed its beam into the huge, silent darkness of the bell chamber.

Directly above him hung the bell, a bronze behemoth with a silver ring in its rim, pitch dark inside where no moonlight penetrated. Railed catwalks went all the way around the inside of the wood-framed belfry, bolted to the walls. Above the catwalk, tall, narrow arched windows slatted over by shutters loomed on all four sides; the openings between the slats let the sound out.

Over hill and dale, Bob thought irrelevantly, the phrase from another of the children's books he read. But the image of his little girl's bedroom didn't belong here; he shoved it away, knowing someone else's child lay below him, bloodied and dead.

He knew whose child, too. Bob wasn't sure which of his duties he hated most tonight, finding her or telling her father about it. Not that it mattered; he'd done one, and he would have to do the other. *Mine is not to reason why . . .* Christ, though, Hank Hansen was going to be a crazy man when he found out.

Pouring between the slats of the big shutters piercing the walls, the moonlight formed a striped pattern on the old floor. Bob hauled himself the rest of the way through the opening into the belfry, his flashlight's beam picking out the long-forgotten items lying around: a coil of ancient rope, a pipe wrench lying in a mess of rust flakes.

On the floor near the rope spread another pool of blood, and then a smear mark. *Because he dragged her. The son of a bitch cut her and then he—*

"Bob?" It was Waters, calling from below. "One of the girls at the Boarding Hostel saw someone, maybe. And I found something."

Nobody up here. Bob aimed the flashlight around once more to make sure. "Waters," he shouted down, "don't—"

"Yeah, first I picked it up and handled it," Waters cut in before Bob could finish, "got my prints all over it and messed up anyone else's, and then for good measure I spit on it."

In addition to being smart, Waters was a smart-ass. "No, I marked it and left it," he added in conciliatory tones. "You all right up there?"

Bob climbed down the ladder. At the foot of it, a local girl named Karen Hansen lay dead. From the color of her face, white as a page from one of Bob's own little girl's storybooks, almost all of the blood had been drained out of her.

"Yeah, I'm just ducky," Bob managed. "You got the boarding home woman squared away?"

He didn't want her talking to anyone before he got to her. When people in Eastport started gabbing, what started out as an unusually dressed tourist snapping vacation snapshots at one end of the island would be a squad of terrorists taking surveillance photos in preparation for an imminent invasion by the time the story got to the other end.

He descended the stairs, careful as before not to step in any of the blood pools or touch the smeared walls. Outside in the Vic, Tiffany Whitmore sat in the front passenger seat smoking a cigarette and poking at her cell phone.

Tiffany wore a blue scrub suit, white sneakers, and a zipped navy hoodie. Her peroxide-orange hair was skinned back in a ponytail held by a fabric scrunchy. She was a nice woman and a hard worker, and those cigarettes were the worst of her habits, but she had a big mouth and on top of that the car was going to smell like an ashtray.

At least she had the door open. "Hey!" Bob yelled.

"Put the phone away, Tiff, would you? And get out of the car if you gotta smoke."

She scowled, but grudgingly did as he asked. On top of not wanting her to tell anyone else her story before she told it to him, he didn't need half the town here standing around gawking at everything, which he would have if Tiffany got yapping.

Would anyway before long, he realized glumly, turning to Waters. "What do you think you found?" he asked, imagining a gum wrapper or a cigarette butt.

Waters aimed his flashlight into the evergreen shrubbery by the church steps. Crammed up between the dark, gnarly twists of the box-hedge roots lay a wad of tissue, a faded Hershey bar wrapper, a plastic bag from the IGA, and—

"Huh," said Bob. The thing Waters had spotted had a taped wooden handle, an index finger groove for improved grip, a short row of rip teeth near the guard that divided the blade from the handle. And a trailing swage point, wickedly tipped.

All of which made it a professional-grade hunting knife, its blade stained thickly with . . .

Blood. Lab tests would say for sure, of course, but to Bob's eye there was no question about it. And he knew who owned this large, very distinctive-looking knife, too, because he'd seen it before.

Oh, hell, he thought as an approaching Maine State Police cruiser's distinctive high-low siren howled eerily.

"Don't touch it. Let the state guys deal with it," Bob told Waters, then left the young officer standing over the weapon while he went to talk with Tiffany

Whitmore, before the presence of her cell phone became just too much of a temptation for her.

"So are you coming, Dweeby, or are you gonna sit there like a scared little kid?"

Flicking away his cigarette, Bogie Kopmeir hopped onto the bike he had just stolen out of a garage on Evans Lane and pedaled it in a circle, his oddly babyish face gleaming greasily under the streetlamp.

"Put it back, Bogie." David Thompson sat hunched on the front steps of the house that the garage belonged to, wishing he'd stayed home. Across town, church bells were ringing and the sound of police sirens rose eerily in the thickening fog.

David wished he was in bed under the covers, unable to hear them. He hated these late-night outings with Bogie, hated being jolted awake by stones tossed against his bedroom window, hated the way his heart thumped anxiously from the time he slipped out until the moment, always way too much later, when he sneaked back in again.

And he hated being called Dweeb. In fact, there wasn't much about hanging out with Bogie—crude, cunning in an animal way, and possessed of a temper that could explode into spitting rage for no reason at all—that David didn't hate. But what choice did he have?

It was that or get the crap beaten out of him every morning at school, where David was a sophomore on the honors track and Bogie, despite being sixteen and a year older than David, was still a freshman. Slight, bookish boys like David were fresh meat for the guys who played sports and went deer hunting, many with their own guns. They regarded David as merely another variety of prey animal.

Hanging with Bogie—and by extension, with a crew of butt-ugly, thuggish mutts just like him, all led by the repulsive but weirdly charismatic Harvey Spratt—kept David safe.

"Hey, *Dweeb*!" Bogie yelled, circling on the bike, heedless of the lights coming on in the dark houses all around. "Dweeb, hop on!" Bogie reached back and patted the rack behind the bike's seat demandingly while at the same time he attempted to circle around again under the streetlamp.

Bogie was especially wired tonight for some reason, but at least he wore clean clothes for once. Thinking this, David got to his feet just as a man in pajamas came angrily out of one of the houses. Hopping with fury under his porch light, he yelled what men like that always did: "Hey, you kids!"

Bogie laughed wildly. "*Hey, you kids!*" he cackled. "*Yah!*" But then the bike's tire hit a pothole and he swerved out of control, careening into a barberry thicket that marked the lot line between two yards.

Jesus. Bounding off the porch, David shot into the alley behind the house where Bogie had crashed. The place they'd stolen the bike from—Bogie picking open the garage door lock with a tool that resembled a dentist's instrument, as easily as if he'd held a key— was vacant, the summer people who tenanted it gone home for the season.

But all the other nearby houses belonged to locals, year-round Eastport residents. Many of them were probably calling the police right this minute. "Bogie!"

David whispered urgently, crouching to peer into the thorny thicket.

No answer, and for a moment David felt relieved. Around him the only sound was the faint rustling of dried vegetation in the summer people's perennial gardens, the pale globes of hydrangea blooms like ghostly heads hanging against a picket fence. But then a stream of curses sputtered out of the gloom and Bogie appeared, the porkpie hat he always wore jammed down crookedly and his lip oozing blood.

"Come on," he snarled, grabbing David by his jacket collar. Out in the street now, the householders were gathering purposefully; this wasn't Bogie Kopmeir's first visit to the neighborhood, apparently.

A door slammed; a car started. A cell phone jangled out a mechanized tune, and then—horror of horrors—a dog barked.

A *big* dog. "Move it, Dweeb! You wanna get us caught?"

Bogie was short, but he was built like a fireplug, and he was strong. Fast, too; gasping, David let himself be half dragged and half shoved up the alley behind the houses until the stabbing of flashlight beams and the voices of angry men had faded.

Finally they reached the cemetery, scuttling in among the mossy old gravestones where the silence was complete. David fell exhausted against one of them, not even caring that only a few feet below, human bones moldered. If he'd had his way, he'd have been down there with them, he told himself miserably.

God, what kind of a life was this? Beat up by one bunch of cretins or bossed around by another even stupider bunch. Meanwhile, the school's anti-bullying program kept yammering about how they should all just be *nicer* to one another.

Yeah, *nicer,* like that was going to—

"Dweeb."

Suddenly Bogie Kopmeir's thick, stubby-fingered hand was at David's throat, choking him while pinning his head back against a century-old carved granite angel's unyielding wing.

"Freakin' fag," Bogie spat. "Why'd you run away, huh?"

His breath stank of cigarettes and unbrushed teeth. David jerked his head to the side. "Didn't," he gagged out past Bogie's merciless stranglehold. "You *told* me to . . ."

But there was no reasoning with Bogie. He gave David's throat a sharp shove, slamming David's head against one of the angel wing's pointy-ended stone feathers. If it had pierced his skull and killed him, he'd have been glad at that moment just to let everything end. He was tired, so tired of being scared.

But *better days are coming,* his father always told him; David remembered the phrase now, found in it the strength somehow to squirm free of Bogie's grasp and speak, croaking out the only thing he could think of to defuse his companion's unpredictable energy.

He didn't want it, didn't like it, felt his gut roil already in anticipatory disgust. But:

"Gimme a cigarette," David said.

Chapter 3

*Never cut
toward yourself.*
—Tiptree's Tips

My name is Jacobia Tiptree—Jake, to my
friends—and when I first came to Eastport, Maine, I
thought that moving here would solve all my problems.

At the time, though, I also had a young teenaged
son; a Very Old House™ whose state of repair suggested tenancy by the Addams Family; and an awful

ex-husband—his name, appropriately enough, was Victor—whose quirks only intensified after he'd followed me here so he could go on torturing me.

So much for the geographic cure. And then I started getting involved in murders. Not Victor's, although the idea was incredibly tempting. He was such a notorious cheater that the nurses at the hospital where he worked—Victor was a brain surgeon, which was perfect for him since he interacted best with unconscious persons—used to send out mass emails to the nursing school graduates every year, to warn them about him. But instead, after I divorced him, snatched our son Sam out of a drug haze, and got the hell out of Dodge, it was other people's untimely demises that I wound up concerning myself with:

Eastport's town ne'er-do-well, hung upside down from the cemetery gate, for instance. Or the local butcher, whose parts were found wrapped and labeled in his own freezer. For a while, it seemed that just crossing the causeway onto Moose Island could earn you a place either among the wanted posters or in a grave.

And I am sorry to report that I found it all fascinating, and so did Ellie White, my best friend here in Eastport and the other half of what became a sort of unofficial sleuthing duo. But eventually, after chasing a murderer and instead nearly becoming a murderee one too many times, I decided to give snooping a rest.

Firmly, I told Ellie that from now on whatever time I didn't spend fixing up my big old house would be devoted to gardening, dog walking, and perhaps knitting tiny garments for those few of our friends who had not yet negotiated the hell-on-earth known as child-rearing.

Well, in my case it was hellish, at any rate. But then, I was perhaps the most unlikely mother in history, possessing no instinct for it and having myself been raised by people who were only a little more civilized than feral cats. By the time Sam was five, he could work the microwave and figure out which of the packages in the icebox was a TV dinner and which was frozen margaritas, which I'd told him was "applesauce for grown-ups."

Perhaps unsurprisingly, not much later my son began opting for the applesauce, and soon after that he stopped bothering to hide his marijuana from me. Next, while his father and I fought World War III over a succession of girlfriends so trampy that I wanted to install a decontamination chamber outside our bedroom door, Sam went on adding illegal substances to his intake regimen until the list of what he consumed each day looked like the class notes of some incredibly ambitious toxicology student.

But that was then. Nowadays, fifteen years after we'd first moved here, Sam was thrillingly, delightfully sober, and my long-lost father (the only nonferal of my direct forebears still living; I was three when my mother was murdered) had been found and persuaded to live with me. His wife, Bella Diamond, insisted on keeping us all clean, well fed, and dressed in fresh clothes that felt soft and smelled wonderfully of sunshine and bleach.

And finally, I had a new husband. Wade Sorenson was a hardworking, plainspoken man, well thought of around town as a good fellow to have with you in a pinch. Also he was funny, smart, and gorgeous—when he put his arms around me, I tended to drop whatever I happened to be holding—the kind of guy who had a shotgun racked in his pickup truck and a book open on his bedside table.

In short: life was sweet. And when the whole terrible thing about Sam's friend Chip began, I wanted to keep it that way.

Too bad somebody had other plans.

On the November night when it all started, Sam had an old friend staying with us: Chip Hahn, his childhood pal from back in the city. In those days, Chip and his catcher's mitt were about the only wholesome items in Sam's life. Meanwhile, as a boy Chip himself was so lonely that he'd have dragged Sam out to the park if need be. But something about Chip's entreaties had cut through the fug of pot smoke and vodka fumes clouding up Sam's room and his head.

Nowadays, it was Chip who needed his head cleared. He was in the process of reevaluating for the umpteenth time his romance with a young woman named Carolyn: smart, talented, ungodly pretty, and the most self-centered, spoiled, moody, and generally maddening person I'd ever met in my life.

Well, except maybe for Victor. But hey, it was Chip's heart, and if he wanted it broken at regular intervals, it was none of my concern, or at any rate none of my business.

So that night when I'd found the boys (both in their mid-twenties, but still boys to me; I'd been a *very* young mother) at the dining room table with a map of Maine spread open between them, I let them alone. A fire sputtered in the fireplace, and the cranberry lamps on the side tables sent warm yellow light up onto the old gold-medallion wallpaper.

The windows were dark; from the CD player in the parlor came the muted sound of Stéphane Grappelli, wringing the pure, authentic essence of what it's like to be madly in love out of some jazz violin tune or another, I didn't stop to identify which one. It was, as I had reason to recall later, just past ten o'clock.

Yawning hugely, I closed the draperies against the rising wind outside. As part of the ongoing rehab of my old house (it's like a battleship; long before you get done painting one end, it's time to start scraping again at the other), I'd spent the day pulling carpet tacks out of the front hall stairs, filling the resulting holes with wood filler, and sanding down the result, which might not sound like much.

But there were fifteen steps plus a landing in that flight of stairs, and each step had approximately four hundred million separate tack holes it, so I was exhausted.

Leaning over the table, Sam pointed out the dirt road they intended to take in the morning to Borden's Brook. "See, we put the kayaks in right here"—he ran the tip of his marina penlight confidently over the map—"and get to about here by lunch—"

I was going around checking the thermostat and making sure both dogs were settled and so on. But I paused to admire the two young men with their heads—Sam's dark and curly, Chip's light thatch already beginning to recede—bent over their plans.

The kayaks were tied in the truck bed, and their backpacks stood ready by the door. "—and come out down here at Portman's Bay in time to get home for supper," Sam finished.

It crossed my mind again that if not for Chip, Sam might not be here at all, since any one of those long-ago days they'd spent in the park playing ball together might otherwise have been the day Sam overdosed or got himself stabbed or shot.

Or got knocked off the top of a subway car he was riding for thrills, that being the kind of crew he'd been running with when he wasn't hanging out with Chip. A burst of gratitude flooded me, followed by a twinge of premonition.

But that, I told myself, was silly. They had life jackets, and Sam was scrupulous about wearing his, while Chip after some experience he'd never wanted to tell me about would barely walk out onto a dock without his own flotation device securely belted.

"Are you guys turning in soon?" I asked, not expecting anything else. In Eastport in November, the phrase "night life" is an oxymoron unless you're a raccoon.

Sam nodded, tucking his penlight away. "Yeah. Early start tomorrow." But Chip shook his head.

"Guess I'm not tired yet." He glanced around the dining room with its olive brocade curtains draped at the old wavery-glassed windows and the ornate carved mantel over the dying fire on the tiled hearth. There was a roll of brass weatherstripping, a tin snips, and a hammer on one of the small bookcases that stood under the windows, all in readiness for a draftproofing job on the lower sashes, once that stairway was done.

But Chip wasn't noticing that, or imagining the work I'd put into the house since I'd bought the old place: miles of wallpaper stripped, woodwork sanded, doorknobs repaired, and plumbing parts replaced, not to mention contracted-out jobs like roof repair. Despite the fact that I am pretty sure my blood now flows best when it is thinned out considerably with varnish fumes, and I hardly recognize my own reflection in a mirror if I'm not gripping a few wood screws or possibly a paint-stirring stick between my teeth, all Chip knew was the result, and I could see him thinking that this was what he wanted to have with Carolyn, this warm safety.

This routine peace, which was for him proving so elusive. So I was unsurprised when an hour later, unable to sleep myself, I returned to the kitchen for an aspirin and found Chip in the back hall, pulling on a light jacket.

He looked up guiltily. "It's okay, Chip," I said, though the pain on his face in the instant before he knew I was there broke my heart. "I won't send you to bed before you're ready."

I got a glass down from the cupboard, poured skim milk and washed my pill down with it. "So, d'you want to talk about it?"

He shrugged, laughing a little. To keep from crying in front of me, I guessed. "Think it'd help? I've tried everything else."

Chip and Carolyn had started simply as business partners, she a writer of popular true-crime accounts, he a researcher whose ability to winkle out the pertinent fact meshed perfectly with her knack for unraveling a tragedy's emotional truth.

But now things had gotten complicated. "I knew that she'd be difficult," he allowed.

A minute ago he'd been ready to burst into tears, but in his own way Chip Hahn was a tough little nut. "Just," he added, "not so—"

Mercurial. Flighty. Available one minute, icy the next. She was a piece of work, our Carolyn, and if I'd had her there, I'd have tried talking some kind of sense into her.

She wrote about crime, the kind of ghastliness that can arise from madness, and often from the madness of thwarted love. Still, she couldn't seem to see when she was inflicting that pain herself, and on someone who least deserved it.

Or maybe she didn't care. "I guess I'm just a poor little rich kid, huh?" Chip said with another laugh, this one bitter. He was the product of wealth, the kind of boy who got packed off to a grim, posh boarding school while still practically gripping a plastic rattle in his fist.

Although in his case, the rattle had probably been platinum. His dad had been the kind of guy for whom the phrase "captain of industry" was invented. Also, the phrase "son of a bitch."

"I wasn't thinking that, exactly," I replied, although I had been. Chip's early life had been a shower of material goods, but a desert where anything resembling emotion was concerned. "I guess I'm just wishing you hadn't gotten so . . ."

Injured, I'd been about to say. Back in the city, it had been my job to manage money for people like

Chip's dad: wealthy, well connected, and so deeply evil it was a wonder they didn't burst into flames and vanish into puffs of foul smoke, like the devils they resembled at heart.

"Too bad I got so twisted?" Chip took up my sentence for me. "Bent out of shape past recognition, past . . ."

"Now, that *really* wasn't what I meant," I began, but Chip only shook his head. I hadn't seen until now just how near the breaking point he was; he was too good a guest.

He looked up, his eyes darkly circled by the hallway's harsh overhead light. "Did you ever know, all that time I was out there tossing a baseball with Sam—"

Back in the city, he meant, when Sam was eleven and Chip was fifteen, though he'd looked maybe twelve—

"—that it was because I didn't want to go home?"

Oh, for heaven's sake, of course I had. Chip's mom had taken off years earlier to a commune for wealthy, wackily disaffected persons, in the desert Southwest. His father was away a great deal; Chip's home, a fifteen-room, four-story, private-elevatored apartment, housed only himself and a housekeeper who spoke Russian exclusively, and who seemed to dislike him.

Chip zipped his jacket. "Guess I'm the perfect guy to be researching deadly obsessions, though, right?"

Gathering my robe around me, I stepped out onto the porch with him. Under the yellowish porch light, the chill night smelled of woodsmoke, salt spray, and winter not too far in the future.

But before that, rain. A foghorn moaned distantly

and I thought about the nasty weather report I'd heard, and hoped that Chip would get his chance to be outdoors tomorrow.

Then it occurred to me that he might not feel that way about it. "Do you want me to tell Sam anything?"

Like, I meant, that Chip had gone out late and might be too tired or even too hung over—one bar was still open in town at this hour and this late in the season, and Sam was adamant that his own strict sobriety not affect anyone else's behavior—to go out for a twenty-mile trip on a wilderness river.

Chip understood, and laughed. "Oh, no. Hey, I'm up for just about anything. I mean, why not?"

Which wasn't quite the answer I'd hoped for. But before I could say more, he descended the steps and strode off into the fog now beginning to creep stealthily in the late-night streets.

When he'd been gone for a minute, I walked out the short sidewalk to the street myself and looked up at the house looming ghostly in the glow of the mist-shrouded streetlamps like some white-clapboarded ship shouldering heavily out of the gloom.

With three full floors plus an attic, three tall red brick chimneys, and forty-eight old double-hung windows each with a pair of dark green shutters, the house had captured me on sight when I first arrived here in Eastport. Built in 1823, it required more maintenance than your average space shuttle, and when the furnace malfunctioned, as it did at least once a winter, it sounded like the whole place might take off like a shuttle launch, too.

But tonight everything was quiet, raw, and damp,

the kind of night that could bring all your demons creeping up out of the murkiness at you. And whatever was going on with Chip, I thought it was more than a brisk walk could cure.

But he was a survivor, so even then, and even a half hour later when the long-silent church bell a few streets over began ringing and wouldn't stop—

Even then, I don't think I was really worried about him.

Not yet.

When I went back inside, the fire on the dining room hearth had fallen to feathery embers; I checked to see that the screen was up securely in front of them and the damper open a crack, and turned out the lamps.

Upstairs in their apartment on the third floor of the old house, my father and my mother-in-law, Bella Diamond, slept. Wade was asleep, too, in our room's massive antique four-poster, and in the kitchen I'd seen the two dogs, Monday the old black Lab and Prill the Doberman, dead to the world in their dog beds.

A burglar, I thought, could have a field day in here and those two wouldn't stir. But in Eastport the odds were still very much against it: anyway, burglars who want home-repair tools and materials are not so prevalent, here or anywhere, and those were the majority of my belongings nowadays.

So I dismissed the thought and went upstairs, where Wade lay with an arm flung out. Easing in beside him, I listened for last sounds that might mean

I'd have to get up again—the furnace running despite my turning it down, a dog needing to be let outside one more time, or my own personal nightmare, a freak fireplace spark jumping the hearth screen to create an inferno, unstoppable unless I heard it early.

But there was nothing except that foghorn. I drifted off, only to snap awake when the church bell began ringing.

And ringing some more.

Piloting her old Honda CRV one-handed and very fast through the streaming darkness of an unfamiliar rural road in the rain, Lizzie Snow turned the heat up and the defroster fan to high, swigged from the thermos of bourbon-spiked coffee on the car's console, and cranked the volume on Steely Dan's "Black Friday" up yet another notch. At the speed she was traveling, and under these conditions, she probably should've kept both hands on the wheel. But . . .

Screw it. Just screw it, she thought as she drove through the rainy night on an empty road in the middle of Who-the-Hell-Knew-Where, Maine, while the Honda's wipers slapped out a flat, back-and-forth rhythm: *I quit my job, I quit my . . .*

"Shit." Two glowing eyes in the murk ahead made her touch the brakes lightly and put the thermos down without looking at it. Two more pairs; she braked harder, her high beams coalescing around several large shapes in the road, wet leaves spiraling down around them.

Deer. She slowed nearly to a stop on the shiny ribbon of wet asphalt. The animals peered incuriously at her, then continued their casual progress across the road, disappearing like ghosts in the tall weeds on the other side.

She muted the CD player and lowered the car window, feeling her heart pounding in her chest. Rain pattered, loud in the late-night silence; ninety miles out of Bangor and she might as well have been nine hundred. Breathing in the cool, acid-wet smell of the last autumn leaves plastered to the blacktop and the whiff of salt in the night air, she was suddenly sure she'd made a mistake. Then the final deer, the very smallest one that she'd known somehow would be still be there, poked its nose from between two old cedar fence posts. Delicately he stepped in front of the car, pausing once to turn and look at her with his huge, dark eyes.

His two fuzzy forehead bumps, she supposed, were nubbins of antlers. Only when he'd vanished into the brush at the far side of the road with the rest of his kin did she let her breath out. *Just a baby.*

But that thought sent her hand out past the thermos in the center console to the photograph on the passenger seat, slipping it from beneath the .38 automatic that she had used to weigh the sheet of eight-by-ten photo cardstock down.

The dashboard's glow lit the photo of a young teenage girl, her thin, freckled face laughing into the camera. The baby in the girl's arms was only a few days old back then, wrapped in a pink blanket and wearing a pink crocheted cap.

The baby's mother had just turned sixteen, and of course had no idea what was coming, so terribly soon. *Oh, honey . . .*

Cecily had sent emails for a while, to let her big sister Lizzie know how happy she was in Maine, how free she felt. That was when Cecily still had a computer and access to the Internet.

But after that, there'd been a job in a bar and then one as night clerk at a so-called motel, and those things had taken their toll. Besides, booze and drugs were effective pain meds, at least in the short run, and Cecily had been in a lot of pain once the baby's dad took off and left her alone.

A couple of months later, Cecily had called to say that she was broke, and could Lizzie send her some money?

Which of course Lizzie had. She'd been up to her eyebrows in work at the time, though, trying to finish a combination master's and bachelor's degree, so she couldn't just drop everything and leave to help Sissy, as she had always called her younger sister.

Besides, Sissy hadn't wanted her to come. "Wait till I've gotten myself situated for guests," Sissy had insisted, so Lizzie had, secretly relieved not to be disrupting her own life just when her goals were so close, they'd seemed practically in her hands.

And for a little while, that seemed like the right decision.

Emails from Sissy grew happier, and the pictures of her baby showed a healthy, much-loved infant. Maine, Sissy had said, was a good place for a kid, not like back in Springfield, where she and Lizzie had grown up, in a neighborhood where creeps lurked on the corners and even the air was dirty.

Nicolette was the baby's name, Nicki for short, and by the time Lizzie got her degrees, it seemed that

Sissy was doing well as a single mom. Drugs no longer seemed to be in the mix, and Sissy never drunk-dialed Lizzie anymore, or sent any emails that read as if they'd been drunk-typed, either.

She still didn't want visitors, promising instead to bring Nicki to Boston "soon." Maybe that should have alerted Lizzie, but instead she'd let it go, concluding that the bad patch in her sister's life was over, that love and responsibility for the baby had straightened her out when nothing else could. And that they would see one another soon; after the Christmas holidays, maybe. Or in the spring, when the roads weren't so bad . . .

Recalling this, Lizzie put the driver's-side window back up and started off again, through the now steadily falling rain.

I should have come. No matter how well she seemed, I should have come up here and checked on her anyway, and met the baby.

When I still could.

Because suddenly, there'd been silence from Sissy. After a week of it, Lizzie had taken personal time and driven up here—*after it was too late,* she accused herself, meeting her own gaze in the rearview mirror and glancing away guiltily.

Still, she had at least done that much. She'd come here and initiated a serious, by-the-book search: every lead, any scrap of information or rumor that might lead to their whereabouts. If for any reason Sissy didn't want to be found, Lizzie had told everyone she talked to, that would be fine. Lizzie only wanted to make sure mother and daughter were all right.

But she learned nothing useful. And they weren't all right. Ten days after Lizzie had arrived in downeast Maine, Sissy's body had floated in on a lunar high tide. A wave flung it up onto some rocks just south of a place called Shackford Head State Park.

There'd been no sign of Nicki, by then almost a year old. Nor had there been any clue to the child's location among Sissy's pathetic personal effects, in a trailer home that was older and in much worse repair than Sissy had let on.

And there never had been any sign of the little girl, ever since. *Until now.* Lizzie reached for the other photograph lying on the car seat, glancing at it once more even though she'd long memorized its every detail: this one showed a little girl maybe nine years old or so, with cornsilk hair and pale eyes staring at the camera.

Eyes just like Sissy's; hair, too. Both photographs had been sealed in a plain brown envelope that bore no return address. They had shown up in Lizzie's mail at her apartment in Boston a week earlier; no note, no explanation.

And with their arrival, Lizzie's dead sister and missing niece weren't just old wounds anymore, guilty sorrows that could be put out of her mind if she applied enough work, enough intense physical exercise, and— *let's face it*—enough alcohol so that she could sleep.

Now another wave of anxiety washed over Lizzie as she recalled what had happened next, after the photographs dropped from a tan envelope, exploding her world. *I quit my . . .*

Job. Just quit it and then boogied, as her old partner Liam O'Donnell would have put it. *Boogied on out of there, and I'll probably regret it.* Still, she'd had no choice: sending the photos—one of Sissy cradling an infant Nicki, and with it a photograph of some other child, the implication being that this was Lizzie's niece now—could've been someone's idea of a joke, she supposed.

But if so, it was a cruel one, and even that was farfetched; who would do such a thing? Bottom line, Lizzie only knew that Nicki had been born nine years ago, and Sissy had been dead for eight. And that now, somebody wanted Lizzie to remember them.

As if I could forget. Someone wanted it badly enough to go to some trouble, reminding her. Suggesting that Nicki was still alive.

So—*why?* Lizzie had no idea about that, either. But she did know that no baby girl's body had ever been found. And if Nicki's bones weren't in a shallow grave somewhere, or in the ocean—

If they weren't, Sissy's little girl would be Lizzie's only living kin, as well as her only link to the sister she'd let down so terribly and, in the end, she feared, fatally.

She opened the thermos again and took a long drink from it. Cold, but the caffeine still packed a jolt and the bourbon was a sweet relief after the long, dark drive up Route 9 with the log trucks and the eighteen-wheelers thundering on both sides.

Beginning to think that she should've reached the turnoff toward Eastport by now, she dragged the back of her hand over her mouth and peered with renewed intensity through the Honda's dark windshield. Only more wet road showed ahead, and a glance in the rearview mirror showed nothing but her own reflection.

Like a poster for a horror movie, she thought, her hair spiky and eyes darkly hollowed, her lips a slash of red, blackish in the gloom. Then behind her reflection she spotted a flashing red light coming up fast.

Very fast. She hit the hazard lights and pumped the brakes rhythmically. Pulling over as far as she dared onto the road's soft shoulder, she prayed that the driver of the car flying up behind her in the dark would have time to react.

The overtaking vehicle's roof bar flashed on, strobing the night with yellow. A single *whoop-whoop* from the car's siren confirmed what she had already figured out: cops. And from the way they roared by, swerving expertly to the left and then back in again before their taillights vanished around a sharp curve, they were on their way to something.

A crime scene, she thought. Or a bad accident, something hot and fresh. The last reflected glow of departing taillights paled and died, leaving her there in the dark with her heart pounding again.

Thirty minutes later she was cruising over a long, curving causeway toward the island town of Eastport. The dashboard clock said one in the morning. Back in Boston, headlights and neon would still be ablaze, but here it seemed no one was on the road. She slid the window down again, smelling salt water and wet sand. In the distance, foghorns moaned guttural warnings to any sailors foolish or unlucky enough to be out on a night like this; nearer by, a bell buoy clanked monotonously.

The sky ahead, though, glowed red. Some natural phenomenon, the northern lights, maybe, she thought, or a house fire. But then she recognized the glow's deep hue: the same cherry-beacon flaring that she'd seen on the dark road half an hour ago.

I quit my job, I quit my job. The words went on thudding in her head. But they didn't matter, she realized suddenly.

That color on the sky, as if the clouds had been pumped full of blood . . . just the sight of it set her heart racing again, her mind fizzing with gritty anticipation.

Cop-car red. Crime-scene red. A *lot* of cop cars . . .

Murder red.

URGENT WEATHER MESSAGE
WEATHER SERVICE CARIBOU MAINE

FOR INTERIOR HANCOCK-COASTAL HANCOCK-CENTRAL
WASHINGTON-COASTAL WASHINGTON-
INCLUDING THE CITIES OF . . . EASTPORT . . . PERRY . . .
PEMBROKE . . . CALAIS . . . LUBEC . . . MACHIAS

. . . WEATHER ADVISORY IN EFFECT UNTIL MIDNIGHT
EDT TOMORROW NIGHT . . .

THE WEATHER SERVICE IN CARIBOU CONTINUES
URGENT WEATHER ADVISORIES FOR HEAVY RAIN,
GALE FORCE WINDS, TIDAL FLOODING

* PRECIPITATION TYPE . . . RAIN HEAVY AT TIMES.
LOCALLY AS MUCH AS 1 INCH PER HOUR.
* ACCUMULATIONS . . . RAIN 3 TO 5 INCHES TOTAL
EXCEPT WHERE DOWNPOURS FREQUENT.
* TIMING . . . STORM IMPACTS WILL OCCUR IN TWO
DISTINCT WAVES WITH A HURRICANE-LIKE EYE OF
RELATIVE CALM, TODAY INTO TOMORROW NIGHT.
* TEMPERATURES . . . IN THE LOWER 40S.
* WINDS . . . NORTHEAST 35-65 MPH. WITH POSSIBLE
HIGHER GUSTS ESPECIALLY COASTAL. CALM PERIODS
MAY BE DECEPTIVE. STAY ALERT FOR DETERIORATING
CONDITIONS.
* IMPACTS . . . EXPECT TRAVEL DIFFICULTIES. WIND
DAMAGE AND POWER OUTAGES LIKELY. LOCAL

FLOODING LIKELY AND MAY BE PROLONGED DUE TO
WIND VELOCITIES.

PRECAUTIONARY/PREPAREDNESS ACTIONS . . .
TRAVEL DELAYS WILL OCCUR. DO NOT UNDERTAKE
UNNECESSARY TRAVEL. IF YOU MUST TRAVEL, PLAN
EXTRA TIME TO REACH YOUR DESTINATION. SECURE
LOOSE OBJECTS, STAY AWAY FROM WINDOWS DURING
PERIODS OF HIGH WIND. DO NOT DRIVE THROUGH
FLOODED AREAS.
THIS IS PRIMARILY A COASTAL STORM. WINDS
STRONGEST ON ISLANDS AND ALONG THE SHORE.
FLOODING AT HIGH TIDES PROBABLE. HIGH WINDS
WILL IMPACT COMMUNICATIONS IN AFFECTED AREAS.
LOCAL EMERGENCY ENTITIES SHOULD TAKE NOTE.

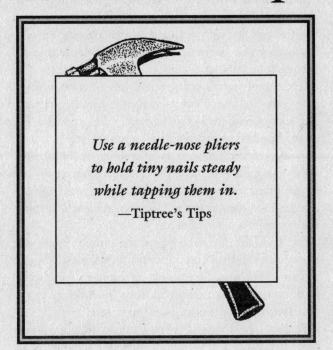

Chapter 4

Use a needle-nose pliers
to hold tiny nails steady
while tapping them in.
—Tiptree's Tips

The Motel East's empty parking lot gleamed like wet licorice as Lizzie pulled gratefully into a space by the Office sign, then turned the car off.

Made it. The trip from Boston had taken eight hours, all of it in darkness and most in the kind of rain that turned driving into an eyestrain exercise, enough to smear up the windshield but never enough to rinse it clean.

Lizzie let her head roll back, then side to side. Not that it would help; since getting the envelope with the unfamiliar pictures in it, she'd felt like an iron rod was stuck between her shoulder blades and up through the base of her neck.

The motel's small office was dimly lit. Five minutes after entering the office, she was letting herself into her new home-away-from-home. She dropped her duffel bag and snapped all the lights on, starting with the ones in the large, reassuringly clean bathroom. Next came the lamps on the bedside tables, the ones by the chair and on the desk, finally the wall sconces and the overhead in the tiny microwave-and-mini-fridge-equipped kitchenette.

She finished by snapping on the pair of lights just outside the sliding glass doors, on the small wooden balcony. The motel was built into a steep bank over-looking the bay, so the drop from the balcony to the courtyard below was at least thirty feet.

Perfect, she thought; pretty much intruder-proof. Sissy had always raved about how safe Eastport was, how hardly anyone even locked a door and how when Nicki got older she could play outside without an adult hovering over her every minute.

But then look what happened to Sissy.

The silence in the motel room was stunning, making the words in her head sound even louder. Lizzie turned abruptly from the sliding glass windows, un-able to see the bay in the darkness but knowing it was there, the ice-cold water that had swallowed her sis-ter. Fiercely she forced her mind back to her own well-being; her drive into town on the main street running along the water's edge had showed only rows of darkened storefronts.

Nowhere open now to eat, she realized, and she'd skipped dinner. But a few individually packaged snack cakes rested in a plastic basket on the room's kitchenette counter; ordinarily, she'd never have touched them. She could fill up on them, though, wash their too-sweet gumminess down with what was left in the bourbon-and-Starbucks thermos, and, if necessary, with a couple of swallows from the bourbon bottle itself.

Why was she thinking about food anyway? She wasn't even hungry. But she knew. It was so she wouldn't think about a certain guy, not even his name, and most certainly not the fact that she was here in the same state with him instead of safely far away, in Massachusetts.

Far away, where she couldn't just call him and he could be with her in a few hours. If he wanted to be, which was another whole questionable subject . . .

Stop. She jumped up, facing herself in the mirror behind the dresser. Glaring back at her was a woman whose three-inch-heeled black dress boots defiantly increased her height; at five foot nine she was as tall as many of the men she'd worked with, taller than a few. She ran an impatient hand over her dark hair, whose short, spiky messiness made her look like a punk rocker, drew a spit-moistened index finger under each eye to wipe away smeared mascara.

None of which helped much, nor did the short denim jacket, slim black Levi's, or black silk turtleneck she wore. *All I need now is a pierced eyebrow to make sure everyone in Eastport thinks I just dropped in from Mars.* Her halfhearted try at mascara-gunk removal hadn't done much good, either. Still . . .

Screw it, she thought defiantly again. She didn't want a shower, and even as tired as she was, the idea of sleep was beyond ridiculous.

Because she was here. She'd done it. And she might very well end up done for, at least professionally, on account of it. *I quit my job I quit my . . .* Oh, shut up, she told the nagging voice in her head, and for once it actually obeyed.

For now, anyway. Turning from the mirror, she dug into her duffel bag for her pink wool scarf. She wrapped the scarf around her neck, noting that a big slug of hot pink improved things immensely, then tucked the scarf ends into her jacket front.

Suddenly she looked decent, if still not exactly ordinary. She made sure that the .38 auto was in her bag, that it was loaded and the safety was on. When she stepped outside, the glow of cop-car lights still pulsed redly on the night sky, only a few blocks distant. The faint but unmistakable sputter of a dispatch radio suggested that this might've been what the squad car was racing toward, on the road earlier.

Damn, though. Because sure, it was interesting. But it could turn out very unhelpful; she'd planned to check in with local law enforcement first thing in the morning, introduce herself and see if anyone remembered her sister and Nicki. But now it looked as if the local cops might have plenty on their plates already.

Still, she had nothing else to do. In the chilly drizzle, she crossed the motel's parking lot and the empty

street and headed uphill past an old red-brick library
with tall arched windows and a cannon bolted to a
concrete block set into its lawn.

Ten minutes later, she was still walking; it was farther than she'd thought. But eventually a steep downhill stretch to a sharp right-hand curve brought her to
within a half block of the bright white crime-scene
lights set up in front of a church; two churches, actually, but only one was lit, the other, its near-twin,
lurking half-visible in reflected glare from the first.

Somewhere nearby, a man's voice kept shouting
something. A name, Lizzie realized, howled raggedly
over and over. Then she noticed another man walking too, a dozen yards ahead of her, and where the
hell had he come from?

He hadn't been there a moment ago. From between
the houses lining the street, maybe, slipping out of a
backyard . . .

But then she caught herself. This was Eastport, not
Boston. Probably the guy lived in one of the white
clapboard houses, each with its bay window, tiny front
yard, and gabled roof, that seemed to have multiplied
like white rabbits here. Still . . .

Tan slacks, light blue jacket, sneakers with some
kind of a silvery reflecting logo on their heels; maybe
she was being silly but she committed the details to
memory anyway, along with his pale hair and the
cautious way he slowed near the corner, as if he didn't
want to be seen by the people in front of the church.

There was a rabbit's foot on a chain dangling
from his belt loop, she noticed. And then suddenly he
was gone; frowning, she quickened her step, but he'd
slipped away somewhere, into one of the dark, nar-

row yard areas between the houses, maybe, or behind one of them.

But *which* one? She didn't like not knowing where he'd gone; automatically her hand went to her bag to find her weapon as she paused under a streetlamp whose anemic glow was sickly yellow. Ahead stood more old houses, some dark and vacant-appearing but others with porch and multiple interior lights blazing, probably on account of all the activity around the church.

You'd have to be deaf not to hear that guy yelling the same name over and over. And the lights made the church front resemble a movie set, the building's massive white front rising up and up into the streaming mist.

The shouting stopped. As she watched, a man dropped to his knees on the church's lawn, face in hands. Cop cars clogged the street and a small but growing crowd had gathered.

Lizzie scanned the personnel inside the crime-scene tape, picking out a man with a medical bag and clipboard. A couple of guys in state cop uniforms conferred by the two big front doors, propped open with folding chairs so the scene lights illuminated a small foyer. A bulletin board on the foyer's wall displayed the words BAKE SALE in green letters.

A boxy white EMS vehicle backed up onto the lawn near the weeping man. The lights in the patient compartment were on but no one was inside; when the doors opened, Lizzie could see the vacant gurney with empty IV hooks dangling over it.

She approached the lit-up scene until she reached the yellow tape barrier. The man on the lawn looked up des-

perately as if he might see—somehow, miraculously—
what had been taken from him.

A pang pierced her. He was probably the spouse,
or parent, maybe, of whoever the victim was here,
someone whose loved one would lie unceremoniously
where they'd been found until all the photos and
measurements and samples had been taken, the careful collection of evidence more important, now, than
the empty husk of a human being.

But not to him. *His child,* Lizzie guessed, certain
she was correct. She'd seen that special hell before,
on too many suddenly bereaved parents' faces, to be
mistaken. And not just on good parents' faces, either;
looking at the man again, she got the sense without
quite knowing why that he was one of the ones who'd
always planned to do better, someday.

Yeah, someday, she thought bleakly. Someday never
had arrived for her own dad, either, hers and Sissy's;
maybe that was why this guy in the churchyard seemed
unpleasantly familiar in his over-the-top dramatic,
it's-all-about-me mourning style.

It was how, she recalled very clearly, her dad had
grieved for her mother. He'd been half in the bag in
the intensive care waiting room at nine in the morning, wailing loudly and pounding the wall so that
the hospital's security officers had had to be called.

An officer she hadn't seen before came out of the
church. Plump and pink-faced with thinning hair, he
wore a blue uniform shirt that was almost all one big
perspiration stain. Spotting the man on the lawn, he
spoke sharply, and soon thereafter two ambulance
guys helped the man to a folding chair.

One got him a cup of water. The other one crouched by him.

Then, as Lizzie was about to turn away, another figure emerged: tall, very slender, with high cheekbones and a lot of dark hair curling over his jacket collar . . .

Lizzie swung around reflexively before he could spot her, a lump suddenly in her throat. *Dylan.*

She'd known he was in Maine, of course; had not, in fact, been able to stop knowing it for a minute, all the way here. But he was supposed to be in Augusta, not out here in the boondocks.

Damn . . . The young uniformed cop approaching her must've thought she was trying to avoid him. "Hey," he called sharply.

She turned back, still keeping her face in profile. She didn't want Dylan spotting her, and she hoped he wasn't coming in her direction.

Or most of her hoped that. Only that damned little voice in her head kept saying, *One more glimpse of him. Just one more . . .*

Please.

The young cop confronted her politely. "Excuse me. You have business here?" He indicated the scene of misery behind him with a jerk of his head, meanwhile assessing her.

From his face she could tell that he was already finding her to be sober, civil, forthright, and at least halfway decently dressed. She saw him place her in the "probably okay" category, and felt the same relief that any other private citizen would.

Especially since, she suddenly realized, she had an

illegal .38 automatic in her bag. Maine required a carry permit, and she didn't have one.

But that wasn't likely to be a problem now; the young cop had begun noticing her on a personal level, his manner suddenly casual as he ducked under the tape to get closer.

Fail, she thought, because she did have that weapon in her bag, didn't she? And despite her probably okay appearance, she could be anyone.

She glanced past the young cop in time to glimpse Dylan Hudson just folding his lanky frame into a car with a Maine state decal on it. The car swung around toward her; she felt a brief flare of panic until the car pulled another fast U-turn and sped off in the other direction.

She looked back up at the cop's blandly handsome face: light hair and eyes, blond eyelashes. The smugly confident expression on it told her that girls around here thought he was the cat's meow.

"Don't think I know you," he said, putting a little twinkle into it. Back in Boston that twinkle would've lasted about five seconds before somebody smacked it off him. But:

Come on, give him a break. He's not working in Boston. He's from here.

She produced ID though he hadn't asked for it, careful not to let him see into her bag, then waited while he examined it with feigned seriousness, giving her the girlie treatment.

"Boston girl, huh?" He gave the ID back. "And your interest here?" Not quite teasing. He had a job to do and he was doing it.

Sort of. She gave him the spiel: just arrived in town,

out for a walk after the long drive, etc. Enough information to satisfy without overexplaining. Then she described the man she'd seen walking ahead of her in the fog minutes earlier.

His look grew more serious and he wrote that part down, at least. On the lawn the emergency workers were helping the weeping man into the ambulance. By the church steps, the plump uniformed guy shot a look her way, noticed his officer still with her, and appeared to be starting toward them. Then at a shout from inside the massive white structure, he went back in.

". . . some very unpleasant stuff going on in there," the young cop told her patronizingly, noting her interest. "Now, why would a pretty young lady like you want to worry about . . . ?"

Her turn to twinkle. She was good at it, too. "C'mere."

To his credit, he hesitated. She crooked a finger invitingly at him. "C'mon, I won't bite."

Smiling, she waited until he'd bent down a little, so she could whisper to him. She took care not to touch him.

"If I were a bad person, you'd be *dead* now," she hissed. "And if you ever talk to me like that again, I'll kick you so hard that you'll be wearing a truss for the rest of your life, got it?"

She backed away sharply, feeling sorry for an instant about his shocked face. But only for an instant.

"Now, you can either take a lesson, or you can go whining to your boss about how the little lady got the jump on you."

Then she handed him his duty weapon, an HK

USP .45, which she'd slipped from its holster while he was busy having his ear whispered into. "Keep your damn safety strap snapped, too."

He grabbed the gun, eyeing her furiously, obviously trying to think of some way to take her into custody without risking the real story getting out. But there were just enough people around and near enough so that someone could have seen the incident.

And in a town this small, "see" quickly became "tell." His face crimson, he ducked back under the tape.

"Make this a short visit," he advised over his shoulder as he stalked away, his voice harsh with wounded dignity.

Yeah, or I'll end up kicking your ass the rest of the way around the block, Lizzie thought at him. But as she watched him go she knew it was her own rear end that really deserved kicking.

Nice work, she scolded herself as she sidled around to where a lot of gawkers had gathered, some in heavy jackets, others in sleepwear with fuzzy slippers and layers of sweaters. A bunch of teenaged boys peered wide-eyed from the rear of the crowd, their mouths hanging open in fascination at all the exciting goings-on.

Good work, Lizzie, way to antagonize the local cops. That'll get you a lot of help. Idiot.

Still, the guy had been a creep, trying to lay that load of patronizing crap on her, and anyway she'd never been a fan of the catch-more-flies-with-honey routine.

Or at least not when a solid shot of vinegar was an

option. "What's going on?" she asked as she approached the onlookers.

"Dead girl in there," a man said in a thick Maine accent: *they-ah*.

He was in his fifties, wearing a red plaid wool jacket and heavy trousers plus thick-soled work boots. A woman in pink foam rollers frowned disapprovingly at him, as if he'd revealed some family secret.

He didn't notice, busy swiping a clear droplet from the end of his nose. "Like a slaughterhouse," he went on. " 'Least if what Tiffany Whitmore said is true."

He gestured with his swiping finger at a squad car parked at the curb. In the car's front passenger seat with the door open was a heavyset young woman in a scrub suit, the white turtleneck under the scrub top making her look even bulkier.

"She was inside," said the man in the red jacket. "She found the body," he added.

No, she didn't, thought Lizzie. If that were true, the woman wouldn't be sitting there alone. Every minute that passed risked blurring important memories; besides, you didn't want the media—or anyone else—getting to even after-the-fact witnesses, giving a defense attorney ways to demolish testimony later.

Not that there seemed to be any media here, she realized: no reporters' notebooks were visible, and neither were any cameras. No one was even holding a cell phone up.

Also, no one was hassling the cops, no catcalls or bottles were being thrown, and since there was no video being shot, no junior comedians were capering and mugging in hopes of ending up on the TV news. Even the EMS techs weren't keeping an eye on their vehicle's doors to make sure no one reached in and stole something from it.

I guess we really aren't in Kansas anymore. Fatigue, held off so far by wired nerves and spiked coffee, hit her suddenly between the shoulder blades with an ache like a dull drill boring in. She should go lie down, stare at the motel room ceiling for a few hours.

And tomorrow, start trying to find Nicki. That was her job here, not—

"Not going to stick around and tell them how to proceed?" The voice was low, wryly amused. *And familiar . . .*

Unmistakable. She froze, not turning. Barely breathing.

Dylan. "Not like you. I mean," the voice went on, "you're so good at knowing what other people should do."

No. I saw him leaving. Don't let it be . . .

Don't let it be him, she prayed desperately.

But of course it was.

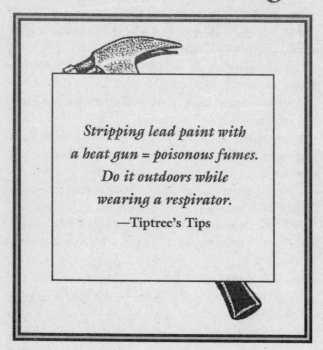

Chapter 5

*Stripping lead paint with
a heat gun = poisonous fumes.
Do it outdoors while
wearing a respirator.*
—Tiptree's Tips

"This is Jake Tiptree, how can I help you?"

Deep in my own thoughts, the next morning I answered the phone the way I used to do back in the city, when the call was almost certainly either business- or neurosurgery-related.

Or possibly from one of Sam's drugged-up pals,

but that's another story, too. "Jake," the voice on the phone said now, "it's Bob Arnold. Is Wade still there?"

Not business this time. Not neurosurgery, either. I was in Eastport, Maine, in my big old house on Key Street, and this call was homicide-related.

"No, Bob, he's with George over at the Hansens', trying to help." With my friend Ellie's husband, George Valentine, I meant, trying to keep Karen Hansen's dad, Hank, from putting a gun to his head.

I personally thought Hank Hansen could have demonstrated his love for his daughter a little better before she died, if he was going to be so histrionic about it afterwards. Everyone in town knew the poor kid got food money by recycling Hank's beer bottles a six-pack at a time. But now, of course, he was heart-broken.

"Bob, d'you have any idea yet who might've done it?"

They'd taken Hank to the hospital and sedated him, but he was out again, and from what I'd heard, it was touch-and-go as to whether there might be another violent death soon. It depended, Wade said, on him and George finding all Hank's weapons; in addition to his other stellar qualities, Hank was the kind of guy who believed the Chinese might invade any day now, and that they would probably come ashore right here in Eastport.

"No." Bob's tone, usually friendly, was curt. "We don't have a suspect. Listen, Jake," he went on, "let Wade know I want him to find me just as soon as he gets a chance, all right? I have," he added resignedly, "no idea where I'll be."

"I'll tell him. And I expect he'll find you." In our town on an island four miles wide by seven miles long, you could usually locate just about anyone without too much trouble.

"Take care, Bob," I said, and went back to the kitchen, where Sam and Chip Hahn were at the breakfast table, which Bella was trying to keep supplied with food. But two healthy young men, it turned out, could eat even faster than Bella could cook.

Or Sam could, anyway. Chip's roundish, usually amiable face looked pale green, and his toast and eggs were mostly untouched.

He fiddled with a slice of bacon. "I don't get it. How did this girl get into the bell tower? Don't they keep it locked?"

The question startled me, because it was so close to what I was thinking. "Um, no," I said, and then went on to explain that security in the tower itself wasn't what you might call strict.

"You and Ellie were in there yesterday, weren't you?" Sam asked. Yet another question that hadn't been designed to pluck my worry-strings, but did.

"Yeah," I said unhappily. "Right up there in the belfry, we were looking for rehab and repair chores that might need doing."

The Chamber of Commerce was going to write grant proposals, and if the church wanted in on this there'd need to be a list of specific tasks lined up for funding. And on the simple principle that it was good to do something civic-minded occasionally, Ellie and I had said we'd see if anything obvious like a roof leak or a case of dry rot jumped out at us, just on preliminary inspection.

But the place had turned out to be in a lot worse repair than we'd thought, so we hadn't gotten finished. We'd even left our tools and notebooks up there, thinking we'd be back.

That wasn't my problem now, though. My problem now was not recalling whether, on our way out, we'd locked the church door. If we hadn't, I was afraid that was how the murdered girl got in.

And her murderer, too; outside, the sky spat cold rain. Between vintage tunes like "Purple People Eater" and "Hand Jive," radio station WQDY advised mariners to stay in port.

I gathered that the kayak trip was also canceled. "You were out last night, Chip, right?" Sam asked. "Did you see anything?"

Sam drank down a cup of coffee, got halfway up for another, and was met by Bella, already wielding a fresh pot. Meanwhile I thought Chip's hand with the bacon slice in it paused on its reluctant way to his mouth.

"Um," he said, chewing manfully. And when he had swallowed: "No." He frowned at his eggs. "No, I walked out Deep Cove Road and back, came home in the other direction from the church."

He glanced at me. "I had some thinking to do," he said.

I poured my own coffee while Bella put a bowl of fruit salad on the table, sliced pears and the last frozen blackberries. "So," I said carefully, "I guess you must've slept very well after all that fresh air and exercise."

"Yeah," Chip replied unconvincingly, "I slept great." He got up, scraped his plate, and took it to the old soapstone sink to rinse it. "So, Sam, what's on our agenda instead of kayaking?" he asked, running the water a little too hard.

To cover, maybe, the quaver in his voice. "You can come to the boatyard with me," Sam offered. "I mean, since we're not going anywhere, I guess I might as well put the hours in." He got up. "You could hang out, bring your laptop, and do some work if you want. There's wi-fi," he added.

He stacked his breakfast dishes in the sink without rinsing them, this being the way that Bella preferred, and if you knew what was good for you around here, you tried hard to do things the way she liked them.

"But we gotta get going," Sam finished, and with that the two of them hustled from the room, headed upstairs.

"How come the boy lied, d'you suppose?" Bella said, scowling into the dishpan when they had gone.

I turned down the radio. Rawboned, henna-haired, and with a face like a hatchet that has been used to chop concrete blocks, Bella was fond of Chip Hahn, too.

But she wasn't fond of falsehoods. "I don't know," I replied as the two young men thundered back downstairs and out the door together, calling their goodbyes.

"I heard him come in." Bella scrubbed at a stubborn bit of egg residue. "Last night, after everyone else was in bed."

She rinsed the plate in water so hot, you could've poached another egg in it. "I was looking south over toward the churches on Two Church Lane from the high upstairs window . . ."

From the third floor, she meant, where she and my dad lived in the apartment Wade and I had built for them up there. From its lofty windows, you could look out over half the town and the bay beyond.

"And I saw that boy walking. Came right up Key Street, the opposite way from what he just said."

She rinsed a sudsy juice glass in the barely liquefied steam issuing from the faucet. "Way he came, he couldn't have missed the commotion down there. A dead man," she emphasized, "couldn't have missed it."

A sudden, stiff breeze tore the last autumn maple leaf off a branch, and it slapped wetly flat up against the kitchen window, splayed out like a bloody handprint. At the same moment, the back door flew open and Ellie White rushed in, her red-gold hair breeze-tangled and her green eyes anxious.

The chill outside had put pink roses in her freckled cheeks, but the rest of her face was pale. "Jake? Is Sam in some kind of trouble?"

I hadn't thought she'd be able to trump the question I was about to ask her, but that did it. "No, not that I . . ."

It struck me suddenly that after I'd heard Sam's car doors slam outside, I hadn't heard what should've come next: an old engine roaring to life with a chug-and-rumble, parts reluctantly shuddering into motion, then the *pow! pow!* of an engine firing off random explosions before settling to the regular *bam-bam-bam*-ing that on Sam's car we called idling.

No start-up at all, in fact, and none of the desperate *err-err-ERR* sounds of it not starting up, either. I hurried outside and out the front walk, where a squad car was pulling away. Through its rear window I could make out the shape of someone in the back seat.

Then I spotted Sam on the sidewalk with a woman. Tall and ramrod straight, she had a lot of short, spiky black hair, and a lot of attitude in the way she faced Sam while he yelled at her.

"What the heck did you just do? What did *he* do? Who the heck *are* you, anyway?"

He turned as I hurried toward them. "Mom, Bob Arnold just took Chip away. To *question* him! Because *she*—"

He stopped. The woman was walking away, briskly but not at all hurriedly. "Hey, wait a minute! You can't just—"

She looked back over her shoulder. "I'm sorry about your friend, but he was there last night. At the crime scene. When I got asked about it, I said I'd seen him, that's all."

She kept walking. Gesturing at Sam to stay where he was—by now he was practically foaming at the mouth—I caught up to her, and when she glanced back again at my approach, I could see how pretty she was: dark, wing-shaped eyebrows and dark lashes, high cheekbones, a heart-shaped face.

"Excuse me, but would you mind telling me how you knew it was our friend that you'd seen?"

While I spoke, my mind went on racking up the details: exquisite skin, huge blue eyes, lovely makeup. She wore a pair of black jeans that fit her so perfectly, they appeared to have been tailored, and high, black stack-heeled boots.

Her black leather jacket looked soft as butter and

had a red-wine-colored silk lining. "Rabbit's foot," she said simply.

My heart sank, even as the hairs on the back of my neck went on bristling with instant mistrust. To cover it, I stuck my hand out and introduced myself, and she did the same.

"Lizzie Snow," she said. Her grip was cool and surprisingly gentle. She didn't need to emphasize anything, obviously.

Meanwhile, Chip was in trouble. I still didn't know what kind, exactly, but I did know he had a rabbit's foot key chain that he carried obsessively.

"The young man you saw last night is my houseguest," I told Lizzie Snow. "I feel responsible for him, his welfare, and so on, you know? So could you tell me a little more about what you saw?"

I gestured across the street at my big old house: white clapboards, forest-green shutters. Towering over us with its old-fashioned respectability and its clear need for chronic TLC, it fairly trumpeted my own solid good citizenship. After all, with a house like that, how would I have the energy for anything else?

"Why don't you come in?" I coaxed. "I've just made coffee."

Which was a lie. But Bella could do it fast, and I was still putting things together in my head about Lizzie Snow: a no-nonsense woman, new in town or I'd have heard about her already, who looked . . . well, she looked like just about everything I'd left behind when I turned my back on the city in favor of Maine:

Good haircut, expensive makeup carefully applied,

clothes that had been chosen, not just thrown on because they were clean. Even more striking was a sense
of purpose she radiated so clearly that it practically
came off her in waves.

Not a happy sense, necessarily. More like a *probing*
sense, the way she took in my face, the house, Sam's
unhappy expression. When a car approached on the
street, her glance went from the license plate to the
windshield sticker and then to the driver's face, bing-
bing-bing . . .

A *hunting* sense. It didn't make me like her any better, but it gave me a hunch.

"Come on in," I repeated, because what the *heck*
was she up to, anyway? "You never know, I might
have information that you're looking for, too. Or I'll
know someone who does."

Bingo.

Back in the city where I was a financial advisor,
I used to have to finagle people's money stories out
of them: the size of their alimony payments, amount of
their delinquent income taxes, what they owed to
loan sharks, bookies, and the purveyors of the substances they used to help them forget all the other
money they owed.

So I wasn't expecting Lizzie Snow to be much of
a challenge, spilled-guts-wise. I brought her inside,
Ellie came with us, and half an hour later, as we three
sipped fresh coffee by the kitchen woodstove, I had
an astonishing story out of her: a possibly murdered
sister, a missing child, photos in an envelope with no
return address but with an Eastport postmark.

But it wasn't the *whole* story; I got the feeling that there was way more to this stranger than she was telling, even though what she did say rang true: The sister's body, I now recalled, had indeed been found in Eastport.

"So I decided to come up here," Lizzie explained. She sat in the bentwood rocker pulled up to the stove. "Because someone who knows something sent me the pictures from here. I just don't know why."

I hadn't forgotten about Chip. But when you're trying to get something from someone, it's just good manners to pay attention to what they want first.

Also, it's good strategy. "Someone," said Ellie to Lizzie Snow, "who knows what happened back then, maybe. And thinks that something still needs to happen about it now?"

Lizzie looked appreciative. "Exactly. Or maybe some new thing has happened, even after all this time. It would have to be someone who knew who and where I was, too, of course. But—"

"But why not just go to the police?" Ellie asked. "If you have information about an old murder, or about a missing child, that would be your first move, ordinarily, wouldn't it?"

Lizzie looked down at her coffee mug. "Mmm. But I don't have information, do I? And no one else thinks it was a murder."

She took a sip of her coffee. "Anyway," she went on, "that's not really what I'm here for, my sister's death. I came to find Nicki, if I can. That's the long and short of it."

"Really" was all I could say for a moment. "After all this time, you . . ."

"Yeah." Her rueful smile said she understood. "Wild-goose chase, huh? Maybe so," she allowed.

Then she looked around my big old kitchen with its antique built-in cabinets, tall bare windows, and pine wainscoting. Bright rag rugs warmed the hardwood floor, and the stove radiated cozily. "Nice place," said Lizzie, changing the subject.

Or I thought she was, at first. But on the kitchen shelf, snapshots of my family and Ellie's smiled from among Sam's boat school diplomas and the various ribbons and mugs he had won in sailing contests out on the bay.

"Nice family, it looks like, too," she added.

Then I got the point: Nicki was her family. Maybe all of it, and she wanted it. It didn't make me like her any more or trust her any better, but I thought that part of her story at least was true.

"So if you find your niece," I asked, "you'll try to take her back to Boston with you? Raise her?"

At that she looked uncomfortable. "I'm not sure. I want to know if she's alive, first of all . . ."

In other words, she had no idea. My turn. "So what did you tell Bob Arnold about Chip?"

She shrugged. "Not much. I stopped in to see your police chief just to introduce myself. I said I knew he had a lot on his plate, and no time for my problems. But I figured I'd better let him know what I'm doing here in town, since I doubt it'll take long for rumors to start."

She had that right. In Eastport if you sneeze at one end of town, they'll be getting out the aspirin and hot lemonade for you at the other end in ten seconds flat.

"One of his officers saw me near the commotion at the church last night," she went on, "and I'd mentioned then that I saw your friend. Although I didn't know then that he *was* your friend."

"So that's why Bob wanted to talk to Chip?" Ellie's tone was doubtful. "Because you saw him walking by?"

The rabbit's foot dangling from his belt loop had identified him, of course. Bob Arnold had stopped in to see Wade a few days earlier, on the morning when Chip arrived, and commented on it as a way of making conversation while he was meeting Chip.

Bob had said he could use one, too, and so of course later remembered the thing. It wasn't like Chip, though, ignoring a crime scene; he was, after all, a crime-book researcher.

Or lying about it afterwards, either. Just then Sam rushed back in. "Mom! Chip's been arrested!"

Then Wade came in, looking even more unhappy than Sam. "Jake, did you by any chance take a knife out of my workshop? A big one, with a black taped handle?"

"Ellie, did we lock that church door yesterday?" I asked as soon as Lizzie Snow had gone.

I hadn't taken Wade's knife, of course. Ellie's face fell. ". . . I think we did. Don't you remember doing it?"

I didn't. I might have locked it; we'd been in a hurry, her to get home before her daughter, Lee, returned from school, and me to try to get in a few work hours on my own house, after half a day of assessing what repairs were needed inside the church.

As to why our offer to do this had been accepted, all I can say is that something about keeping your own house from falling down seems to make people think you can do it for other antique structures, too. Next thing I knew, I was marking dry-rot patches and measuring for new support beams and trying to figure out why the plaster in the belfry stairwell was cracked diagonally in one direction on one side, and the other way on the other.

None of which seemed very important right now. "Jake," Ellie said troubledly, "if we didn't lock it, that means . . ."

Yeah. I'd already thought of it: that if we'd left that door open, we'd as good as let the victim *and* her murderer inside. "I wish I remembered for sure," Ellie said.

But we didn't, and there was no help for it. "What'd you tell Lizzie?" Ellie asked. She'd left Lizzie and me alone in the kitchen for the final few minutes of our visit.

"I said we'd help her if she'd help us," I replied. "I mean, if any of us got the chance."

Lizzie planned to go around Eastport asking questions about her own family, not about Chip. Still, she might come up with something, and I'd run the photos of her niece and sister through the scanner built into Wade's copier so I could make more or even email them if need be.

"And what about the knife?" asked Ellie.

"I don't know," I replied, thinking, *Dear God, the knife.* Because Wade was definitely missing one that matched the description of the murder weapon. And you could explain being in one place when you'd said you were in another, I supposed.

So maybe Chip still could finesse that, somehow. But explaining the presence at a crime scene of a big, sharp knife that everyone knew had come from the house where you were staying, *after* you'd lied about where you were . . .

Ellie took some copies of Lizzie's pictures, slid them into her bag. "The thing is, though . . . ," she began.

"Right," I replied, catching her thought: that even if we had forgotten to lock that church door, how could anyone *know* we had?

Outside the windows, the sky darkened suddenly. Sleet began tapping the panes, then dissolved to fat raindrops slapping.

"No one would know that door was open unless they'd been watching us," I said. "And who'd do that just on the chance they might see us forget to lock it?"

I put the kettle on. "It doesn't make sense. And the worst thing is, we might never know for sure."

Not that our consciences were the important victims in this situation, but still. "Meanwhile, maybe we'd better start getting ready for whatever *that* is," Ellie said with a worried nod at the rain-slashed windows. "It's starting to look nasty."

"Gettin' wild," agreed Bella, coming in with a dust rag and a can of Pledge in her hands. "Gale flags are flying, I heard on the radio. It's a real old-fashioned nor'easter."

So she got busy fetching candles from the butler's pantry and gathering up our kerosene lamps, flashlights, and batteries, while Ellie and I decided to head downtown to see if we could do anything for Chip, while it was still possible to go out at all.

Maybe that would distract me from my lingering reaction to Lizzie Snow: that I didn't like her or trust her. For one thing, she'd put our friend Chip in a jam. True, he'd helped her do it with his own inexplicable deceptiveness on the subject of where he'd been last night. But that didn't change the fact that she was hiding something, too, I'd have bet my new claw hammer on it.

And on top of that was the undeniable pang of envy I felt, meeting a woman as smart and stylish as I'd been, once upon a time. Not that I didn't love my life, but still: back then I could hike fast from Times Square to SoHo in three-inch heels, not even breaking a sweat. Nowadays I couldn't take two steps in the kind of high-stacked boots Lizzie was wearing; was there such a thing as *too* comfortable? I found myself wondering.

So yeah, maybe a walk in the weather would clear my head, I thought as I confronted the shiny makeup-free zone that was my face in the hall mirror. Nothing snazzy had magically appeared in the closet, so I pulled on an old denim jacket of Sam's, thinking it would at least keep me warm and—I hoped—reasonably dry. I mean, the weather couldn't have gotten that much worse in the short time we'd been indoors, could it?

Wrong: as soon as we stepped out into the rising storm, I knew we'd made a mistake.

But hey, at least I wasn't worrying about how I looked.

* * *

Half-frozen rain pellets hit my face like a barrage of icy bullets. All the way down Key Street, the wind buffeted us first one way, then shoved us the other.

"We should've taken the car!" Elllie shouted, but driving in this wouldn't have been any picnic, either. On Water Street, spray surged up over the rocky riprap lining the harbor, rain hammered the plate glass windows of the stores, and wind howled like a wild animal demanding to be let out of a cage.

Staggering, we let ourselves be blown toward Bob Arnold's new office in the old A&P grocery store building, across from the massive granite post office structure. Fighting to keep the glass door from tearing off its hinges when she hauled it open, Ellie shoved me inside, hurled herself in after me, and muscled the big door closed again with both hands.

Bob Arnold saw us from his desk, in his new headquarters' large open-plan office area. Scowling, he heaved himself up out of his new office chair and came from behind his new desk. Pausing to sneeze twice—the place smelled like fresh drywall compound—he advanced upon us.

"What're you two doing out?" Pink and plump, with a few hair strands slicked back from a domed forehead, Bob had a round face, light blond lashes around light eyes, and a pink rosebud mouth that didn't look at all as if it belonged on a police officer.

His harmless appearance served him well, however, since on account of it many guys didn't put up a fight early, and by the time they realized their mistake he'd already snapped the handcuffs on them. And even if they did fight, they learned pretty swiftly that looks can be deceiving, which I hoped they were now because Bob looked mad as the dickens.

"What," he demanded again, "do you think you're—"

He stopped in frustration. Past him in the office area were six identical desks, each with a phone, a laptop computer, a chair, and a wastebasket. On one wall hung a classroom-sized whiteboard, a large calendar, and a big white-faced clock.

The opposite wall, on the street side, had been the front of the old A&P where the weekly specials on pot roasts, paper goods, and sweet corn had been postered. Now white venetian blinds covered the windows, their louvered slats almost shutting out the rattle of rain mixed with sleet outside.

"Ugh," I said, pulling off wet outerwear. After the walk down here, I already felt like somebody had been hitting me with one of my own hammers, and this place wasn't helping any. Besides the drywall compound, it smelled like latex paint, chemicals from the whiteboard markers, and glue from the indoor-outdoor carpeting, recently installed.

Bob hated it in here, though, and I didn't blame him. All this new, supposedly better location needed was a spray-textured ceiling with glitter in it to make the ticky-tacky look complete.

But that's not what was eating him now. "I've got a dead girl. I've got her *father.* I've got the state cops, the medical examiner, the DA, and the *Bangor Daily News* all crawlin' up my rosy red—"

I cut him off. "Bob, have you got Chip? The kid who's staying at my house, that you picked up just a little while ago on Key Street?"

I'd already seen copies of Lizzie Snow's photographs on the office corkboard; Bob must've made them when she was here introducing herself. But what I didn't see, back there among the new desks and chairs all lined up like an ad for Office Depot, was my houseguest. I had a mental picture of Chip Hahn being whisked off for a brief courtroom appearance, followed by a long sojourn in prison while a case against him was meticulously assembled.

And putting Chip into a prison population was going to work out about as well as dropping a tame mouse into a room full of hungry cats. His only hope would be trading that rabbit's foot of his for a tommy gun, somehow.

Bob didn't answer. Instead, he yanked his slicker and sou'wester from the doorway area's carved wooden coat-tree, the only item he had managed to salvage from the old cop shop.

"Bob," I pressed him, "I really need to—"

He turned on me. "No, you don't, Jake."

He stomped his feet into rubber shoe covers. "There are people in this situation who need things. You're not one of them."

His tone was as harsh as a slap, betraying, I supposed, the pressure he felt.

He shoved the heavy door open, then relented. "But I guess you won't give up until you get what you've come for, will you?"

He squinted up into the thinning rain, and when he did I saw that some of the drops running down his face were tears.

Shock kept me silent. I'd known Bob for a long

time; he was a friend. I'd never seen him this way before.

"Come on," he ordered gruffly. "I'm going to take a ride around town, make sure no other catastrophes have hit while I've been busy with all this—"

His own daughter Annie, I realized, would be a teenager in a few years, like the girl he'd found in the church. "If you want to hear what I've got to say meanwhile," he added as we followed him through the chilly drizzle across the parking lot, "you can."

I climbed into the squad car's back seat, grateful as I was sure Chip also had been for Bob's habit of wiping the seat and door panels with spray cleaner regularly; Ellie got in the front.

"You can hear it," he repeated as we belted ourselves in and he started the car, twisting his thick neck to peer past me as he backed it out. "But you're not going to like it."

"Hey, *Dweeb*!" The shout came from somewhere down the hallway where the guys on the Shead High School basketball team gathered each morning right before first period.

"*Dweeb! Hey, Dweebles!*" Shoving his geometry book back into his locker, David ignored their taunts. It was the morning after the late-night stolen bicycle escapade, and his throat still felt sore and bruised from where Bogie had squeezed it.

More catcalls followed him as he slammed his locker door and merged with the jostling, chattering mass of kids headed for the gymnasium, where a schoolwide assembly had been called. The guys weren't trying to be friendly; far from it. Instead, by using the nickname that Bogie had given him, they were reminding him that if not for his association with the thuggish little freshman, David would be dead meat. As if he needed reminding . . .

In the gym, which still smelled of popcorn and grilled hot dogs from the refreshments sold at last night's basketball game, the mood seemed oddly subdued. Clusters of girls huddled in their usual cliques, their faces shocked and their eyes, he noted with puzzlement, red from crying. Teachers came over and patted them on their shoulders; David hadn't seen any TV yet today or been on his computer, and he wondered if there'd been a big terrorist attack somewhere. Or maybe the president had been assassinated.

He found a spot on the bleachers and sat, positioning himself between the area customarily reserved for teachers and the nearest exit as he noted that Bogie wasn't here today. Not that Bogie's presence was necessarily required to ensure David's safety—Bogie found out everything that happened in school, sooner or later, and he carried a grudge—but David didn't see any sense in letting himself get trapped, just in case.

The first-period warning buzzer sounded as the principal made her way to the center of the floor. Bogie, David imagined enviously, was still asleep in bed, having blown off school again. They'd parted last night at the cemetery gates, David to hustle on home, where he'd sneaked back in holding his breath, mindful of his parents both snoring at the top of the stairs, and Bogie to head down to the breakwater, probably, where Harvey Spratt and the rest of his crew would still be hanging out even that late at night.

The principal, a white-haired, gravel-voiced woman named Mrs. Krause who also taught math and whose sharp-eyed gaze missed nothing, gestured once for silence and got it. David thought that if she called down a lightning bolt to strike them all dead, she would probably get that, too; she was that kind of teacher.

"Today," she intoned, "is a sad and terrible day in the life of our school."

A sob from somewhere high in the bleachers interrupted her; she glanced up impatiently, then went on. "We have lost an important member of our community, a young person whose life had barely begun."

Some in the audience, mostly the girls, seemed to know this already. Others didn't, and looked either frightened or bored.

"Jeez, cut to the chase, will you, you old hag?" one of the basketball players muttered, loudly enough for her to hear. His pals elbowed him appreciatively, but the flicker of her answering glance made David glad he hadn't been the one who said it.

She went on: "Last night, sometime around midnight—"

Home, David thought automatically. *When whatever it was happened, I was still—*

". . . Karen Hansen, a beloved member of our freshman class and valued citizen of our school community . . ."

A cold feeling came over David. That must've been what the sirens last night were all about, he realized.

Around him the sounds of weeping intensified, and even some of the boys looked troubled.

". . . murdered . . ."

At the word, loud sobbing broke out somewhere behind him. A girl got up and ran from the gym. The first-period late buzzer sounded, loud and obnoxious as an alarm in a nuclear power plant, he imagined, but nobody seemed to hear it.

Sitting there, silent and still amid what felt like utter chaos, David struggled to make sense of it all. *Karen Hansen?* A girl he knew slightly, funny-faced, faded clothes, just someone he'd brushed past in the hall sometimes—

Karen Hansen got killed last night? Murdered?

"Christ," breathed one of the basketball guys, whose name was Bub Wilson, and his buddies looked stunned as well. David felt a mean pulse of grim satisfaction at this evidence that the guys had feelings, that they could be made unhappy, too, even if it took a murder to do it.

Mostly, though, he kept circling around the other thing Mrs. Krause had said: ". . . *sometime around midnight* . . ."

Now the assembly was ending, and she was talking about grief counselors, a memorial project, and getting together in groups to discuss their feelings. David got up. The idea of talking about his feelings only intensified his certainty that very soon he'd need to run to the boys' room and vomit.

Because he'd been home, all right. When the clock on the living room mantel struck twelve last night, he'd still been in his own bed. Bogie hadn't shown up until about twelve-thirty. But . . .

Bogie . . . and Harvey Spratt.

A full-on druggie and all-around creep, Harvey was the downside of being protected by Bogie Kopmeir. Harvey had Bogie's back the same way Bogie had David's, or anyway Bogie thought Harvey did. David had his suspicions about what would really happen if Bogie ever actually tried to depend on Harvey. He was pretty sure that Harvey's ideas of loyalty only ran one way, toward himself.

But right now that was neither here nor there, David decided as he made his way out of the gymnasium with his classmates. Right now what he knew was that *after* their outing together, Bogie would've probably gone downtown to the breakwater to meet up with his unsavory older friend.

What one of them might've been doing *before* Bogie came to roust David from his bed, though, was David's question. Because Bogie was tough and violent, but Harvey was another can of worms altogether.

Harvey was *nuts*.

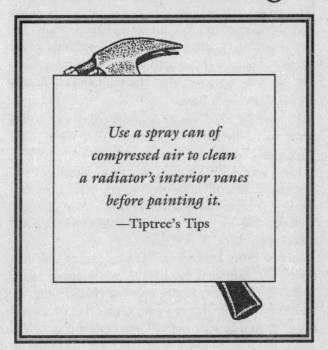

*Use a spray can of
compressed air to clean
a radiator's interior vanes
before painting it.*
—Tiptree's Tips

"**R**ats." Lizzie Snow faced herself in the motel room mirror. "Of all the damn fool . . ."

A knock at the door stopped her. Great, she'd come back too soon and the maid wanted in. "No, thank you," she called, making her voice sound as cheerful as possible.

Which wasn't very. *Nice work, genius. In less than*

twenty-four hours, you've made an enemy of a local cop, gotten a pair of town busybodies involved in your private business, and fixed it so some poor guy just out for a late-night stroll is sitting in an interview room right now, wondering what hit him.

If they even had interview rooms here. Eastport was pretty, but that was about all; as far as she could tell, the only hot spots were the hardware store and the marine-supply shop.

At least if I need a boat hook or belaying pin, I'll be all set. Not that she actually knew what those things were, nor did she want to. Most everyone else in town seemed to, though, at least to judge by their clothes: jeans and sneakers, mostly, with here and there—on men and women both—a pair of work boots so big and clunky, you could drive railroad spikes with them.

Among them, her own skinny black pants, polished boots, and leather jacket looked wildly out of place, and so did her careful makeup, which back in the city had looked normal, even restrained. *But up here I might as well be wearing a clown costume, a big red nose, and some floppy shoes. Maybe a squirt-gun daisy in my lapel.*

Defiantly she ran a comb through her hair and freshened her lipstick. Pretending to be one of the gang hadn't ever gotten her anywhere, and she doubted it would here, either, no matter what the accepted costume might be.

Or pretending she was anything but what she was. She'd begun brushing more blush onto her cheeks when the knock came again.

"I said I don't need any maid service, thanks," she

called, somewhat less pleasantly than before, because what she really didn't need was more hassles, not even of the well-meant variety.

"It's not maid service I'm offering," came the reply. *That voice . . .*

Dylan's voice. Her heart punched the inside of her chest. Until last night, she hadn't seen him in over a year, hadn't thought she'd ever see him again. But now—

One year, three months, and five days, a sly whisper in her head commented knowingly before she could shut it up. *D'you want to know how many hours and minutes?*

Oh, but I forgot—you already do. She strode to the door and yanked it open. "What the hell are you doing here?"

He stepped past her into the room, taking in her bag messily unpacked with its contents strewn all over the bed, makeup scattered across the dresser, and the new bottle of bourbon on the bedside table, beside the room's plastic ice bucket.

"Made yourself at home already, I see." He let his gaze rest a little too long on her unmade bed, the sheets in disarray from where she'd tossed and turned in them, unable to sleep.

Thinking of him, replaying the glimpse she'd caught of him at the crime scene last night . . . *Damn, damn.*

He caught her expression and a look of innocent hurt crossed his lean face. "Aw, Lizzie, don't be that way. It's me."

Tall and slim, with dark, thick-lashed eyes and high cheekbones, he held his arms out the way he used to, for her to step into them. "You know I don't bite," he said.

The look of innocence changed. "Not too hard, anyway," he added softly. "Remember?"

I do, indeed, she thought. *But if you think that's going to get you anywhere, you can go piss up a rope.*

"Hello, Dylan," she said. "What are you doing here?"

The night before, she'd turned her back on him and walked away, not giving him more than a flat "hello." *Yeah, like that was really going to work.*

"You look great, Lizzie," he said, ignoring her question. "A little thin. And sad, as if you haven't been having enough fun."

His eyes said he could remedy that last part, if she would let him. *Dream on, Binky.*

"I'm fine. Working in Boston until recently. You know the drill, guns and knives, a poisoning now and then, and—oh, yes, a disemboweling a couple of months ago. That one was a pip, you probably read about it in the papers."

She'd been censoring her thoughts since even before she'd arrived in Eastport, knowing that the first rule of keeping a secret was keeping it from yourself. People here didn't need to know what she was.

But Dylan already knew. She turned back to the mirror, began combing her hair again though it didn't need it.

"Tons of fun," she said. "A laugh a minute, actually."

He came up behind her, not touching her. "Oh, really. That why you quit?"

She met his gaze in the mirror. "How'd you know

about that? And how'd you find me, anyway?" She'd have sworn he hadn't followed her from the church last night.

His answering glance was mocking, as if he'd read her mind. But then he gave up the Lothario act. "I saw your car outside."

Which *could* be true. She'd had the same car back when they were . . . *but no, don't think about that,* she ordered herself. "And I know you quit because I keep track of you," he added.

He let his hands rest lightly on her shoulders. "Or is that not allowed, caring about what's happening to someone I was close to?"

She stepped briskly sideways, out from under his touch. "I'm not in charge of what you do or don't care about. But I can tell you that you're wasting your time."

"Come on, Lizzie, I've really changed—" he began again, but she cut him off roughly.

"No. No, you haven't. You're a *liar,* Dylan. And that's never going to be different."

She took a shaky breath, fighting tears suddenly. But no, she was done weeping about him, had been for a long time. "But maybe you don't remember. Maybe it's slipped your mind, what you told me."

He looked caught. *Too late, buddy. You bought this trip by knocking on my door after all this time. And now—*

Now he was taking it. "You told me she was leaving," Lizzie snarled the words out at him. "You said your marriage was over. While you and I were in bed together, you said she'd be *glad,*" Lizzie finished, feeling again the fresh anguish of his betrayal even though it had happened over a year ago.

Not that a year was long enough. A century wouldn't be long enough. Her nails stabbed the palms of her hands.

He stared at his shoes, his easy, charming line of chatter stopped in its tracks by her outburst. "I'm sorry," he said.

And to his credit, he actually looked sorry; sounded it, too. That didn't undo any of what he'd put her through, though. And anyway, this could all be a charade; Dylan was an actor *par excellence,* as she knew only too well.

A master at the art of keeping a secret. After a long moment, he spoke again. "We did have a good time together, though, didn't we?" His tone softened as he reached out and plucked her bone-handled jackknife from the dresser top, then put it back. "I mean, come on, Lizzie, admit it. It wasn't all bad."

"I don't have to admit a thing to you. I thought I'd never see you again. Which was fine with me," she retorted.

Lies, lies . . . and then you accuse him of being deceitful? His glance went to the bottle on the dresser and then to her face, questioningly.

Right, like you care. It never bothered you before. "No, I was not having a drink," she told him. "That's for later."

There'd been a while there, right after she found out about his wife, that she'd hit it a little hard. But bottle-emptying was a fool's game, even more than he had been. "And anyway, may I remind you that until I met you, I'd never tasted a drop?"

Strange but true; her tenement upbringing, in a neighborhood known for drug busts, domestic abuse, and arson, had featured a dad so deadbeat that he couldn't even be bothered to leave. She might've just numbed herself to it, but after their mother died she'd needed to stay alert to protect her younger sister from her dad's drunken outbursts and—just once—his midnight attempt at groping Sissy.

Once had been enough. By the next morning, both girls—Sissy fourteen, Lizzie four years older—had left the house, never to return. It was the start of Lizzie's path into law enforcement as a career . . . and of Sissy's much different route, one that ended in her body getting washed up onto some rocks.

And led to this, to what I'm doing now. To finding my niece if I can, or finding out what happened to her.

And Dylan's no part of that. "So you can keep your advice to yourself," she finished, "and everything else to yourself, too."

If she'd known last night that he would find her today, she would have gone back to Boston and waited until this other thing, this local murder case, was over, and Dylan was back in Augusta.

Uh-huh. The skeptical voice in her head was relentless. *Sure you would. Give me a break, when you saw him across that church lawn last night, you could've eaten him up with a spoon.*

Like right now . . . and you know it. So does he. He always did.

And he always will. "Lizzie," he said simply, letting his hands drop to his sides again.

But knowing is one thing and doing's another. And

no matter what kind of chemistry they'd had in the past, he was bad news. Turning away, she grabbed a sweater from the dumped bag on the bed and began folding it.

"Yeah," he said after a moment, shrugging. "Well. I guess I couldn't expect open arms, could I? Not even if I . . ."

Oh, enough. She flung the sweater down. "Not even if what, Dylan? You had a wife, she loved you, and she was wrecked when she found out about me. And you'd never told me."

He looked down once more, no doubt remembering just as she did the awful scene: Lizzie's apartment, the wine and the candles and silken caresses. They'd already drunk most of the wine; the music, she recalled, was a guitar concerto they'd discovered together in a used-record shop that afternoon.

And then the door bursting open. Locked, of course, but Dylan's wife had had a key, a copy of the one she'd found on her husband's key ring and hadn't recognized. After that it had been a simple matter of following him on several evenings, then finally staking out Lizzie's apartment and waiting.

At least Dylan's wife hadn't had a gun. All this time later, Lizzie was still grateful for that little detail. It was the only thing she was grateful for about that night. That night, and all the ones since then . . .

"But go ahead, Dylan," she said bitterly, "tell me, what else could've happened, what's different that might change anything? I mean, that you haven't lied to me about already?"

Lies like the one he had told her about him and his

wife being separated and planning to divorce, about how Lizzie wasn't hurting anyone by loving him.

She waited. No answer. "Well?" she asked softly. "How about it, Dylan?"

He wasn't wearing a wedding ring, but that was meaningless. He hadn't worn one back then, either. "What's the big difference now," she persisted, "that makes you think you can just waltz in here like you own the place? Like you own *me*."

Still frowning at his shoes, he appeared to consider his answer, or whether he would answer her at all. Then: "She died."

And as Lizzie felt her mouth drop open wordlessly, "Sherry got sick just . . . it was only a month or so after we'd stopped, you and I. That she started having symptoms, I mean."

She stared as he hurried on. "And we were living right there in Boston, so of course we saw all the best doctors, went to the best centers for that kind of thing. Tests, surgery . . ."

A humorless grin touched his lips, vanished. "And you can say what you want about the union, but it turns out they really wangled us some decent health insurance out of the last contract. Everything she needed, nurses at home, the hospice . . ."

"Dylan. I'm very sorry."

Lips pursed, he nodded. "Thanks. It was fast. Only four months, can you believe it? It was like a forest fire, like . . . it just went through her. Nothing they did could stop it, or slow it down, even."

Lizzie couldn't help herself. "Did she ever . . . ?"

He laughed ruefully, knowing what she was about to say, as usual. The feeling that somebody really *got* her, *understood* her, had been one of the first things that had attracted her to him.

"Did she forgive me?" he finished her sentence for her. "Yeah. Yeah, she did."

She couldn't tell if he was shaking his head at his wife's foolishness, at what he'd managed to get away with, or what he'd done that needed forgiving. *Not that it matters . . . does it?*

"At first it was just that all of a sudden we had so much else going on," said Dylan.

He spread his hands expressively. "I mean, we had to fight this thing, you know? This . . . this monster that was attacking her, we thought at first we could beat it, and we had to at least be speaking to each other to do it."

Watching him as he spoke, she saw how the battle he was describing had marked him, tracing thin lines around his eyes and softening his expression, especially when he didn't know she was looking.

"So there was that, for a while," he said at last. "The shared fight we had to face, just getting through each day, it was the glue that was holding us together. Until . . ."

His voice trailed off while she imagined them, Dylan and the wife he'd betrayed, sitting quietly together somewhere. Shame swept over her when she recognized the emotion she felt. *Jealous of a woman who was fatally ill . . .*

And now was dead. *Nice. Very nice, Lizzie. Gotta hand it to you, you're a real sport.* "And then what happened?"

He met her gaze squarely. The dancing light she recalled in his eyes back then was a steady flame now;

another change. "Then everything went too fast, like fast-forwarding. First a hospital bed. Then hospice care. And then she was gone. Just . . . poof."

His look recalled the stunned shock he'd felt. But Lizzie had seen people at the ends of their lives, up close; two of them she'd put there herself, once dropping a fleeing psycho who'd slashed his mother, the other time when a perp wouldn't release the beat cop he'd taken hostage, one arm around the trapped cop's throat, the other hand waving the cop's service revolver.

That time, she'd had to put one in the guy's head. It was, she realized now, why she'd been so angry with the smart-ass cop last night: the unsecured weapon. Anyway, she was pretty sure that for Dylan's dying wife it had been anything but "poof."

The pain lingered on his face. Lizzie wondered if it ever went away completely. "She liked Maine, though," he added with a half smile. He'd taken the new job here just a dozen or so weeks after he and Lizzie had . . . what? Broken up? Imploded?

She still didn't know what to call it. "She said if it had to happen anywhere," he went on, "she was glad it was here."

"Yeah, well. Somebody's got to like it, I guess." Lizzie couldn't repress a grimace.

What the hell, it wasn't as if the dead woman knew she was being contradicted. And as far as Lizzie was concerned, one tree, one moose, one old backwater seaside town—they were all pretty much like one another, and ditto for rocky coastlines.

She liked sandy beaches, preferably with azure water, warm sunshine, and plenty of muscular, swimtrunked waiters scurrying around carrying drinks with little umbrellas in them.

And don't even get me started on lighthouses. Or, God help us, hot dog buns stuffed with mayonnaise-glopped lobster chunks.

She'd take the broiled tail, garlic butter, and a good, cold Chardonnay, thanks, leek mousse and possibly a nice barley pilaf. She wondered what would happen if she ordered that at the eatery just down the street from the motel, called, if she remembered it right, the Muddy Duckster.

From the aroma of french fry grease wafting from its vents even early this morning, she thought a blank stare was the best she could probably hope for. But the thought of food at all reminded her that the last thing she'd eaten was a Little Debbie cake in the middle of the night.

"Yeah. Well, I'm sorry about all of it, Dylan. I really am, but . . ."

She walked past him toward the door and opened it. "And it's been nice to see you again." *Much more of this and my nose will start growing.*

Outside, the deluge of half an hour earlier had diminished to drizzle, but the sky still roiled with clouds and there was an unnatural look to the midmorning light, as if it angled upward from the earth instead of slanting down from above.

It said this break was a reprieve, not an end to the rough weather. That there might be even worse to come.

"But I have a busy day planned, and I'm sure you must, too," she added, thinking, *Go. For the love of God, just . . .*

Dylan stepped outside. Then he turned, tipping his head to look at her with that wry, crooked-lipped grin she remembered so well. That, at least, hadn't changed.

No, it hadn't changed at all. "Not even curious, Lizzie? That's not the girl I remember."

"Curious about what?" But then she realized he was talking about what he was doing here in Eastport.

"I'm on a new task force out of Augusta. I'm supervising the investigation of violent crimes against women."

She couldn't help her curiosity. "So it's not your case? At the church last night?"

"Nope. I'm an observer." He was leaning over her now, one hand on the doorframe. "So what's the deal with the kid?" He changed the subject abruptly. "The one the chief of police picked up on Key Street this morning?"

It took her a moment to understand. "You . . . you were watching that? Dylan, have you been following . . . are you *stalking* me?"

Suddenly it all made sense: his knowing she'd quit her job, that she was here in Eastport. There was no reason at all for him to have noticed her car, no decals or bumper stickers to catch his eye and jog his memory; he hadn't just found her by chance.

But: "I was in the coffee shop across from Bob Arnold's office when you went in there this morning," Dylan explained. "You looked," he added with his trademark brand of easy charm, "like you just stepped out of a French fashion magazine."

At this, a little burst of pleasure exploded in her

heart; following at once, however, was the fresh real-
ization that she stuck out like a very sore thumb here
in Eastport, Maine. "But you haven't said yet why
you're in town," he added.

None of your business, she wanted to retort. She
hardened her voice.

"Cut to the chase, Dylan, okay? Tell me what *you*
want. Maybe I can help you, maybe not." Because
this was all well and good, this blast-from-the-past
stuff . . .

Or maybe it wasn't, she corrected herself wryly;
her peace of mind was definitely taking a hit. But she
could handle it, now that she'd gotten her breath
back, and meanwhile if she knew one thing about
him, it was that despite his history, he didn't let anything or anyone lead him around by the zipper on his
pants.

Back then, he'd gotten involved with her for the
same reason he'd slept with other women before her:
because *he* wanted to, not because he couldn't resist
some random impulse. And as flattering as it might
be to think he'd found her again now for sentimental
or even just sexual reasons, she knew better than
that, too.

Because at heart—*Oh, at heart,* something deep in
her own whispered softly—Dylan Hudson was a serious man. And the only question was what he wanted
from her, not whether he did.

His answer at once confirmed this. "Actually, I
thought we might be able to help each other," he admitted. "See, I know what happened here to your sister and . . ."

Of course he did. She'd told him about Sissy. ". . . her little boy?" he finished.

"Girl," she corrected, waiting, willing herself not to be disappointed; after all, this was no surprise.

He nodded, returned to the pitch he was making. "Anyway, I think I also know the only reason you'd ever come back here."

She stared past him at the gray wet street, the beat-up vehicles moving in it—vehicle-wise, keeping up with the Joneses was a foreign concept around here, apparently—and the elderly white clapboard houses set far apart in the neighborhood uphill from the motel. Yeah, she disliked it, all right.

A lot. "Something happened, didn't it?" asked Dylan. "That is, recently. You found out something about your sister, or—"

Gazing down acutely at her, he guessed correctly as he had always been able to; not just serious but smart, too. Give him two dots and Dylan could produce a third like a rabbit out of a hat, then connect them in a line that led straight to an answer everyone else had missed.

"Or about her child," he suggested. "Something new, that's made you come back for another look."

She drew her gaze back to him, unaccountably furious all at once at how easily he'd drawn these accurate conclusions about her and unwilling to confirm them as a result. But she didn't have to.

He knew that, also. It wasn't an act, an interrogator's strategy. Or even a smart cop's trick; he'd simply always known how she thought and felt, what she wanted and what made her feel afraid.

And what made her feel other things. Probably he

knew now how near she could be to reaching for him, drawing him back in to where the sheets were already in comfortable disarray, and shutting the door.

"That's none of your affair," she told him instead. But he had an answer for that, as well.

Of course he did. "It is if we can help each other. Because, look," he went on before she could say anything, "I've got an in with these cops. You don't. I mean, sorry, kiddo, but . . ."

I quit my job I quit my . . . Local police chief Bob Arnold was the one person she'd confided her past to, not wanting him to find out later and feel deceived. She'd asked him to keep it quiet for now and believed that he would.

Eventually she'd hoped to parlay her bona fides into inside info from cops who might recall Sissy's death, or who might have heard things since. But her plan, she realized now, wouldn't have worked; Bob Arnold had been polite and she pegged him as trustworthy, but law enforcement was probably just as territorial here as the cops were at home.

Meanwhile, Dylan was *already* an insider, wasn't he? And he'd thought of that, of the need she would have for someone like him.

"What would I have to do?" she asked him dully. Because her own feelings were one thing, but his were another, and probably quite different; he'd seen her and thought of a way he could use her to his advantage, that was all.

Nothing more. "Easy. My insiderness with the Maine cops," he said, "traded for yours with the woman that guy's staying with on Key Street, the guy Bob Arnold picked up. Just information."

"Who, you mean Jake Tiptree? It's her name," Lizzie added at his mystified expression. "The woman who owns the house. If it isn't even your case, though, why would you want to know what she says about anything?"

But then . . .

Not his case, she thought. That didn't mean he couldn't end up a hero by solving it, though, did it? A hero, back on active duty, with his own cases again—

. . . *then* she understood.

"Come on, let's go get something to eat," Dylan said, and this time she followed him.

"Mark my words," Bob Arnold said sourly, peering through the squad car's rain-streaked windshield. "This thing's bad enough now, but before it's done it's going to get evil."

We'd started out near the breakwater, where men in pickup trucks were arriving to secure their boats against the coming storm. Down on the floating docks, those who had already arrived were throwing extra lines onto their vessels, checking bumpers on the pier's massive wooden pilings, and grabbing any loose items that had been lying around on the decks, to stow them below.

"The storm or the . . . ?" Ellie hesitated. We didn't yet know what to call what had happened in the church last night. "Death," she finished inadequately.

Bob shot a dark sideways glance at her. "Both. And there's no need to be delicate about it, it's all over town now. Karen Hansen was murdered."

He drew a plump finger across his throat; the

crudeness of the gesture was unlike him. That more than anything else told me how deeply upset he was. "In all of my career, I have not seen anything like it. And I don't want to ever again."

He turned up Sullivan Street past the marine-supply store, which to judge by what the men coming out carried was doing a big business in bilge pumps and coils of rope. A fisherman before a storm could never have too much of the latter, but if that didn't work you'd need the former, and fast.

Then what Bob had said hit me. "What do you mean? You're not really thinking of quitting, are you?"

There'd already been rumors. His wife, Clarissa, and their little girl had been spending a lot of time in Arizona; the child was asthmatic, and the air in the desert agreed with her. And I knew Bob had thought of moving; lucky for us, though, he'd always reconsidered.

Now as he drove he kept slowly swiveling his head from left to right, matching what he saw of the houses and parked cars with what he'd seen last time, noting the people he saw and what they were doing, and with whom. Looking, in other words, for anything out of place, which he always said was 99 percent of small-town police work. But it was the other 1 percent that was bothering him now.

"What, me worry?" He answered my question with a quip. But there wasn't any humor in it, or any real answer, either.

Nor was there any amusement in his eyes when he glanced at me again in the squad car's rearview mirror. "So, d'you know your little pal has a criminal record?"

Chip, he meant. "Oh, Bob, he does—" *Not*, I'd intended to finish. But then I stopped, because Bob wasn't asking.

He was telling. Ellie shot me an incredulous look. "What kind of record?" she asked as he turned onto High Street, then down Washington Street back toward downtown.

"Kid's a peeper." Bob's inspection took in Spinney's Garage, the enormous old white-clapboarded Baptist church, now home to the Eastport Arts Center, and the apartment building just uphill from the post office, where a work crew hurried to put a lot of new lumber and other construction materials for the building's rehab under blue tarps. "I mean, the kind who peeps in windows."

I looked at Ellie, and she looked at me: *Wha-a-at?* The idea was absurd. Then I found my voice. "Bob, there must be some mistake. Chip's not that kind of—"

Bob had never liked Chip, even though on Chip's previous visit here he'd acquitted himself heroically, in my opinion, when a combination con man/killer pretty much scared the wits out of the rest of us. But Bob just thought Chip had enjoyed better luck than he deserved in the con man/killer department.

Between the granite-block post office building and his own new headquarters, Bob turned right: back onto Water Street again but this time in the opposite direction. Here small businesses and offices crowded both sides of the street: a flower shop, two galleries, a bakery, the water company, some gift stores, and an attorney's storefront. Hurrying to beat the weather, storekeepers hauled down their awnings, pulled in "Open" flags, and retrieved merchandise from the big plate-glass front window displays.

Workmen were even screwing plywood sheets over the windows; the whine of electric drills and circular saws echoed between the buildings. Bob slowed for a guy balancing a stepladder on one shoulder and a bundle of two-by-fours on the other.

"What exactly are we talking about here, Bob? With Chip's criminal record, I mean. And"—it occurred to me that I hadn't asked this yet—"where's Chip now?"

We could talk about Bob maybe quitting his job later; I had a feeling that trying to convince him not to while he was driving a squad car whose transmission sounded like a banshee was being ground up in it—his departmental budget was even tighter than the collar around his fleshy neck—wasn't exactly strategic. He popped a hard candy from the car's cup holder into his mouth and crunched it, looking as if he would rather be crunching the bones of whoever had killed Karen Hansen in the church last night.

"State boys've got him at the command post they've set up, at the Youth Center." Yet another reason for Bob's sour mood, I realized; a small wood-frame community building with a kitchen, restrooms, and a meeting area with cafeteria-style tables and metal folding chairs, the Youth Center on County Road was used mostly for bingo—or as they called it around here, beano—on Wednesday nights.

Despite its name, no self-respecting "youth" would be caught dead in the place. But the state cops were using it, instead of running their operation under the same roof as Bob's department. He caught my eye again in the mirror, grimaced.

"Yeah, that's right. I'm good enough to find the girl. Fell right down outta that trapdoor onto me, got so much blood on me I hope to hell the poor kid didn't have hepatitis."

She could have; from what I'd heard, Karen Hansen's living situation with her neglectful dad was just this side of criminal. But of course I didn't say so to Bob, who went on fulminating.

"Good enough to secure the scene, best I could considering it was all four flights in a stairwell, plus a belfry. Grabbed up the witnesses, got all the right people here . . ."

We passed the wide parking lot that led out onto the wooden fish pier, with the colorful statue of a bearded, slicker-and-sou'wester-clad fisherman clasping a silvery codfish sticking up from the middle of it. The statue resembled a cartoon character dreamed up by a chain of seafood restaurants, but everyone else in Eastport liked it, so I'd kept my mouth shut about it, mostly.

". . . even closed down the port and the airstrip," Bob went on. "Which I'll hear about, and not in a good way, at the next county commissioners' meeting."

At the far end of Water Street, the business part of town gave way to wood-frame houses set close together right up against the street, their front doors almost touching the sidewalk. Bob turned at the corner, downhill toward the island's south end.

"Not that anyone tried getting in or out, anyway,"

he added. "But you know those yahoos'll have to chew my tail about it, just 'cause they can."

I did know; in Maine, county commissioners had lots of odd-seeming powers, left over from when the county seats were even more remote and difficult to travel to than now. Also, politics was part of it.

"Exceeding my authority, my fanny," Bob grumbled. "Let them see how they'd handle a goddamned bloody—"

"Bob. What're they doing with Chip?" Because if he'd been arrested, as Sam had said, he should've been getting transported somewhere else by now, and if he wasn't—

"Questioning him," Bob said flatly as outside the car two seagulls clashed over what looked like a fish head. One of the seagulls speared the fish head with its long orange beak and flew off with it, leaving the other gull looking around peevishly.

We crested the next hill onto the bluff overlooking Prince's Cove and out across Johnson Bay.

"And there's no mistake about the peeping charge, Jacobia." Bob used my full name, which meant he was really serious. His tone, despite his own personal dislike of Chip, was grudgingly regretful.

"I ran my own check for warrants and priors on him, since the state cops aren't sharing anything with me. I am," he added a little huffily, "allowed to do that. So I did, and saw the faxed arrest records myself."

I could still barely believe it. "But . . ."

"Look," said Ellie, pointing across the bluff to the edge of a field overlooking the sea. The bluff ended sharply in a forty-foot drop to the beach, though the cliffs weren't visible from here.

The two men at the edge of them were, though. One was Karen Hansen's father, Hank, whom I could tell even from here by his wild head of flame-red hair, sticking out in all directions like a fright wig.

But that wasn't the only frightening thing about him: with one hand thrust out toward his companion in an angry warding-off gesture, he held the other hand close to his head. And although I couldn't see it clearly, from his desperate-looking stance and the way the other man seemed to be pleading with him, I'd have bet anything that in *that* hand was a gun.

"Hell," Bob pronounced in disgust at the sight. Hansen was a fixture around town, a foolish talker and a mean drunk who'd been rumored to smack his wife around when she was alive. But even a guy like Hansen could have a come-to-Jesus moment, I guessed, the kind that made him feel he'd be better off dead.

That, or he was the kind of guy who thought everything, even his own daughter's bloody murder, was really about him, and it was this latter theory that I tended right now to subscribe to. Meanwhile, the other man was my husband, Wade Sorenson.

Spotting the pair, Bob pulled the Crown Vic over onto the shoulder and slammed on the parking brake. After hauling himself from behind the wheel, he shoved the door closed hard behind him and without hesitation lumbered against the wind across the bumpy headlands toward Wade and Hansen.

"Hey!" Bob yelled. "Hey, put that damned gun down! Damn it, Hansen, I'm talking to you!"

Which might've been enough to put another man over the edge. But unlike Wade, Bob was an authority figure. Also, he made it his business to know and understand the subjects of his policing, the people it was his job to protect.

So he knew Hank Hansen. Still yelling, Bob went on motoring across the grassland. But by the time he got halfway to the now-wavering man, his step grew ragged, and although he went on shouting out orders, his voice was wheezy, with long pauses between the words.

I looked at Ellie. "Not doing so well," I said, meaning Bob.

She nodded gravely. If you didn't know Bob, you'd think he was having a heart attack; maybe him quitting his job wasn't such a bad idea after all. But the idea was still hugely unwelcome; if only, I thought, he'd take better care of himself.

Not that he was getting the chance right this minute: nearly to Hansen's side, Bob stood bent over with his hands propped on his knees, catching his breath. Still, he hadn't given up.

"Damn . . . you . . . Hansen. Now . . . get over here . . . and . . . give . . . me . . . the . . . damn . . . *gun!*"

The final word was almost all air, like a whistle. Hansen, though, heard it. He stood indecisively a moment before letting his hand fall. Then, turning his back firmly on Bob, he raised both arms as if about to leap over the edge of the cliff—

And sank to his knees abruptly, burying his face in his hands; as Bob had known, when push came to shove, Hansen followed orders. The onshore wind that had carried Bob's shouts to us now brought the ragged, tearing noises of Hansen's sobbing.

Wade approached the car, brushing his big hand sheepishly over his blond crew-cut hair. Tall and solidly built, with a big square jaw and eyes that were either blue or gray depending on the weather, he had a smile that still made my heart go pitter-pat, but he wasn't smiling at the moment.

"Hansen got away from me," he explained when I opened the car's door. "Slippery as a bucket of eels, that guy. I tried the bars first, of course."

Of course. Where else would you go the morning after your daughter was murdered? My sympathy for the guy dropped another notch, and what had a four-teen-year-old been doing out at that hour, anyway?

"But I couldn't find him in any of them, and then somebody said they'd seen him heading out here," Wade said.

He peered into the car and spotted Ellie. "So, are you two okay?"

I assured him we were just ducky. That is, unless having your houseguest suspected of a ghastly crime counted; the guest with the previously unknown po-lice record for spectacular ickiness . . .

Out on the bluffs, Bob put his hand on the grieving man's shoulder and just stood there with him, not talking. Eventually Hansen got up and the two men came together across the grassland toward us, the dark storm clouds looming behind them as huge and solid looking as a giant hammer getting ready to slam down.

Wade looked troubled, his eyes now the exact same gray as the clouds lumbering monstrously toward us.

"My knife was the weapon," he said, confirming my earlier suspicion.

Because, of course, there'd been another reason to pick Chip Hahn up; no one gets taken in for questioning just for carrying a rabbit's foot. There had been a customer visiting in Wade's shop earlier in the day, I seemed to recall.

But whoever that customer was, he hadn't been spotted near the crime scene later, as Chip had been. And Chip had also been up there in Wade's workshop with Sam that afternoon. Probably he had seen the knife then, or he could have.

That's what a prosecutor would say, anyway.

"Somebody," said my husband, while Hank Hansen pushed the toe of his boot disconsolately into a clump of earth, "used my knife to slit that poor little girl's throat."

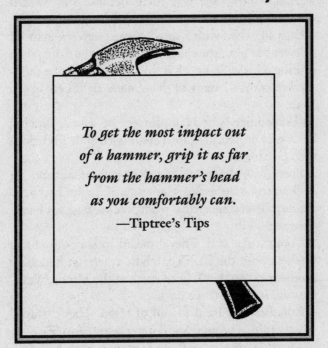

Chapter 7

*To get the most impact out
of a hammer, grip it as far
from the hammer's head
as you comfortably can.*

—Tiptree's Tips

Dylan was still driving the old red Saab
900 sedan that he'd had in Boston, its tan cloth seats
and the brown leather steering wheel cover as homey
and familiar-feeling to Lizzie Snow as the inside of
her own apartment.

Ex-apartment, rather. As they headed through the
rain out of town in the Saab, she still had no clear

idea what he wanted from her, only that he wanted something. But that wasn't why she was in the Saab with him now. She was there because she wanted something from him, just as he did from her.

Even so, when with a small inward sigh she glanced sideways at him, she caught him doing the same, then smiling a little. So he felt it, too, the weight of a thousand memories, many of them made right here in the Saab.

"Remember New Hampshire?" he asked, slowing for a pickup truck heaped high with split firewood, then passing it.

There was almost no one else on the road, though back in town the grocery store's parking lot had been jammed. Everyone getting ready, she guessed, for heavy weather.

"Yeah," she said. They'd meant to stay only for a weekend, but the Saab's catalytic converter had gone on the fritz. So they'd been stuck at the Mount Washington Hotel for three days.

It had rained hard for all of them. They'd stayed mostly in their room. She'd never wanted to leave.

"Yeah, I remember." *And now I wish I didn't.* "What're you up to, anyway, Dylan? I mean, now you've got some kind of a boss's job, something supervisory?"

Which, as she'd realized earlier, would mean no cases of his own, and he wouldn't like that. Dylan on a case was like a dog with a meaty bone; he just kept at it till the marrow was gone, meanwhile enjoying the hell out of it.

They reached the Route 1 intersection: huge old evergreen trees looming on three sides, an out-of-business gas station and convenience store on the fourth. A log truck roared by on the wet road, huge tires spewing.

He turned north, past a small white rural post office and over a wide tidal inlet thick with cattails and roiling with an inward-rushing current.

"Yeah. Supervisor," he replied sourly. "That's where they put you if you light a fire under the wrong boss's butt."

"I see." She could've guessed as much. That same dog-with-a-bone quality made him stubborn in work politics, too, especially if he thought someone was, as he put it, too dumb to live. The trouble being that Dylan would say he thought so right to the person's face.

"Doesn't matter what the beef was," he told her before she could ask. "Guy I had it with had favors he could pull in with a top boss, and he got mad enough, so he pulled 'em. Got me back but good."

He turned left, into the unpaved parking lot of a low, red-painted roadside restaurant. The sign said that it was the New Friendly—she wondered where the old one was, maybe fallen into the tidal inlet?—and the number of cars in the lot said that it might even be halfway decent.

For around here, anyway. He parked the Saab, and by the time she had her seatbelt undone he was out and had her door open for her, leaning in over her with an umbrella raised.

Swinging her legs around, she looked up incautiously and was hit full force with his smile. He put his arm out but she refused the physical contact, knowing too well what it might lead to.

If he even wants that, she cautioned herself. But then, *Don't be silly, of course he does,* she realized. *He always wants that.*

He just wants something else first. And learning more about what it was meant coming out for a meal with him, playing along. After all, she did need what he had: cop access, instead of the make-it-up-as-you-go-along method of getting information out of police officers she might manage to cultivate on her own.

And good luck on that one, anyway, after the ass you made of yourself with that young local cop last night . . .

The bottom line being that Dylan was a straight shot in to where somebody might really know something about where Nicki was. *Some small fact that nobody else thought was important . . .*

If there was something like that, Dylan could find out, and he would tell her—if she played all her cards right. Deftly he lowered the umbrella and ushered her into the restaurant ahead of him.

"Thank you," she murmured, knowing he'd be surprised that she'd returned his courtesy with no sarcastic comment.

And knowing, too, that whatever game Dylan was playing, on her side at least it was about to get much more difficult. Because common sense and rational decisions were one thing, but physical reactions were entirely another; all it took as she passed by him was a whiff of that shampoo he'd always used, the woodsy scent of it more evocative than anything so far, to convince her of that.

They went in. The New Friendly featured a long counter with round, red leatherette stools, some tables at the center, a pass-through to a kitchen where a white-aproned cook labored. Booths lined the walls, and a trio of waitresses whisked trays around, avoiding collisions with one another as if by radar.

He allowed her to slide ahead of him into a booth by a big front window looking out onto the rain-swept parking lot. Once they were settled, she leaned forward across the Formica table.

"So, Dylan," she began, "let's dispense with the sentimental stuff for the moment, shall we? Tell me what you want."

Almost surely what he sought was any inside info she could get out of the Tiptree woman, something he could use to break a case whose investigation he was supposed to be only observing. No doubt he thought that way maybe he could get back into active duty. In other words, he wanted to use Lizzie, and after all, she told herself bitterly, there was nothing new about that.

But as her knee brushed his under the table, she had her own ideas about how their arrangement should go.

Because when it comes down to being the used or the user, she thought, *guess which one I intend to choose this time?*

On the bluffs overlooking the bay's dark gray, racing waves, Wade took charge of Hank Hansen again, once Bob Arnold had relieved Hansen of his gun. Wade strode back to his pickup truck with Hansen in tow, speaking consolingly to him, and Ellie and I got back into Bob's squad car; not much later Bob dropped us off at my house.

"Yeeks," I said, looking up at the old place.

Not that it was a shambles, exactly. Over the summer, the white clapboards had been freshly painted and the dark green wooden shutters repaired and rehung. Also, the roof got patched, new pipe was laid from the municipal water line in the street to the house itself, and the front porch railings had been replaced.

And yet . . . "I guess a couple of those wind gusts got pretty lively," said Ellie inadequately.

"Yeah," I replied. With two of those green shutters hanging askew, a gutter dangling, and a whole patch of shingles flapping on the roof I'd thought was all set for the winter, the old house was already looking the worse for wear, before the big storm had even arrived.

"Yeah, too bad my bank balance isn't as vigorous as what's still on the way, weather-wise." What we'd had so far was just the preview.

"In fact, after all I spent on the house this past summer, if I buy much more than a pack of gum it's the checks I try writing that'll be bouncy," I said.

I was a rich woman back when I managed money for some of the biggest crooks on Wall Street. But after fifteen-plus years of keeping an antique house upright, my older parent provided for, and a son fed, clothed, and educated to the point where he could do those things for himself, I was about as prosperous as most people in Eastport.

Which is to say not very. And then an even worse thought hit me. "Ellie," I began as the sky darkened suddenly and another downpour opened up, fresh gusts lifting a corner of tin flashing from around one of the red-brick chimneys.

Two bad thoughts, actually. A strip of flashing tore off and flew away. "Ellie," I repeated. "Remember when we were up in the bell tower yesterday and we noticed all that . . ."

We weren't even supposed to go up there. All I'd said was that we'd look around a little, make a list of repairs that a pot of grant money could be used for: replacement windows, leak fixing, possibly new wiring if the old knob-and-tube electrical connections looked dangerous enough. But what we'd found was so much worse than I'd been expecting—a new foundation and floor were just the beginning of that old building's to-do list—that I had decided to come back to document everything, with a camera.

And that should've been that. But Ellie had never been up in a two-hundred-year-old church tower before—neither had I, actually, but that was all right with me—so before we left, her curiosity sent her scrambling up four flights of stairs plus a ladder and into the belfry itself, with me grousing and complaining behind. And that was where we'd seen the—

"Sawdust," I said. Old-house repair causes plenty of it, so when I'd spotted the powdery heaps of it in the belfry of the All Faith Chapel, I didn't think much of it. I was used to the stuff.

But now it occurred to me that my own house had gotten lots of structure-bolstering attention over the years . . . and the old church hadn't. And *that* meant the sawdust in the belfry wasn't the by-product of carpenters. Instead—

Instead it was almost certainly from carpenter ants: wood-munching, building-devouring insects as hungrily destructive as termites, and hardier in cold climates. Carpenter ants *eat* wood, and they especially enjoy big structural beams; they hollow them out and live inside, enlarging their dwellings by the power of their appetites, the sawdust piles they make merely crumbs that have fallen from their constantly chewing mouth parts.

Constantly chewing. As in right now, and we had gale-force winds coming; meanwhile and as far as I knew, no repair work had even been scheduled on the old church.

On top of which it was still a crime scene, and no cop in the world was going to let a carpentry crew in to work until each and every scrap of potential evidence had been photographed, gathered up, bagged, tagged, recorded in an evidence log, and carried away.

All of this I hurriedly explained to Ellie while she made coffee and rummaged in the refrigerator for lunch stuff—today was Monday, so Bella was upstairs scrubbing the bathroom faucet handles with a toothbrush and bleach, wiping down every surface with antiseptic spray cleaner, and generally making the place so clean you could do organ transplants in it—and I tried finding the church caretaker's number in the phone book.

". . . Mahan, Mahaney, Mahoney . . ." I slammed the book shut. No number for the caretaker was listed. Probably it was on a Twitter page or a Facebook page or his website.

Or whatever, I could Google for it, if I had all the

time in the world and even a tiny bit of patience for that kind of thing. Ellie was the Web-guru one of us; with an eight-year-old at home she was required to be, just to stay ahead of the kid.

So while I corralled and assembled what she had plucked out of the refrigerator—Swiss cheese, dark rye bread, a tomato, and a container of Bella's home-made hummus, this enriched with enough garlic from Ellie's garden to ward off every possible vampire on Moose Island—she used her Google-fu, and then I used the phone.

Ten minutes later I'd finished trying to convince a church caretaker who hadn't actually been up in the belfry for at least ten years that it was about to fall down.

"He says he'll have a look at it after the police get out of there," I reported through a mouthful of garlic and rye. Ellie's fresh coffee washed it down nicely.

"Did you tell him that if he waits too long, he'll be able to inspect it without going up into it?"

Because it would be on the ground, Ellie meant. Probably in several, to put it mildly, pieces. "Yeah. Or-ville Morgan isn't the easiest guy to alarm, though."

Also to put it mildly. If a bomb went off under Orville's chair, he might consider getting up. But then he'd think better of it and stay, as he'd put it, "where the good Lord flang him."

While we were eating, Bella came down and sat with us after putting together her own lunch of about a tablespoon of rice left over from dinner the night before, plus half a macaroon.

I privately suspected her of downing cans of Ensure

when I wasn't around; with that angular face, those bulging green eyes, and those big every-which-a-way teeth of hers, Bella was no beauty contest winner, but she was among the most vigorous late-sixtyish (she wouldn't tell her age) persons I'd ever known.

Vigorous in her opinions, too: "Orville Morgan," she said, swallowing a tiny bite of half-macaroon, "is a perfect example of a man who thinks he's way too good for his job—"

Another tiny bite, another swallow. "—and is mistaken," she finished, clicking her cup down into its saucer for emphasis.

Well, I didn't agree. Orville swept, dusted, and mopped the place for free, and took the trash out after events in the church basement, too, hauling it upstairs to the curb without complaint even though he was eighty-five (Orville did tell his age, often and to anyone who would listen).

But in this case, I needed a person with some authority to act, someone who would understand that something needed to be done over there, pronto, and someone who wasn't already involved somehow in last night's ghastly event. Which ruled out Orville. And it also eliminated just about everyone else on the island who was ambulatory and had a pulse, since finding a murderer was at the top of a lot of to-do lists around here today.

And the looming storm occupied everybody else. So finally I called Ava Wilmot, the town dogcatcher, whose husband was a roofer, so he wouldn't be working at that today, and he didn't own a boat, either, so ditto.

Once I'd explained, she put him on the phone and

he agreed to go over there and tell the cops that the City Manager had sent him, and if they didn't let him in to inspect the belfry right now, it might fall down on them.

All of which was true except for the City Manager part, and I thought I could probably fix that later; as an ex–money whiz, I'd been able to show him some perfectly legal tax strategies that had saved Eastport a lot of cash.

So he owed me one. "Great," said Ellie when I'd hung up.

Now I just hoped we'd thought of the carpenter ants in time, since outside the kitchen windows the wind had given up blowing intermittently and was now howling steadily, whipping the last of the autumn leaves across the yard and blowing snapped-off twigs against the antique glass panes. If we hadn't been in time, I expected to see that belfry sailing across the sky, soon, too, possibly with the dogcatcher's husband clinging to it.

"But . . . ," Ellie added, not looking quite as pleased as I'd expected. "There is still the other thing . . ."

Right. Chip Hahn. "Okay, next project," I said, and reached again for the phone book. "We've got to get Chip a decent lawyer, and get ourselves in to see him, and—"

"Nope," pronounced Bella flatly, meanwhile washing her rice dish and spoon with soap, then pouring boiling water from the teakettle over it.

She was, as I may have mentioned earlier, a big believer in hygiene. "Why not?" I asked.

Bella wiped her hands on a pristine dish towel. "Because he's got a lawyer already. He called here while you two were out, said Chip had called *him*— the lawyer, I mean—earlier this morning."

She named a top-flight New York criminal attorney, Maury Cahill, a guy I knew; in fact, I'd once had his firm on retainer for a client whose teenager was handsome, smart, and a complete sociopath.

"But—" I began. This could be bad. This could be very bad. Because how would Chip Hahn know he needed a lawyer so early in the morning, when Bob Arnold hadn't scooped Chip up and taken him in for questioning yet?

"And," Bella went on, carefully brushing macaroon crumbs, if any, off the red-checked tablecloth, "you won't get in to see him anytime soon, either. They follow the rules down in Machias."

The town forty miles to our south that was the county seat, she meant, where the county jail and the courthouse were located. "Yeah," I conceded, "you're probably right."

Before she came to work for me, Bella had been married to a man who got hauled in so often on drunk-and-disorderlies that the squad car in their town used to cruise down his street a couple of times each night just to see if he'd gotten around to starting that evening's fight yet.

They'd never let her in, either; not until she'd signed up to be a visitor and gotten herself cleared. I could only imagine the security around a homicide suspect would be even more rigid.

"So we won't even be able to ask Chip what's going on. What did you tell the lawyer?" I asked Bella, who by now was polishing the cut-glass knobs on the kitchen's old beadboard cabinets.

"Who picked Chip up, what they think he did, where they took him, and the name of the lead investigator on the task force that is working on the case," she replied, rubbing off a particularly stubborn streak from one of a knob's crisply cut glass facets.

I just stared. "I heard it all in the IGA," she explained, "while I was buying a can of scouring powder."

Preparatory, of course, to cleaning that upstairs bathroom so thoroughly that light bouncing off the porcelain was probably blazing out through the bathroom window right now, blinding any unwary passersby.

"And," she went on after satisfying me that Chip Hahn's new lawyer was at least as well informed as your average Eastport IGA shopper, "I heard something else."

She paused with a wet paper towel poised over the handle on the refrigerator door. "I heard Bob Arnold is quitting."

Ellie shook her head. "Bella, you must've got that wrong. Why, Bob's been the police chief here forever! His wife's working at the community college in that new pre-law program they have, and his little girl is in kindergarten here, and . . ."

But she didn't sound convinced and finally her voice trailed off entirely. "Forever," she repeated softly.

"He's been gaining weight lately," I said into the silence in the kitchen. Because really, why shouldn't he leave?

People did. "He always eats when things aren't going well for him," I added. For Bob, the phrase "comfort food" didn't even need the word "food" in it; it was a given.

"And his little girl's asthma isn't getting any better," Ellie reluctantly conceded. "A couple of doctors at least have told him that Arizona would be better for her."

Or somewhere else dry; here, when we use the word, we mean not actually raining, snowing, sleeting, misting, drizzling, fogging, or otherwise precipitating. Speaking of which, at the moment it was raining so hard and so sideways that little water jets were squirting in between the storm window and its frame.

"And now this," said Bella quietly.

Murder, she meant, and all its difficulties, from strange cops and other investigative personnel to the inevitable special city council meeting later, at which Bob would have to justify doing whatever he'd done and defend not doing whatever he hadn't.

"I wouldn't take the job for a million bucks," I said. Not that Bob got paid a twentieth of that. And—

"How long has he been chief, anyway?" I asked Ellie. He'd already had the top Eastport cop position when I arrived here, a little over fifteen years earlier.

She thought about it, while Bella began taking down and wiping each jar, vial, and bottle on the kitchen mantel.

"Twenty-five years," said Ellie at last, wonderingly. "He started so young . . . why, he's probably eligible for a pension."

Bella ran a wet paper towel over the kitchen counter, in case it might've had a crumb on it. Then she crouched to run the paper towel along the baseboards, where yet another crumb might possibly have fallen.

Finally she followed the baseboard right out of the kitchen and down the hall, wiping as she went. When she had gone, Ellie spoke again. "So how come you don't like Lizzie Snow?"

I glanced at her in surprise. "It showed?"

"Well, kind of. The same way the spines on a porcupine show. Or the stink on a skunk. No more than that, though."

"The stink on a skunk doesn't show," I retorted, but then I gave up. "I just get the sense that there's something she's not telling us, that's all."

Outside, it was still raining hard, but Ellie's little girl was due home from school any minute, so I offered to drive her home, and in the car with the wipers flapping madly, she continued.

"That's not the only reason, though, is it?" she asked. "That you don't like her."

The windshield looked as if a firehose had opened up on it. Squinting through it, I turned onto Water Street, where the wind off the bay abruptly ratcheted up to gale strength.

"No," I admitted. A massive gust hit the car, rocking it on its wheels briefly. A cardboard box tumbled end over end across the street; signs hung on lengths of chain outside the shops flew violently, threatening decapitation or a skull fracture to anyone walking below at the wrong moment.

"I just . . . Ellie, she's everything I used to be. Great hair, great makeup, lots of pizzazz . . ."

Fortunately, there were no pedestrians out. Except for a few cars parked in the angled spaces outside Wadsworth's hardware store, Water Street was deserted, and at just past noon the sky was already so dark that the streetlamps had gone on.

"And on top of all that, as if it weren't enough that she reminds me of everything I left behind in the city . . ."

"Are you sorry?" Ellie asked acutely. "That you did leave, that you came here and—"

Found a new home, a new love, and saved my son's life in the bargain, she could have finished, because that's what happened.

"No, of course not." We rolled through a hubcap-deep puddle. "I just—"

In the boat basin beyond the breakwater, fishing vessels were getting tossed around like bathtub toys. Half-million-dollar bathtub toys, many of them; the gear and electronics even a modest fishing boat needs nowadays would stun Daddy Warbucks.

"She reminds me, that's all," I said, inadequately. "And she is lying about something, by omission at least. Something about her just doesn't add up. And that makes me nervous."

Also, it made me *mad*. But right now I had enough to worry about just driving the car in what was shaping up to be a real gullywhumper, as the guys around here would've put it.

So far, nothing down in the basin had broken loose, the work boats rafted together so tightly you could walk across them, from shore to the breakwater. Beyond the massive concrete dock's twenty-foot pilings, though, the bay was nearly black, huge foam-topped waves chugging along it like cars on a freight train.

"If this keeps up," Ellie began unhappily. Roaring

into the breakwater, the waves slugged the pilings and exploded up onto the deck, sending great gouts flying over the automated weather station, the Port Authority's little red security hut, and the picnic tables on the observation pier built out over the water.

"Uh-huh," I said distractedly, absorbed in the tricky task of staying in the proper lane. But it was a worrisome sight, that boat basin: if there was a boat in it that was paid for, I didn't know about it, and as for repairs, I could count on no hands the number of fully insured fishermen in Eastport.

Making our way on outer Water Street, we passed between small houses with vinyl siding strips peeling away, trash cans rolling down driveways, and here and there loose chimney bricks already fallen. Also, a fractured limb from an enormous old oak swung dangerously over a power line, right next door to Ellie's house.

I pulled in as near to her front door as I could get, past her old Ford pickup truck, which at the moment was sitting up on concrete blocks. Her husband, George Valentine, was the man you called here in town if you needed something done, stat: a skunk trapped or an old shed taken down, for instance. But doing nonpaying work just wasn't economically feasible for him right now, so the truck, which needed its fuel tank replaced to pass annual inspection, had been on blocks since Easter and would likely be frozen solid to them at Christmas.

"All right, then," said Ellie, contemplating the short run through her dooryard to her house. Outside, the wind positively shrieked, blowing cabbage leaves and eggshells out of her compost heap and yanking at the plastic sheets George had found time to nail up around their bungalow's foundation. "Let me see if I've got today's news straight. Chip lied about where he was. He had access to the weapon. He apparently has a record of peeking in windows, which doesn't sound good."

"No, it doesn't. And yes, you've got it straight," I said unhappily. It sure didn't sound good to me, anyway, and to the police it must sound even worse.

"And," Ellie went on thoughtfully, "can we reasonably assume that a man with one previously unknown, unpleasant fact in his past might have another?"

She glanced at my face, which probably looked defensive on Chip's behalf. "Emphasis on 'might,' of course, but still," she added.

"Yeah," I agreed reluctantly. "Yeah, I guess we'd better factor in the idea that this could get worse, although I don't see how."

O ye of little imagination. "All right, then, so here's our plan," said Ellie. "First, we'll . . ."

I felt a sudden spasm of guilt at getting her into this. What she would do first once she got inside, I happened to know, was make a good home-from-school snack for her daughter, Lee. She'd supervise homework: drawing letters and numbers, practicing a simple song—"I'm a Little Teapot" was what they were working on now, if I remembered correctly—and learning to spell "cat."

After that: laundry, dinner, dishes, and maybe a spin around the place with the vacuum cleaner; my best friend Ellie was nearly as picky as Bella about household cleaning. She might go over the business accounts with George, sending out bills and making up deposits to take to the bank. And she would do some reading of her own if she could keep her eyes open; Hilary Mantel was her current favorite.

Finally at midnight she would fall into bed for her usual five hours of shut-eye; George started work early, and as a matter of family solidarity she insisted on rising with him.

"Ellie, are you sure you're up for this? I mean, we said we weren't going to snoop into murder anymore."

"Jake, we're not snooping. That's what you do when you don't know the people involved. We're just helping your friend Chip."

"Yes," I agreed dryly, noting her bright eyes, rosy cheeks, and lively expression. No doubt about it, snooping suited her.

"I mean, I'd rather no one had been killed, of course," she went on. "And especially not a young girl."

Her expression darkened. "Especially not," she emphasized. Having a daughter of her own had put a particularly hungry smile on the face of my friend Ellie's inner tiger.

"If Chip didn't do it, then someone else did," she summed up efficiently. "But as it is . . ." A large blown-off branch from a nearby leafless maple tree whirled across her front lawn and smacked hard into the car's back window; she didn't even flinch.

"As it is," she finished, "the police seem to think they've already got their culprit, don't they?"

"Yes. So they're probably not searching too hard for someone else. And as for his lawyer, as much as I don't like the way it looks that Chip called one so early, he could probably use one."

Maury Cahill, I happened to know, was licensed to practice in Maine and Rhode Island, as well as in New York; I assumed Chip must've known that, too.

"But," I went on, "this weather's getting worse. I wouldn't be surprised at flight delays in Bangor, and even if the lawyer made it that far—"

If he was coming here physically, I meant, and I assumed that Cahill was; back when I'd known him, the attorney had struck me as a street brawler in a good suit, a guy who knew how to pick a fight if need be.

And how to win one, usually while enjoying it. Meanwhile, the money in Chip's past had extended to the present, enough to make Chip look like a client who could pay his bill and then some.

"—getting here," I finished, "could still be a trick."

Blown-down trees, power outages, car accidents, or just-hit moose carcasses that blocked roads anywhere along the way . . . what I'm saying is, I can't stress enough that Eastport is remote. All kinds of things up to and including overturned tractor-trailers could delay an Eastport-bound traveler in a storm, and even after the storm was past.

Ellie turned to me, her look beatific; that tiger had a pretty smile. But there was something else going on behind it. Again it struck me that I'd had a different existence before I came here: city living, fancy apartment, a job that I supposed must've at least looked glamorous.

Not to mention the high heels and fancy makeup.

But Ellie's life was Eastport. Always had been and always would be, probably, and she wanted all of it.

The whole shebang, murders included. "So, no assistance from that department, either, probably," she said, meaning Cahill. "Or at least not soon."

Then she added the zinger, which by then I'd figured must be coming:

"You know, Jake, I'm beginning to think the only way we can help Chip Hahn is to find out who killed that girl ourselves."

"Listen, Carol, I'm kind of busy here."

Sam hauled six more just-delivered cartons of teak oil off the pallet and hoisted them onto the metal shelving behind the counter, then checked them off the delivery sheet with his penlight pen. Stock handling was boring, but it was part of his job at the boatyard two miles out of town on Deep Cove Road.

He wished he could be with Chip, trying to help. "I mean, I'm on the clock here, you know?" Sam told Carol, who did not seem impressed. Sucking on a cherry Tootsie Pop, she toyed with a box of paper clips on the counter.

Heck, Chip couldn't have done anything like what they said. Sam knew Chip, and he was sure of it. But there was nothing Sam could do about his friend's troubles until the cops got finished questioning him, and released him.

Which Sam had no doubt they would, but the whole thing was very worrisome, and meanwhile Sam was stuck out here instead of at the breakwater in town. That was his next choice for where he'd rather be, helping guys secure their vessels against the big blow that was coming.

But the boss wanted him at the boatyard in case customers needed a new cleat or more line to tie to the new cleat. And for sure he'd already sold plenty of those, plus blue tarp, deep-cycle batteries, boat bumpers, and the kind of chemical hand-warmer pads you could put in your gloves so your fingers wouldn't freeze while you tried like hell to keep your vessel from sinking.

"You don't look busy." Carol leaned on the counter, a cell phone in one hand and the glistening Tootsie Pop in the other. At intervals, her cherry-red tongue flicked out at the Tootsie Pop.

Sam tried not to watch, but it was difficult. "Sam," she repeated insistently. "Where's your friend?"

Sam heaved the last carton of teak oil up, then turned to grab another few boxes of battery cables. He'd have gone outside to escape her if he could; she wasn't supposed to be here, anyway, and if the boss came back and found her, he'd be in trouble.

But with the storm raging the way it was, the only work he could do around the marina was indoor stuff. And Carol, of course, had figured that out.

"You mean Chip?" He hung the cables on display hooks mounted in a pegboard behind the counter.

"Who do you think I mean? You have some other guy staying at your house?"

She eyed him mischievously over the Tootsie Pop. With her dark hair in a ponytail and her long, athletic legs covered by a pair of gray sweatpants, his old high school football jacket over her shoulders and battered sneakers on her feet, she looked just barely plausible as a boat-supply customer. If the boss did come back, it was what Sam intended to tell him.

That is, he would if Carol didn't decide out of spite—she was still irked that he hadn't come out to the party last night—to put the moves on the boss, first. She was just bratty enough to do it, too.

"What d'you want with Chip, anyway?" Sam had introduced them when Chip first got here, a few days earlier. He dropped fuses of varying sizes into their proper small clear plastic drawers in the display case. "I didn't know he'd made an impression on you."

"He didn't." She sounded bored. "I just wondered. Why, is that a crime?"

No, of course it wasn't. Just thinking about Chip made him feel anxious, was all.

"Sorry," Sam said as a customer came in wanting cotter pins; motoring over here to get his Chris-Craft onto a safer mooring on the lee side of the island, he'd strayed near shore and hit an outcropping of granite ledge with his propeller.

Then as the customer went out, the phone rang. "She's there, isn't she?"

It was Maggie. "Uh . . ."

"I saw her heading out Deep Cove Road in that little car of hers."

Carol's red Mazda Miata, Maggie meant. Anybody else would've had the car safely under cover for the storm, but for Carol danger only made things more fun.

Still, was it his fault Carol had shown up? *Grow a damned spine, Tiptree,* he thought. "Yeah. She's here."

He didn't quite add *Wanna make something of it?* But from Maggie's reaction, he might as well have.

"You know, Sam, I understand that she's pretty, and that she has nothing to do all day but hang around revving your motor."

Ten feet away, Carol touched the cherry-red Tootsie Pop very deliberately to the tip of her tongue, then slid the candy slowly between her lips. *Oh, holy criminy.*

"But I'm getting pretty tired of playing second fiddle to a woman whose only real assets are in her . . . assets," Maggie added.

In the background at Maggie's, a string quartet was playing. "And it's not like she'd ever settle down with you, be part of a team, you know, to do anything worthwhile."

Carol, she meant, the girl batting her long lashes at him right now, her mouth making kissing movements and her eyes bright with suppressed laughter.

"I mean, I know her type," Maggie went on. "She'll play with you, but in the end she just wants some guy with a lot of money."

Carol, whose other-woman radar had twigged instantly to the fact that it was Maggie on the telephone, flapped her fingers and thumb together in a "blah-blah-blah" motion.

"Seriously, Sam," Maggie said, "don't you ever get tired of her? I mean, all she's doing is yanking your chain."

Yeah, Sam thought, transfixed by the sight of Carol doing something he hoped to hell his boss didn't walk in on.

Or anyone else. *Pull your shirt down,* he mouthed

urgently at Carol, and in response she began undoing her sweatpants drawstring.

"What?" said Maggie.

He swallowed hard. "Maggie, look, I've got a whole lot of customers here, I've got to—"

"Forget it," snapped Maggie, whose own radar was nothing to fool around with, either. "I'm not going to try talking to you if she's . . . what's she doing, a striptease or something?"

Carol kicked off a shoe. "Carol!" he hissed urgently at her as his boss's big Chevy Silverado pulled into the lot outside.

"Goodbye, Sam. I'll give you a few days to think about it. If you're not wised up by then, though, don't bother to call me."

Oh, hell . . . Through the shop's front window, Sam watched his boss hop down from the truck and sprint hard through the pounding rain. Kicking off her other shoe, Carol turned, giving Sam a view of that gorgeous backside of hers.

Then, spotting the boss, she snatched her shirt up off the floor, snagged both her shoes, and ran, hiking her pants back up first one leg and then the other, giggling as she went. She'd just made it behind a display rack loaded with boat cushions and hatchway covers when the bell over the front door jangled and the boss rushed in, dripping and cursing.

Luckily, he'd only come for the bank deposits, and he was in such a hurry that he didn't smell the cherry-candy perfume still wafting in the air. Two minutes later he was gone, and soon after that Carol was, too, but not before protesting petulantly that she'd just wanted to have some fun, and couldn't he, Sam, loosen up a little once in a while?

"You're as bad as Chip," she complained.

Her car was right outside. Sam wondered if maybe the boss had noticed it; how could he not have?

Then what she'd said hit Sam. "What do you mean? Have you been pestering Chip?" He wouldn't have put it past her.

Not that Chip would've cooperated; he was so crazy about his own girl back in the city. Too crazy, maybe, but there was nothing Sam could do about that, either.

Carol pouted, tossing her glossy dark ponytail. "No. Chip's not my type, I told you."

"Yeah, well." He ushered her toward the door. It was still raining pretty hard, but she'd made it in here from her car all right. She could make it back out again, too.

"Just make sure you don't, that's all. He's got enough of his own problems." It came over Sam again just how much trouble his friend might really be in. But . . .

It's a mistake, though. I mean, it's got to be a mistake . . . doesn't it?

At the door Carol kissed him, reaching up with both hands to pull his face down and plant her warm, moist lips on his. The shock of electric pleasure this sent through him immobilized him for an instant, long enough for her to let go of his head and let her hands roam over his body lingeringly.

"There," she said finally, pulling away when she was sure he didn't want her to. "See if Miss Goody Two-Shoes can match *that*."

Gasping, he straightened. "Wait," he managed.

But it was too late. The bell over the door jangled and with a mocking laugh she was gone, dashing to her car through the pounding rain, spinning up wet gravel as she accelerated out of the parking lot.

Not until his vision had cleared, his heart rate slowing from its thud-thud gallop, did he notice the other car, idling at the far end of the lot. *Damn* . . .

It was Maggie's beat-up Toyota. Knowing her, she'd come out to . . . well, not to apologize. This was Maggie, after all, and she actually hadn't said anything unreasonable. But to put things on a better footing, maybe; they'd been friends for a long time.

More than friends . . . But now, through the Toyota's fogged-up windshield, he could just make out the white of her face, two dark smears for eyes, and a downturned mouth. Guiltily he reached for a slicker from the rack by the door, but before he could pull it on, a puff of exhaust bloomed from the Toyota.

"Maggie!" he shouted, scrambling out to catch her before she could race off. Obviously she'd seen Carol leaving, but how much else?

"Maggie, wait, I can—" *Explain,* he'd meant to finish, but before he could reach it the Toyota swung hard through a three-point reverse out of the lot and sped away. Watching it go, Sam felt Carol's kiss still on his lips, and at the same time heard Maggie's voice—her melodious, sensible, *indispensable* voice, so dear and familiar he hardly knew what he would do without it—issuing its really quite sensible, understandable ultimatum.

Me or her. And why not? Guilt washed over him as he turned and slogged back across the wet parking lot, its crushed-stone surface deeply rutted by Carol's flashy departure.

Inside, he paced angrily, disgusted with himself. Maggie didn't deserve this. Hell, even Carol didn't. *And I don't. Man, this kind of behavior is effed up.*

So I'm going to stop it. Now, before being a dumb jerk began sliding irresistibly—and at least in his own experience, also inevitably—into being a drunk dumb jerk.

Because that was how it always went: first behaving like an ass, then drinking like one. Grabbing up the phone, he called his boss's cell and said what he had to say, and hung up before he could change his mind. Then he dialed his own home phone number.

"Mom? Yeah, it's me. Yeah, I'm okay. No accidents, no, I haven't gotten injured or anything. Everything's fine. That is, I mean, not *fine* fine. But—"

It had stopped surprising him, how relieved she always was to hear that he was still alive and intact. Hey, he'd bought that trip. "Mom, I quit. Yeah, my job. Until Chip gets out of whatever this is that he's in, I'm going to—"

Outside, the big Silverado roared back into the parking lot again, its big tires digging their own ruts in the gravel as it braked hard to a stop, wipers sloshing ineffectively through what looked like rivers on the windshield.

"And, listen, Mom? If Carol calls, or if Maggie does? Say I'm busy, I'm not seeing anyone for a while. But make sure neither one of them thinks I've dropped her to go with the other one, all right? Because I'm not. Going to, I mean."

I hope. He half listened while the burly figure of his

boss loomed larger outside the front window, shoulders hunched in the deluge. Frowning, Sam turned away from the figure.

"Fine. See you soon," he said hurriedly into the phone, and hung up as the bell over the front door jangled violently.

Turning back, he faced the music.

The fried haddock sandwich in the New Friendly restaurant was delicious, the white flesh moistly flaky and batter coating perfectly browned.

"Not bad, huh?" Dylan ate a french fry from the single order they'd agreed to split, while outside the rain-splashed window the weather went on deteriorating swiftly.

Lizzie sipped her Pepsi, which had come in a tall glass with a lemon slice in it. "Excellent," she agreed, and then, "So tell me about this thing last night."

Getting Dylan talking about something he was interested in had always been the way to get other information out of him. His answering shrug-and-headshake combination, though, meant that in his opinion there wasn't much to tell.

"Girl got killed. Throat cut. You ask me, they got the guy. Case closed." He bit into his own sandwich, captured an escaping drip of tartar sauce with the tip of his tongue.

She looked away. "Who, that kid? Come on. I know he was at the scene, but he looks like Mr. Respectable to me."

"Yeah, well." Dylan ate another french fry, first

dipping it in the blue cheese dressing he'd ordered on the side. He'd never had to pay attention to calories, always just burning up whatever he ate.

"He might *look* innocent." He drank some of his milk shake, another of his quirks. Dylan could pack the booze away with no problem, never even seeming to get tipsy. But with his meals, he chose kids' drinks, a root beer float or maybe a frappe.

"That guy's got so many skeletons in his closet, he could rent 'em out for Halloween. Got a sheet for peeping in some girl's window in New Hampshire, first of all."

She looked up in surprise, taken aback that she'd misread the guy so badly. "Really? What was the dispo?"

How, she meant, did the situation get resolved: a plea, a trial, what? Because anybody could get accused of something, but that didn't mean they'd done it.

"Pled out," said Dylan, which told her that Chip Hahn hadn't wanted to go to trial, but not why.

"No other arrests, though, before or since. Of course," Dylan added, "we don't know if he never did it again, or if that was just the only time he got caught."

"I guess," Lizzie said, thinking it over. The arrest record was no problem for law enforcement in Maine to get hold of, even this quickly. The "dispo"—how the case eventually turned out—was another matter.

Ordinarily, it could take days to get someone to dig up the relevant records. That Dylan had the answer now meant he'd gotten it himself, by calling, say, an assistant DA with whom he already had a relationship.

He was good at relationships, she thought to herself dryly. Or at starting them, at least. "I thought you were only observing this investigation?" The fish really was very good; she finished the last bite.

He tipped his head before attacking the french fries again. "Hey, it doesn't hurt me to be useful once in a while," he said, dipping one in ketchup. "Work my way back into the higher-ups' good graces."

So that's what this was all about. Just as she'd thought, he'd been kicked upstairs as a time-out for bad behavior. But he wanted active duty again and she was supposed to help him get it.

Showing her how easily he could get information out of back channels might kill two birds with one stone: demonstrating his skill and moxie to the bosses, while also further persuading her that he could be useful in helping to find her niece.

If she's alive. Glancing at him again, she found him studying her. "I see you're catching my drift," he said.

His gaze lingered unnervingly on her lips. She broke the moment by saying, "How do I know you'll come through with what I need, though? I don't even know there is anything to—"

He laughed without humor. "Yeah, and it's not like I haven't burned you before, huh?" He ate a pickle slice.

That wasn't like the Dylan she remembered. In the past he'd have tried wriggling out of any blame, no matter how slight. She thought again of how fast he must've had to grow up when his wife was dying, as across the pleasant room a pair of good old boys in bib overalls tucked into plates of meat loaf.

"That's why I figured that you might need a sample of what I'm promising," said Dylan.

He pulled a photograph from the inside front pocket of the sport jacket he was wearing over a black turtleneck. "Does this look familiar?"

Lizzie took it. The photo was a picture of Sissy as a child: white-blond hair, pale eyes, gap-toothed grin. Only—

Only it wasn't Sissy. "Where did you get this?" The child in the photograph was holding a small American flag in one hand and a red, white, and blue banner in the other.

In sparkly script, the banner said HAPPY 4TH! Lizzie stared. She'd been sent a photograph of this same child, just in different clothes.

Also, this photograph was date-stamped. "This was taken—"

Dylan nodded. "Uh-huh. Last summer."

Last summer, Sissy had already been dead eight years. And Nicki was nine.

About the same age as the child in the picture. "This came to me in the mail," said Dylan, "about a month ago. Plain manila envelope, no return address, no note, no explanation."

He shook his head frowningly. "I've been carrying it around with me ever since, wondering why. Never made the connection with your thing back then, but when I saw you and realized what you must be doing here, then I got it."

He laid the photograph on the table between them as Lizzie tried to find her voice and couldn't. Leaning back in the booth, he waited while the waitress cleared plates and offered coffee, which Dylan accepted for both of them. Then:

"I didn't know," he repeated, "but even if I had, if I had tried calling you about it would you have given me the time of day? No, you wouldn't," he answered himself, "and I don't blame you."

Her hand moved unbidden to touch the picture, her finger moving lightly over this new bit of evidence that after all, she might not be alone in the world.

That she still had family. Her eyes prickled with tears. "No," she replied finally. "You're right, Dylan, I wouldn't have. You were dead to me."

And now he wasn't. He was here with her right now, no longer the perennial bad boy but instead a grown man, owning frankly up to his past mistakes. Here just the way she'd dreamed, with his dark, knowing eyes and his expressive mouth and his dark forelock perpetually begging to be tugged very gently—

Stop that, she ordered herself.

"And why would anyone send this to you, anyway?" she added, because it made no sense. Who from around here would have known enough about them both to do so, first of all, and—

"I have no idea." He plucked up the photograph, glanced at their lunch check and got his wallet out.

"Tell you what, though," he said, laying a twenty and a five atop the check; he always had been a generous tipper.

"Of course you have your doubts about me. I didn't exactly earn your respect as a guy you could depend on, did I?"

Oh, I could depend on you. To lie, and cheat, and . . .

And break my heart. "But I think we could find out the why of all of this. I think we could help each other," he finished.

He let his hand rest on her shoulder again briefly as she went ahead of him out the door. Then they were in the pelting rain once more, dashing through it together toward the shelter of his car. In the few moments before they reached it, he took her hand.

"Come on, you're getting drenched!" he laughed, and pulled open the car door with a sweeping, mock-gallant gesture.

Heaven help me, she thought as she ducked in, laughing, too, now, in spite of herself, feeling only the giddy exhilaration she recalled so well, that pure happiness.

Except it wasn't so pure. By the time he'd hurried around and climbed into the driver's seat, she'd gotten control of her emotions again, or enough so that she could talk and think.

"So listen, how come you and Liam never got together?" he asked casually, as if back in the restaurant he hadn't just made her search for Nicki even more troubling and confusing than it was before.

Because . . . why *would* someone send that picture of the child to Dylan? Or send the other ones to Lizzie, for that matter?

Now the one Dylan had received lay on the Saab's center console. She glanced around uneasily, filled suddenly with the sense of some unknown person out there somewhere, knowing more than she did. But then it hit her, what Dylan had just said.

"Liam? You mean . . . God, Dylan, he was my partner."

As she spoke, the memories rushed back of her job as a cop with the Boston PD, first on patrol with her partner, Liam, later as a homicide detective; a murder cop, those whose work it was called it. Getting promoted had been the proudest moment of her life, leaving the job the most difficult.

But now that she'd quit, it wasn't the detective work she'd done that rose vividly in her mind. It was the memory of all the shifts on patrol with Liam that assailed her, the bond they'd shared along with the fast-food sandwiches and take-out coffee.

Liam had been the most honest man she'd ever known, before he died trying to stop a convenience store robbery. She wondered what he'd think of the way she was lying to everyone in Eastport, now, hiding her cop past.

Lying her head off, at least by omission. Keeping her true self, her real feelings, secret.

And not only about having been a cop. "Why do you want to know, anyway?" she asked Dylan.

Dylan shrugged. "Just wondered. Is there . . . anyone now?"

None of your business. But she answered. "No." She didn't elaborate; let him make what he wanted of it. Her personal life—*not that I have one*—wasn't his concern anymore.

He nodded judiciously, not prodding slyly as he once might have, instead waving at the photo to change the subject again. "Anyway, think it over. You never know what somebody in the house where the Hahn kid was staying might've seen or heard, that could nail the lid down on him."

Backing out of his parking spot, he turned on the Saab's heat; the rush of warm air carrying the smell of freshly cleaned car upholstery sent another rush of nostalgia through her.

He'd always kept the old car up beautifully. Memory flooded her: *late-night Boston traffic, the lights and cars, flaring of neon through a rain-streaming windshield* . . .

And afterwards. *Oh, afterwards* . . . She wrenched her thoughts back to the present. "But what if it doesn't? Nail the lid down, I mean. Are you so sure this kid is your guy?"

Surprised, he glanced over at her as he made the left turn back toward Eastport, the road ahead a shiny, dark gray ribbon pelted with rain, the drops hitting so hard that they bounced up again, and the roadside puddles seemed to be boiling.

"I mean, so he's got a peeping arrest," she went on. "That doesn't mean he carved up some girl with a hunting knife."

Another glance, this one bemused. He drove fast and well, as she remembered, unfazed by the wet and murk outside the car.

"No, Lizzie, it doesn't. But something about his story just doesn't jell. That's why I want everything you can get, no matter how unimportant it seems," he replied.

A sudden downpour flooded the windshield; he turned the wipers to high. "Especially if he comes up with an alibi of some kind; as it is, from what I understand, he's sticking with his original story, that he was out for a walk, nothing more. But we're not buying it."

"But if he had an alibi"—one that was verifiable, Lizzie meant, not the goofball out-for-a-late-night-walk nonsense Hahn had tried to make fly—"why wouldn't he have told you about it already?"

Dylan shook his head. "No idea." He changed the subject. "How'd you know what kind of weapon it was?"

She explained about being there in the Tiptree house when the husband came in asking about the knife. "And from the look on his face, I didn't think he'd just misplaced it."

"Aha. You must be a detective." Zipping along through the rain, he attempted a comically mysterious expression, succeeded only in looking lovably goofy, and then several things happened:

A van in the oncoming lane slowed suddenly, its turn signal flashing, fat waves of puddled rain sluicing away from its front tires. From behind it, a pickup truck swung out wildly, crossing the center line straight at the Saab.

"Damn," Dylan said tightly, swerving right. There would be, Lizzie realized as the pickup truck kept coming, room on their left. By straddling the center line, the truck headed straight at them could get by them.

But the pickup didn't *stay* on the center line. It crossed all the way over, and now she noticed the van that had originally slowed for its turn, somehow lying in the ditch on its side.

The pickup must've rear-ended it, she realized, sending it out of control. That wasn't the important thing, though. The important thing was the pickup truck itself, now filling up the whole windshield even though Dylan kept on trying to evade it by swerving onto the shoulder.

Lizzie tried to relax, remembering how loose-limbed drunks always seemed to survive their driving mishaps. As a patrol cop, she'd shoved her own share of slurring fools uninjured into the back seats of squad cars . . .

Then came a massive *thud* that stopped everything: the truck, the Saab, the world as she knew it. She felt the seatbelt yank itself viciously tight across her chest, her left arm flinging out as if reaching for the Saab's front bumper, her neck stretching impossibly as her head flew forward and then was slammed back again, against the headrest.

And then silence. *Breathe in. Breathe out.* Part of her knew she was alive and that any minute, she would have to do something about this. A whole laundry list of tasks had to be completed in the event of a serious motor vehicle accident.

The trouble was, she couldn't recall what any of them were. She blinked deliberately, hoping her mental switches would clear, but they'd been hit very hard by that pickup; just sitting there drawing slow breaths one after the next seemed to be all that she could accomplish at the moment.

In fact, some small part of her felt good just being able to do that much. *The part that says you're lucky to be alive . . .*

Steam rose from the Saab's radiator, boiling up in white billows into the dark afternoon of pouring rain. The smell of hot antifreeze confused her until she realized that the windshield was gone, shattered into a thousand greenish-white granules that lay all over her lap and the front passenger area.

What was left of it. The whole dashboard seemed to have been moved back several inches toward the passenger seats, and most of the center console was crumpled, accordion-like, halfway into the rear compartment.

No movement from the pickup truck. None from the van that had gone into the ditch over there, either. Really, it was very annoying that she couldn't seem to think, couldn't . . .

Outside, other cars were stopping, people's voices seeming to come from a distance. A cherry beacon flared rhythmically out there somewhere, getting nearer very fast.

Now she could hear its siren. *Good,* she thought dully. It was good that the cops were coming now. But the Saab was a mess, and oh, Dylan was going to be so upset.

He'd loved this car. He hadn't said anything about it yet, but . . . *Dylan.*

She turned very slowly. Her neck didn't hurt yet, but it was going to. *Careful, a little more* . . .

Shifting gingerly, she angled her body around toward the driver's seat, while outside, the sirens screamed nearer and the rain hammered down.

That was when she saw the blood.

Twenty minutes later she sat in the front seat of Eastport police chief Bob Arnold's squad car, its roof rack strobing the rainy gloom with red and its radio sputtering intermittently. The heater was on, but she shivered uncontrollably despite the warm jacket someone had thrown over her.

The EMS guys had tried cajoling her into an ambulance, but she'd refused; as far as she could tell, sore muscles in her neck and shoulder would be her only injuries out of this mess.

Dylan, though, was another story. From across the road, she watched them remove him from the bent and broken Saab, secure him to a stretcher, hustle him through yet another downpour, and hoist him up through the brightly lit back door of the emergency vehicle.

He wasn't bleeding anymore that she could see. But he wasn't moving, either. A plastic oxygen mask covered his face; one of the EMTs held up an IV bag. She bit her lip hard as Bob Arnold appeared, leaning in through the open squad car window.

"Here." He thrust in a steaming-hot paper cup of coffee.

She took it gratefully. "Thanks. Is he—?"

Bob shook his head. "Breathing. Got a pulse. That's all I know. Pickup driver bumped his head but that's all, and those people in the van ended up okay, too, don't ask me how."

She nodded, sipped some more of the hot liquid as Bob strode off again. Now that the adrenaline from the crash was fading, she felt flattened, as if most of her own blood had been drained from her. In the wind and rain, flashlight-carrying figures moved in the road, routing cars over onto the shoulder to get by, waving them along.

The boxy red ambulance's rear doors were closed, so she couldn't see Dylan anymore. But he had a heartbeat, and he was breathing . . . *Please,* she thought. *Just let him be okay.*

Even her anxiety over Dylan's condition, though, didn't wipe out her doubts over what he'd been saying just before the crash. He'd told her he wanted to hear anything she found out about Chip Hahn's activities the night of the murder, incriminating or not. But the trouble was, she realized with deep regret as she sat in Bob Arnold's squad car getting her wind back . . .

The trouble was, she didn't believe it. He was after the bad stuff, if there was any, or anything about Chip Hahn that Dylan might be able to make look bad. Not that she had any particular loyalties to the suspect, or to his hostess Jake Tiptree, either.

Still, she'd rather liked Jake and her redheaded friend, Ellie White. They'd both seemed to be pretty straight-up people; she'd felt bad about, in effect, lying to them about who she was. So to stay straight with herself, Lizzie realized as she sat gathering her wits, there was one more thing she was going to have to do about this whole situation.

And there'd be no need for Dylan to know what that one thing was, either, she thought . . . because of *course* he was going to be okay, of *course* he was.

The ambulance backed up, turned sharply, and sped toward her, activating its lights and siren as it went on by. Then a cop who'd been helping the EMTs sprinted over, one hand tucked into the front of his jacket as if protecting something he held.

It was the young Eastport cop she'd gotten herself into the beef with last night, at the church. *At the murder scene . . .*

When he reached her, his face changed, official courtesy giving way to recognition and personal dislike. "He said to give these to you."

"Who—?" Squinting through the gloom, she made out only the shapes of cops and fire department personnel, and of a tow-truck guy ready to haul the Saab up onto a flatbed. Confused, she took the sheet of paper the young cop held out.

But then she saw what it was, and realized: Dylan must have been alert at some point after the crash, awake enough to—

Hope energized her suddenly; she sat up straight. "Thank you," she called after the departing officer, then looked down again at what Dylan, even injured and in pain as he must've been, had wanted her to have.

It was the picture of Nicki—*if it is her,* Lizzie reminded herself—the photograph he'd received at about the same time as Lizzie herself had been getting two of them. But that wasn't all. Folded behind the picture was a sheet of paper, a printout of something that someone had emailed to Dylan.

Today, to judge by the date at the top. It was an annotated list of odd, alphabet-soup-like website addresses.

Private websites, Lizzie realized, with addresses consisting of meaningless letter sequences; they could be accessed only by people who already knew about them, not casual Web surfers.

The practical result, she knew from an Internet security in-service she'd taken in Boston, was that the sites were "members only," but why?

And then, from the websites' real names noted

alongside the scrambled ones—names with the words "death," "women," and much worse things figuring prominently in them—she understood why.

Bub Wilson stuck his close-clipped blond head up through the moonroof of the car filled with his buddies as it pursued David slowly up the steep hill of Adams Street.

"Hey, *Dweeb*!" Behind the wheel was Jerome Kadlick, a thin, fox-faced teenager with dark eyes and a sullen expression. The boys had caught sight of David on Water Street on his way home from the library, and noticed that he was alone.

Bogie Kopmeir was keeping a low profile today for some reason; David hadn't seen him yet. With the boys in the car still keeping pace with him, David walked faster. *Just don't look at them,* his dad always said about situations like this. *Don't antagonize them, don't give them anything to—*

Something buzzed fast past his face with a quick, hot *zzzzt!* At the same time he heard the *snap!* of a BB gun being fired.

"Hey, Dweebles, pay attention when I talk to you," ordered Bub. Glancing sideways at him, David noted the BB pistol in Bub's hand. "You ain't got Bogie with you now, punk, so listen up."

Another shot. This one smacked the street, sending sharp grit spraying stingingly up into David's face. Head down, fists jammed in his jacket pockets, he felt hot tears filling his eyes. Half a block now, past the quarter acre of scrub woods and partly emerged granite boulders of a vacant lot, and he would be able to turn onto the narrow back lane leading to his house.

He didn't think the boys would follow him there. The rarely used lane's ruts were deep, with a rise at the center that would take out the muffler of Jerome's dad's car.

Between here and the lane, though, was the hill's steepest part. *Zzzt!* Bub's third shot caught the bill on David's baseball cap, nipping a few threads from its tip.

David flinched hard, provoking guffaws from his tormentors keeping pace with him in the slowly moving car.

"Dweeb! Look at me, you little mutt."

David stopped, transfixed by the sight of the tiny tear in his Red Sox cap. He'd gotten it at an actual game, in Boston with his father and his uncle Joe, who'd been skinny and pale and who had died a few weeks afterwards of pancreatic cancer.

"Shut up," he said, taking the cap off to hold in both hands as he turned to Bub.

At the same time, he was calculating the distance through the vacant lot to his house. Too far; he should have thought of that before he opened his stupid mouth, he realized. But the words had just come out of him.

"What?" said Bub incredulously, hauling his slim frame out through the moonroof and leaping easily from it to the street in a single, liquidly athletic motion.

He stalked toward the sidewalk. David took off running but Bub was on him in a heartbeat, one big splay-fingered hand clamped around David's arm and the other clutching a fistful of his hair.

"You little dirtbag," he snarled, muscling David backwards until he had him shoved up hard against the old gatepost marking what once had been a driveway, curving into the vacant lot.

Bub's face contorted menacingly, teeth bared, small ice-blue eyes glaring. His breath smelled like pizza. Pinning David, he drew his fist back, ready to punch and punch for the sheer animal joy of it, and then out of nowhere Bogie was on him.

Bub staggered backwards, flailing ineffectually, while Bogie clung to the basketball player's back with his short legs wrapped around the bigger boy's torso. The amount of blood suddenly gushing from Bub Wilson's nose shocked David, as did the number of blows Bogie managed to deliver to Bub's face while essentially slugging him from behind.

Bogie spat curses, kneeing Bub in the kidneys, scratching and headbutting while the boys from the car scrambled out but then hesitated, unwilling to get within punching range. Bogie aimed a last, open-handed slap at the side of Bub's head, cocking his arm back and slamming his palm flat to Bub's red, bitten ear: *smack!*

Bub dropped like a felled tree. The other boys started forward. Bogie whirled, screaming, pounding his chest with his fists, which were spattered with Bub's blood.

"*Yah! Yah! You want summah this? Yah!*" he screamed as he advanced on them, whereupon they scuttled back to their car and raced off in it, leaving Bub lying there.

David stood shakily by the gatepost as Bogie stomped back, not sparing the moaning Bub Wilson a glance. "Come on," he said.

Looking back as he followed Bogie into the vacant lot, David faintly suggested that maybe they should call help for Bub.

"Call him a freakin' hearse," Bogie responded irritably. "I hope he freakin' *dies* there."

By now Bub was struggling up. So he could still move, anyway, David thought with a combination of disappointment and relief. Bogie chuckled, spinning the BB pistol he'd taken from Bub around his index finger as if it were a six-shooter. He looked happy, like a little kid with a new toy.

What just happened back there? David wondered. It was as if he'd witnessed some violent force of nature in action, a volcano erupting or something, and now it was over.

They came out of the vacant lot, crossed the lane into the rear yard of David's house. A pie was cooling on the small cast-iron café table on the back porch, set on a blue gingham-checked dish towel, and the sight suddenly made David feel like bursting into tears.

URGENT WEATHER MESSAGE
WEATHER SERVICE CARIBOU MAINE

FOR INTERIOR HANCOCK-COASTAL HANCOCK-
CENTRAL WASHINGTON-COASTAL WASHINGTON-
INCLUDING THE CITIES OF . . . EASTPORT . . .
PERRY . . . PEMBROKE . . . CALAIS . . . LUBEC . . .
MACHIAS
. . . WEATHER ADVISORY CONTINUES IN EFFECT UNTIL
MIDNIGHT EDT TOMORROW NIGHT . . .
THE WEATHER SERVICE IN CARIBOU HAS ISSUED A
WEATHER ADVISORY FOR HEAVY RAIN AND GALE
FORCE WINDS.

* PRECIPITATION TYPE . . . RAIN HEAVY AT TIMES.
LOCALLY AS MUCH AS 1 INCH PER HOUR.
* ACCUMULATIONS . . . RAIN 3 TO 5 INCHES TOTAL
EXCEPT WHERE DOWNPOURS FREQUENT.
* TIMING . . . TODAY INTO TOMORROW NIGHT.
* TEMPERATURES . . . IN THE LOWER 40S.
* WINDS . . . NORTHEAST 35-65 MPH. WITH POSSIBLE
HIGHER GUSTS ESPECIALLY COASTAL.

* IMPACTS . . . IMPACT FROM THIS STORM WILL BE
CONSIDERABLE. EXPECT SOME TRAVEL DIFFICULTIES.
WIND DAMAGE AND POWER OUTAGES LIKELY, LOCAL
FLOODING LIKELY.

PREPAREDNESS ACTIONS . . .

TRAVEL DELAYS MAY OCCUR. TRAVEL WILL BE
DIFFICULT. PLAN EXTRA TIME TO REACH YOUR
DESTINATION. MARINERS SHOULD STAY IN PORT.
SECURE LOOSE OBJECTS. POSTPONE TRAVEL AT
HEIGHT OF STORM IF POSSIBLE. DO NOT DRIVE
THROUGH FLOODED AREAS. HIGH TIDES. HIGH WINDS
MAY IMPACT COMMUNICATIONS TOWERS ESPECIALLY
DOWNEAST. EXPECT OUTAGES.

Chapter 8

> *The more time you spend*
> *steaming old wallpaper,*
> *the less time you'll have*
> *to spend scraping it off.*
> —Tiptree's Tips

Whenever I got back to my house after dropping Ellie at hers, I had every intention of staying home for the storm's duration. But then I went upstairs to wash my hands, and calamity ensued.

This way: I turned the hot and cold water faucet handles on together, which in my old house is the only way of not either boiling or freezing yourself to death.

The faucet gurgled. Some water spat out. Then the water cut off, but the gurgling didn't, and the next thing I knew, there was yelling down in the kitchen, followed by the banging of pans and clanking of buckets.

All of which, I knew from my sadly extensive experience in This Old Money-Pit, represented a broken pipe in the downstairs hall ceiling. And since every plumber in town was busy putting sump pumps into cellars not already equipped with them (in towns to our south it was rumored that the animals were lining up two by two), I had little choice but to put on my own plumber's hat.

Which resembled a dunce cap, and some people said was made of tinfoil, but I had to do something before it started raining even harder inside the house than out. So I raced to the car, backed out of a driveway so flooded that the animal story started sounding halfway believable, and drove toward downtown and the harbor, where I expected to see an Ark floating.

There wasn't, but if it kept raining like this, everything else would be soon. I left the car in a lagoon that hours earlier had been a parking lot, then rushed across the street through what was already a running stream. In the store, clerks hurried to keep up with sales of downspouts, drainage tiles, and spray caulk, gutter sections and connectors, and—for when all else failed—truly enormous blue plastic tarps, plus plenty of bungee cords to lash them down.

In the narrow old building with its wooden floors, exposed brick walls, and wide-bladed fans turning slowly near the high, stamped-tin ceilings, I found my way to the pipe section, where braided steel, copper, PVC, and PEX were all displayed, cut in lengths or dangling from big reels.

The store smelled as usual of paint, sawdust, and 3-in-One oil, mingled perfumes that always encourage me in fond beliefs that I'd be much better off without. Such as, for instance, the idea that no matter how bad the trouble is, a little elbow grease and an insane amount of determination can still make everything all right.

Well, that and the right tools. Buoyed by this notion, I chose two pieces of PEX pipe and an installation kit. It held a crimping tool, various sizes of compression fittings, and pipe cutters. The whole thing was more expensive in the short run than it would've been to splice in more copper piping, but over the long haul I figured I was saving on the psychiatric care I'd be needing if I ever had to work with copper piping again.

Because of two words: "soldering gun." Personally, I'd rather try fixing a pipe with an AK-47. As I pondered this, the chatter around the cash register up front began penetrating my plumbing-obsessed brain. And despite the emergency at home, when I heard Lizzie Snow's name, I couldn't resist a peek around a display of work gloves—cloth, leather, insulated, rubberized, and thin plastic, just to name a few—to see who was there.

"She won't arrest anyone," said Beanie Rumford, leaning on the cash register counter. "She'll just nag 'em to death. Make 'em wish they were in jail, y'know? Like their wives do."

"Har har," said his audience, a quartet of Eastport's

least admirable citizens. Lounging by the garden supplies were an enlightened crew of benchwarmers, second-guessers, and armchair quarterbacks, none of whom would ordinarily have been caught dead in the hardware store, since it reminded them too much of work.

But of course it was raining outside, so they were making an exception. "She ain't no cop. She's too good-lookin' for a cop," another of them chimed in; I guessed the rocket science programs Dinty Dutton had applied to must've been full. "Those legs of hers look like they go all the way to heaven, don't they?"

As he glanced around for approval, Barron Hallie spoke up. "Don't know what a woman'd want with that job," he commented from behind a shrubby mustache. "Decent one wouldn't, anyway."

They didn't know I was down the aisle, listening. "Oh, she's decent, all right." Beanie sniggered. "I wouldn't mind her workin' with me undercover, you know what I mean? Get it? Under covers?"

Apparently they all did, which surprised me considering that their combined IQ barely exceeded today's temperature. More hilarity followed until I appeared with my pipes and my pipe-putting-together kit, which I may have set down on the counter a bit more firmly than necessary.

"Anyone working under cover with you would need a gas mask," I told Beanie as the clerk rang up my purchases; the cloud of garlic and chewing-tobacco fumes hanging around Beanie today was even more stunning than usual. "Haven't you got anything better to do than gossip?"

Because the idea of Lizzie Snow being a cop was

silly. For one thing, cops didn't have to go wandering around on their own snooping into things like missing nieces and possibly murdered sisters; they had all the snooping resources in the world.

"Ain't gossip," Barron protested stoutly.

The clerk went to check a price. With the pipe stuff, I'd picked up a can of Spackle, some plaster buttons, a putty knife, and a can of white ceiling paint, since the burst pipe was above the ceiling and that meant taking some of the ceiling down.

"Heard it straight from Paulie Waters," Barron said, but I ignored him, still busy with my own thoughts.

Of course, taking the ceiling down meant patching it back up again; besides, I could always use ceiling paint. Oh, the happy life of the old-house fix-up enthusiast; tra-freaking-la.

"He thought there might be something hinky about her, so he went an' ran her licence plate," said Barron. "Turns out she's a Boston police officer, sure as shootin'."

Which got my attention, even if he had mispronounced it: *ossifer*. I turned sharply to him.

"That's right." Barron looked delighted with himself. "And that's not all. Paulie says he thinks pretty soon she's gonna be our brand-new Eastport chief of police."

So there, smarty-pants, his defiant expression said, and I was about to reply, but just then, as the clerk returned, Paulie himself came in, the bell over the door jangling brightly. The good-looking young Eastport cop was Bob Arnold's second-in-command, and so might reasonably have thought the chief's job would be his should it become vacant.

But the scowl on his face said something had disappointed him recently. As he caught my eye his mouth formed a bitter line, then he turned away, pretending to compare the advantages of a tack hammer versus a rubber mallet.

So maybe, I thought with dismay as the clerk told me what I owed—if there were taxi meters for old-house fix-up expenses, mine would've overheated and burst into flames by now—*maybe the stories about Bob leaving Eastport were true.*

And maybe *that* was Lizzie's secret: she was replacing him. No wonder Paulie's face looked stormier than today's weather . . .

So forbidding, in fact, that although I approached him, when I got up close he looked exactly as if he might bite my head off, and I decided to ask Bob Arnold about it instead.

If the rumor was true, though . . . oh, man, just what I needed: a smart, energetic, and slim-as-a-switchblade cop zipping around town, reminding me every day with her edgy style and her fearless attitude that she was, as Sam would have put it if he weren't so mad at her, *da bomb.*

And I wasn't, anymore. Not to mention that if she had lied by not saying she was a cop in the first place . . . well, why?

Oh, I didn't like it a bit. Or what I found when I got home, either: when I walked in the door, I found that the pipe leak had enlarged quite a lot, and as a result my back hall bore a strong resemblance to a certain famous watery honeymoon destination.

So I spent the afternoon not only replumbing the bathroom but also exploring the mysteries of compression fittings, which when you're perched atop a stepladder with your head stuck up through a hole in the ceiling is not exactly a cakewalk. But finally I got it sorted:

First, shut off all the water in the house. Next, hacksaw out the broken part of the pipe. Measure the cut end's diameter, slide on the correct compression fittings, butt the new piece's ends up to the existing-pipe ends, and slide the fitting over the two mated pieces like a sleeve. Then crimp the fitting and repeat the process at the other end of the replacement piece, and . . .

Presto, no more Niagara Falls. And with any luck, that would be the day's final emergency, since besides fixing the leak I'd also done what I could about that carpenter-ant-weakened church steeple; not much, but at least it would get looked at soon.

As for Chip Hahn, he had a lawyer, so we didn't have to set that up for him. I'd called the courthouse, talked to a pleasant clerk, and discovered that yes, he was still there, but no, he had not been arrested. I asked the clerk to find out if he wanted us to come and stay with him, or bring him anything.

Which wasn't strictly in her job description, of course. But she did it and the answer came back no. Meanwhile, Ellie and I had agreed that we'd start asking around in the morning, once the storm had gone by, in case anyone in town knew anything we might find interesting on Chip's behalf.

Ellie had said she'd email Lizzie Snow's photos of her niece around, too; what that increasingly odd story was really all about I couldn't begin to guess. Could the guys in the hardware store be right?

Looking out into the rain-swept evening, I hoped not, and not only for my own sake. As a potential police chief, Lizzie fit Eastport the way a roofing tack fits a finishing nail's pre-drilled hole: you can hammer it in there, all right, but it's not going to do the job like you wanted and it'll always look funny.

For now, though, all I could do about any of it was stay home, with no plans to go out any more tonight. But that just goes to show how life can turn on a dime, doesn't it? Because not much later I was in a strange car, sneaking down a dark street through wind-driven rain while following a possible murderer.

And that was the good part of the evening.

"That's them." Lizzie pointed across the dark expanse of rainswept Water Street.

"I'm telling you, they were there last night, and they were watching."

At the church, she meant, right after poor Karen Hansen had been knifed to death. "I mean they were fascinated. Way more than the rest."

She'd arrived at my place while I was in the hall, cleaning up after the pipe repair.

"Jake," she'd said, standing on my back porch with the rain hammering down behind her, "can I come in?"

"Sure," I said. What I wanted to say was "Liar, liar." The more I'd thought about it, the more believable that rumor about Lizzie being a cop sounded.

But I didn't feel like confronting her about it; for one thing I had no control over who the next Eastport police chief might be, and for another, with my hair still full of Spackle globs and my eyes gritty with plaster dust, I didn't give a hoot if she was secretly Bozo the Clown as long as I could get into a good hot shower real soon, now.

So I just stood aside to let her past the stepladder, the spackling tools, the hacksaw, a tub of Spackle, a plastic drop cloth, the opened can of plaster buttons, and the electric screwdriver.

Due to the leak, I'd had not only a water emergency but also a ceiling emergency, and when I reached up to smooth Spackle onto a plaster button, I'd nearly had a ladder emergency. But she didn't go past the mess, because she wasn't staying; instead, she wanted me to go with her.

"I've got an idea about your guest's situation," she'd said, blinking raindrops out of her long dark eyelashes, "something that might help him out, and I'm going downtown to check into it a little more."

Phooey, I'd thought, looking out past her at the rain; also, who knew what she was really up to? On top of that, she looked scrappy and determined even in her current wet, bedraggled state; good heavens, this woman annoyed me. But it was Chip she was talking about, so of course I went and got my raincoat.

Now the three boys she'd pointed out stood huddled in a doorway of one of the closed shops on Water Street, while we sat in her Toyota in a dark parking lot half a block distant.

"You're sure?" I asked. "They were outside the church last night?"

The boys pushed and jostled, smoking and rough-housing as well as they could in the tight space. I didn't know their names, but the scruffy trio was a familiar sight most evenings on one downtown corner or another. I'd even seen them in snowstorms.

"I'm sure," Lizzie answered quietly. "I barely noticed them last night by the church, but when I was driving through town a little while ago . . ."

She'd spotted them and remembered. Her scarf slipped, exposing a deep bruise forming on her neck. Feeling my gaze, she touched it lightly. "Seatbelt got me."

But she didn't want to talk any more about the accident she had been in. Then Sam spoke up for the first time from the back seat. "Those guys are trouble."

At the last minute, he'd hustled out and hopped into the car with us uninvited, still in work clothes and with his penlight stuck in his shirt's boatyard-monogrammed breast pocket; seeing it reminded me of how much I wished he hadn't quit the job.

"One of their usual crew isn't here tonight. But that tall one down there now is especially bad," he added. "Harvey Spratt."

"Uh-huh." Lizzie's gaze returned to the youths. "I didn't figure any of them for charity workers."

Sam still blamed Lizzie for the fix Chip was in, but even a hint that there might be other suspects was catnip to him. So he obliged her by naming the other boys horsing around in the doorway.

"Not that you couldn't get their names from Bob Arnold, too," he added. "He knows 'em all real well."

To his dismay, though, once he'd ID'd the foursome she went on to grill him about Chip: Work? Hobbies? And the big questions: How did he get along with women? Any problems in that department?

Oh, man. She sure sounded like a cop. It was all I could do not to skewer her with accusations right then and there, but if I did that, I might not get what I wanted out of her: help for Chip.

So I shut up while Sam sighed impatiently. "I don't get it. Why's everyone so fixated on him? I had access to the weapon too, you know. We all did, everyone in our house."

Which was not at all the tack I wanted him taking. But she brushed his protest aside.

"Look." She thrust a sheet of paper out; he snapped his penlight on so we could all see it.

"It's a list of websites your friend visits regularly. The cop I was in the car crash with this afternoon gave it to me just before they put him in the ambulance, and I think you'll find it pretty interesting."

So she'd been riding with a cop when the accident happened; yet more evidence for the truth of the rumor about her. I glanced sharply at her. She didn't seem to notice.

"Huh," said Sam. "That was fast work, getting hold of his browsing history." He squinted at the list. "What're all these weird numbers and letters, though?"

"Private Web addresses. You name your website something gibberish-y, no one stumbles onto it by accident. Look at the handwritten notes by the Web addresses, though. If you went to the websites, you'd see those were their real names."

Sam frowned at the sheet again. "Aw, come on. Chip wouldn't go for anything like this."

I looked, too. But not for long. After years in the money business, I'm not easily shocked, but just the names of those websites turned my stomach.

"Anyway, isn't that invasion of privacy or something?" Sam demanded. "Checking on what websites someone visits?"

And why, I wanted to add, *did that cop give the sheet to you?* But we were here to help Chip, not express my indignation.

Lizzie turned to Sam. "Maybe. Law's murky on that point. But investigating the sites themselves isn't invading anything, and that's how that list got generated. He's on the list because he's visited them a lot. Sites," she added, "where you can see pictures and watch videos of women being hurt, even killed. Where people go who like that sort of thing."

She took the list back. "And who like doing those things, themselves. I guess a court will have to decide whether he had an expectation of privacy while viewing that material."

Her tone said she thought not, while I noted with interest her familiarity with phrases like "expectation of privacy." She had some kind of law enforcement expertise, for sure. What kind, though, and why the hell was she hiding it?

Across the street the young men grew tired of hunkering in the doorway and began venturing out; at each effort, the rain drove them back in again. Meanwhile, Sam wasn't giving up.

"Chip writes about all that stuff. I mean, researches it. Professionally. So he must've—"

Lizzie watched the youths. "Yeah. Everybody's got a reason for what they do. And research is always a big one."

She sniffed scornfully. "Do a bad deed, claim you're writing a book about it," she said, and when Sam tried to say again that Chip really was a researcher, she cut him off.

"Oh? Is that why he lied about where he was last night?"

That silenced him. I gazed uphill at the granite-block post office building on the corner. The massive old edifice with its high, arched entry, wide granite-slab stairs, and marble interior floors was once home to Eastport's customs office, and sported no-nonsense iron grates on its street-level windows.

Lovely, and familiar, I'd seen it a thousand times. Tonight, though, it reminded me of something I'd heard recently, something that—now that I'd been thinking about it without realizing it for a while—didn't make sense. Only . . . what?

While I tried figuring it out, Lizzie leaned back against the car seat. "Ah, this is all just getting impossible," she said with sudden fatigue in her voice.

I turned, surprised, as she went on. "Look, I've got a small confession to make. All I want is to find my niece."

"But?" I'd already known that.

"But the state cop I was riding with earlier today is an old pal and he wants me to help him nail your friend."

Sam's face flattened with outrage.

"He thinks I might get info out of you. Now, he says he wants evidence that might help your guy, too," she went on as Sam opened his mouth to blast her.

"But that's not what he *really* wants," she said. "And you want the opposite."

Um, yeah, that about summed it up, all right. "So what are you going to do?" I asked, putting out a hand to keep Sam from coming right over the seat at her.

She sighed heavily. "At first I wasn't sure. I mean, I do need all the help I can get. From everyone."

That much was true. "So you were thinking maybe you'd play both sides? Tell us you're working for our team, and the cop that you're on his?"

My own fists were clenched pretty tightly by then, too. The way she was going, it was a wonder those pants of hers weren't actively ablaze. "Lie to us," I added angrily, "some more?"

Because the hell with it, she wasn't just deceiving us, she was *playing* us. "You're not out here to help Chip, you just want us on your side so maybe we'll tell you—"

What? I wondered suddenly. Because the fact was, there wasn't anything more to tell. Before I could finish processing this thought, though, Lizzie half-turned to me. And as she did so, that butter-soft leather jacket of hers fell partway open.

If it hadn't been such a good jacket, so generously cut and softly drapey, it might not've fallen open so far. But it was.

Sam happened to be leaning up over the seat at the time and glaring sideways down at her. "Gun," he pronounced flatly at the sight of the handgun in its black nylon shoulder holster.

Me too; I just didn't get the word out as fast as he did.

"Okay," Lizzie sighed. "Look, I'm a cop, all right? Or I was until last week, anyway."

She plucked a slim wallet from her inside breast pocket, let it fall open as she passed it to me. There was just one photo in the clear plastic photo sleeve: Lizzie in a patrol uniform, maybe five years younger than now, standing beside a handsome redheaded guy who was also in uniform.

"That's my partner there with me, Liam O'Donnell. Ex-partner. He died trying to stop a convenience store robbery a few years later. I'd been promoted by then."

"To?" I handed the wallet back.

She tucked it away. "Detective. Youngest woman detective in the Boston PD until I quit. Couple days ago, that was."

"I don't understand. Why didn't you just—"

"Tell you? Because I didn't want to, that's why," she snapped. "I didn't think it was any of your business. Although good luck with that idea, around here," she added in disgust. "Look—let's say that somebody here does know something about Sissy or Nicki, and some stranger comes around asking a lot of nosy questions. Who're they likelier to tell, just a plain private citizen or a homicide cop?"

"Yeah." I thought about it a moment. "That makes sense, I guess."

She blew a breath out. "Well, thank *you*, Little Miss Expert on the Topic. So glad you approve. I

mean, I might've told you before if I'd thought anyone in this town could keep their mouths shut for five
freaking . . ."

She took another deep breath, let it out slowly.
"Anyway. If I quit my damn job so I could come up
here and do what I thought was right—"

She paused, composing herself. I recalled that in
the past twenty-four hours she'd driven over three
hundred miles, gotten involved with a murder, and
been in a car accident.

But when she spoke again, she was rock solid.
"Well, I can't very well start knuckling under to other
people's agendas right away, can I? So what I've decided is, I've got to stay straight with myself." A small
laugh escaped her. "Not very original, huh? But I've
got no other option but to try finding out what really
happened with your friend Chip, and then be perfectly honest about it with everyone. You, my cop
pal . . ."

Sam nodded slowly. "You mean play it straight.
Not try to clear Chip or to convict him, or be on any
side of it, yourself. Just . . ."

"Yup. Just the facts, ma'am," she replied.

Yeah, maybe. But I still wasn't convinced. For
someone who wanted to be honest, she had an awfully good poker face, was my ongoing opinion. At
the same time, I kept trying to capture the elusive
memory I was still puzzling over, while half a block
distant the enormous granite post office building
stood smugly silent. Then:

"Hey," said Sam as across the street one of the boys
in the rain-swept doorway suddenly seemed to notice
Lizzie's car. Its headlights were off but the wipers

were still back-and-forthing slowly over the wind-shield; without them, we wouldn't have been able to see at all.

Glancing around as well as they could with the rain sheeting down, the guys who'd been crammed in the doorway stepped briskly into the weather, collars up, hands in pockets, hustling quickly toward the break-water and away from the business district.

Eyes narrowed, Lizzie waited for them to be out of sight on the other side of the post office building. Once they'd gone, we pulled out and crept slowly downhill after them, still without headlights.

By the time we spotted them again, they were two blocks away: heads down, shoulders hunched, skinny, jean-clad legs scissoring in unison. Lizzie stayed well behind them: hands loose on the wheel, face more relaxed than I'd yet seen it, eyes bright. She looked interested, almost amused.

Almost. We inched up outer Water Street where the shops gave way to houses on either side, the lights in their windows looking tiny and frail compared to the storm out here.

"As you can see, I'm not one to ignore other reason-able possibilities, even when a slam dunk's staring me in the face," said Lizzie, touching the brakes briefly.

The slam dunk being Chip; from the back seat Sam nodded in reluctant agreement. She kept the boys in view expertly, pulling nearer when they hurried ahead and falling back when the gale winds slowed them.

"And when the victim's a teenaged girl, and some local guys are eyeballing the crime scene like their own lives depend on it, well, I'd be stupid not to pay them at least a little attention, wouldn't I?"

"You sure they weren't just curious last night?" I asked. "I mean, they're just a bunch of teenagers, naturally they'd want to see what all the commotion was about."

She shook her dark, close-clipped head. "Not sure at all. But she was a teenager, too. Small town, maybe they knew her. I'm just sort of noodling around at this point, you know? Trying things out."

That much I did understand. Bottom line, snooping is just poking at things and waiting to see which ones poke back. "So what're you going to do next?" Sam wanted to know.

Lizzie answered casually. "Just follow them around a little, see where they go, what they do."

She popped a mint into her mouth from the tin of them on the car's center console. "Hey, it could be they really were just curious. Maybe they weren't up to anything suspicious last night. But the thing is, none of us know what your buddy Chip Hahn was up to, either, and he's not saying."

I felt Sam stiffen with fresh anger behind me. "You just don't know him the way—" he began.

"Quiet," she cut him off, snapping the wipers to high and the headlights on, peering around tight-lipped.

The boys were gone. The wind yowled, hurling small objects around: a lobster buoy, a For Rent sign broken off from its signposts, a jacket with a red fake-fur collar that startled me badly, looking like something bleeding.

"Yeah. You're right, I don't know him," she answered Sam at last as the wind rocked the car. "But you know what?"

The downpour eased slightly; we could see again. But no one was out there. They'd vanished like wisps of fog.

"Your pal Chip's got a big problem," Lizzie said, "and the sooner you quit pretending that what's coming next is all about his good *heart,* about how he couldn't *possibly* have done the bad deed the cops're thinking he did—"

Out in the rain, no iffy-looking teenaged boys hustled along, not on Water Street or on any of the cross streets, as far up them as we could see. Finally she headed back toward downtown.

"The clearer you see it, the better off he'll be," she said. "Because, trust me, his good heart's not the issue here."

A limb broke off a massive old elm on the corner of Water Street and Adams, crashing down in front of us and bouncing once very hard on its splintered end, just missing the car. In the next instant, it was gone, tumbling away downhill toward the Coast Guard station building with its triangular gale flags snapping, across the breakwater from the lit-up boat basin.

"I don't know him," Lizzie repeated, peering about one last time for the young hooligans. But there was no one, only a white foam bait box blown up from the harbor, tumbling along the rainy street. She met Sam's gaze in the mirror again.

"But the people who are questioning him now don't know him, either. And if you want to help him, maybe you'd better open your mind to the possibility that neither do you."

"Bogie, come on." David stood in the trashed living room. A row of engraved plaques, small trophies, and framed photographs had been swept from the mantel. Books flung from their shelves, a lamp smashed, papers from the desk stuffed into the fireplace and set ablaze . . .

In the glow from the flames' sullen flicker, he spied a small silver clock Bogie's frenzy of destruction had somehow missed. It chimed sweetly as he stared at it, nine clear bell tones.

"Bogie, we need to get out of here, it's late, she's going to—"

The house belonged to Mrs. Krause, who was probably at the gathering they were holding tonight at the high school for Karen Hansen, so people could get together and commiserate about her death. Her *murder*, David reminded himself numbly; it still didn't seem real that such a thing could have happened in Eastport.

". . . fat old *bitch*." Bogie's voice, low and furious, came from the kitchen amid the crash of breaking glass. The teacher had sent a letter to Bogie's dad about Bogie's chronic absence.

"*Bogie*," David pleaded as a car hissed by in the rainy street outside, its headlights briefly strafing the ruined living room. He wasn't even sure how they'd gotten here, only that Bogie had lured him with the promise of something cool, and the next thing he knew—

". . . here, kitty. Here, kitty, kitty . . ."

David's blood turned to icy slush as an orange cat crept out from behind an overturned phone table with Bogie right behind it, thick hands outstretched. Spotting David, the cat froze.

No! David thought as Bogie pounced on the animal, and then a lot of things happened at once: the cat squirmed and scratched Bogie on the face. Bogie yelled, flinging the cat away.

And a key turned, loudly and unexpectedly, in the lock of the front door. Instantly Bogie was gone, out through the kitchen and the back door, down the steps and into the dark night, with David sprinting behind, leaving the squalling cat in the trashed house full of breakage and the stink of burning letters.

"*Yah!*" Bogie shouted triumphantly as they ran, but David barely heard him, small bare branches slapping his face as they hurtled through backyards, over fences, and between sheds.

How? he wondered as he sprinted along, unable to believe he had just been part of a behavior so . . . so *bad*.

Ahead, Bogie laughed crazily, his squat, powerful figure troll-like in the streaming rain. "Oh, man, wait'll Harvey hears about *this*!" Bogie crowed.

But David didn't care about what Harvey Spratt thought of this escapade, this . . . this *crime*. All he knew was that the next time Bogie started something like this, David had to act.

He didn't know how. He didn't know if he could. But his dad's advice and his dad's hands-off attitude—*just ignore them and they'll get bored*—had been no good. And there were more weapons where Bub

Wilson's BB pistol had come from. Bigger ones, probably, too, not to mention Bub's fists and those of his pals.

So David still needed Bogie, but he couldn't be part of this awful stuff, he just couldn't.

Which meant that somehow, when Bogie got insane like this again—and he would, that was obvious from the whacked-out dance Bogie was doing now atop a backyard picnic table, whirling and thudding like some kind of crazy man in the pouring rain—

"*Yah! Yah!*" Bogie bellowed, heedless of lights coming on in the houses nearby.

—when *that* happened, David would have to stop him.

Back on Key Street, Lizzie pulled over in front of our house and Sam got out, slamming the car door and dashing across to the porch without a word.

Lizzie watched him go. "Sorry if I upset him."

Upstairs, his bedroom light went on, which meant he hadn't even stopped to talk with his grandfather or Bella. "Chip's been a good friend. Sam's worried about him, and so am I."

Her face was unreadable in the dashboard's glow. "I wish I could be encouraging. What he needs is an alibi, you know? He needs to tell the truth about whatever it was that he was doing when . . ."

"Uh-huh. I guess he's still not saying, though."

Or maybe he'd be back by now. Which he wasn't; the guest room window was dark. "Are you going to follow up on those boys?"

She shrugged. "If I can. But I have no authority,

Jake. I'm not a cop anymore, I'm just a private citizen here, and I don't need a harassment charge."

Or to get tarred with a reputation for browbeating people, either, if she wanted help with her own search. And if she wanted to be accepted as Eastport's police chief later . . .

But before I could ask her about that, she went on: "Those guys probably know Sam, though. He might be able to get something useful out of them."

"Maybe," I said doubtfully. I understood Sam's impulse to want to spend all his time helping his friend. But Sam had a job, after all, or I hoped he still would once he asked for it back.

It was a move I meant to encourage. And the thought of him approaching Eastport's punk brigade wasn't a welcome one, either. I changed the subject: "Had any luck on the other thing?"

Finding her sister's child, I meant. She looked down at her hands, which I understood to mean no. Outside the car, the wind flung everything it could find, gutters and downspouts crumpled like huge drinking straws tumbling down the wet pavement.

"Actually, I was hoping maybe you'd had news." Something big and black unreeled itself in the street; after a moment, I identified it as a roll of tar paper, unfurling itself as it went.

"Sorry," I said. The photographs of her sister's child were being circulated; Ellie was emailing them around to everyone she knew. "Nothing yet. Ellie's going to keep trying, but . . ."

But I don't know quite how or what good it'll do, I thought. I didn't say it, though. I didn't quite have the heart to.

And anyway, from the look on Lizzie's face in the dark car that stormy night, I didn't need to.

Even as miserable, scared, and ashamed as he was, Chip Hahn still treasured Sam Tiptree's good opinion. Sam was his friend, the oldest and best he'd ever had, and if Sam ever found out what Chip had done . . .

Well, it didn't bear thinking about. Having the clerk come down with the message from Jake Tiptree, asking if he needed anything, had buoyed him immensely; more, maybe, than was good for him. Because being able to come here to Maine, to stay in the Tiptrees' cozy, old-fashioned guest room and be treated like a member of the family—the only normal-seeming family he'd ever known—seemed more than ever unbearably precious to him now.

Now when he'd nearly lost it all, and through his own stupid selfishness, too. If Sam ever found out . . .

So he won't, Chip resolved as he sat waiting for his state police interrogator to return. *He just won't, no matter what.*

They hadn't arrested him; not yet. But they'd put him here and left him, after several lengthy questioning sessions that made him feel so filthy, so thoroughly *guilty,* that he didn't know how he'd ever be able to look anyone in the eye ever again.

He wasn't sure what might come next. He'd have asked to call a lawyer but he felt that would only increase the suspicion the police felt about him. He still hoped they'd figure out their mistake soon. Meanwhile, though, his questioners kept ratcheting up his discomfort without ever actively doing anything to him.

Charles, they'd called him, for instance. Not Chip, which threw him off; no one but his father had ever called him by his full name, and the Old Man had never said it without contempt that Chip could remember. Then, once they had him off-balance, they'd peppered him with questions he had at first not even been able to understand.

Because they were horrible. Did he like little girls? Boys? Dirty pictures? They'd actually called them that, leering as if Chip were some heavy-breathing fourteen-year-old, salivating over the centerfolds in *Playboy*.

And after that it only got worse. Did he know Karen Hansen? This girl? They'd shown him a snapshot of a skinny child with masses of freckles, and a Band-Aid on her knee. A Band-Aid—for God's sake, she'd probably gotten it falling off her bike.

No, he'd told them politely. That was when he still had the strength, the inner wherewithal, to keep his replies civil. He'd never seen her, never met her, never spoken with her, never made a date with her or lured her to any church, or anywhere else.

Never, never. No, he hadn't killed her. Hadn't seen her, or touched her, or . . . what kind of a monster did they think he was?

Then he'd felt his mouth snap closed like a trap before he could say more and incriminate himself somehow. Because that, of course, was exactly what they did think: *monster*. He knew for sure as soon as they started asking about his online browsing habits.

At once he'd realized they must've learned somehow about his visits to the snuff-film sites and the hideous chat rooms he had discovered while researching background for Carolyn's next book, the websites devoted to the exploits of supposed "thrill killers," with pictures and text that made his skin crawl.

He'd thought that if he just put up with their interrogation for long enough, they'd let him go. After all, they didn't—they couldn't—have any real evidence against him. And eventually, he knew, even the DA would say enough was enough, that they had to either arrest him or cut him loose.

His Web history, though, had pushed that possibility further out into the future, made them even more reluctant to let go of him. Meanwhile, he didn't want to demand to be either released or arrested, since they might choose the latter option even without a strong case against him, and once he was in the system it would just take that much longer to get out of it. Besides, the truth was that he was afraid of going to jail, even for a little while.

And deep in his heart he feared that it wouldn't be just a little while, that it would end up being much longer. Hey, it happened. People got wrongly convicted. It could happen to him. Better to wait, he decided; to answer their questions patiently.

To cooperate as best he could without revealing his secret; yet another reason he didn't want a lawyer involved quite yet. A lawyer, after all, would wind up being just another person trying to pry it out of him.

Thinking this, he put his face in his hands, his elbows propped on the metal table bolted to the floor of the small cinder-block room in the basement of the combination courthouse and jail, thirty miles south of Eastport. He'd been ushered in with a cop on each side, so fast his feet barely touched the floor. Down a flight of stairs, through a short tunnel with no one else in sight . . . they had brought him in a back way, he realized with shock, in case some citizen tried delivering a dose of frontier justice.

Because they think I hurt—murdered—*a girl.* Which was ridiculous; part of the reason that he'd been able to keep his resolve steady was that he still couldn't get his brain around it. But it was starting to sink in now, because he was here, wasn't he? Alone, friendless, and despised; with their lacerating glares, some of the cops he'd seen on his way in here might almost have cut his throat using their eyes alone.

An entirely unwanted mental picture of throat-cutting came forcefully to him as he thought this; to banish it, he focused on his surroundings. The walls were painted a harsh, institutional yellow, the linoleum tiled floor was dark green. One locked door, one large window, mirrored.

And that was it. Just him, and the distant sounds of office activities: phones, footsteps. He was, he knew, being watched from the other side of that mirror glass, both during questioning and now, while he sat with his face in his hands and waited. They'd confiscated his cell phone when they took the rest of his valuables; with his permission, but still.

So he couldn't call Carolyn; by now she'd be wondering about him; worrying, maybe. Or not; he didn't know which to wish for, her not noticing or her fretting, wondering where he was and what he was doing. *The way I do over her, day in and day out . . .*

But there was no joy in that line of thought, either,

so he abandoned it. A chair stood pulled out from the opposite side of the table from where he sat. Soon one or another of his interrogators would return, start in with the questions again.

Where'd you meet her? Did you know she was only fourteen? And despite his denials, *How'd you get her to go with you into the church? Oh, you didn't? Then which of you got there first?*

All wrong, all beyond the realm of any possible reality—

Then from another angle: *Come on, man, don't you just get angry with them sometimes? Women? Hey, we understand, we're guys, too. So don't you just get so pissed off once in a while, you could just grab a knife and—*

Worst of all, though, was the jackpot question, the one he absolutely couldn't answer. Over and over, in every combination: straight out, sideways, up front, or as an afterthought: Where was he last night? Where had he gone, and if as he insisted he hadn't been killing a girl in a church tower, what had he been doing?

It was the thing he refused to say: not to a lawyer, not to anyone. He didn't even dare think about it, for fear the pressure of interrogation would force the truth from between his lips: the thing he wouldn't, *couldn't* tell.

No matter what.

"So how is he?" I asked. After Sam had gone in, I'd lingered in Lizzie Snow's Honda CRV for a while.

I had something to tell her and she wasn't going to like it.

"Your cop friend from the car accident, I mean," I added.

It had been on the evening news, that he was air-lifted to Bangor after being assessed at the hospital in nearby Calais. Lizzie looked up gratefully, confirming the sense I'd had when she first mentioned him that "friend" might be understating it.

"Better," she said. "Broken collarbone, he needed surgery. But okay now."

"That's good." Oh, she wasn't going to like it a bit.

"Listen," I said. Outside the rain poured down. "About that envelope you got."

With the photographs in it, I meant. I'd finally remembered what I'd been trying to recall, in front of the post office.

Now I dug in my bag, rooting around there among newspaper clippings, an old issue of *Working Waterfront,* and a delivery slip from the fuel oil company, detailing how many more millions of dollars I owed them after the most recent fill-up.

There was an envelope in there, too, from a Halloween card Ellie's daughter had made and sent me a few weeks earlier.

"I've been thinking about what you told me," I said. "You came here because the postmark on your envelope said 'Eastport.'"

Lizzie nodded.

"And forgive me," I went on. "I know you're an experienced cop and I'm not. But you're missing a big thing."

Her face went still. "What do you mean?"

She took my envelope from me, studied it in the dim glow of the dashboard lights. Ellie's entire return address was on it, as was the postmark it had received.

It wasn't marked "Eastport," though. It couldn't be; we'd stopped processing our own mail years ago. It all went to Bangor for sorting, and was postmarked "Eastern Maine" before proceeding to its destination.

Even if that meant it got sent right back here again for delivery, as my card had been. "So there's no such thing as . . ."

"Right," I said. "I don't know what your friend's envelope looked like. But I think someone faked the postmark on the one you got."

She sat silent a moment. Then: "So someone *wanted* me to come here? But—"

She turned to me, some enlightenment she didn't want to talk about dawning on her face. "You know what?" She laughed ruefully, a little "hah" at the unwelcome conclusion she'd come to. "I don't know what it looked like, either. The envelope, I didn't even ask . . . Oh, God," she finished, shaking her head. "I'm an idiot."

Outside, the rain pounded down and the wind made a sound like the hounds of hell had escaped. "You're not sure it's her, either, are you?" I asked. "The newer picture of the little girl, you don't know for a fact that it's your sister's—"

She bit her lip, perhaps thinking that she'd given up her life for a prank. Or worse, a trap.

"I don't see how anyone else but Sissy's daughter

could look so much like her. But no, I don't know it for sure."

"And how do you get your mail? A post office box, or—"

She pressed her red-tipped fingers together. "I live . . . that is, I did live, I've given up my apartment . . . in a very secure building. The doorman gets the mail and lays it out every day on a table in the lobby, all sorted by apartment number."

She looked up at me. No doubt the arrangement had seemed okay at the time. "There's never been any problem."

I got it. Living in a building so exclusive that you don't even need a locked mailbox must've felt very special; back in the bad old days in Manhattan when I lived in a penthouse with a view of Central Park, I'd enjoyed that feeling, too.

Also, the doormen I have known have been lovely individuals. But exposing them to temptation is, in my opinion, neither kind nor wise; as I discovered while managing money for men who on the outside looked rich as Croesus, you never know what financial pressures someone else may be under.

Or not, speaking of which: "A doorman building, huh? On a cop salary?" Hey, she'd have asked me. I mean, really?

"Yeah, well. My partner who died? He left me some money." A flash of sudden pain crossed her face; I watched her stomp it out mentally, like putting out a little grass fire.

"He left me an insurance policy," said Lizzie. "And since I'd never be able to get a great place like that on my own . . . I mean, a real home, you know? That I could stay in a long time."

Put so simply, it was perfectly understandable; if she'd been my client I'd have told her that a quality-of-life purchase that would also appreciate was a great place for the money.

But at the moment, that was neither here nor there. I took the envelope back. "See, what I'm wondering is if somebody got into your building's lobby and put that envelope in your mail pile, or got your doorman to do it."

She nodded, still thinking more than she was saying. "Here I quit my job, put the condo up for sale, everything I'd worked for given up just to come on a wild-goose chase all the way up here to this . . . this . . ."

"Godforsaken chunk of granite in the middle of nowhere?" I suggested gently. "More moose per square mile than people?"

She managed another laugh, but it wasn't really funny. Back in Boston, I guessed, police work was at least interesting, maybe even exciting sometimes. But if Lizzie Snow really did mean to take up Bob's job as Eastport's top cop, she was facing a rough transition.

And considering what I'd heard in the hardware store, a rude one in some quarters: women did almost all kinds of work around here just as they did in the city. But those jerks making their jokes represented an attitude that wasn't so rare, either, that a woman who took a man's job and a man's paycheck . . .

Well, from some people, at least, she could expect a ration of crap, is what I'm saying. A few minutes later when I got out of the car, the pavement was a running river, the yellow glow under the streetlamps hazy with rain. From inside the house, I watched her drive off in water so deep, her tires formed a foaming wake.

Then I closed the door and leaned against it, listening to the storm pounding and screaming out there and thinking of Chip, wondering where he was right now and if he was listening, too, or if in the past few hours he'd been arrested for murder, and was already locked away in some cell where he couldn't hear it.

Chapter 9

*To make a sticky wooden
window sash slide easier,
spray the channel
with furniture polish.*
—Tiptree's Tips

"**S**he's not doing you any good, you know."

By morning, the first part of the storm had moved out over Nova Scotia and was heading for the Atlantic.

"She's bad for you. Also, she's *mean*."

Not heading harmlessly, as the forecasters all tended to say of these violent, ocean-bound weather behemoths; if you were on a freighter, say, or a scientific research vessel, or God forbid a sailboat, you probably thought those gale-force winds, torrential downpours, and sixty-foot waves were very harmful indeed.

Sam lay on his bed with the phone pressed to his ear, snapping his penlight mechanically on and off while Maggie—his *real* girlfriend, his possible-future-with-her girlfriend—went on with her litany of Carol-criticisms.

"I mean, you keep saying it's okay to drink alcohol in front of somebody who doesn't drink," Maggie said.

Which was true. He'd quit, but he didn't see why anyone else should have to just on his account. It was his job, not theirs, to make sure he avoided whatever he needed to.

"Come on, Mags, I've explained and *explained* it to you—"

Outside, wind still rattled the gutters. But the rain had at least stopped, this brief relative calm a welcome breather before the second half of the gale roared in.

"—but it *isn't* okay to taunt someone with it," Maggie went on, not listening. "And don't tell me she doesn't taunt you. I've seen her practically pouring it down your throat."

He sighed; Maggie was right. Carol made no secret of her wish for him to drink with her. "Oh, come on," she'd wheedle, her look kittenish. "What can it hurt?"

He wondered what she'd say if he told her: the binges, the rage. One time a few years ago, Bob Arnold had actually had to throw a net over him to bring him home.

He tried changing the subject. "Listen, I'm going out soon, see if I can find Harvey Spratt."

But that wasn't a safe topic, either; he could practically see Maggie frowning doubtfully. "That kid? What d'you want with a little gangster like him?"

Sam sat up, leaning his back against the headboard of his narrow pine bed. He liked the bed, with its faded plaid bedspread and carved wooden bedposts. Homely and plain, it felt normal to him, and all he wanted nowadays was normal. Except sometimes . . .

Oh, those sometimes. "I'm not sure," he answered Maggie's unhappy question. "But he might know something about all the trouble my friend Chip's in. So I'm just going to ask Harvey."

"Uh-huh," said Maggie, her tone cautioning. "He sells Oxys, you know. Not just pot and booze."

Sam had known, actually. Irritation seized him, that she'd thought he was ignorant and that he needed the warning.

And that she was the one to give it, like she was his mom or something. "Yeah, well, I'm not going to buy any pills from him, if that's what you're worried about."

He stuck his pen in his pocket, swung his legs down off the edge of the bed. "Look, I've got to go."

Silence. Maggie was a babe—a smart, talented, crazy-in-love-with-him babe, and he loved her, too, most of the time—but she was impossible to talk to when she got like this. Finally:

"All right," she gave in. "Do what you want. You will anyway, I know that much about you. But this is how it happens."

He pulled his boots on. "How what happens?"

Not that he needed an answer. "First hanging out with party girls. Then socializing with druggies. Next thing you know—"

"Maggie, I'm not *socializing* with him. I'm just going to ask him a few questions."

"Like what?" she snapped back. "Have you planned this? Do you even know what you're going to say?"

He finished tying his second bootlace, wondering if maybe she thought she should be doing that for him, too. *And wipe my nose for me, maybe. And my . . .*

"No. I don't, okay? I have no freaking idea. All I know is, my friend is in trouble. And if Harvey Spratt's going to talk to anyone, he'll talk to—"

Me, he'd been about to finish. But that way lay disaster, because Maggie didn't know the half of what trouble Sam had been in himself before he got sober. Bad enough to need a cop's net thrown over his squirming body while half the town looked on, bad enough to need an AA meeting (or two, or in the early weeks even three) every day for a year.

Bad enough, at the bitter end there when he really could've used hospitalization, to be buying prescription painkillers from Harvey Spratt. But no one knew that, or needed to.

"He'll talk to another young guy like me," Sam said.

A silence. Then: "Sam. I'm sorry I sounded pushy. But—"

"Aw, Mags." He knew what she was about to say.

". . . but the way things are between us, you need to make some decisions, because . . . because I've made mine."

She sounded definite. *No,* he thought. *Don't.* But even as he thought this he continued pulling his jacket on and flinging his long scarf, the navy striped one that she'd knitted for him, saying that it made him look like a Harvard man, around his neck.

A Harvard man. Yeah, that's a hot one. I can't even keep a boatyard job. "Maggie—"

"Don't call me," she interrupted. Not harshly, but that only made it worse. "And don't come over here, all right?"

His heart cracked. A vision of his future, full of wild, glassy-eyed girls like Carol and sullen thugs like Harvey Spratt, opened up before him, bleakly compelling.

He wanted a drink. "Listen, I'm sorry, okay? I've been a big jerk about all this, but—"

"No," she repeated. Not angrily; not anything, really. Just the one word.

Vodka, he thought. Or Jack Daniel's, tall glass, no ice. *Down the hatch.* If he started now, he could be loaded by noon. Maybe he should call Carol, give her the thrill (*the triumph,* his mind corrected him accurately, *a win for her team*) she'd longed for.

He turned his mind from the thought, from the warm, blurry-visioned comfort it promised, with the ease of long practice. But it was still there, lurking just out of sight, deeply imprinted.

It always was. Maggie went on: "You know how I feel about you, so you decide what you want, me or her. A happy life, or all this . . . all this *racketing around* that you don't seem to be able to give up."

"Maggie . . ." Outside, the sky lightened briefly, darkening again as more clouds scudded by overhead.

"But, Sam?" In the background at Maggie's he heard music, a chamber trio, he thought, and a volley of barks as her brindle cur, Roscoe, spotted a squirrel through the window.

"Don't take too long, Sam, okay? 'Cause I love you, I do."

The barking stopped. The music did, too. He stood there, no words coming to his mind that would fix this.

"But even I have my limits, Sam," said Maggie. Then:

Click. She'd hung up.

"This is Jake Tiptree." I'd been waiting for Sam to get off the phone, but it rang again before I could pick it up.

And the news wasn't good. "Yes, Lonnie," I said, "I know you've got other work waiting."

Lonnie Porter was the local roofer whose wife I'd called, to ask him to visit the church steeple, now unfortunately a crime scene, in hopes of keeping it from falling down on all our heads. But Lonnie was, to put it mildly, not enthusiastic about this.

Much less enthusiastic, actually, than I'd thought. "Ayuh," said Lonnie. "Other work's not the whole trouble, though. It's them cops." *Cawps*, the Maine way of pronouncing it. "Don't matter what I say to 'em. Ain't goin' to let me in there."

They-ah. Just then Sam came downstairs, dressed in jeans, jacket, and boots; with the long striped scarf looped around his neck, he looked just like a Harvard man.

What's up? I mouthed at him, but he only waved, grabbed an apple from the bowl on the kitchen table, and headed out, looking determined and as if, wherever he was going, when he got there he wasn't planning to take no for an answer.

Me either. "Lonnie," I said, "if you tell them the steeple could actually *fall,* that it might not even be there for them to collect evidence out of unless they let you inspect it—"

"Won't matter." *Mattah.* "Them cops is thick as mud. I told 'em, I said, you guys is gonna get your heads knocked off."

You-ah. "But they didn't care. They just looked at me like I was a dumb ol' Eastporter."

Eastpawtah. "So I says, okay, then. Don't come cryin' to me, that there tower flies off in that big wind, next thing you know you'll all be investigatin' it down the bay in Lubec!"

Thet they-ah towah. "Okay, Lonnie," I said. "You tried, and that's all you can do, I guess."

I peered out the dining room window, just to make sure that Mother Nature hadn't moved the investigation to Lubec already. At this distance I couldn't see the whole steeple, but the copper weathervane in the shape of an arrow still juddered in the stiff breeze up there, pointing due north.

So we were still okay for now. "I mean to go back, take the Eastport zoning guy with me. Maybe he can talk sense into 'em. Way that shaky steeple's creakin', maybe they'll get smart."

Smaht. "I appreciate it, Lonnie," I said, and hung up to confront something else that was shaky: my own house. A patch of shingles approximately the size of Texas had torn off in the storm, or it looked

that big anyway when I'd gone out front to try esti-
mating how much tar paper to buy.

Also I'd need shingles and roofing nails, and while
I was at it the chimney flashing looked iffy. And I'd
need somebody to do it all, too, since the idea of me
going up a ladder to reroof a house was about as
likely as me going up one to visit the moon.

The one in the church tower had been bad enough,
and that one had only been about one-fourth as tall
as the distance up to my shingling project. Maybe
when Lonnie was free again, I'd ask him. Meanwhile,
the resulting roof leak had brought down a small
patch of plaster in the guest room; luckily, I had half
a can of Spackle left over from yesterday's pipe explo-
sion. So while I worried about Chip being in jail, Sam
being jobless, Lizzie Snow finding or not finding her
niece, and the church steeple blowing down onto the
town's citizens—including *moi*—I would at least
keep busy.

Or I could have if fat, wood-stained water droplets
weren't still seeping through what was left of the
guest room ceiling. Upstairs, I watched them ooze,
each drop forming and quivering awhile before falling with a plop into the pail I'd set beneath, thinking
that what I really needed was a blowtorch.

With it I could either dry out the area above the wet
spot or burn the house down. At the moment both
options seemed equally acceptable; very-old-house repair is satisfying, it's confidence-building, it's even
tranquilizing sometimes.

But other times, it's a pain in the behind. Still, with
more rain forecast I'd be better off waiting; no sense
doing the job twice. So finally I went back downstairs

to smooth out my state of mind with coffee and one of Bella's freshly made blueberry scones, and that's where I was when the phone rang and I learned that the murdered girl's dad, Hank Hansen, was missing once more.

He'd slipped out of his house again, reported Wade, who'd been with the bereaved man. But this time, he didn't have a .22 pistol so old and bunged up that—according to Wade, who'd examined the weapon after confiscating it—you could hold it to your forehead and pull the trigger and still not be sure of hitting anything.

He'd have sworn, Wade said, that Hansen didn't have any more firearms handy. He and George Valentine had questioned Hansen very closely and looked through the house as well as they could.

Nevertheless, from the sales slips and customer literature that Wade had found scattered around the place after Hansen came up missing for the second time, it looked as if on this trip he'd taken along a box of cartridges and a Marlin 336 rifle with a telescopic sight on it.

Hank Hansen drove carefully out Route 190, past the bank and the Mobil station and around the long curve at the edge of town. He didn't want to get pulled over by any of the cops swarming all over the island, investigating his daughter's murder.

Not that it needed any investigation; not anymore. Hank knew the suspect was already in custody. Bob Arnold had said so while he'd tried calming Hank down, the day before out on the bluffs.

City guy, Bob had said. State boys had him in a locked room down at the county courthouse in Machias. Right next door to the jail, Bob had informed Hank soothingly, while Hank slumped in the police chief's embrace and tried hard to get hold of himself.

Tried to stop weeping, shaking, all but screaming, which was what he'd really wanted to do. Screaming to be allowed to go back to when Karen was alive, to when she'd still been sassing him and defying him, and he'd still had a chance to do right by her.

But now he never would. His chance to turn it all around—not today, not tomorrow, but someday—had been stolen from him. Floating around the periphery of his mind was the truth: that it was the murdering of his fantasy—a dream that he *could* change, that anything would *ever* be any different between him and his only child—that truly enraged him.

He couldn't look straight at it, though. *All my hopes, all my dreams* . . . That the operative word in all his pain was *me,* that it was about *him* and how *he* felt—didn't penetrate. Only *his* loss, mostly of his ability to go on fooling himself, sank in.

But his anguish . . . well, that was real, certainly. Jesus, how had it come to this? Wondering, he clutched the steering wheel, fighting the impulse to drive straight into a tree or maybe a loaded log truck barreling down Route 1 like an oh-so-convenient engine of destruction, trailing the smell of pine sap in its turbulent wake.

But that wouldn't help Karen, would it? Karen was past and gone, like everything else in his life that was ever any good.

Because he'd ruined it all. A sob escaped him; he

swallowed it down as a cop car came over the hill at him in the opposite lane, heading toward Eastport. He straightened behind the wheel, did his best to look normal, ordinary.

Not-crazy. Which for him was a stretch, he knew. Stringy hair, broken nose, lips like liver slabs . . . he was no oil painting, and the look in his eye under the best of circumstances suggested a recent encounter with a booze-fueled hallucination or two.

And on most days, that suggestion was accurate. He summoned what presence of mind he could, his hair drenching with sweat from the effort of looking as if he weren't making any effort at all, and was rewarded by nary a glance as the cop sped by.

Phew. He let his breath out. He'd borrowed this car from the shed he'd rented to one of the summer people in Eastport. Key was in it, full tank of gas . . . and the best part was, nobody was going to miss the vehicle, since no one knew it was there. He had simply driven it away, right under the nosy nose of that damned Mr. Big-Shot do-gooder, Wade Sorenson.

Like *he* had an idea what Hank was going through. "You aren't gonna do anything stupid, are you, Hank?" he'd asked, out on the bluffs yesterday.

Even crazed with grief as he was, Hank had nearly laughed in Sorenson's face. *Who, me?* he'd wanted to giggle.

Giggle forever, giggle himself right into a freaking grave. *The worms crawl in, the worms crawl out . . .*

Oh, Jesus. Don't think about that. About Karen, his sweet baby girl, lying on an autopsy table with her throat . . .

Stop, his mind instructed itself sharply, but it was

too late. The bloody vision of his child, violated beyond all human reason, *taken* from him . . .

So now, his mind cut in and instructed him calmly, now he would take back; easy-peasy, simple as that. The Marlin hunting rifle in the back seat had belonged to his father and was one of the very few items of any value Hank owned that he hadn't lost, sold, or ruined somehow; he'd even hung on to the box it came in and the instructions and safety literature that had come with it. Because it ejected to the right instead of out the top, he'd been able to mount the scope he'd bought for it himself.

Over the years, in season and out, with and without the help of a dashboard-mounted jacklight, he'd shot deer numbering in the hundreds with his dad's Marlin. Dragged them home, hung them from a tree to bleed and age them, then dressed the carcasses out, cut the venison in pieces and wrapped them for the freezer.

Ate them, too. Venison sausage was Karen's favorite, doused in ketchup with fried potatoes and eggs for breakfast. Or for a late-night snack, even, the two of them sitting up watching old movies until the wee hours. At least, they had on nights when he hadn't drunk himself into a stupor by nine . . .

An axe blade of anxiety chopped the thought off as the cop he'd passed going the opposite direction now came up on him from behind. Suddenly the rifle in the back seat—out of sight under a blanket, but still— glowed radioactive green in his head.

Pulsing its presence, neon flashes of *gun! gun! gun!* flared through the car's trunk and out the rear end, into the cop's mind. Or so Hank felt certain; glancing into the rearview mirror, he was met by the twin mirrored lenses of cop sunglasses, and by the cop's flat expressionless face.

Reflexively he let up on the gas, but that was a wrong move, too; the car slowed suddenly, the cop roaring up practically onto Hank's bumper now. Another glance; the cop's head tipped sideways a little, one hand reaching out for . . .

Lights. Siren. Damn, he's pulling me . . . Hurriedly Hank tried to come up with some reason for having a concealed rifle in the back seat. A *loaded* concealed rifle . . .

The sudden high-low howl from behind drilled through his head, bloodying his eardrums, though part of that might have been his awful hangover. The squad car's red light strobed mercilessly, lobbing his eyeballs around like bloodshot Ping-Pong balls.

Then, with a roar of its big V-8, the squad car surged past him, the cop staring straight ahead, one hand on a dashboard knob and the other barely touching the wheel. As he passed, he didn't even seem to know Hank and his Marlin existed, so intent was he on whatever sudden errand had arisen.

Hank huffed another breath out, the sudden absence of that awful siren like an intense vacuum, sucking the air out of him. Relief thudded in his chest as sudden rain spritzed thinly out of the low clouds racing overhead, dull gunmetal gray.

Trees went by, long swathes of them on both sides of the road. Here and there small houses sagged in discouragement at the ends of long, rutted-mud driveways. His tires sang over a bridge, crunched through graveled sections, flung bits of tarry hot-top material up into the car's underside.

Twenty miles still to go, and then fifteen; the road wound over a saltwater inlet where geese rested among cattails, logs rotted to pitchy blackness, and the edge of an abandoned apple orchard sprawled, the autumn fruit all gone up as high as a deer on its hind legs could reach.

On the passenger seat sat the box of .35 Remmies. With it: a pair of sunglasses, in case the forecast was wrong and no second part of the storm materialized. If there was sun, he wanted to be sure he could see well enough in any glare to make his shot good.

Also: a night-vision scope. He'd used this often enough on darkness deer expeditions—completely illegal, but who the hell cared?—to be able to exchange the sighting scopes on the Marlin without difficulty. So he was set for day or night.

He'd brought supplies, too, assembled in the dawn hours long before Sorenson or anyone else showed up. Coffee in a jar, bologna on Wonder Bread, cheap but filling, and a sack of mixed off-brand candy left over from Halloween, the gaudy wrappers thin and stained with the imitation chocolate liquefying inside them. He had a bottle of Bushmills, too, as well as an empty jumbo soda bottle for comfort purposes, since once he got to his destination he did not intend to leave the car for any reason.

The wheels turned, and the tires hummed beneath him with a singing tone. *Ten more miles, nine miles, eight miles, and then . . .*

The words rang in his ears, urging him on with their promise of a sure destination and a happy arrival. Hank had a feeling it was going to be something else entirely, that in the actual event things wouldn't be so cheerful.

That there would be blood and screaming. But for the moment, he let imagination take precedence over reality; over the fact, for instance, of his little girl's murdered body lying right now on a morgue table somewhere, cold and alone.

No, better not think of that. Instead he gazed ahead as he crossed bridges over streams flowing down out of Orange Lake and Gardner Lake, then wound through a series of hairpin turns. A sharp left led out to Cutler and Little Bay, where a boat trip to see the puffins had long been on Karen's wish list.

But he'd never taken her. Ignoring the turn, he continued across a long causeway, its summer throng of vegetable stands, fish sellers, and Maine-made trinket hawkers thinned now to only a few desperate used-furniture and craft-item merchants. A few blocks later, past the old railroad station, Helen's Restaurant—*Try Our Famous Pies!*—and EBS with its sweet smell of recently milled pine, he turned onto Court Street.

Uphill between ornate old wooden mansions now sagging with neglect or divided into office suites, he slowed as the traffic for the county seat thickened. Lawyers and their clients, jail visitors, courthouse workers and dog license applicants, real-estate title searchers, seekers of building permits, applicants for assistance . . .

They all came here, and they all needed a parking spot. So when one opened up right across from his target area, Hank took it as a sign and nipped straight into it, earning a glare from a guy in a Prius who clearly thought his right to the spot trumped Hank's. A sickly whonk from the Prius's anemic horn emphasized this, but Hank ignored it, not even flipping the guy his tobacco-stained middle finger.

Because the guy meant nothing and neither did his vehicle. Only this place was important, and this time, and the shot Hank would get off from the Marlin in the back seat, loaded and ready.

Across the street, the Washington County court-house was a three-story brick building with a massive brick archway over the front door; inside, Hank knew, a wide hallway with doors along it led to the courtrooms, and to the grated window of the public information desk. Downstairs, a cramped but orderly reading room resembled a library, filled with books of real-estate records. A sort of perfume hung in the air there, of aged paper and leather bindings, the constantly running copy machine, and floor wax.

Hank knew all this because at one time it had been his job to clean down there, to dust the big old books of deeds on the metal shelves and polish the floors, vacuum the venetian blinds, and empty the waste-baskets. A time when he had been clean and sober, with a pretty young wife and a new baby girl at home . . .

He shut off the thought. The main courthouse building wasn't his focus now, anyway; rather, it was the section to the right and rear of it that interested him, the newer structure where the bars on the windows were barely visible from outside.

But they were there. It was the county jail, whose interior layout Hank also knew well, although not from cleaning it. He'd spent many a night there while waiting to be arraigned on charges stemming from whatever shenanigans he'd been up to.

Now Hank waited until no cars or pedestrians

were near, then leaned into the back seat for the rifle, laying it across his lap with the blanket covering it from view. Business as usual went on in and around the courthouse, whose entrance had a metal detector just inside and a cop standing just beyond that, Hank happened to know, in case of . . .

In case of guys like me. Angry, mistrustful, and determined to get a job done, one no one else would do: just blow the damned head off a murdering bastard and get it over with.

Don't have enough to charge him yet, Bob Arnold had said. Hank snarled at the thought, gripping the gun reflexively. That kind of BS was everywhere nowadays, keeping creeps out on the street. Keeping the guy who'd killed Hank's baby girl from getting what he deserved, pronto.

But, surprise, Hank thought. *I got news for you.*

News, and something else. The box of cartridges on the seat beside him still contained eighteen of its original twenty rounds. One in the magazine, one in the chamber . . . that was the rule he'd always followed for hunting, and he'd stuck with it today.

Big news. Because the guy they had in there would do one of two things, sooner or later. Either he'd be released, and walk out the side door of the jailhouse section of the building, or he'd be charged and they'd take him upstairs to one of the courtrooms, for a hearing. After that, the state cops would take custody of him, to transport him to one of the Maine state prisons where he'd remain for who knew how long.

Years, maybe, comfortably awaiting trial while Hank Hansen's daughter lay cold in the cold ground.

Eating, sleeping, watching TV, while Karen could do none of that. Which was . . . unacceptable.

Intolerable. But Hank knew from his experience as a janitor here that when the state cops took custody of someone, they did it in state-cop style, marching like soldiers with their prisoner between them straight out the front door.

Which was where Hank and his dad's old Marlin would come in, when the guy came down the hall from the courtroom, out past the metal detector's aluminum turnstile, and down the wide front steps, the son of a bitch blinking, maybe, his eyes unaccustomed to daylight after the fluorescent overhead lights inside.

Forty yards away, the guy would be if he came out directly across from where Hank was parked. If it was the side door, maybe eighty yards.

But through long practice, Hank's shooting eye was good, and his hands never shook when there was a gun in them. And the Marlin's deadly range with those Remmies in it was two hundred yards for a bear or deer, less for a man, especially if Hank got a head shot.

So: sooner or later, one door or the other. In a strange car that nobody was looking for and with the rifle across his lap, he settled in to wait for as long as it took.

"Dylan. Dylan Hudson?"

He lay in a white bed, in a white room. In a white haze, the load of painkillers they'd given him—how long ago?—only now beginning to wear off.

The nurse called his name again. "Time to wake up, bud."

She smiled down at him. "You were in a car accident, you're in Eastern Maine Medical Center, and you're fine," she recited. "Just a seatbelt injury, it turned out. You're a lucky man."

Pretty girl, young, wedding ring, he assessed automatically as she bustled around the hospital room. But he didn't really care; now that he was conscious again he had other things on his mind. She took his temperature and blood pressure, adjusted his IV, and opened the curtains.

It was light outside. "You're going to have an X-ray soon. That's why I had to wake you up."

She left the room. *Good.* He wanted out of here. Hospitals all smelled the same to him, like medicine and boiled cabbage.

Or like his wife's illness and death; he shook the memory off as best he could. So: peel the tape, slide the needle out. He tied the IV tube in a knot to stop its leaking onto the floor.

Next: feet over the side. Fortunately, the nurse had put the bedrail down. He had a woozy moment but it cleared.

His clothes were in a locker, unlocked. He hauled them all to a chair, sat, and got them on, keeping one eye on the door for the promised X-ray technician. He got the sling back onto his arm without much trouble, but his jacket was a bitch, heavy enough to hurt his shoulder even when he'd gotten it settled and snapped. But never mind; checking the inside pockets, he found his things there. Keys, wallet, phone . . .

No weapon. He glanced around frantically before realizing that he'd handed it and his badge to Bob Arnold, just after the accident. At the sink he splashed water on his face; *gah,* he thought at the red-rimmed eyes and beard stubble in the mirror, but there wasn't time to do anything about it.

Out on the street, he caught a bus to a nearby Hertz place and rented a car, then threaded his way through Bangor traffic to the bridge over the Penobscot. Twenty minutes after that, he was on Route 9, zipping between tall granite ledges topped by stands of spruce and pine, speeding across foaming rivers, and powering past loaded log trucks.

Dumb, maybe. His collarbone already felt as if broken glass was in there, grinding around. But back in Eastport, Lizzie was doing who knew what.

Finding out who knew what, too. He had to be there to keep things under control, or . . .

Without warning, a huge deer bolted out from the forest that lined both sides of the highway and sprinted across, causing a propane truck in front of Dylan to brake, swerve, and just miss a vanload of kids. The deer vanished into the trees on the other side, no doubt laughing its head off.

Exhaling, he sped through a series of S-turns and up a hill that would've been better managed by about a ton of dynamite and however many trucks it took to haul it away. Everything in Maine was like this: trees, animals, and inconvenient land features.

He'd only come here because Sherry had said— through a haze of morphine and the static of the tumor already fritzing up her brain's wiring—she'd always wanted to live here. Hell, it was the least he could do; buried her here as well, and now here he was, himself. *Wherever you go, there you are . . .*

Stuck. And in job limbo, too; heck, you choke the

shit out of some pill-pushing little weasel, you'd think Dylan had spat on a lighthouse, or defiled a lobster trap with a blueberry pie on top of it from all the fuss the suits had made. But unfortunately, the pill hound had beat the charges by using a color snapshot of the fingermarks around his neck, so the suits probably hadn't had too much choice.

At least he hadn't been fired, Dylan thought as the piece-of-crap car he'd rented struggled up the last big hill before the long glide down to the coast. He'd hung on and all he cared about now—besides the anguish in his shoulder, which felt as if one of Maine's meanest wild animals was biting into it—

All he cared about now was Lizzie. A careful plan, a few bold moves, and a piece of tremendous good luck—good for him, anyway—had gotten him this far: back into her life, and even halfway into her good graces.

Which was where he wanted—needed—to be. Seeing her again had made him certain, and now all he had to do was stick with his plan a little longer . . . he hoped.

He took the turn off Route 9 onto the River Road— *damn, but that hurts*—headed toward Eastport, feeling strongly that his luck was about to change. He had lost big-time but soon he would win again.

That is, if he got there in time. He had something to tell her, something she absolutely had to learn first from him, not by figuring it out for herself.

He hoped he wasn't already too late.

Chapter 10

*Use a magnet to
pick up spilled nails,
screws, etc.*
—Tiptree's Tips

Bob Arnold pulled the squad car up the long, rutted driveway to Hank Hansen's house. The place stank of a burn barrel whose fire had been doused by the recent rain and of a septic tank that urgently needed attention.

He could've delegated this trip to Paulie Waters, but Paulie was sulking today, like a bratty kid who thought

all his siblings were getting a treat and he wasn't.
Showing up for work late, he'd tossed his newspaper
onto his desk with a snotty flick of his wrist, then
sneered at Bob's perfectly civil greeting before stomp-
ing out again, blasting out of the parking lot like his
hair was on fire and his tail feathers were catching.

So Bob had decided to let Paulie get over whatever
it was, and instead had come up to Hansen's place
himself, to see if he could figure out where the soz-
zled old coot might be going. And in what vehicle,
too, if he wasn't on foot, since the first thing Bob
saw when he pulled in was Hank's rusty old Toyota
4Runner, sitting on a flat.

And Hank had no other vehicle; hell, from the
looks of it he barely had this one. Climbing out of
the squad car into the muddy yard, Bob nearly stepped
on an old brown mutt, well fed but its eyes pleading
anxiously with him.

"Oh, hell, Maxie." He patted the dog. "I'd take
you home, but my kid's got asthma."

Maxie followed him up to the asbestos-shingle-
sided house. A long time ago, those shingles were the
hot new thing: cheap, easy to maintain, and halfway
decent insulation to boot. An easy sell in a part of the
world where paint peeled nearly as fast as you brushed
it on, he reflected; his own home back when Bob was
a kid had been sided in asbestos, too.

Nowadays, of course, it was a health hazard. But
asbestos was the healthiest part of this dump, Bob
thought as he climbed a shaky set of cinder-block
steps and yanked open the back door.

Inside, the smells were different and thicker. Burnt

food, an overflowing garbage pail, bad drains . . .
Bob popped a mint into his mouth and made his way
through a squalid kitchen, its frilly curtains falling to
pieces at grimy windows overlooking a rancid, trash-
strewn backyard.

Bob found some dog kibble, poured some into
Maxie's bowl and refilled his water basin at the dish-
heaped sink before setting it down, then proceeded to
the dining room.

Another horror: mouse droppings, sodden cardboard stuck over missing windowpanes, moldy
magazines—*Outdoor Life, Field & Stream, Gun
Digest*—and unidentifiable stuff piled nearly to the
ceiling. So Hank was a hoarder on top of everything
else . . . Wishing he'd brought a dust mask, Bob tried
not to breathe in the yeasty-smelling mold spores bil-
lowing from the filth-grayed carpet at his every step.

Maxie appeared, wagging his tail after his good
meal. A thud of sadness hit Bob at the sight of the
animal, who couldn't very well be made to stay here
and fend for himself. But the only alternative Bob
could think of was worse.

"Come on, fella," he sighed. "I don't like it, but I've
got to go upstairs. You might as well come."

Cocking its head alertly, the dog woofed once as if
in agreement and followed, as on his way to the stairs
Bob peeked into the ghastly parlor with its cobwebs
hanging like draperies. A small TV with a pair of
foil-tipped rabbit ears perched on it stood atop a lobster trap with a shriveled bait chunk still in it, nestled
inside an orange plastic-mesh bait bag that was the
only brightly colored thing in the room. A black plastic trash bag brimming with empty beer cans added

its own sour aroma to the stew of stink, slumped by an ancient recliner whose yellowed stuffing erupted from it in a dozen places.

Bob turned his back on it all, paused in the paint-peeling front hall under a bare lightbulb dangling from a jerry-rigged extension cord. He hadn't known it was this bad. No one had, or the girl wouldn't have been allowed to stay. The state would've placed her in residential care, which of course was why she had never told anyone about the conditions here; kids rarely wanted to leave home, no matter how bad it was.

To them, home was normal. Upstairs, the dog padded ahead of him along the hall, stopping to whine at a closed door. Bob followed, picking his way through fallen plaster and past patches of exposed lath.

The state guys had been here already today, look-ing for Hansen so they could question him about his daughter and who might've wanted to hurt her. But Hansen had been gone. Bob opened the door the dog had plopped down in front of.

And stood there, gazing around wonderingly like a man who has been let into a fairy-tale world, one that a moment earlier he'd have denied existed. *Or could ever exist, with this other awful place stinking and sliming all around it . . .*

But it was real: the pink curtains, carefully washed, ironed, and hung at the spotless windows. The white chenille bedspread, a plush teddy bear nestled on the plump pillow.

The braided rug by the bed on the otherwise bare wood floor, a few brown hairs on it saying that's where Maxie slept. A well-chewed Nylabone was on the rug; with the air of one retrieving a thing that was rightfully his, the dog marched over and grabbed the bone, dropped with a satisfied thump to the rug, and began gnawing happily.

Bob crossed the neat, sweet-smelling room past the mirrored dresser, its surface clean and dust-free, to where a suitcase lay open. In it were a few clothes, some toiletry items that had probably stood on the now-uncluttered dresser, and an old library book entitled *Becoming a Model*.

Under the book was a sheet torn from a spiral notebook, with names and addresses printed on it in a firm but childish hand: the Bangor YWCA, a career center office in the same city, and the Bangor bus terminal. Below that were listed a half-dozen names and New York City addresses for what he guessed might be modeling agencies, though he knew little about such things.

While Maxie's yellow teeth clicked enthusiastically on the chew toy, Bob opened the library book, and at the information on the first page felt another wave of sorrow wash over him. The girl had done her homework, all right; she'd done what smart kids do when they want to find something out.

She'd gone to the library, borrowed a book on the subject, and read it. But one thing hadn't occurred to her, and of course she hadn't been able to ask for advice. If she had, she might've been told to get more recent information.

But she was only fourteen, and she lived in Eastport, Maine, which was about as far from the streets of Manhattan as a person could get and still remain on the planet. And here was the result, Bob thought as he gazed sadly at the volume in his hand:

She'd based her plan to run away, to move to the big city and get hired as a model, on a thirty-year-old library book. Even her preliminary scheme, which from the notebook sheet he guessed included living at the Bangor YWCA, was heartbreakingly outdated; there hadn't been a room for rent at the Y in Bangor in who knew how long. Hell, Bob didn't even know if there ever had been such a thing there.

Never, maybe. In the bigger cities, possibly, but not there. He laid the book back in the suitcase, looked around again at the pristine space Karen Hansen had created for herself. A dorm-room-sized refrigerator served as her bedside table. On a bench made of two milk crates and a two-by-six board, she'd set up a hot plate and microwave, both with $1 tags from the thrift shop on Water Street still stuck to them.

A little collection of utensils plus a plate, cup, and glass stood under the board. Bob left the room, made his way to the only bathroom in the place, and found it, like Karen's own living chamber, utterly spotless.

Worth it, he supposed, cleaning up after the old man if she could also have it clean for herself. Catching his own reflection in the medicine-chest mirror, he wondered what she'd seen there to make her think modeling was in her future.

From what he recalled from seeing her around town, she'd been a gap-toothed, messy-haired child, awkward the way they all were at her age. Nothing to make anyone think twice about her.

Not until someone murdered her. Turning to find Max grinning in the bathroom doorway with the bone clutched in his jaws, Bob realized what he hadn't seen in this hideous little hovel:

Money. Because it was one thing for Karen to have planned, however unrealistically, to find a job in Bangor. But first she'd needed to get there, and live somehow meanwhile. And from the look of her room, she'd have planned for that, too: for a roof over her head, and food, and a way to stay clean and warm.

Those things were important to her. Meanwhile, from what the rest of this place looked and smelled like, Hank Hansen had no cash. And even if he had and his daughter had taken it to use for her getaway . . .

Bob strode back quickly to the neat little bedroom, rifled through the suitcase, turned out the drawers and the tiny closet while Max stood in the doorway looking puzzled. But . . . nothing.

No cash anywhere. Still, she'd had a *plan,* and it must have included a few dollars to survive on, at least.

So . . . where had she been *planning* to get it?

Standing in silence behind a shelf loaded with plumbing parts and equipment in Wadsworth's hardware store, Lizzie Snow debated between two models of coffeemaker. She'd toned down her makeup and costume today, and on the way here from the motel had felt a little less like a sore thumb on account of it.

Today's outfit of slim jeans, white sneakers, and a black down-filled vest over a turtleneck were a far cry from the more stylish things she usually wore, and she still preferred her leather jacket and heeled leather boots. But the looks she'd been getting in them weren't worth it.

The cash register's *briing!* brought her mind back to her task. She'd come in here for the coffeemaker—in addition to hardware store staples, Wadsworth's also carried everything from stationery supplies to Maine-themed souvenirs, snow globes with lighthouses in them and so on—because the one at the motel had broken. And she might as well have her own; she wouldn't be staying at the motel forever.

But when the cash register's ring had faded, she heard a voice she recognized. ". . . seen that skinny bitch in the tight pants this morning?"

"Come on, Paulie," the store clerk began, "that's not a nice thing to be saying about . . ."

She didn't catch the rest, which she knew was directed at the young cop she'd tangled with two nights ago; he must have come in while she was back here in the household goods aisle. And why the hell was everyone so concerned about her pants, anyway?

She grabbed a package of filters to go with the basic Mr. Coffee she'd chosen and prepared to march to the front of the store, summoning a few pointed phrases in case they'd be needed. But before she could turn, a hand came down lightly on her shoulder.

She spun on her heel, one arm automatically pulling back to punch with. "Get your freaking paw off my . . ."

"Hey, hey." Dylan Hudson backed away, laughing. "Don't hurt me, I'm a wounded man already."

She almost dropped the coffeemaker; he took it from her with his good hand. The other one hung inside his jacket, in a sling.

He looked like hell. "Dylan . . . what are you doing here? You were supposed to be . . ."

The information desk at the hospital had told her—after she'd lied, saying she was a cop investigating the accident he'd been in—that he'd be a patient for at least another full day.

But obviously not. "Why'd they let you out?"

He grinned as well as he could with that fat lip. It had clearly met up with the steering wheel despite his seatbelt.

She could relate; she'd been wearing hers, too, and her neck still felt twisted, the livid bruise on it barely covered by the high neckline of her sweater.

"They didn't let me. But I just couldn't stay away from you," he added only half jokingly.

He put his arm around her; she shrugged it off. "You're an idiot, you know that, right?"

Bruised face, tired eyes, his neck beneath his open collar even more seatbelt-torn than her own . . . "You look wonderful," he said. "But are you okay?"

"I'm fine." She snapped her body away from his and headed down the wood-floored store aisle, between the faucets and pipe-thread tape, drain traps and washing machine hook-up hoses.

At the counter, the clutch of men gathered there chatting backed away. She could feel them avidly cataloging her clothes, hair, and makeup for later discussion. *And they say women are gossips.*

She set her things next to the register, not acknowledging the men. The store clerk's eyes were curious but kind, unlike the others' flat assessments.

"Have a nice day," he said gently as he returned her change, and in his tone she heard apology for the others, especially the young cop whose stare was anything but friendly.

"Thanks," she said, just wanting out of there.

But as she passed him, the young cop made a spitting-on-the-floor motion with his lips; in response she felt a strong urge to smack the snotty look off his face.

Instead, she stopped. Turning, she motioned Dylan to stay out of it. And spoke: "I'm sorry we got off on the wrong foot the other night. But do you have another problem with me?"

The surprise on his face was naked, that she'd confronted him. He opened his mouth but she cut him off:

"Because if not, I wouldn't think a skinny bitch like me would worry you so much," she said, and added a smile, playing it to the peanut gallery of men.

They ate it up, nudging one another. The clerk turned away, too, hiding his own smile. *Aha,* she thought; *so our boy Paulie is maybe not the most popular kid in town. Otherwise these guys wouldn't like it so much, seeing him get taken down a peg.*

"Can't even run very fast in these tight pants of mine," she added, swaying a little to emphasize the way they fit; hey, she hadn't given up looking good entirely.

Laughter now, from the audience; she'd gotten them on her side. And she could run in the pants, all right.

She could run just fine. Dylan scrutinized his shoes, trying not to laugh. He knew she'd apprehended men twice Paulie's weight and three times her own. They didn't see you coming when you were smaller, and quick. And that was key, because no amount of skill or practice beat muscle mass unless you had another advantage.

Like brains, for instance. And a pinch of don't-give-a-good-goddamn; a big pinch. "Don't worry, Paulie," she said softly to him while his face got redder. "I'm not going to hurt you."

She took her coffeemaker off the counter, then stepped up so close to the tall cop their shoes nearly touched. "Not unless you make me," she added softly, and got out the door before the laughter stopped.

Dylan followed. "Lizzie, someday somebody's going to knock your block off. You know that, right? You know they'll—"

She spun on him. All the anger that she'd held down boiled to the surface. "Hey, Dylan, mind your own beeswax, okay?"

She had her own bone to pick with him, but not out here. She stalked up the street ahead of him, toward the motel. A pickup truck dragging its muffler chugged by, its bed loaded with wire lobster traps. Sparks spat from the truck's muffler-on-pavement action, jumped into the puddles that spread everywhere from the recent rainstorms, and fizzled out.

The driver grinned at her, his whiskery face creased with appreciation, around the chewed-looking cigar stuck in his mouth. "Lookin' good," he called, as sweetly as if he were at church saying good morning to the minister's wife.

The truck belched exhaust, pulling away. Lizzie shook her head tiredly; the driver had meant no harm, and it was better, she supposed, than being thought ugly. It got old, was all.

"So tell me," she said over her shoulder to Dylan, "when you walk away from somebody, is it always your ass they watch? And if you're approaching, do they stare at your chest?"

The hill felt good on her calves; it struck her that she'd had no real exercise since leaving Boston. "It's one thing to compliment someone," she went on at Dylan's puzzled expression. "It's something else to look at them as if they're an ice cream you're thinking of licking."

Or, she added mentally, *to identify them as "that skinny bitch."* Dylan nodded as if he understood, but he didn't and she didn't care. "Oh, forget it," she said, "I might as well complain about the sky being blue."

Which it mostly was at the moment, but not for long. At the corner in front of the red-brick library, she stopped, sucking in big breaths of the fresh salt air. One good thing about this place, you couldn't beat the smell; it made just breathing into a bracing tonic. Not bad scenery, either: to her left the bay spread choppy gray-blue with whitecaps racing atop it and the tide surging in, while to her south a wall of clouds rose from the horizon, the distant bridge spanning the water there like an ink sketch on the looming weather.

Dylan kept pace with her, crossing the street. On the motel parking lot, wide puddles reflected clouds scudding across the unsettled sky. He followed her to the door of her room.

"Look, Lizzie, there's something I need to tell you, and . . ."

His jacket hung open on the sling-arm side, exposing what looked like the manila envelope that Nicki's photo—*my niece. My sister's baby, my only family in this world*—had come to him in.

If it had. And if it was even Nicki. Giving the door a shove open with her foot, she clasped the coffeemaker and filters in one arm and grabbed his good arm with her other hand, and yanked.

Inside: clothes everywhere, makeup on the dresser, a bra on the bedpost . . . oh, the hell with it, she thought impatiently. He'd seen her underwear before, and Holly Homemaker she wasn't.

"Sit down while I make coffee," she ordered him, clearing a place on a chair by removing her leather jacket, a few sheets of motel notepaper, and an almost-empty Cheetos bag.

"Don't talk to me," she cut him off when, as she unpacked the machine, rinsed it, and loaded it with water and a packet of coffee from the motel kitchenette's supply, he tried again.

Her not thinking of the postmark detail was bad enough, but that he hadn't thought of it was . . . well. If he hadn't.

That being her big question now. And she didn't want him confusing her with his smooth line of chatter until she asked it. She sat across from him at the room's small table, reached across to pluck the envelope from his pocket, and slapped it down. Beside it she put the one she had gotten, the postmarks on both envelopes clearly visible. The *faked* postmarks.

"Lizzie," he began, "what I need to say is—"

"Shut up. I'm talking now. Because it turns out we've got a little problem," she said, and watched as his expression turned wary. *As,* she thought, *it most certainly damned well should.*

Then, with a sudden, sharp *bringg!* that startled her, the motel room's telephone rang.

Harvey Spratt was approximately the last person Sam Tiptree wanted to talk to, ever again. For one thing, he reminded Sam of his old life, much of which was mercifully hazy and Sam preferred it that way.

But Spratt was also a bully, the kind of guy five minutes of whose toxic personality could sour a whole day, Sam reflected as he strode past the big old clapboard houses of Key Street toward downtown.

Why anyone who wasn't buying substances from Spratt would want to be around him, Sam couldn't fathom. But somehow Spratt always managed to attract other boys into a sort of posse, its members always younger than he was, since for one thing, no one his own age would take his crap.

To audition guys for his group, Spratt liked to see how many supposedly friendly shoulder punches they'd put up with. That was the main test; besides being craven little sociopaths with hardly any reasoning skills and fewer social ones, the other rule was that they couldn't hit back. If after plenty of provocation they never did, just sucked up for even more abuse, they were in.

Thinking about this as he turned onto Water Street, Sam noted the choppy bay, still ragged from last night's storm. Work boats hustled busily, getting the fish food, antibiotics, and supplements out to the underwater cages of salmon farms. The sky was blue, but now the racing clouds of earlier had coalesced into a milky look that made the sunlight tentative.

Spratt and his crew had a few places they liked to hang, and these were Sam's destinations. On the corner by the post office, where they'd been last night, was one, but in broad daylight they wouldn't be there; too visible. The breakwater was another, at a picnic table on the platform over the boat basin; not as exposed to the town's comings and goings but from there they could still see a cop car or somebody's parent in time to tuck away a beer or a baggie of forbidden smoking materials.

The breakwater's proximity to Rosie's hot dog stand was a plus, too; some of those smoking materials could make a person thirsty, Sam happened to know. But the boys weren't there today, when the stiff breeze off the bay made any exposed location too uncomfortable; Sam zipped his jacket.

So it would have to be the beach behind the seaweed factory, as it was called; a boarded-up warehouse built on a wharf over the water a quarter mile from downtown. Sam quickened his step, a pang of anxiety hurrying him along as he thought of Chip, still in Machias and still apparently being questioned about—and actually suspected of, to Sam's continuing shock—a local girl's murder.

Past the breakwater, where men in boots and sweatshirts ran up and down the metal gangs, adding lines and bumpers to boats already so trussed up that the floating piers looked spiderwebbed with lengths of rope, Sam spotted a car he recognized. Carol's car, the red Miata, zipped from a side street and turned, but not in the direction he was headed.

Watching it go, he let his breath out in relief. If she saw him, she'd start teasing him to take a ride with her, or go to a house party. Just something, she'd beg; something fun, something lively.

But Chip's predicament got worse by the minute; as long as no one else was being investigated, he'd look better and better as a suspect. So Sam had to help, somehow, and anyway if Maggie should happen to come by and see Sam and Carol together . . .

Well, that didn't bear thinking about, and anyway he was too busy for either of them now. Stepping quickly past the ice-cream store and the tattoo shop, he patted his pocket to make sure that his penlight pen and the small spiral notebook he'd grabbed off his desk before leaving were still there.

In general, he was not a note-taking kind of guy; dyslexia, which in his case manifested itself as a tendency to spell "dog" as g-o-d and vice versa, among other things, caused writing in general not to work out so well for him. But in this instance he figured he might really want to remember something, and later he could get Maggie or his mother to help him transcribe what he'd written into normal, non-dyslexically spelled English, he hoped.

And if not, then at least he'd tried. Meanwhile, the Spratt crew might be on the beach, or in one of the caves in the cliffs that rose up from it, out of sight from any passersby. He'd try there, he decided, and if he found them he'd feel them out, see if they'd heard anything useful about the dead girl.

Not that he really thought that bunch would have. Why would a little girl like Karen Hansen have anything to do with them, anyway? Even Carol, who knew Spratt at least to talk to—she had a lot of sketchy friends around town—said Harvey was creepy. But Sam knew she still bought pot from him occasionally anyway; heck, maybe Karen Hansen had, too, it occurred to him suddenly.

So he might as well try. A couple of blocks uphill from the breakwater, he crossed the street, jogged down a short dead-end lane, and picked his way among old bricks, rotted driftwood, and slimy patches of rockweed tossed up here by last night's storm until he reached the beach. To his left loomed the warehouse on the old wharf, its thirty-foot pilings crusted with barnacles and swathed in draperies of dripping seaweed. To the right, a stony beach meandered between the waterline and a set of granite cliffs rising up suddenly, slabs of rock slanting massively this way and that. Watching his step among the rockweed patches, he made his way toward the caves.

Fifty yards down, he was out of sight of everyone but the boats out on the water. Above, the cliff tops jutted out, hiding the beach from anyone up there; ahead and behind, thrusting boulders and sand ridges blocked the view.

He didn't like it, suddenly. Too isolated, too . . . something. He wasn't sure, only that it gave him pause. But knowing Chip was stuck in an even worse place kept him moving on the wet sand, the raw breeze stinging his eyes and his feet trying not to slip.

He'd forgotten this stretch of shoreline was so desolate, and the crying of gulls as they wheeled overhead didn't help, not even a little bit. Good place for a hideout, though, and now even in the wind he smelled cigarettes. A few more steps and he'd found the bowl-shaped depression that led into an open-mouthed cave about the size of a one-car garage.

The five young men hunkered around a sputtery driftwood fire in it looked up, eyeing him with heavy-lidded hostility. One lumbered to his feet.

"The hell you want?" Harvey Spratt demanded, flicking away his smoke. The medal on a chain around his neck glinted evilly. A Saint Christopher, Sam thought; what a joke. Harvey looked stoned as usual, only on him it didn't translate to mellowness.

"Got a question for you."

Behind Harvey, who wore his usual outfit of skinny black jeans, black sweatshirt, a pair of black pointy-toed boots, and a denim jacket whose sleeves didn't quite reach his gangly wrists, the other four scowled.

Or rather, three of them did. The fourth, a slender youth in chinos and a warm-up jacket with a Red Sox logo on the sleeve, wore a look on his pale face that suggested he'd wandered in among these guys some-how and didn't know how to get out.

"We ain't answerin' no effin' questions, man," one of the others declared belligerently. Sam recognized that one.

Harvey's head snapped around quick as a snake's toward his mouthy pal. "Shut up, Bogie."

Harvey looked at Sam again, red-rimmed eyes nar-rowed sulkily. "Yeah? Like what, how to—" The ac-tivity he mentioned was not only disgusting, it was anatomically impossible.

Sam took a few more steps toward the cave. When

dealing with guys like this, it was important to show that you were not afraid of them. Although he was, a little; anyone would be.

The fourth kid, the civilized-looking one, hung back, but the trio of tough guys stubbed out a cigarette apiece in the damp sand before advancing, glowering menacingly.

"No, Harvey," said Sam, ignoring them. Wally Belknap, Todd Verdun, and Bogie Kopmeir were only the latest in a long line of Harvey Spratt wannabes. But unlike their hero, they were all too dull and lazy to start any trouble on their own, and too scared of Spratt's unpredictable temper.

Well, all but Bogie, Sam realized. The Kopmeir kid had some possibilities of his own as a dangerous little dude: nastier than Harvey's usual follower, for one thing, and smarter for another. A wild, unpleasant grin twisted the kid's lips.

The kid in the Sox jacket looked worried and as if he still wanted to get away, but then a grimly determined expression filled his face. "Bogie," he said warningly to the Kopmeir kid. "You don't want things to get out of hand, do you? So maybe you should calm down a little and—"

Bogie spun hard at the same time as his fist shot out fast, stopping the kid's mouth with a solid punch that broke the kid's two front teeth. His other fist swung around, knocking the kid's head sideways; Bogie punched it back the other direction, one-two one-two, finishing with an uppercut that lifted the now-woozy kid off his feet and sent him flying backwards.

His head hit the rocky overhang of the cave's mouth

with a wet-sounding *crunch* that turned Sam's stomach. "Jesus," he said to Harvey, "put a leash on that thing, will you?"

He reached for his cell phone. "You guys want to get out of here, that's fine, but I'm calling an—"

Ambulance, he would have finished, but by then Harvey was advancing purposefully on him.

"Hey, look, all I wanted was to ask you about Karen Hansen," Sam began, trying to wave Harvey away, possibly even defuse this situation, which, he was just now beginning to realize, was more fraught than he had at first understood.

"I mean, if you knew any—" Then Bogie was on him, the kid's surprisingly strong arms wrapping around his shoulders and hauling him downward. His feet slipped on the weed-slimed rocks; in the next moment, Bogie knelt on his chest, gripping his throat in tough little hands that stank of nicotine.

And of something else. Bogie's eyes were spark-spitting pinwheels; too late, Sam realized that more than cigarettes were being smoked in the cave. *More than pot, too.*

"Whatta you wanna know about her for? We dunno nuthin' about that, whatta you want? You try'na get us in trouble? Huh?"

Bogie's hot breath stank. His fingers tightened their grip. Sam heaved his body but couldn't break free.

"No! Jesus, Spratt, get him off me, what the freak is the matter with—"

Bogie drove a kneecap into Sam's solar plexus. "Shut up!" he grated out, spit spraying from his lips. Without warning, he reared back, clenched a fist tight, high in the air, and punched Sam in the side of the head with it.

Everything went gray. Sam's body felt floaty, as if he might just rise right up off the stony beach here and sail, cloudlike, into the sky. If only he could remember what direction *up* was . . .

Somebody kicked sand at him, his eyes painfully blinded all at once. One of the other boys protested. "Hey, come on, Bogie, don't get us all in—"

Bogie released Sam suddenly and jumped up, pulling something from his belt. Sam couldn't see what happened next but the other kid's voice rose in a shout that thinned to a short, sharp cry, half shriek and half horrifyingly wet gargle.

Cursing foully, Spratt grabbed Sam by his hair, hauling him up, then kicked him hard in the chest with his pointy boots.

Once with each boot. Sam gagged, dropped back to his hands and knees, and swayed there, trying to summon something.

Anything . . . "Hey, what's going on? Stop it, you . . . damn, let go of me! Get your . . . *stop* it—"

It was Carol's voice and it sounded like she was in trouble. But he couldn't do anything about it.

"Where's Sam?"

It was ten in the morning and Bella was in the kitchen, scouring the insides of the cabinets. I'd told her that I would paint them anytime she liked, but she'd decided to clean them first; just knowing the grime was still under there would keep her up nights.

"Don't know," she said, wiping back a hank of her

henna-red hair with a rubber-gloved hand. When she cleaned a cabinet, she really cleaned a cabinet. "And don't," she added, "you dare paint this until I've given it another going-over."

It looked to me as if another going-over might reduce that cabinet to toothpicks. But I promised I wouldn't, and went into the parlor where Wade was looking over the bills.

"I wish I did know," he said when I asked if he knew where Sam was. "I'd tell him those cable movies he and Chip have been watching cost four bucks each."

He looked at me over the half-glasses he wore for reading. I thought he looked adorable in them, but now was probably not the time to say so. "Expanded cable service," he said, "sure costs us a lot of money."

"But without it we wouldn't get all the sports stations in the universe," I replied, and left him to digest this while I tried the dining room.

"Nope," said my dad, thin and wizened with a braid of gray hair tied in a leather thong, a ruby stud in one earlobe, and a face like a winter apple. He was frail since a car accident the previous year, but still cheerful in his chair by the fireplace, with his jack-knife in hand.

Having given his answer, he smiled very sweetly at me and returned to his job of carving clothespin dolls for a craft shop downtown. Clothed in Maine-themed costumes sewn out of brightly colored remnants from Ellie's scrap basket, the dolls had become a surprise hit, and he had orders to fill.

"How do you know Sam didn't ask for his job back and then just go out there to the boatyard to do it?"

asked Ellie, twenty minutes later when she picked me up out front.

We were going over to the church to see if any inspection progress had been made, or even was imminent; judging by the cop cars and other official vehicles still out front, though, I did not have high hopes for this.

"Because his boss from the boatyard called him," I replied. "And *he* says Sam's not there."

Ellie pulled to the curb outside the yellow crime-scene tape, now windblown into shredded tangles.

"*He* says that what with the second half of the storm coming and all, he'll forgive and forget as long as Sam shows up for work this afternoon," I said.

On the sidewalk, Ellie glanced up uneasily. What had been a nearly clear sky just an hour earlier was thickening to murk. A mean breeze, damp and penetrating, put its cold hand on my neck just as Paulie Waters came out of the church.

"Hey, you two," he began angrily, hurrying toward us with a frown. Paulie was a nice enough guy, but he was not very sure of his own authority and that made him touchy.

"Don't worry, we're not going inside. We just want to know when the work can start." I peered past him through the propped-open church doors.

"Work?" He looked at me like I was nuts, and this, to be honest, I suppose was not a completely unreasonable notion on his part. He'd once had to get me off the top of an extension ladder by calling in a utility crew, complete with forty-foot bucket truck.

I'd been trying to unclog the gutters at my old house at the time; the episode accounted for both my ongoing fear of ladders and Paulie's ongoing doubts about my mental stability. Anyway:

"No work going on here." He shot an unhappy look back over his shoulder. "Unless you mean top-secret state police work, too super-confidential for a low-on-the-totem-pole guy like me."

Oh, so that was the trouble. Paulie felt dissed, not a good mood to find him in if you wanted any cooperation out of him. A man in a sport jacket and tie appeared in the church doorway.

"Hey, Waters! Go find us a hacksaw or something, will you? DA wants a piece of that ladder."

Interesting; I supposed he meant the one that went up to the belfry, too large and cumbersome to bring in whole if only a part of it was needed for evidence. Skin shreds were snagged in its splintery rail, maybe, I thought. Or hair, or . . .

"Yeah, yeah." Paulie's voice didn't hide his scorn as he turned back to me. "Those guys. They'd haul the whole building away if it wasn't attached to the ground."

I looked up, awed as usual by the sheer, soaring height of the spire, no great shakes in a big city but still so tall within the context of a small Maine village that its perspective seemed off, almost as if it was . . .

Leaning. The really high part, where the steeple soared up to a point from the bell enclosure was . . .

"Paulie." I caught his sleeve. Alerted by my expression, Ellie gazed up at the steeple, too.

"Jake?" she said uncertainly. "Jake, is it just me, or is that thing—"

"It's not just you. Paulie, you go in there and tell

those guys that if they cut one more piece out of that church . . ."

In my own old house, over the years everything had become so shakily dependent on everything else that you could take out a curtain rod and a ceiling would fall down, drain a radiator and the furnace could explode. For all I knew, the belfry ladder was the only thing keeping this whole building from collapsing.

". . . it could come down on their heads," I finished. "I'm not kidding, the place is termite food."

I wasn't sure Paulie was familiar with carpenter ants. "They should at least be wearing hard hats," I said. "Really, you go on in there and see the sawdust piles everywhere, that's what those insects spit out."

I took a breath. "And from how big those piles are, you just imagine how much of that place those bugs have *eaten*."

"Jake," said Ellie urgently, "it's moving. When the wind blows hard up there, it's actually—"

Paulie looked unconvinced. But then his gaze followed hers. "Holy jeebus," he breathed. "Holy *criminy* jeebus."

He ran for the church. "You guys? I think you better . . ."

The sky blackened as we got back into the car. "What next?" said Ellie, since obviously we weren't going to accomplish any more here; if the state guys treated Paulie like a gofer, it was a certainty that they weren't about to be taking advice from a couple of snoopy local women.

Besides, it was not my ambition to die by having a two-hundred-year-old church steeple squash me. "Next?"

I settled back into the passenger seat. "Next," I grated out as premonitory spatters of rain washed a maple leaf down the windshield, "next we're going to find my son, the job quitter."

Ellie wisely decided not to say anything. "And *then*," I said as a particularly harsh gust of wind flung the leaf away, "*then* he's going to tell me just what the . . ."

I paused. Crude talk, Bella always said, was unladylike and unbecoming; an intelligent woman could surely find some other way of expressing herself besides uttering filth.

". . . what the *freak* he thinks he's doing," I finished.

Uncrudely. Unprofanely. Unfilthily, even.

But very, *very* sincerely.

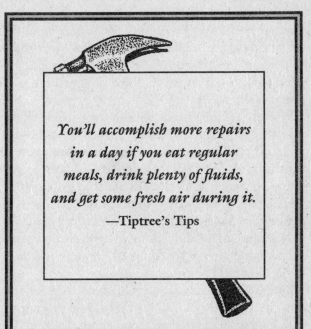

Chapter 11

*You'll accomplish more repairs
in a day if you eat regular
meals, drink plenty of fluids,
and get some fresh air during it.*
—Tiptree's Tips

"**W**here're we going?" asked Dylan.

They passed a small wire paddock with two ponies in it, across the road from a tiny airfield whose apron sported a fuel system, a small wood-frame office, and a handful of Quonsets.

"That was Bob Arnold on the phone, back in the room just now," she said. "Asked me if I'd take a drive, keep an eye peeled for that Hansen guy. The dead girl's father, he's gone AWOL, apparently."

It was why Paulie Waters had been looking for her, she guessed, but she'd managed to annoy him enough to make him forget his errand, confirming again her doubts about the hotheaded young cop. Meanwhile, this was not at all what she wanted to be doing, but she meant to stay in the Eastport police chief's good graces if she could.

Besides, reacquainting herself with this territory was not a bad idea. The road S-curved along the edge of an inlet where the tide was just now beginning to turn inward, the sloping shore littered with storm-flung driftwood and clots of dark green seaweed. Coming out of the turn, she put her foot on the accelerator, then had a new thought and slacked off again.

"I should take you back to your own crime scene soon, though, right? I mean, you have your own work to do, I shouldn't have assumed—"

But he was already shaking his head. "Those guys don't need me, they know their jobs. And they sure as hell don't want me in their faces, either. To them, I'm just a spy for the bosses."

He half-turned to her. "So, you really think somebody faked those Eastport postmarks just to get us here?"

Lizzie shrugged. "Can you think of any other explanation?"

She could, but she didn't want to tell him about it. Not yet.

He settled back against the seat. "I guess not. Weird, though. I'm going to have to cogitate a little on this one."

Yeah, she thought. *You cogitate on it.* Ahead another Quonset hut, this one long abandoned, bore a rusted sign proclaiming that it had once sold FRESH C-FOOD!

"So, what's this Hansen guy look like, d'you know?" Dylan asked. "I only got a little glimpse of him at the scene the other night."

Uphill away from the water, the road ran straight between stands of scrubby trees, their slender trunks and bare, spidery branches silver-gray in the weak sunlight. Lizzie remembered this stretch from back when she was here looking for Nicki, right after Sissy died.

It hadn't changed. Neither had Dylan, relaxed in the passenger seat, unaware of her suspicions.

"Me too. But I'm guessing he looks like someone whose last living relative is gone," said Lizzie.

She didn't know if it was true about Hank Hansen or not. But it was about her, and Dylan knew it.

Let him cogitate on *that.*

"What are you doing here?" Sam whispered. Carol lay beside him at the rear of the cave that faced onto the beach.

"What are *you* doing here?" They were tied hand and foot with lengths of the plastic rope that floated in on the tide all the time around here, from salmon pens, fishing boats, and renegade lobster buoys.

In the gloom at the back of the cave, he could just make out Carol's lips tightening. It would've been darker except for his penlight, which while plundering Sam's pockets Harvey Spratt had at first mistaken for drug paraphernalia.

Eyes narrowing with sudden interest, Harvey had closed his hand around the pen and clicked it on, then flung it away in disgust when it proved itself to be not smokable or shootable. Now it shone brightly from where it had landed and rolled, clinging precariously at the edge of a granite ledge, above and behind Sam and Carol.

"What I'm doing here is none of your business," she snapped in reply to his question. "Honestly, Sam, I don't see why you act like you're my father all the time. It's a real drag."

Sam was against hitting women, or hitting anyone in fact. But at the moment he felt lucky that his hands were tied. "You came back here with money, didn't you? You wanted Harvey to sell you something, but he wouldn't front it to you."

Let her have it on the promise of payment later, in other words; something like marijuana or pills. Carol liked fun, the kind that made her forget where she'd come from and what sorts of things she'd done prior to meeting Sam. And sometimes, that kind of fun needed a little help.

Meanwhile, you could yell your head off inside this cave and no one outside it would hear you over the wind and waves. Carol sighed heavily.

"Yes," she conceded. "But what do they want with us now?" She'd clocked that little idiot Bogie a pretty good one when he'd lost his grip on her for an instant. But the blue-green shiner above her left cheekbone was Bogie's reply, and seeing it gave Sam a bad feeling.

Icy water oozed down the granite behind his head, and into his collar. "Where'd you park your car?"

"Why?" Carol snapped back at him. "You want to criticize how I did that, too?"

He rolled hard toward her. "Where'd you *park* it, damn it?" If it was nearby, someone looking for him might draw a connection and get the idea that he might be around here.

"On the breakwater." She sniffled theatrically. "Why're you being so mean to me, Sam? I didn't do anything, I just wanted—"

"Yeah, yeah." He knew what she'd wanted, and ordinarily it wouldn't have been a big deal, a couple of joints or whatever. Although—

"It was just pot, though, right? I mean you're not using—"

The hard stuff, he meant to finish. She sniffled again. "No. I mean, yes, I wanted a few joints and he had them, so I said I'd come back down here with the cash. Sam, why is he doing this? Did you make him mad, somehow?"

Her eyes brimmed with tears, smearing her mascara. "No. I mean, I don't know. I wanted to ask him about that girl, the one Chip Hahn's in trouble over."

Outside, Spratt and his boys were arguing. The wind blew bits of their disagreement into the cave.

". . . don't know what you're so freakin' pissed over . . ."

". . . get us all in a lot of . . ."

". . . didn't even *see* her after the breakwater . . ."

And then: "Shut up! You all better just shut your mouths and do what I say. Or I'll make damn sure you *all* go to prison, right the freak along with me!"

It was Spratt. "What's he talking about?" Carol whispered worriedly, easing up closer to Sam. For warmth, he realized; it was getting colder in here. Also, the tide was coming in.

"I don't know." Sam did the math: The tide rose three feet per hour, it was only a dozen or so feet now from the mouth of the cave to the waterline, and the cave's interior sloped down sharply from front to back.

There was another brief flurry of guys' voices from outside, and then nothing except the waves and the sound of wind moving past the cave's mouth, a low musical fluting like someone blowing across the top of a large bottle.

"I don't know what Harvey's talking about," Sam repeated. *We never saw her after the breakwater . . .*

But he did know. He just didn't want to scare Carol. He'd been, he realized, an idiot to come here.

Lizzie turned left onto a twisty, unmarked road leading into Quoddy Village, once a World War II settlement of Seabees and other Navy personnel. Now the area was a patchwork of mobile homes, small bungalows, and tiny lots where only cellar holes remained.

"Sissy lived out here somewhere," she said, scanning as she drove. But no distraught man walked along the road's shoulder, or lay in the yellowed weeds beside it.

"Nicki was just a baby then, though," said Lizzie.

A short stretch of graded dirt road ran through an area of abandoned house lots; she turned onto it, thinking that if she were the distraught dad of a newly murdered child, she might want just this kind of desolate-feeling privacy.

Dylan sat up. Deep ditches bounded the road on both sides, and its washboard texture made the car judder unpleasantly even at slow speed.

"Hey." She slowed further. "Is that . . . ?"

"Yeah." He craned his neck toward the ditch on his side. "Damn, that sure looks like—"

A body; of course it was. And no big surprise; she'd known when she agreed to Bob Arnold's request that a recently bereaved dad of uncertain mental status might end his own life.

From behind the wheel, all she could see was the one shoulder clad in a black windbreaker, and a shock of brown hair. When she got out and peered into the ditch, it was clear this victim would not be getting up again.

"Dylan, call this in, will you? Nine-one-one, and tell dispatch we've found Bob Arnold's . . . no, wait a minute."

"Wait?" Dylan looked impatient. "You mean so you can do some detecting?"

The sour twist he put on the words reminded her that he must be in misery, and that he could have stayed at the hospital, where they'd have kept him pain-free for another day at least. But he'd rushed back here instead; she wanted to wonder why, but she was afraid she knew.

Not that it felt very important right this minute. Crouching at the edge of the ditch, she found to her surprise that the victim was not Hank Hansen, after all. This guy was only in his late teens; she examined the weedy area all around where he lay.

No weapon. She picked up a thick branch and gingerly shifted him with it. *Christ* . . . It wasn't a body after all. It was *two* bodies. And the one underneath was breathing.

Hurriedly she hauled the still-living victim from under the deceased one, laying him out flat by the side of the road and checking him over swiftly for anything first aid might be able to fix. Meanwhile she ran through the obvious:

Unconscious young white male, chinos and athletic jacket, his pulse, airway, and breathing all adequate for now, no active bleeding or other obvious acute distress, multiple cuts, bruises, and abrasions to the face and head, and . . . she noted the dark, sodden mess of his hair at the back of his skull at the same time as she took in the Red Sox patch on his sleeve . . . severe blunt-force head trauma, or possibly a gunshot wound.

But probably blunt force. You didn't beat somebody that way when you could shoot them. When she was done, she gently let the body down again, turning the head to the side so the blood oozing from the battered mouth wouldn't obstruct the kid's airway.

Dylan was in the car making the call. "Tell them it's not the guy Bob Arnold's looking for," she said, glancing around again. No drag marks, no smeared or spattered trail led out of the wooded area. But if the victims had been assaulted here—especially the dead one—there'd have been more blood.

A lot more; at first glance the mark on the deceased kid's throat was barely visible, covered by the windbreaker's neckline. But when she'd shifted the body, his head didn't move, because it had been almost severed, attached only by a strip of skin and gristle.

Dylan got done describing their surroundings and made sure the dispatcher understood their location— the road had no street sign—then snapped his phone shut.

"They want us to wait here," he said.

Well, of course they did. To wave the cavalry in, and the surviving victim might still need emergency CPR, for Pete's sake, or the perps might even come back. Had Dylan always been one to state the obvious like that? Or had she just not noticed before? She got back in the car, keyed the engine on, cranked the heat, keeping an eye on the kid's slowly rising and falling chest.

Dylan shifted uncomfortably, trying to arrange himself so that his collarbone didn't grate so painfully, she supposed. They sat in silence that way while she averted her mind's eye from the nearly severed head and instead thought about how easy it would be, faking a postmark.

Having a rubber stamp made was all it would take, and it would not even have to resemble a real one precisely; after all, who looked at postmarks closely enough to detect a phony?

Not me, she reflected bitterly. And Dylan hadn't had to.

He'd already known. The sky darkened stealthily, mist beading on the car's windshield, and the branches in the softwood scrub clattered ominously in the rising breeze.

"You know," said Dylan, apropos of nothing, "I never stopped thinking of you."

"Really," she said flatly, and if he thought that was odd he didn't say so. In the distance a siren wailed, coming nearer. The rain thickened, blurring her view of the body lying where someone had thrown it, tossed away like trash.

Like Sissy's, only she ended up in the water. The siren got louder abruptly as the squad car rounded the corner and blasted toward them on the unpaved road, its tires flinging wet stones.

"Whoever did this, though," Dylan declared, gesturing at the manila envelopes with the photos in them, "we'll find out who it was. That'll be one good thing, you have to admit that much."

Funny way to put it, she thought. And—*No. No, I don't have to admit it.*

She looked down at his hand, now resting atop her knee. Only a day earlier, his touch would've been thrilling whether or not she had wanted to admit it. But now . . .

"Take your hand off me." The squad car skidded to a halt and the driver jumped out, hand on his sidearm. As she'd expected, it was Paulie Waters, his handsome face grim and alert.

"I said get your hand off me," she repeated, not bothering to see how Dylan took this.

It didn't matter how he took it. "Or," she added in the same mild tone, "I'll break your other freaking collarbone for you."

Slowly he did as she asked. "Okay. If that's the way you—"

Paulie crouched by the ditch. "I don't understand,

though," said Dylan. She put her window down, called to the frowning cop.

"Hey. Thanks for coming out. We were just cruising around, Bob Arnold asked us to let you guys know if we spotted the girl's dad, Hank Hansen?"

Paulie nodded. "And instead we found this," she finished.

Later, after they'd given brief statements and Paulie had sent them on their way, Dylan tried again. "Listen, Lizzie, I know you're still angry about the way I abandoned you, back in the city."

Along the water on the way back toward town, foamy waves broke on the weed-strewn beach, the tide rising swiftly and the dark clouds on the horizon looming high, like massive boulders getting ready to cascade down.

"What?" She glanced briefly at him, still thinking about the victim back there, the surviving one. "No, I'm not angry about that," she replied. "I mean, it's what people do when they go back to their wives, isn't it? They cut off all contact."

She took the S-turn at speed, pushing it until the Honda's rear end lost a bit of traction. His good hand clenched the seat edge slightly.

Good. He deserved to be scared. "It bugs me a little, though, to hear you were thinking about me. Obsessing, even? Would that be a fair way to put it?"

At the Mobil station, she slowed for the 35 MPH sign, got a full breath at last in past the fury that had a stranglehold on her. "While she forgave you. While she was dying, even. I was on your mind even then, do I have that part right?"

Getting one of those manila envelopes delivered to

Dylan had been easy, of course. He'd simply put it into his own pocket.

The one to her, though; somehow finagling it into a pile on the table in her building's lobby, where the doorman on the day shift sorted the heap into a stack for each tenant. That had been a lot more difficult to do, but hey, even difficult things could be accomplished when you were a cop.

Back in town, she pulled into the motel's parking lot. "You didn't come back here today to be with me, though, did you?"

She bit the words off. "To help me in my time of need," she added, "in spite of the awful pain you were in."

He stared straight ahead. "But Dylan," she went on. "Listen, now, it's important. I want an answer to a question, but before you do answer, think. Make sure your answer is truthful."

She reached inside her vest. "Because I've given up a lot, you know? My home, my job . . ."

She angled her head at the manila envelopes, which either did or did not contain photographs of her only living relative. Of her murdered sister Sissy's child, a little girl by the name of Nicki. If she was alive and Lizzie didn't find her, the girl might grow up in conditions even worse than the ones Sissy and Lizzie had endured, back when they were children.

And that, while Lizzie herself was still alive, could not be allowed to happen. "So I'm going to ask you a question and you're going to answer, and if I get any sense at all that you're lying to me, Dylan . . ."

He began looking alarmed, too late. In the old days, he could've charmed his way out of this. But now when she brought out the .38 auto it was already aimed at his kneecap. "Ready?"

One in the chamber, safety off. "I'll take your silence as a yes," she said. "So start talking, and don't stop until you've told me absolutely everything about what you're up to."

A full day had passed since Bob Arnold had handed Chip over to the Maine State Police investigators, and for all that time, other than brief bathroom trips with a cop watching, he'd been in this small room. Concrete-block walls, acoustical-tiled ceiling, fluorescent lights whose faint buzzing seemed to be coming from somewhere inside his head . . .

The hard straight chair he sat on was a torture device, the table where he rested his head on his arms only a little less so. At regular intervals, they asked him if he was hungry (he wasn't) or thirsty, which he was, but those trips to the bathroom with the cop watching him were so creepy he tried to limit his liquid intake.

"Mr. Hahn, will you get up and hold your hands out for me, please?"

Confused, he shook his head to clear it. "What? Uh, wait a minute, why do you want me to—?"

The detective's face was impassive. "I'm placing you under arrest for the murder of Karen Hansen," he said, not in answer to Chip's query but because the script he was following required him to say this.

The detective, a dark-skinned man of about fifty, had short salt-and-pepper hair and a lot of old acne scars. He wore a good blue suit over a blue-striped dress shirt and a maroon tie. His aftershave smelled expensive, and his nails were neatly clipped, each tipped with a slender white crescent.

He'd been the one questioning Chip all this time, and until now Chip had liked him well enough. Or as much as you could like someone who was trying to get you to confess to slaughtering a teenaged girl, anyway.

Now, though, he wasn't so sure. He hadn't even known the girl's age, for instance, until this guy—Osbourne was his name, not that it mattered—told him. But then Osbourne had managed to work it around later so it seemed Chip had known.

Now Osbourne stood waiting. "Come on, Chip. Let's just do this thing, okay?"

Shakily Chip got to his feet. Moments ago he'd been worried about Carolyn, back in Manhattan. Was she eating? Was she staying at home, wondering where he was and waiting to hear from him? And what had happened about the attorney she'd asked him to call—did she still need one? And if so, why?

"Look, just let me make my call first, okay?" Confident that sooner or later they would release him, he hadn't called a lawyer himself, which he now realized was a huge mistake.

"Absolutely. You want to make a call, that will of course be arranged. Phones are out right now on account of the storm, but as soon as they're up, you can use one, no problem."

Osbourne held the handcuffs ready. Chip stared at them as if they were a pair of poisonous snakes, poised to wrap themselves around his pulse points. "But . . ."

The detective leaned over the table, snapped the cuffs onto Chip's wrists. "Come on, son. There's no way around this, okay? And anyway, it's just a hearing we're headed to now. Just a prelim for the judge to say where you're going next, is all."

Osbourne's voice, Chip noted dully, had changed subtly. It had been kind, even confidence-inspiring, before. A guy like Chip, it had said, could depend on Osbourne not to screw him over.

But now it had lost its veneer of friendliness. "Get up, bud," said Osbourne. "I'm not going to ask you again."

Chip met Osbourne's gaze, which had been bright with feigned personal interest and now did not give a damn as long as the prisoner did what Osbourne said he should do, went where Osbourne told him to go, and didn't get anything on Osbourne's good suit in the process.

"Can I just ask you something, though?" Chip paused halfway to the door. "Why are you all so sure I killed that girl?"

Osbourne looked down at the small yellow steno pad he'd been taking notes in throughout Chip's interrogation. He flipped back several pages until he found his place.

"Let's see, now. 'Girls Dying Badly,'" he recited. "'Stab City.' 'Underage Screamers.' Oh, and here's a good one. You can upload your own videos. It's called 'Slice Her and Dice Her.'"

He looked up. "Thirty-seven homemade videos on this site, of real girls being killed. Including one from you."

Osbourne snapped the notebook shut. "Does that

answer your question?" He ticked off on his fingers: "Access to the weapon, a sick Internet habit, no alibi . . ."

Stricken, Chip let his head fall forward. It was the price of being admitted to that disgusting secret chat room, that you had to upload a violent video of your own or the guys wouldn't trust you, they'd think you were a cop trying to bust them.

Which in a way Chip was; he'd pirated his video from another website, of course, but good luck getting anyone here to believe that. He doubted they'd be any swifter at corroborating his claim that he'd told the Wisconsin authorities about the sites, either.

Hey, there were a zillion nutballs in the world, and for all they knew, he was just another one of them. He moved obediently to the door of the small, bare room.

"Good man," Osbourne said approvingly. "Now, before we go out, there's one thing I need to caution you about."

Chip balked in the doorway but Osbourne gripped his arm and hustled him on through toward an open stairwell at the end of the cellar corridor.

"There's people up there," said Osbourne. "Word's gotten out that you're here, see. Reporters, curious citizens . . ."

Angry citizens, Osbourne didn't have to add. Chip could hear raised voices and clomping footsteps from upstairs.

"But they're all at the rear of the building, in front of the courtroom you're scheduled to be in. So they won't see . . ."

"What?" They started up the steps, paused to let a

deputy hurry past them on his way down, and began climbing again.

The cuffs were already beginning to hurt, and Chip was starting to wish he'd drunk more of that last soda Osbourne had offered him, too. Then he'd need to visit the bathroom again, and could put off whatever was coming for a little longer.

"What do you need to caution me about?" he persisted as they reached the first stairway landing. A plump, gray-haired lady in a skirted suit, pleasantly grandmotherly-looking, began a smile as she approached them, then realized who Chip must be.

"*Hsst.*" She aimed the sound at him on her way by, as if shooing away an animal. Chip felt wounded at this, then realized:

This was his life now. Like an animal's, yes; one who had already torn someone apart. Osbourne gripped his elbow.

"The people are all gathered in front of the rear courtroom where they think you'll be," Osbourne repeated. They paused by a barred, electronically locked door. You needed a card to put into the card slot to get outside the building.

Osbourne peered through the small square of wire-reinforced glass in the door. "We're going to wait for a couple deputies," he informed Chip. "Otherwise we'd have to go the rest of the way up this stairwell, and right out into the crowd."

He glanced at his watch. "Any minute now," he told Chip, as if they were waiting for a taxi to go somewhere pleasant.

Somewhere without handcuffs. "We're going to fool the folks up there," said Osbourne, seeming pleased at the cleverness of the subterfuge the authorities had come up with.

"Take you in through the front door, zip you right into a different courtroom from the one where they're expecting to see you. Soon as the deputy gets here."

Osbourne glanced at his watch again, a big round Timex with a brushed-aluminum body and leather band.

"But to do that," he added, "we'll have to bend the routine a little." He looked up at Chip, his dark brown face now devoid of any personal feeling whatsoever.

"Because to go around and get in through the front door of the building," he finished grimly, "we'll need to take you outside."

He could have made it all better eventually, Hank thought again. He could have gotten his daughter's love back, made them a real home. Somehow, someday . . .

Which particular day it would've been didn't even matter now. Because instead, the man they were holding in the courthouse for Karen's murder had taken them all.

Hank didn't know why. But he knew the phrase "an eye for an eye," all right. And he meant to put that phrase into practice.

Soon. As soon as they brought him out, Hank meant to get off his shot. Or ideally, two: one in the head, one in the chest.

After that, he'd be arrested, possibly even shot to death by the police, depending on how trigger-happy those state boys turned out to be. Either way, though, it was a cinch he wouldn't be driving the car home tonight. So he ran the engine, burning up gas, kept the heat on while he sat there, watching and waiting.

His butt was sore, and his legs felt cramped. But the ache in his chest was the worst part. Hank wondered if, after he blew the head off of the son of a bitch who'd slit his little girl's throat as if she were a meat animal, the ache would go away.

Or if maybe it never would. But that didn't matter, either. What mattered was that Hank had a clear view of the courthouse steps, and of the sidewalk leading up to them, and that sooner or later they would have to bring the son of a bitch out.

Transport him to prison, where he would get three hots and a cot, plenty of free TV, any medical care he needed. A tight grin stretched Hank's lips, which were beginning to bleed from the constant, nervous way he kept licking at them.

Yeah, he thought, *life of Riley for the girl-murderer, huh?*

Not.

Chapter 12

Keep a record of your work, including before-and-after photographs, samples of removed wallpaper, etc.
—Tiptree's Tips

"You had snapshots of her in your apartment, remember? Back when we were still seeing each other. Sissy had sent you pictures of her and the baby."

Dylan spoke in a monotone. The pain of his broken collarbone was getting to him, it seemed, his hair damp with perspiration and his face pale.

But what must've been even worse, Lizzie thought, was feeling all his plans crashing down all around him; plans that had included her whether she agreed to them or not, or even knew about them.

"After you told me your sister's little girl had gone missing, that you'd tried once to find her and couldn't, I took a couple of those pictures off your desk. You had a bunch, I figured you might not miss them."

This had been long after Sissy died, she realized, and she hadn't missed the photographs. Back when she was alive, Sissy had sent dozens, many of them near-duplicates. One or two gone hadn't even been noticeable.

They sat in her car in the parking lot of the Motel East. A huge wall of clouds from the south advanced slowly across the sky while he went on talking.

"I wanted to find the kid for you," Dylan said. "Produce her for you, grant your wish. You know? Be a hero." He made a face at himself.

"So I had a bunch of copies made of the pictures," he went on, "sent them around to people I knew. Organizations for missing children, cops in other states, figuring maybe a lead would turn up."

But none ever did. And—"That doesn't explain where *these* came from." She tapped the photographs of a smiling nine-year-old with an impatient index finger.

"Age-advanced," he explained. "Digitalized to show how a little kid like your sister's toddler would appear as an older child."

So the pictures of the older girl weren't even really Nicki, just a computer's idea of her. Lizzie shook her head, watching a line of rain squalls march up the bay like a heavy gray curtain.

"So you just wanted to get me here. Is that it? Nothing had changed, no new evidence about Nicki. It was all just about what you wanted."

He half-turned toward her in appeal. She twitched the gun she held. "If you touch me, I swear to God I will kill you. You lured me here, you *faked* all this to—"

He drew back, his face bluish-gray in the fading daylight. "That's how it began. But Lizzie . . . the photographs are real. I mean, I used Nicki's real toddler snapshots to get them made. A guy at the missing-kids organization owed me a favor, so . . ."

Yeah, and God forbid Dylan should leave a debt uncollected. "Why, you got lonesome? So instead of finding a new woman, one you'd have to spend time and money getting to know, you figured you'd just yank the string on the one you already knew was a sucker for your nonsense?"

"You still don't get it. I know that I screwed up, okay? And I'm sorry, it was stupid, I shouldn't have done it. But the pictures are good, they're what Nicki *would actually look like* at that age. I've sent them all over the state multiple times. I kept at it. To make it up to you, or try."

He paused. "And the reason I had to get you here one way or another now," he added, "is that I finally got a nibble."

She stared while a heavy rumble of thunder shook the car and he kept talking. "Town up in Aroostook County, way up in the northern part of the state. Allagash, the town is called."

She lowered the gun, put the safety on. "Someone thinks they've seen her," he said. But then his shoulders sagged. "Probably not, you know, though. It's probably some other kid."

"Why here, then? Why Eastport, and why didn't you just call me? Let me decide whether or not to—"

But she knew the answer to that last one, at least. Even if he had called, she'd have hung up on him, deleted his email without reading it, or in the unlikely event she had heard him out, she'd have thought it was a trick.

An empty lure he was dangling, to get her where he could work on her. The most he could've hoped for was that she'd take his flimsy lead on where Nicki might be, and follow it herself.

But this way—a supposedly accidental meeting, an imaginary plot by some shadowy third person, targeting them both—this way he had a chance of getting close to Lizzie again.

Or so he'd thought. He turned toward her once more. "This was more believable, Eastport. The last place Sissy lived . . . I figured you could go on from here, I'd get you up to Allagash somehow once you were in Maine."

His face turned rueful. "But I'm sorry," he repeated. "You were doing just fine without me. I should've had somebody else get in touch with you, tell you what I'd found. I should've left you alone."

Doing just fine . . . She had been, actually. Sort of: work, the gym, the Friday night fish dinner with Liam's family, with the series of nice Catholic guys they kept inviting to sit next to her in the dining room where Liam's medals and commendations were still ranged out on the mantel like a saint's relics.

Just fine, the life she'd given up for Dylan's lie. But she didn't miss it, she realized suddenly. Since arriving here in Eastport, she hadn't missed it at all, not even the apartment she had been so very proud of. Hardly thought of it, even.

He glanced over at the gun she still held. "So, are you going to shoot me with that thing or what?"

She shrugged. "No." She put it into the nylon holster under her jacket. "So . . . tell me something. After we . . . after it ended. You never called. Was it because you didn't want to, or . . . ?"

He closed his eyes, leaned back against the headrest. "I'd promised her I wouldn't. Sherry, that is. And for once I thought I ought to keep a promise, you know?"

He took a deep breath, grimaced at the pain, and let it out. "Just for once. And then she was gone. For a while I was sort of stunned, too paralyzed to do anything, and after that so much time had gone by that I figured you would be too pissed off."

"You were right. I was." And yet she was glad he'd managed to keep his promise. One tiny bright spot in his character . . . it was something, anyway. It gave her hope for him.

She glanced up from the age-progressed photograph of Nicki. A pretty little girl with cornflower-blue eyes, flaxen hair . . . she looked just like Sissy had at that age.

Just like her. "But now here we are, anyway."

Outside it was getting dark, though it was barely

three in the afternoon. Raindrops skittered warningly across the puddles on the paved parking lot.

"Just one thing, Dylan." She started the car.

He was already nodding. "Yeah. I figured you'd have to ask. I was at a bachelor party in Augusta when I got the call. Guy in my old squad's getting married."

The call about a dead girl in an Eastport church, he meant. "Don't worry, I've got alibi witnesses," he added lightly.

Witnesses to say, that is, that he hadn't been here killing a kid just so he'd have an excuse to be in Eastport when Lizzie arrived. Terrible thought, but she was a cop, so she'd had it.

She shrugged. That kind of coincidence was . . . well. It could have happened.

Stranger things had. "How were you planning to get together with me? I mean, before the girl got killed and brought you here as part of your job, how did you think we'd run into each other?"

"Um," he said. "I hadn't quite figured that part out yet. But . . . just take a ride, end up here, make it my business to run into you on the street or something. Since I knew you wouldn't meet with me on purpose."

Which actually reassured her more than anything else he could have said; a pat answer was her least favorite kind, in the believability department.

"Where are you staying?" He must've hoped to be staying with her by now. *But then, we all hope for a lot of things, don't we?*

And we don't get them. "Ah, there's a cot at the

cop shop; I'll bunk there again if Bob Arnold lets me," he replied.

She turned that direction, out of the motel parking lot. On the street the other cars had their headlights on, their wipers slapping at the rain gusting cross-wise in bursts. A few pedestrians hustled along leaning sideways, holding on to hats or gripping plastic shopping bags to their chests.

At the corner she slowed for an eighteen-wheeler headed for the breakwater. A massive freighter with open cargo bays was tied up to the outer berth; near it, men in reflective vests directed the truck traffic under swaying dock lights.

Then, just as she was about to turn into the police station's asphalt parking area, a familiar car—where had she seen it?—approached from the opposite direction. Before she could glimpse its plate, it pulled a U-turn and raced away.

Instinctively she hit the gas, only then recalling where she had noticed the fleeing vehicle before. Oh, for a dashboard beacon, a radio, anything . . . because she wasn't a cop here and didn't play one on TV, either. But she was about to behave like one.

Oh, was she ever. A dead girl with her throat slit, and then a dead boy with *his* throat cut, too . . . now *there* was a coincidence worth pursuing.

At the corner she swung the wheel hard to the left and hit the gas, accelerating into a narrow, tree-lined lane. Dylan glanced at her questioningly.

"Detour," she told him flatly. The car ahead made another sharp left, fast, as if the driver knew she was following and had a guilty conscience.

She peeked at Dylan again; he looked . . . interested. Then she noticed something else about him.

"Dylan, buckle your damned seatbelt."

The car ahead shot up over the top of the hill. Lizzie hit the gas again, gripping the wheel with one hand, reaching inside her jacket with the other. Dylan went after his own weapon, came up empty, and uttered an oath, then stuck his hand out for hers.

"Give it here. Come on, I know you're a hardass at heart, okay? But on paper . . ."

She'd have argued, but he was right. A civilian did not get to fire from a moving vehicle at another moving vehicle, not for any reason. Not unless she wanted a lot of trouble.

No matter what she'd been empowered to do two days ago in another state. "Here."

She passed the weapon to him without looking. As it crested the hilltop, the CRV caught air, slammed down onto its tires, and shot forward again after the fugitive car, which blew through the stop sign at the approaching corner and swung around it. Lizzie floored the Honda, flew around the same corner, and raced down a curving slope through what turned out to be a sprawling cemetery spread out on both sides of the road, entered by way of iron gates set into granite-block posts.

The gates were open. In the thickening gloom of approaching evening, the marble gravestones gleamed wetly under rain-haloed streetlights. Ahead, the fleeing car showed under them, too, as it entered the cemetery. It was a small red sports car with a black cloth top.

A Miata, Lizzie thought. More power, less weight . . . the Honda was great for off-duty, the little four-banger under the hood as economical as hell. But right now she'd have killed for a V-8 and to hell with better gas mileage.

Inside the graveyard with the Honda trailing, the Miata cut between two large stone angels onto a grassy track, paralleled the graveyard's cast-iron fence for a hundred yards, then found the cemetery's open iron gates once more and shot back out onto the road. The fleeing car's brake lights flashed briefly at another corner, then rounded it faster than she'd have thought possible. The driver was nuts—

Or guilty of something, and Lizzie was betting hard on the latter. But why run from her? No one here even knew her, and they certainly didn't know she was a . . . but then she realized:

Dylan. They could've glimpsed him through the windshield, and he'd been at the church right after the murder. He'd been there in an official capacity, inside the crime-scene tape with all the other . . .

"Cops," she said. "They know we're . . ."

In the dim glow of the dashboard lights, his face was tight with pain, but his grip on the gun looked solid. "Yeah. I betcha you're right."

The next turn put the Honda on two wheels momentarily, but it set down solidly again when instead of panicking, she floored it and let the car's engineering do what it was designed to: not roll them. They raced down a dark, twisty road between big pine trees whose branches thrashed heavily in the rising wind.

"Hey. One other thing." Dylan spoke calmly, just as if they weren't exceeding the posted limit by triple or so.

"Yeah?" Taillights still glowed intermittently ahead each time she raced around another sharp curve, tires squealing. But unless she had her directions mixed up, they were approaching a larger thoroughfare where there could be more local traffic.

Storm or not, it was getting to be the hour when working people would be on the road going home. And whoever this jerk up ahead was, he wasn't worth the collateral damage she could cause by chasing him much farther right now.

"When this thing here is over, you're going to let me help you," Dylan said.

"Hah." The mirthless laugh got punched out of her by a bump in the pavement. "Are you kidding?"

Then she concentrated again on catching up with the small red car. It had disappeared around a curve ahead, but if memory served, the main road was still a little ways distant.

So she might still catch up. "Yeah, they're still up there," Dylan said as she pressed the gas pedal harder. "And if whoever's running from you is doing it 'cause they saw me in your car . . ."

Then maybe it was because they'd seen him at the church, she completed the thought silently. *Because they'd done the crime.*

"Or if it's you they recognized . . . ," Dylan added.

Right; she'd been at the scene, too. Not only that, but she'd been in this very car not twenty-four hours ago, watching four punks until they twigged to her and split.

Four punks who could've known the dead girl; it was why she had been watching them in the first place.

Punks who could be in that car right now; as soon as she thought it, she knew it was true.

"I owe you, Lizzie. I got you here, it's my fault. So if Nicki really is still alive and in Maine, maybe in Allagash—"

"Yeah. But listen, we'll talk about it later, all right?"

Because for now it was all she could do just to hurtle down this wet, barely familiar road. Gripping the wheel, pushing the CRV as fast as she dared—faster, even—she frowned into the thickening drizzle. But no taillights showed ahead now, just the swaying evergreens lining both sides of the dark road.

Until suddenly she did see . . . "Dylan."

She touched the brakes. The road, slick and wet in what was rapidly becoming another downpour, felt like ice under the tires. She braked to a stop by the side of the road and put the flashers on. Beyond a row of pine trees, a low, dark shape sent up plumes of steam.

She hoped it was steam. She pulled her cell phone out. *No signal . . .*

Yet another charming fact about downeast Maine: crappy cell reception, or at least it was with the phone she had. Fifty yards away, though, house lights glowed through the trees.

"Get out." He obeyed while she yanked her own seatbelt off, swung the car door open, and jumped out into rain pouring down in a nearly solid stream. Cursing, he headed for the house up behind the line of evergreens while she slogged into the field where the little red sports car lay on its side, wheels still spinning.

Nothing else moved there but the steamy spew of whatever was rising, smokelike, from the hood area of the crashed vehicle. A *lot* like smoke . . .

The rain on the road's pavement sounded like bullets. Lizzie forced her way through a thicket of some kind of thornbush, then into a ditch full of cold muck. Hauling herself out, she slipped and fell, clambered up again and forced herself on. Slogging into the field, she scanned the wreck for any sign of life.

And if I see any, it'd better have its hands in the air the very instant I say so, or . . .

But she didn't see any. The stink of antifreeze mingled with a sharp, familiar smell that sent a pang through her: gasoline. And even though the rain would douse any fire outside the car . . .

Then, through the vehicle's torn canvas top, she saw flames flickering. Tiny at first, they lapped up briefly and then with a bright *floof!* they were everywhere.

And so was the screaming.

What happened next was a confusion to her, then and later: shouts. A stabbing anguish in her hands, sounds of rain sizzling on a hot surface, a blood-slick gripping on her arm. Then she was staggering, half urging and half carrying someone.

There was the smell of sweat and blood, but it was okay, she was getting somewhere, she thought. Hauling someone out of a car fire, alive, until something hit the side of her head very hard; then came the taste of blood, sickening her, and stars flaring behind her eyes.

Somebody grabbing her again, dragging her away. The rain in dizzying circles . . . falling again.

Falling and falling.

Bob Arnold thought that if anyone in Eastport knew where the murdered girl, Karen Hansen, had been planning to get enough cash to run away on, it was probably local bad boy Harvey Spratt. He knew everything about anything bad that anyone was ever planning; it was a talent of his, that and taking advantage of whoever was planning it.

Harvey was bad, and dangerous to know, and sooner or later Bob intended to catch him at something serious, a plan that Harvey with his animal-like cunning had so far thwarted.

Bob also knew that foul weather rarely kept Harvey from his haunts: the picnic tables on the breakwater, the old scaffolding under the defunct canning factory, or the storefront doorstep at the corner of Water and Washington Streets, where he could stand under the brick archway and see everyone coming and going.

Especially cop cars, so Bob left his squad car at the Mobil station and borrowed one of the station's junky loaner vehicles. By now it was past dusk, the clouds heavy overhead and the wind-driven rain coming down in earnest again. Down at the breakwater, men in slickers waved baton lights to herd the last freight trucks away from the big vessel tied to the massive pilings. Deck lights on the ship shed a silver-white glow onto angular cranes hovering mantis-like over the cargo holds; most of the fishing boats and other vessels in the boat basin were lit up, too, their owners unwilling to leave them with more ugly weather imminent.

As Bob passed the breakwater's entrance he ran a practiced eye down the row of pickup trucks parked on the dock, thinking about whose wives might be home alone tonight with kids and need help if later on the storm got extra nasty. Then he was at the corner where he'd expected to find Harvey.

But he didn't. Instead, Bogie Kopmeir loitered in the arched doorway of the brick storefront, smoking a cigarette and peering around as if waiting for someone.

Bogie was a short, solidly built kid with a round baby face; his porkpie hat and leather jacket were no doubt intended to make him look older. Instead he resembled a large, oddly dressed baby, and this pretty much required him to be good with his fists and any other fighting tools he could get his hands on.

Also, Bogie was kind of nuts. Pulling up alongside the boy, Bob rolled down the loaner's window. "C'mere."

Bogie sauntered up to the car, flicking away his smoke.

"Where's Harvey?" Usually Bob chatted with youngsters for a moment or two before hitting them with questions; there was no sense in creating unnecessary hard feelings. But he avoided small talk with Bogie and his thuggish cohorts.

Give them an inch of familiarity, they'd take a mile

and you wouldn't like the result, Bob knew from un-happy experience.

Bogie tried looking sly, but on his smooth, round face the result was the expression of an infant with colic.

"Get in the car, Bogie."

Colic vanished, replaced by peevishness. "Whaf-for? Din't do nothing, why're you always—"

Bob grabbed Bogie's sodden jacket front. "You can tell me where Harvey is, or I can take you home and hand you over to your old man. I hear he's been in a bad mood lately."

Bogie's eyes widened; he twisted away. "Awright, jeez, you don't hafta—"

Bogie's mother was long out of the picture. His fa-ther was a locksmith who'd worked for the mill in Woodland, a town forty miles to the north, which left Bogie on his own most of the time. But the mill was on shutdown until the lumber market picked up again, so the old man was out of work and drinking heavily lately as a result, and he was even quicker with his fists than Bogie.

Bogie backed sullenly into the doorway. "Took off in that chick's little car," he said dismissively, pulling out another cigarette.

"What car?" Bob demanded, thinking *Aw, hell*. Har-vey behind the wheel was even worse news than Harvey just walking around on two legs.

"The little red car, you know the one? But I dunno where he went. Just took off," Bogie said in the same wondering tones he'd have used if Harvey Spratt had vanished into thin air.

Yeah, vanished like a magician's trick, Bob thought

sourly. He knew the car Bogie meant, though. "How long ago was that?"

Bogie pretended to think: that colic expression again. Then he brightened. "Uh, twenny minutes?"

He squinted to see if this answer would get him off the hook, and Bob off his case, meanwhile lighting the new smoke.

"He have anybody with him? The girl?" Although what a girl like Carol Stedman would want with Harvey Spratt, Bob didn't know.

Bogie puffed. "Nah. She gave him the keys, though. He, like, didn't steal the car or nothin'."

"Uh-huh." In Bob's experience, people gave Harvey things when Harvey made them do it, one way or another. But there was no sense trying to parse that out with Bogie, whose thoughts about people rarely extended beyond their immediate usefulness (or lack thereof) to him. To Bogie, defending Harvey wasn't so much an act of friendship as an effort to escape a beating from him, should Harvey ever learn of this conversation.

But Bogie still looked shifty. "What else?" said Bob, then repeated himself when Bogie toed the wet sidewalk evasively.

And when Bogie continued silent: "Hey." Bob got out of the car, never mind the rain. Bogie stood his ground, knowing that he could run but not hide.

Not in Eastport, anyway. Bob seized his collar, snapping the cigarette from Bogie's lips with a flick of his index finger. "So what's this?"

He brushed Bogie's jacket back to reveal the leather knife scabbard on his belt. Empty, though. "Where's your knife?"

Bogie always carried one, small but wicked looking. The boy scowled. "Lost it."

"Uh-huh. You know anything about a kid getting stabbed in the neck today? And another one, younger kid, beat to within an inch of his life?"

The stabbed kid dead, the other one clinging to life in the hospital, as if Bob needed any more mayhem today. Bob eyed the kid in front of him, who sure as hell looked guilty about something. But Bogie wouldn't be going far; he was the kind of little punk who thought he could tough-and-bluff his way out of anything. And it was Harvey that Bob needed to talk to now.

"So how come Harvey wanted the car?"

"Dunno," began Bogie in aggrieved tones, "how should I know what he—" but Bob cut in.

"Your dad's home, isn't he?" And before Bogie could reply he went on: "I think maybe I ought to take you there. Drag you right in and drop you there in front of him, like the little sack of—"

"No!" For the first time, real fear showed on Bogie's face; even sober, which at this hour of the early evening was unlikely anyway, his dad was worse than Bob Arnold.

Way worse. "He just wanteda get away," Bogie jabbered. "He wanteda take that car outta Mr. Hansen's garage, nobody ever uses it. But he sent me over there and it ain't there, so . . ."

"What?" Bob gripped Bogie's jacket front, hauled the young man up close to him despite the kid's stinky nicotine breath. "What car out of Hansen's garage?"

Hansen's shed, the kid meant, and there hadn't been any car in it when Bob was there. The only ve-

hicle on the place had been the junker sitting on flats.
But . . .

An awful idea began blooming in Bob's head, one
that had nothing to do with Bogie or his unsavory
pal, Harvey Spratt. It was the idea that he himself
had missed something, and now that something was
about to bite him in the behind.

A car, he thought, sitting in Hank Hansen's shed.
But now that car was missing, and so was—

He let go of Bogie's jacket just as a huge gust of
wind howled down the street, rattling signs and vibrating behind the sheets of plywood nailed up over
the storefront windows. Bogie staggered back into the
relative protection of the arched doorway while Bob
flung himself back into his loaner again. As he started
it up, Paulie Waters's squad car shot down Washington Street at him, its tires throwing up a foot-high
spray of water at the bottom of the hill.

"Hey. No comms," said Paulie, waving his radio
handset. "The wind musta took out one of the towers
on the mainland, I think. No phones, no radio . . .
we are in-freaking-communicado, boss, and I don't
know when it's comin' back."

Bob nodded—yet another of the benefits of island
living, he thought sourly, was the dependency on
mainland communications arrangements—as Paulie
went on:

"But before it went kablooie, I got a poke from dispatch. Accident on outer Clark Street, one of those
state-cop dopes came across it and called it in from a
residence? Says maybe there's injuries. I've got our
EMTs on their way."

"Great. Handle it all, will you, Paulie?" Bob glanced

at Bogie, who was listening wide-eyed. Bogie still looked sneaky about something, some shenanigans he hadn't revealed. But Bob didn't have time to find out what.

He turned back to Paulie. "I gotta go to Machias."

Paulie made a *What?!?* face; a less opportune time for a trip to the county seat forty miles to the south could hardly be found, his expression said.

But Bob didn't have time for that, either. "Listen to me now, if the radio doesn't come back right away and you can't get dispatch to relay a message—" Because Paulie was right: heaven knew what had gone wrong or how long it might last.

"—then I want you keep trying, however long you've got to. Try to let 'em know not to let that kid out of their sight."

He sucked in a breath. "That Chip Hahn kid, the one they got for the girl up to the church last night. I mean it, Paulie, he's got to stay indoors, locked up, no one gets at him. Got that?"

Paulie still looked puzzled, but he didn't argue. "Got it, boss. I'll keep at it. And listen, one more thing."

Bob felt so impatient, he thought the top of his head might just pop right off, spewing steam like one of the characters in his little girl's picture books.

"I don't care, Paulie, don't you understand? I've got to—"

Hank Hansen has another vehicle, and it— probably with Hank behind the wheel—is missing.

And betting that they'd actually managed to find all Hank Hansen's weapons was purely foolish.

"Up at the church there, they got a problem," said

Paulie. "That steeple is *leaning*, Bob. This wind, it's just—"

"Yeah. Whatever." A pang of urgency shot through him. *How long has Hank Hansen been gone, anyway? And what else does he have besides a car no one knew about? A gun? Bomb materials?*

"I don't care if that church *sails away*, Paulie, all right? I don't care if it *blows the freak down*. Get it safe if you can. I'll sign for any money you spend. But I can't help you with it."

On shoring up the structure, he meant, not that Paulie was likely to get anyone around here to do that on a night like this.

"'Cause I've got to go *now*," Bob finished, and sped away.

Headed up Washington Street, his car trailed a wake like a speedboat's; out Route 190, rain thundered down onto the roadway ahead of him. *Hank must've rented out the shed,* Bob realized. To a summer person, maybe, for a few bucks a month which of course Hank would've jumped at, and how the hell had Bob missed thinking of that? Back in the day, he'd known everything about everyone in town. But now . . .

Never mind. Water under the bridge. At the Mobil station, he traded the loaner back in for his squad car again and got back on the road; if he reached Machias in time it wouldn't matter what Hank Hansen had or didn't have or what he intended doing with it.

If.

* * *

My hands are tied, my hands are . . .

Tied. Sam's hands were tied tightly together behind him. He'd tried to wriggle out of his bonds, but no luck. He'd tried hard. "S-Sam?" Carol's voice quavered with cold and fear.

"What?" His did, too, but on the inside. No sense scaring her even more than she was.

"I'm s-sorry." She sniffled miserably.

God, it was cold. "Not your fault."

Harvey Spratt had taken her purse and car keys from her, and her cell phone was in her purse. Not that it would've worked in here anyway. *My hands are . . .*

Tied. And what, Sam wondered a little desperately—well, it was more than a little, really—was he going to do about that?

It was dark in the cave, the only light coming now from the penlight still glowing on the ledge behind them. Outside, the last of the daylight hadn't quite vanished; falling rain caught the pearly gray illumination of evening, making the cave's mouth resemble a snowy TV screen.

The hissing sound was the same, too, but beyond that another noise crept nearer: the rush-and-thunder of waves rolling in with the rising tide. "Can you lean over at all?" he asked Carol.

Her hands were tied, too, with the same thick orange line that held his wrists and ankles tight. The lines' long loose ends were square-knotted behind both of them, around an iron bar someone had driven into the granite ledge long ago.

What the bar had been for back then, Sam didn't know; to tie a skiff to, maybe, or anchor a floating dock. Now it kept the orange lines taut, imprisoning him and Carol at the rear of the cave, in the glow of the small penlight.

"Could you pull a knot apart with your teeth?" he asked. But instead of answering, her voice rose in a shriek, and then he felt it, too. Something *moving* . . .

Moving and cold; *snake*, he thought at first; though that was impossible he stifled a yell of his own. But then he realized the truth and his moment of fear was replaced by a deeper fright.

Icy, implacable. "Shh, it's okay," he told Carol. "It's just water." Creeping in, pulling back . . .

He leaned against her, trying to send some of his own fake courage into her. "Just a little wave, that's all. You'll just get wet, a little."

Fake, because the truth was so much worse than that. From the mouth of the cave to back here where they hunkered was only a distance of about twelve feet, but the downslope was acute, so that where they sat was a good eight feet lower than sea level at least, he estimated.

In other words, at high tide the cave was filled with water; *completely* filled. "Carol. Inch forward, can you? Drag with your feet and scoot on your butt if you can, as much as you can."

"What?" She was weeping now. But she did as he said, and he did likewise, inching along on the wet shale.

When they'd reached the end of the orange line that tethered them to the iron bar, they rested. Cold, tired, scared . . . the words didn't begin to cover how he felt, and it was amazing what that kind of emotion took out of you, he was noticing.

But it didn't take as much as being drowned would. Drowned *slowly*, one wave at a time until . . .

"Okay. Now roll on your side with your back toward me."

Shivering, she obeyed him again. But: "Sam," she complained, "it's *wetter* up here! The waves are coming in, why did you—"

"Lean forward." He didn't have time to argue with her, and anyway, he didn't want to have to tell her the truth:

That, yes, it would stay dryer for longer, farther back in the cave. But when it did start filling up, it would happen fast and from the rear. "Just stay still."

He angled his body sideways, then let himself fall onto his side with his mouth against her tied wrists. Working the line's tightly plied nylon strands furiously with his teeth, he found the knot.

Here's hoping, he thought as he began pulling at it with his front teeth. Another wave came in, foaming around them and giving him a sudden mouthful of cold, sandy seawater.

Choking, ignoring Carol's unhappy cries, he went to work on the knot again as soon as he could breathe. It was tied tightly, but as a boat guy, Sam knew a knot's tightness was not the only measure of its security. More important was the kind of knot and how well it was tied.

Another wave, another intensely salty mouthful.

Here's hoping our pal Harvey Spratt wasn't ever a boat guy himself. Or . . .

More seawater. Sam held his breath, spat. Then back to work.

Or a Boy Scout.

* * *

"Sorry about this." After waiting half an hour for their escort without result, the plainclothes cop named Osbourne had finally returned Chip to the interrogation room and left him.

When he came back, he set a steaming paper cup in front of Chip on the metal table. "Turns out the deputies are all jammed up working calls in the storm. And I can't take you out of here without them, so . . ."

Chip looked up at Osbourne. "It's okay, I'll go upstairs. The people waiting up there, I'll face them."

He summoned a deep breath. "I don't have anything to . . ." But then he stopped. *Hide,* he'd been about to finish.

Only he did, and Osbourne knew it. Chip could see it in the cop's face. Osbourne knew there was something Chip would rather die—or even go to prison—than tell.

He just didn't know what.

And I'm keeping it that way, Chip thought stubbornly. Being here, so miserable and desolate, only reminded him of what his life would be like without Sam Tiptree and his family in it.

And he wasn't risking it; he just wasn't, and nobody could make him. *End,* he thought grimly, *of story.*

The coffee was so bitter that it made his eyes water. Holding the cup in both cuffed hands, Chip swallowed some despite this. During his long wait at the rear entrance of the courthouse, through a reinforced-glass window in the door he'd watched the storm whipping itself together outside.

Trash tumbling, branches flying, people battling their way across the parking lot, gripping their jackets and hanging on to their hats: despite their discomfort, Chip had envied them.

And watching them had at least been something to do. In here there was nothing, only the buzz of the overhead fluorescents and the efforts of Osbourne, still trying to get Chip's confession.

And if Chip were somebody else, Osbourne might have. Gotten him to talk, that is. If, for instance, Chip thought with a quick, hot burst of resilient steeliness, he had actually *done* what they all accused him of doing.

Instead of something else, something that wasn't murder. Or not of a human being, anyway.

But something that in Chip's own eyes was nearly as bad. He took another sip of the bitter coffee and sat back to wait some more.

Outside the red-brick Washington County courthouse on Upper Court Street in Machias, Maine, Hank Hansen leaned back in the car he'd borrowed, biding his time. Full dark now, and the rain thundering, thumping the car's roof and sluicing down the front and rear windows, the wind slamming and banging things around out there.

But sitting there with the long gun across his lap and the radio on, Hank liked it all right, considering. He had plenty to eat and drink, enough smokes for the duration, and the heater was running now and again, too, just enough to take the chill off.

Like hunting, this was, sitting out in a blind waiting for a moose or a deer to stroll by. Waiting a long while sometimes, but in the end it was usually worth it, and this time he was certain that it would be. Because sooner or later, they'd have to bring that girl-murdering little bastard out of there, wouldn't they? On his way, Hank supposed they all must be thinking, to a cell in a state prison.

That is, unless they flat-out released him, which was what the guy must be hoping for. But prison wasn't the worst thing that could happen to a person, Hank knew; a man could get his teeth fixed behind bars, have whatever medicine he needed given to him. Eat a meal, take a shower, sleep in a bed.

Meanwhile, each day that guy enjoyed would be another one in which Hank's daughter's body rotted some more, and the more he pulled on the bottle of Bushmills, the clearer he saw his little Karen: bits falling off, eyes liquefying. Hank let the ghastly details dance in his mind, strengthening his resolve, his holy *intention,* to blow off the head of the son of a bitch who'd killed his girl. Who'd slit her throat like an animal's . . .

Movement caught his eye, people gathering on the courthouse steps across the street. Hank sat up with one hand on the long gun and the other on the window crank. Once the whole thing got started, it would go fast, he knew, like in the woods when the animal finally appeared and it was all just sight and shoot, no time for anything else.

Hank swiveled sideways with one hand under the weapon's barrel, propping its end on the door panel while he rolled the driver's-side window the rest of the way down. Rain drove in, slapping his face with its bracing cold, bringing smells of wind-thrashed pine and the salt tang of nearby Machias Bay.

He couldn't have sat here in broad daylight with a weapon, but as it was, no one noticed when he stuck the rifle's barrel out, its blued steel blending with reflections on puddles, headlights' glare flaring on wet surfaces, the street's slick neon-ish sheen.

The clutch of people on the steps parted to reveal a lady on crutches exiting the building. A helper hustled along holding an umbrella just as a van pulled up, blocking the view briefly. When the van pulled away, the steps were empty again. There hadn't been time enough for anyone else to come out . . . had there?

Hank thought not. A couple of Bangor TV stations' news vans still sat in the darkened parking lot, too, which let him know that something newsworthy was yet meant to happen here tonight.

Something like a local girl's killer being led out of there, for instance. Hank lowered the rifle and settled back to wait some more. He had time.

All the time in the world, until the camera crews could get their live shots. *Yeah, he'd give them live shots, all right.*

One in the head, one in the heart. And after that—

Well, after that Hank didn't really care what happened. He'd already absorbed his one in the heart, or felt like it, anyway. And it would take a minute or so for the cops to figure out he'd shot their prisoner to death.

In that brief interval, he expected he could self-administer his one in the head, as well.

What the hell, save them the trouble.

Chapter 13

> *A clean,*
> *well-lit cellar is a*
> *thing of beauty.*
> —Tiptree's Tips

"...asked him and *asked* him not to go out
and stay out like this, not even telling me where he
was going..."

Fuming aloud to keep my anxiety at bay, I drove
down Water Street with Ellie beside me in the passenger seat. We'd been all over the island twice, looking
for Sam, past uprooted trees and swathes of shingles

and tattered tar paper and shredded sections of vinyl siding that the wind had torn off and scattered around.

And the storm wasn't really even here yet. We'd checked the forecast, locating on the computer screen the low-pressure system in the Gulf of Maine, and found we were on the edge of it, which meant hours to go, still, of winds, rain, and tides rivaling even the 1976 Groundhog Day storm, which shoved a twenty-foot surge up the Penobscot River as far as Bangor, flooding the downtown.

"Where's Wade?" asked Ellie, peering out into the murk.

"At the freighter terminal." Two ships were headed in here, both trying to get sheltered before the worst hit. "Fortunately, there wasn't time before the weather boom lowered to get a harbor pilot out there," I said.

Ordinarily, ships headed to Eastport get guided in by a local pilot who knows the area's hazards and features; Wade had qualified for the job long before I met him. But tonight was too wild to get him out there, so the guidance was by satellite radio, which he was helping to supervise.

So Wade wasn't my worry now; Sam was. "Where *is* he?" I repeated, slowing for another trash can rolling in the street.

He wasn't at the boatyard or on the breakwater, or at his friend Maggie's, or—I'd called, just before the phones went out—at the jail in Machias, trying to see Chip. And now I couldn't call anyone else, and it was pitch dark and pouring, so an answer to my question wasn't looking likely anytime soon.

A huge crash, followed by the collapse of a massive tree across the street in my rearview mirror, emphasized the "we should go home" thought that I knew Ellie was having, too.

"Okay," I said, turning left onto Clark Street. "We'll go up to Route 190 and back that way. Unless you'd like me to—"

Take you home first, I meant to finish, but she knew that; we'd been friends a long time. "No. George'll be out with one of the crews," she said resignedly.

Her husband's part-time job with the city meant handling the worst tasks in the worst weather, and especially any emergencies. "And Lee's with her great-aunt in Orono."

They had family all over the state. "So I'd just be there all—"

Alone. "Yeah, okay," I said, and then, "Hey. What's—"

"*. . . that?*" I hit the brakes, skidding over onto the gravel shoulder. Just ahead at the side of the road, a small car sat with its flashers blinking slowly, as if the battery was running down. But that wasn't what made me stop.

In the nearby field, a fire burned merrily. That was strange, because there was no reason for any fire to be burning there, now or ever, and besides, it was raining like hell, which should've—

"Uh-oh," said Ellie, and then I spotted them, too: a set of tire tracks running off the road into the field, two mucky ruts.

We jumped out of the car and scrambled down through a ditch and across the field, slogging in thick, viscous mud. The burning vehicle lay on its side, slime-coated and demolished, but by the flickering light of flames leaping around it, I recognized it, and when I did my legs went as watery as the falling rain.

It was Carol Stedman's red Miata, the black cloth top torn nearly off and the red paint skinned from it. *Sam,* I thought, but I couldn't make my voice work, so I didn't say it aloud.

And anyway, Ellie knew. Hurling ourselves toward the car, we checked frantically through the open top for victims still inside the vehicle and found none; then came a voice nearby, faintly:

"No." With the word, grated out harshly as if by someone in pain, came scuffling noises.

"Give it to me, you—"

"Hey!" I charged at the sounds. Someone was *choking* someone. "Hey, cut it out!"

Beyond the car, in the flames' leaping glow—gasoline, I realized as the stink hit me, that's what was burning—a pair of figures struggled. The bottom one I couldn't see, only its long red nails flashing. Then one of those red-nailed fists connected.

The top one rolled back as if smacked by a two-by-four, its jaw slack with shock, and fell sprawlingly face-up. Bloodied nose and mud-smeared features hid his identity at first, but then . . .

"Harvey Spratt," snapped Ellie, coming up fast behind me. "You get up and start talking to us right this minute!"

She marched up to him, grabbed his hair, and gave it a yank that lifted Harvey as if by magic. "Owww!" he complained, but not from the hair pulling; a bone end stuck jaggedly through the hole in his pants, and he'd just noticed it.

"Ow, ow, ow . . ." Shock does funny things, I guess. But now that he'd seen his compound fracture, it held his attention.

Lizzie Snow hauled herself up irritably, shaking out the fist she'd just used as a battering ram against Harvey's jaw. "I didn't need those knuckles anyway," she groused, wincing.

She noticed Harvey. "Listen, you little—"

What she called him next made even his eyes widen. "Why're you out on a night like this, anyway?" she went on. "Guy like you should be holed up in a cave with the other snakes."

At the word "cave," his eyes widened anxiously. Seeing this, she stepped up to him, seized his shirtfront, and spoke straight into his face. "How'd you get that car? Where's its owner? Huh? You think your leg hurts now? How about if I—"

She drew her own foot back menacingly, like a kicker in a particularly nasty game of soccer. But just then a man I didn't recognize came jogging across the field at us; "tall, dark, and handsome" would've described him if he hadn't also looked ill and injured. Split lip, one arm in a sling . . .

"Okay, cops're coming, and an ambulance too," he said, a bit out of breath.

In fact, from what I could see of his face in the streaming darkness, he could've used an ambulance himself: ghost white, lips tightly clamped in what looked a lot like pain, a trickle of blood leaking from his nose. He swiped carelessly at it, just as a cop car screamed up the road and skidded to a halt behind mine.

Paulie Waters started across the muddy field toward us. "Ow," Harvey moaned again, and when he realized Paulie was there: "She hit me," he began whining. "She started it, I was only—"

"Shut up, Harvey," said Paulie with about as much concern as if Harvey had a hangnail.

I didn't want him to shut up, though. He knew where Sam was, I could practically feel it coming off him in poisonous waves, a secret that had somehow compelled him to steal the car, to race down a dark, wet road in it, to—

Paulie turned to Lizzie. "You haul him out?"

Of the burning vehicle, he meant. She shook her head. "No. The gas tank blew, the bang knocked me down. And when I came to, this ugly little critter was already on top of me, going through my vest."

Harvey scowled, hearing himself called "critter."

"But she clobbered him," Ellie put in admiringly.

"Yeah, well." Brushing this off, Lizzie glanced over at the smoldering wreck. "I guess we need a wrecker, some transport to custody for this creepster here, and I suppose he ought to get a look by a doctor, too."

She stopped short. "But you know all that, don't you? I'm kind of making a fool of myself trying to tell you how to do your job. So I should probably shut up."

Paulie looked at Lizzie, down at Harvey's now-subdued form, and over at the car's wreckage again. He stood thinking a moment, possibly about the fact that she'd meant to haul Harvey from the burning vehicle, if he was in it; that's why she'd approached it.

Harvey just hadn't been, was all. "Nah, don't shut up," Paulie said. "You might turn out to be worth listening to after all. You'll want to get that eye looked at, though."

He waved his flashlight at her; from the purple lump forming over her left eyebrow, Harvey must've clocked her a good one. She touched it curiously, winced, then turned to Ellie and me.

"What're you two doing out?" she wanted to know.

By then I could hardly contain myself. The whole thing burst out of me, including the part about this being Carol's car, and Carol being Sam's friend, and us not having seen Sam lately and being worried about him.

And how sure I was now that Harvey had something to do with it. But all the while, I knew they weren't going to do anything to Harvey to get the truth out of him: they couldn't. They were cops, I realized as I poured the rest of the story out; they had to obey the law. But I didn't, and by the end of it, I *couldn't* contain myself:

"You know, don't you? You know where he is." In reply Harvey just smirked at me, a look so snottily defiant, it tipped me over the edge. The others weren't expecting it, so when I hurled myself at him no one stopped me at first, not even Harvey himself.

But what I did next shocked even me. I slammed into him, smelling his sweat and blood. Grabbing his hair in my two fists, I shook his head so that his eyes rolled.

And then I *headbutted* him, so angry and scared when I did it that it didn't even hurt. "You know where Sam is. Carol, too, you took that car from her to get away from whatever you did to—"

My hands were around his throat. "Tell me!"

A keening sound was coming from him, high and breathy like the air escaping from a punctured inner tube. Around me, people kept shouting and grabbing at me, but I didn't care. "Tell me, you—"

Paulie dragged me off, finally, by seizing my shoulders and hauling me backwards while Harvey staggered and was grabbed by Lizzie again. Her captive sniffled resentfully while she spoke.

"You know, Paulie, I think I'll ride with these two ladies," she said, turning and giving Harvey a shove. Paulie caught him.

"Unless," she added, "you want to leave our pal here with me for a few minutes." She touched the knuckles of her punching hand with the fingertips of the other. "My fist's not broken . . . yet."

Because on her face in the glow of Paulie's flashlight I saw the same notion I was worrying: Harvey Spratt had gotten Carol's car somehow and I couldn't imagine Carol letting it go willingly.

Harvey looked nervous for a moment, but he knew Lizzie's threat was empty. His upper lip, even bloody and swollen as it was, curled triumphantly at me.

"Meanwhile, Dylan needs to see a doctor," she added sternly. "Make sure he does, please." Dylan, apparently, did not have a vote in this; Paulie either.

"Aye, aye, sir," the young cop said, yanking Harvey along by his collar.

After that, Lizzie strode with Ellie and me over the dark, muddy field, through the streaming ditch, and between the spruces whose boughs thrashed wildly

in the rising gale. At the road she ducked into her car
to turn the flashers off and grab her boots, and hurried to mine.

"Okay, now let's go find your kid," she said.

But only Harvey Spratt knew where Sam was, and
Harvey wasn't talking, so I didn't really see how we
could.

"Sam," said Carol.

She'd been crying, but now she'd stopped.

Sort of. "Sam, we're not going to make it, are we?"

"Cut it out. Of course we're going to make it."

Of course they were. He just had no idea how. Or
even how long they'd been here, tied up in a beach-
front cave with a storm howling outside and the tide
rising.

"Just let me catch my breath a little, and I'll go
down and try it again."

Try untying the knot binding her arms together, he
meant. To do so, he was using his teeth, clamping
them onto whatever part of the line he could get at,
then worrying and tugging at it like a dog playing
with a rope. The trouble was, doing it underwater
was difficult.

Because the tide kept rising, and each time a wave
broke over the sand ridge at the front of the cave,
more water slopped in; now the place where they sat
was three feet deep in ice-cold, intensely salty and
gritty seawater. He had to put his face under it to get
at the knot securing Carol's wrists, and of course he
couldn't hold his nose because his own hands were
also tied; thus the task was an exercise in gag-reflex

suppression plus not panicking while also feeling that he was drowning.

It was why he was resting now, just for another minute.

Or two. "Carol. What did you want from Harvey Spratt?"

Sam let his head loll back, hoping it might allow more air into his windpipe. He felt her shrugging beside him.

"Just . . . a little taste," she answered reluctantly. "Mostly he's had pills. Pot's too tame for him nowadays. But—"

"Taste? Of what?" But then he realized: "Heroin? Are you telling me you've been injecting, that Harvey's been selling . . ."

Shock silenced him. The pills were bad enough, but at least you knew what you were getting. But with heroin, it might be a hit of euphoria or a shot of cyanide, and you'd never know until it was too late.

"Don't be mad at me, Sam. I just wanted . . . I don't know. To feel better. I mean, I never got hooked or anything."

"Yeah." He understood. He'd said the same thing to himself many a time. "Yeah, okay."

She wasn't telling him everything, he knew from her voice. Another icy wave sloshed in, deepening the cold water they sat in by another half inch. He wondered once more what could possibly be so bad that she still had to hide it from him, then gave up on the thought.

Because it didn't matter, did it? Nothing did except getting free of these ropes, getting out of here before water filled this cave and they—

Drowned. Inch by inch, breath by gasping, struggling breath, until it rose up over their . . .

No. He took a deep breath of his own—*while you still can,* a voice in his head whispered thinly—then plunged his head down into the briny water again, resuming his fight to get out of this mess by, quite literally, the skin of his teeth.

But when his head was fully submerged, he heard something, a crackle-and-whoosh sound transmitted clearly through the water to his eardrums. Thrusting his head up, he blinked away the stinging salt water, hoping he was wrong.

He felt it, too, though, the dark, chilly liquid around him rising very suddenly, from his waist all the way to the middle of his chest in a single *swoosh.*

"Sam!" Carol cried. "What's happening?"

The tide must've washed the sand ridge out from in front of the cave, he realized, so now water could get in much faster. He told Carol this, that it was worse than they'd thought. That they didn't have hours in which to escape, as they had believed.

Half an hour, maybe. "At least we're not sitting here in the dark," he added, trying to find some good news to give her.

The penlight was still on, shining from where Harvey Spratt had tossed it onto the cave's highest rear ledge. *Thank God it's waterproof,* he thought; just the air in here was so damp a person could practically swim in it. And it seemed securely perched on that ledge . . .

But even as Sam thought this, a faint rattle sounded from back there, just the tiniest *click-click.*

No, he thought, but as the waves thundered nearer,

slamming the beach, their vibration made the pen-light perched on the edge of the ledge shiver. Shiver and . . . Sam turned in time to see the penlight start to roll. *Clickclickclick* . . .

"What's that?" Carol whispered.

But before she could finish her question, the pen-light fell, hit the water with a final-sounding *plop!* and sank, still shining all the way to the cave's sub-merged floor, where it lay still.

In its own reflected glow it resembled a tiny sub-marine, one lit-up porthole gleaming. But in the next moment another, larger wave rolled in and claimed it, washing it out toward the cave's mouth. Successive waves tugged it farther, each time rolling it a few inches back in toward them but then out again a little more, until at last its feeble glow thinned, dissolved, and in an awful moment vanished entirely, leaving them in the dark.

With Lizzie Snow and Ellie in the car, I drove cautiously up Key Street. Even as we neared home, all I could think of was getting back out again to find Sam, but Ellie looked blue with cold and Lizzie's teeth chattered, though she tried to hide it.

Through the downpours, my big old house looked like a ship on a wild sea. There were lights in only a few windows, and even those were unusually dim.

Now what? I thought, realizing that the houses all along our route home had been in similar shape. But once inside I caught on swiftly: of course the power was out. With the wind howling and the power lines along the causeway no doubt getting the brunt of it, it was a wonder we'd had electricity for this long.

We stripped wet clothes off and put on all the warm, dry sweatshirts and jeans that I could find, including sneakers for me and Ellie. Lizzie's feet, amazingly, were dry in her knee-high boots; what I'd been taking for expensive leather turned out to be amazingly good-looking and practical neoprene.

Wade was still out, said Bella, who pressed cups of hot, creamy-sweet coffee into our hands, while on the woodstove the kettle simmered and lanterns burned pleasantly on the fireplace mantel.

Bella asked no questions, but her big green eyes fixed me with a look of concern. Sam wasn't back. And she knew I couldn't stay home, not with him still out there somewhere in a gale.

And with, as no one else seemed to be realizing quite as clearly as I did, a murderer still on the loose. When we were warm enough to think straight again, Lizzie spoke:

"So you've called all around looking for him?"

I nodded.

"And the little red car we found wrecked belonged to a girl he's been seeing?" she followed up.

At my second nod, she looked thoughtful. "I first spotted the car on Water Street. It wasn't speeding at first but when the kid saw me behind him . . ."

"Maybe Harvey had just grabbed it?" Ellie suggested. Her wavy red hair had begun drying to ringlets around her face, which had gotten a bit of its color back.

Lizzie nodded slowly. "Maybe. Hadn't put the

pedal to the metal yet," she mused aloud. "Just got behind the wheel, still checking it out . . ."

She looked up. "So where around there d'you think the Spratt kid might've run into her? And Sam, too, if he was with her?"

But I didn't answer, being already halfway out the door with Ellie right behind me, and Lizzie, too.

Bob Arnold drove just as fast as he dared out Route 190 and across the causeway, gripping the wheel against storm-driven wind and noting the dangling power lines being flung about, writhing like angry snakes. At Route 1 he swung left onto the two-lane blacktop headed south, the road past his slapping wiper blades a black gleaming surface, as treacherous as hell.

No one else on the road, though. That was good luck, at least. He tried the radio again, finding only hissing static.

Still no comms, then, he realized, so not only could he not warn the Machias people about Hank Hansen, he couldn't even try to find out what kind of car Hansen was driving, or a possible plate number.

So he was screwed. *Blued and tattooed,* his mind added automatically. Nothing he could do but *keep driving, buddy.* Once he got to the courthouse, he would find Hank Hansen if he was able to, and stop him from doing whatever it was that he intended to do to Chip Hahn, Hank's daughter's accused murderer.

Also if he was able to. Bob let a blip of how *he* would feel if it had been *his* little girl slip in under his mental radar, saw his own hands clenching around the steering wheel.

But then as his squad car sped through Pembroke and over the Dennys River bridge, he calmed himself down. *Take it easy.*

Just get there. Find him, and stop him. Because . . .

But as the dark sky let loose with yet another terrifying downpour, flooding the roadway and his vision at the same scary time, he found for an awful instant that his heart was flooded, too, with brain-paralyzing rage. In that moment, while the tires hydroplaned slightly and the squad car drifted toward the ditch and the trees beyond, he found himself unable to come up with any reason why Hank Hansen *shouldn't* be allowed to kill Chip Hahn.

Just take him out. Out of this world, which would be better and a whole lot less complicated on account of the deed. But then as the deluge eased off and the tires caught traction, the ditch and the collision-inviting trees faded back into Bob's peripheral vision, and reason returned.

Because that's not for me to decide, is it? And I don't want it to be, either. Just—find him. Stop him, damn it—

Stop him because I swore to. Because—

He sighed, alone behind the wheel of the squad car, racing through a storm-torn night because . . .

He didn't know whether to be relieved or sorry. *Because it's my damned job.*

Lonnie Porter stood alone in the sheeting downpour outside the All Faith Chapel on Two Church

Lane, smoking a cigarette under his umbrella and watching yellow crime-scene tape fly around the lawn in the wind.

He was waiting for a truck to arrive. Up here against the church's big front door, the wind wasn't so bad, but if the truck didn't come soon he was going the hell home and to hell with the stupid steeple, he thought. Just then the truck finally did show up, though, all eighteen wheels' worth of it, barely making its way around the corner. On it was a crane, not a little bucket truck phone and cable companies used, either, but a monster of a full-sized industrial contraption.

With a wheezy shriek of its air brakes and a final exhaust-spewing rumble of its diesel engine, the truck came to a halt and a skinny man in rolled-down boots and a yellow slicker hopped out of the cab, pulling his ball cap's brim down sharply and peering from beneath it as he strode toward Lonnie.

The man's name was Terrel Carson. He owned the truck and the equipment on the flatbed that it was hauling. "Hope you know what you're doing!" he said.

"Ayuh. Me too." The wind snatched Lonnie's words away as he and Terrel squinted up at the church steeple.

"Can you get 'er up there?" Lonnie asked as a gust nearly knocked both men off their feet.

Terrel spat. "Ayuh."

He strode back to the big rig. Moments later the flatbed's rear tires were digging muddy ruts in the lawn, and moments after that, two enormous track-and-roller mechanisms were juddering down the flatbed's ramp.

Lonnie lit another smoke. He'd told Jake Tiptree he would try securing that steeple against the gale, so he was going to. But now that the machinery he'd summoned was here, he felt . . .

Well, he told himself, at least Terrel didn't seem nervous about it. He watched Terrel climb into the cab of the machine that had come off the flatbed and begin fiddling with the levers and knobs bristling from its dashboard. Taking a drag, he waited as Terrell maneuvered his machine right up alongside the chapel.

That way, the crane's long, hydraulically controlled arm could send the sky bucket up between the building and the row of white pines, fifty feet tall if they were an inch, along the lot line twenty yards distant.

Jeez, I'm glad I don't have to go up in that thing, Lonnie thought, eyeing the sky bucket, which basically really was just a bucket big enough for one man to climb into.

"Okay!" Terrel yelled from the crane's cab, waving at a cable that ended in the metal-stranded equivalent of a noose. You looped the noose end over whatever it was you wanted to pull on, tightened it via another hydraulic system from inside the cab.

"Okay, what?" Lonnie yelled back, unsure why Terrel hadn't come back down from his seat.

Terrel waved again, a *get-going* gesture with more than a little dose of impatience in it. If not for this chore, Terrel would no doubt be at home, drinking a beer.

Me too, thought Lonnie, not sure why Terrel wanted

him over by the sky bucket anyway. Shouldn't he be in the crane's cab by now, learning how to work the machinery?

But he slogged obediently through the mud to where Terrel's wave indicated, right by the three metal steps leading up to the bucket's doorway hatch.

Up! Terrel gestured sharply. Lonnie could see Terrel's hands on the controls now, too, and in the machine's dim-lit cab could see the intent look on Terrel's face.

Aw, no, Lonnie thought, wishing hard for another cigarette. But when his hand went reflexively to his pocket, he was out.

Me? He pointed at his chest. Terrel nodded, up and down very hard in a way that conveyed just what a fool Terrel thought Lonnie was being. Then Terrel yelled out the cab door.

"Christ, Lonnie, you coulda been down by now! Git yer ass in gear, will ya?"

Lonnie swallowed hard. It was clear what needed doing: that cable noose needed to get dropped down around the big weathervane mounted atop the steeple. Right over the tippy-top, it needed to go, and then fall down around the weathervane's base where it was fastened to the spire's peak with iron bolts. Lonnie had simply misunderstood who was going to do what, but now he did know.

Me, he thought very unhappily. Way up there in the sky with the wind, rain, and . . . He felt his shoulders sag. If he went, he would die, either by falling out of the sky bucket or just from sheer fright. But if he *didn't* go . . .

As if giving him a sign, the wind slackened off a bit.

Not a lot, but enough to keep this from being a suicide mission. Up in the cab, Terrel tapped his wristwatch meaningfully. *Let's get this show on the road.* Lonnie imagined the ribbing he would take if he wussied out. *The condemned man,* he thought bleakly as he patted his pocket once more, *didn't even get a last smoke.*

No doubt if anyone knew what he and Terrel were up to, this crazy-ass rescue mission would have the kibosh put on it. But no one else did know, and meanwhile, this was the church that his mother and dad had been married in and buried out of. A whole lot of other people in town felt the way he did about it, too, he was willing to bet.

That it belonged here. That *this is ours.*

That it should stay. But those people weren't here, and he was, was the long and short of it.

Resignedly, he climbed into the crane's sky bucket.

"I don't get it," said Lizzie as we raced through the storm toward Water Street. "What makes you think—"

"You don't get it because you're new here," I told her, "so you don't know Harvey Spratt. But if you *did* know him—"

I stopped talking; I needed all my wits to steer around the large hole that had just opened up directly in front of me. Water had apparently excavated a cavern beneath the pavement, and then the pavement had collapsed into it.

Hoping very sincerely that more wouldn't collapse right this minute, I got past it, then hit the gas and we swung around onto Water Street, which at the moment seemed aptly named. The few other cars out plowed through foot-deep waves, wipers flapping.

"Harvey Spratt is a pretty well known junior bad guy around here," Ellie explained. "Taking a car isn't that big a deal for him."

"Yeah, so I gathered." Lizzie said. "But what's that got to do with—"

"Well, what if the reason he ran when he saw you wasn't the car he was driving?" I said. "What if it was something else he'd done lately?"

"Something he'd *just* done," Ellie added clarifyingly. "Like maybe to Carol and Sam." The boat basin looked as if somebody was stirring it up with an eggbeater; big choppy waves were tossing boats around and spewing foam up onto the Coast Guard's dock. We sped uphill, then sharply to the right until we reached the old cannery building, its dark windows like rows of unseeing eyes.

"Yeah." Lizzie squinted out toward the bay and the whitecaps racing. "This is where the red Miata was when I first saw it."

I pulled over. "Oh, man. So now what?" I didn't know what Harvey might've had against Carol or Sam. All I knew was, he'd had her car, and—

"Okay, how about this?" said Lizzie. "Ellie, you go door to door to any houses nearby, see if anyone saw anything earlier."

There were half a dozen houses on this part of Water Street where people might've been looking out their windows. Ellie nodded as Lizzie went on:

"Ask if they saw Harvey and his crew, or Carol and

Sam together. Or any one of them individually, any time since early this afternoon."

We got out of the car, hunching against the weather. "And Jake and I will go down there," Lizzie finished.

She pointed at the cannery, and the heaving water beyond. Down on the beach, waves rolled up and hit the rocks with a sound like bombs going off distantly, hissing as they slid away for another onslaught.

"Okay!" Ellie shouted, turning away; then Lizzie and I began staggering together toward the empty cannery, whose roof was in the process of being stripped off.

"So why are we coming down here?" I yelled over the wind.

At low tide, the sheltered space beneath the wharf building offered a meeting spot for local kids, out of sight from parents, police, and other snoopy anti-teenager types. Now at nearly high tide, though, the beach under the wharf was flooded to a depth of fifteen or so feet.

"Just want to get a look, is all!" she yelled back.

Which I supposed we might as well. Who knew if Sam had even been here, or Carol either; it was only a guess on my part that had brought us here in the first place.

But if they had been, maybe some evidence of their presence would still be in the sand or in one of the caves above the rock-strewn waterline, blown there, maybe, or flung up by a big wave. There was another, much grimmer possibility, too, of course, but I didn't let myself think about that as we picked our way down the weedy trail leading to the wharf.

Once on the beach, we slogged along until we got

to a granite outcropping that thrust out into the sea, blocking our way. We'd seen nothing that suggested Sam or Carol had been here.

Lizzie shouted over the wind's shrieking: "He could still be inside somewhere, too, you know, just waiting this out!"

I nodded, turning back toward the cannery's huge, dark shape outlined against the breakwater's lights in the distance. She was right, Sam could be holed up waiting for the storm to slacken.

But he wouldn't be. He wasn't working; he knew Wade would be out and that his grandfather wasn't in great shape. He knew that without him, Bella and I might be alone with whatever the storm hurled at us.

He'd been a wild kid, a troubled teen, and a terrifyingly addicted young adult. But he was different now; he wouldn't have left me alone if he could help it. I had to believe that about him, that he'd changed; I had to, and I did.

Lizzie turned back toward the cannery building and the dock lights through the blowing rain behind it. I trudged behind her, trying hard not to let discouragement overwhelm me.

Anything could have happened to Sam, an accident, or Harvey Spratt could've done something to him after all, or—

Lizzie kept looking back, as if she didn't quite want to go. Then her hand came down hard on my arm. "Look."

She waved back toward the granite outcropping. I peered into the streaming murk. "What? I don't—"

But then I did see. Just this side of the outcropping,

the beach slanted sharply upward for a few feet, and through that up-slanting of sand the tide had washed a channel.

And in that channel, winking faintly but undeniably, was a tiny light. We hadn't seen it before because we were looking from the wrong angle.

But from here . . . we ran toward it, and when we reached it I thrust my hand down into the cold water and grabbed it.

"Oh," I said, clutching it.

It was Sam's Eastport Sailyard penlight.

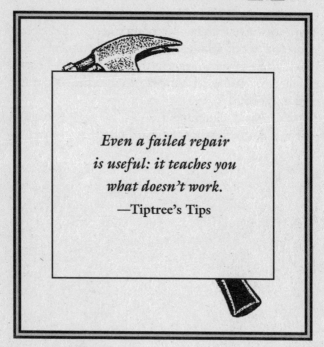

Chapter 14

*Even a failed repair
is useful: it teaches you
what doesn't work.*
—Tiptree's Tips

With Sam's penlight clutched in my cold, wet hand, I scanned the dark, storm-scoured beach for another sign of my missing son, just as another big wave rolled up and then out again, sucking the sand suddenly from beneath my shoes.

I staggered, caught my balance briefly, then went down hard. "Oof," I said, spitting sand and seaweed.

And then: "Hey, Lizzie?" Whispering, not quite yet believing what I'd seen. But there was no escaping it:

Not ten feet away from me yawned the opening of a cave in the cliffs rising up from the beach. The opening was as high as a standard interior house door and about twice as wide; I aimed the penlight into it, but just past the entrance the floor fell away fast so I couldn't see much, only a short stretch of its roof.

At the top of the beach where the bay didn't reach except at very high tide, ordinarily the cave was probably fairly dry, but it was flooded now from waves driven in by the storm. And the penlight had been lying submerged right in front of the opening . . .

"Lizzie," I said slowly, "d'you remember when you mentioned a cave in front of Harvey Spratt and he looked funny about it?"

I turned but couldn't find her in the darkness, then spotted her just to one side of the opening, stripping her boots off. Two minds with but a single thought and all that, I guessed.

"Hey," I yelled, but she didn't even look at me, just tossed the second boot aside, then spread her hands helplessly as if to say it was a cop thing and I wouldn't understand.

The wind yowled a banshee chorus as she plunged in.

Across town at the chapel whose steeple had been rendered so vulnerable by carpenter ants, Lonnie Porter was hearing the wind, too, and not liking it a bit, especially since while he heard it he was rising up into it, in the freight crane's sky bucket.

To steady himself, he recalled that this wasn't nearly as bad as the Groundhog Day Gale. That one took out all the downtown wharfs bing-bang-boom like dominoes falling. It was the biggest blow of his lifetime; he remembered the wild, almost apocalyptic-seeming storm meaning time off from school for him and his pals.

He remembered, too, being at the time still young enough to trust in the adults to take care of everything. And now it was his turn to be the adult; that was how it went here in Eastport.

He didn't know about anywhere else. Meanwhile, the crane here went on lifting him. He clamped his hands around the black rubber safety grips again, hearing the high, hydraulic whine of the crane's motor through the shriek of the wind, still buffeting the bucket: not quite catastrophically, but ferociously.

Oh, sweet mother of Jesus. Because ferocious was bad enough. As the bucket rose, the church's steeple slid by on one side, the wind-whipped branches of the white pines lining the churchyard dropping away on the other. Soon he could see the breakwater at the downtown end of the island, the dock lights running off the generators in the Coast Guard station shedding silver cones of rain-reflected illumination, and the freight terminal itself at the other end, its piers, warehouses, truck yards, and the vessels in its pair of massive berths all bathed in their own generator-fueled pinkish-yellow sodium glow.

Another massive gust made the sky bucket shudder; he caught his breath and clutched the safety handles so hard, he thought they might snap off. But instead the crane kept lifting him, the cable didn't snap, and the bucket did not flip upside down like a car on a thrill ride that he'd never buy a ticket for on purpose, not in a million years.

Now the church clock appeared, so close he could've reached out to touch it. Its pale white face leered immensely at him, its hands thrusting out from a center stem as thick as a small tree trunk and its numerals fastened on by bolts as big as his fists.

Finally came the spire, a narrowing cone atop that supported the weathervane itself. It looked much bigger from up here, with its arrowhead aimed away from him and its thick metal-feathered fletching vibrating only a few feet from his head. As the lift howled beneath him and the bucket juddered upward some more, he could feel sweat balls the size of atom bombs popping out of his forehead; then the bucket lurched and the centerpin began turning the boom slowly to his left.

Closer, closer . . . the boom halted. Now all that was left was to drop the cable's noose over the arrow-shaped ornament, then signal Terrel when to lower the cable.

Which Lonnie did, mentally prying his hands from the grips long enough to wave at Terrel. Then, working the cable controls expertly with both his big ham hands, Terrel lowered the noose as if it were a grappling hook that he was about to grab cargo with.

Down, down . . . that's it, Lonnie thought. *Now a hair to the left . . . more . . .*

A-a-nd done. Yes, Lonnie thought, exultant. At the base of the weathervane's stem were four eyebolts, holding the housing to the spire. Once the cable's noose was looped below them, Terrel would tighten it up hydraulically from below, and—

A stray gust hit the weathervane and turned it slightly just as the noose made its final approach. Half the noose fell down over the arrow end, just as planned.

But the other half . . . oh, the other half.

The other half stuck, resting on the metal fletching. And when Terrel tried to raise it again with the hydraulic lift . . .

Lonnie grabbed the safety grips again, trying not to hear Terrel's shout from the cab of the crane, far below.

"Hey, Lonnie! Climb out there a bit, wouldja? Just hang on to one a them grips—don't worry, you got your safety belt on. And just give that cable a tug!"

Oh, is that all? Lonnie looked upward, but no help from heaven was forthcoming as far as he could see. Only the storm was up there, dark clouds rolling and wind rumbling wickedly at him. The bucket shivered, and the boom lifting it shook like the stem of an old man's pipe, with a quick palsied quiver.

"Lonnie!" Terrel shouted. "Jeez, you wanna be up there all night?"

No, thought Lonnie, he most certainly didn't. In fact, Lonnie put that idea at the top of the list of things that he wanted to quit doing, pretty much instantly. But first . . .

The sad truth hit him: first, he was going to have to go out and settle that damned cable. Get one foot out on the bucket's step-in, reach out and lift the cable off the weathervane's metal fletching so it could drop down below the bolts on the housing.

Just do that. Afterwards Terrel would bring the bucket down and Lonnie would step out onto the good earth, bearing a story he could tell for the rest of his life, one people might tell about him even after he was dead. But first—

He stood up, his bones feeling rubbery and his gut clenched, and opened the bucket's door. He gripped the bucket's body, which was conveniently equipped with a bar for this very purpose, with his right hand, then put his left foot onto the corrugated steel step-in and settled it firmly there.

Finally with his left hand he reached out for the cable loop that needed settling, perhaps three feet away. It wasn't easy but it wasn't worth asking Terrel to shift the boom, either. It was— *Just do it. Just reach the hell out there and get it done. Because you are a man, and this here is Eastport, and stuff like this has to be handled here, sometimes.*

And you are who handles it.

He was looking at the blinking red safety light on the end of the crane's boom and thinking this when his foot slipped.

"Sam?"

They'd scooted back as far as they could, still tethered to the cave's iron bar with the plastic lines tied tightly around their wrists. But there wasn't anywhere else to go, and now the water was up to their chins.

He sucked in a breath. "Yeah?"

"I'm sorry."

He shrugged. " 'S'okay. Nothing to be sorry for."

"Why'd they do this, do you know?"

Harvey Spratt and his pals, she meant. "Something I said. You just showed up at the wrong time."

Silence from Carol, until: "Dark in here," she sighed.

The hopelessness in her voice broke his heart. Then . . .

Carol shrieked, and he nearly did, too, pulling his legs back reflexively as something brushed against his feet.

"*Gah!*" he managed, recoiling in horror.

There was something *in* the water with them.

Bob Arnold didn't know what it was about the big storm that was making the wildlife think getting out of the woods was a good idea; the fact that the wind seemed to be bringing it down around them branch by snapped-off enormous branch, maybe.

As a result, by the time he reached Machias in the squad car the score in this round of roadkill derby was two skunks, a raccoon, and a near miss on a black bear bumbling down the highway, straddling the center line.

In the rearview, the animal still ambled along unfazed; Bob thought Mr. Bear was fated very soon to become a blanket, a hat, and two pairs of enormously black-clawed slippers. But he couldn't do anything about it.

Crossing the causeway in Machias, he tapped the gas pedal again, driving as fast as he dared and hoping he was wrong, but knowing he wasn't. Hank Hansen was sitting right now somewhere very near the courthouse, waiting for Chip Hahn to be brought out.

Knowing he would be. All Hank had to do was stay watchful and then shoot, which Hank, a long-time poacher of anything with fur or feathers, was also well able to accomplish.

Bob started up Court Street through yet another storm squall, with his car nearly lifting off its tires in the rainy onslaught. Halfway to the top of the hill, he spotted a state police van and the flashlight of a transport officer clearing the street.

So they must be getting ready to bring Chip Hahn outside, to take him to—

Without warning, a huge limb on one of the ancient maples lining the street gave way with an enormous snap-*crack!* and came down massively right in front of him, bouncing as it landed and missing the squad car's front bumper by inches. Right away, though, a couple of guys coming the other way in a pickup truck stopped, and pretty soon the three of them had the street cleared.

Drenched, Bob got back in and hit the gas again. But there was no way to hurry very much here as cars and people around the official buildings trundled along, trying despite the storm to deal with whatever unhappy business had brought them. He made his way slowly through them, meanwhile scanning the vehicles parked along the street: their windshields, their passenger windows, the people waiting behind the wheel as if in hopes of a possible fast getaway. Because in one of those vehicles . . .

There. A cracked-open driver's-side window facing the front steps of the courthouse drew his attention.

In the rain, he could not see much inside the vehicle. But why would it be open at all?

At the same time, he took in the movement in the courthouse just beyond the brightly lit glass front doors. Officers, he saw, a whole group of them and in the center of the group was—

The driver's-side window of the car he'd been watching slid down a little more. *No!* Bob thought, but he was still half a block distant, not close enough to do anything about it, and the squad car's radio still wasn't working.

The big courthouse doors opened. The transport officers came through, one signaling the van's driver, the other looking back over his shoulder. A cluster of pedestrians, blinded by their own umbrellas and battling the rain and wind, stepped out in front of Bob, forcing him to slam the brakes on.

No, no, no . . . One hand on the horn, he drove slowly forward again, but now just as he considered jumping out of the car and running, he spotted something—no, *someone*—else.

It was Dylan Hudson, the state cop supervisor who'd come out with the investigating team working on the Hansen girl's murder. He was getting out of an Eastport squad car that Bob had last seen parked out in front of the police station back in town. And then—

Then, judging by the look of horror that appeared on his face, Hudson seemed to see the same thing Bob did: a rifle barrel sliding out of the rolled-down car window a dozen yards away from him. A single look toward where the rifle was pointing must've told him the rest.

"Gun!" Hudson shouted, and in the next instant was in firing position, feet planted, weapon double-handed out in front of him.

"Put down the weapon!" he shouted.

Bob kept driving. Fifty yards, twenty . . . in a trick gleam of streetlight he caught a glimpse of Hansen's face behind the car's windshield, eyes wide and teeth bared in desperate ferocity. The rifle barrel in the car window slid minutely in Hudson's direction.

In the next very few fractions of a second, Hudson was going to kill or be killed. There was no other answer possible. Bob hit the gas, heard the engine cough, glanced at the dashboard gauges.

Empty, read the one with the gas icon next to it. *Oh, holy mother of . . . come on, baby,* he entreated the fuel-starved vehicle. And when against all odds it responded—

Bam. He punched the accelerator. The car shot forward. He pounded the horn hard and he aimed the car straight into where the crossfire would be, if any occurred.

With Hansen to his left, Hudson to his right, and up on the courthouse steps all those transport officers now scrambling in confusion, not knowing against what, Bob felt his heart pounding crazily in his chest and thought of that storm-addled bear, whose mind-set he now felt he understood much more clearly. And as all this happened, he kept driving, waiting until he was almost upon both Hudson and the car Hank Hansen waited in. And then—

Then he yanked the steering wheel *hard*.

* * *

She came up in a stale air pocket, pitch dark and reeking of terror. A *small* air pocket . . . "Police. I'm here to help."

No sense wasting words. Sam Tiptree sat tied and tethered. The girl with him wept.

"Okay. Sit tight. I'm going to cut you loose."

The water around them rose higher. Lizzie cursed mentally, but there was no point clueing these folks in to the fact that she was a little nervous herself, was there?

"Once I do get you freed, you're both going to have to go underwater."

The girl made a sound of despair, but Lizzie wasn't having any of that. What little air remained in here was getting staler by the minute. "Stop. I mean it. You're doing great, okay?"

Sam said something. "What?" Lizzie demanded. Thinking, *We're wasting time.*

"Get Carol out first," he gasped raggedly again.

"Ah, no. You first, without me. I'm going to help her. Don't argue, just when you feel the rope slack off at all, you go."

She pulled out her jackknife, the one Liam had given her because you never know, he'd said, you might need one someday. Plunging her hands into the ice-cold water, she found the thick plastic line wrapped around Sam's wrists and began sawing at it.

And sawing some more.

"Comms are back up!" someone yelled from one of the offices upstairs in the courthouse. "Phones, radio, computers, all working again!"

A muted cheer went up. Chip looked around from the cast-iron-grated counter where he'd been about to sign a receipt for his belongings, which were handed to him in a large brown manila envelope. He'd just finished sorting hurriedly through the things and popped the ballpoint the pleasant gray-haired woman behind the counter lent him when the shout came. Now as he looked back down to complete his signature, he realized what he hadn't seen.

Or rather, whom: Osbourne was gone. The state cop who'd questioned him, sat with him, brought him drinks and a sandwich . . . he'd told Chip that Chip was free to go, that someone else was in custody now for the crime Chip had been suspected of doing.

And now Chip didn't see Osbourne anywhere. Not only that, but in the hour or so it had taken to get Chip's release processed and accomplished, all of the other state cops had departed, too.

"Thanks," he told the clerk in the window, hoping his voice didn't sound as tremulous as it felt. The courthouse was closing, people only now locking their offices and leaving for home even though it was way past five.

A lot of people had stayed late tonight, probably on account of him. Now that was all over, though; he still couldn't quite believe it. He turned back to the window.

"Um, is there, I don't know, a taxi service I can call or something?"

The clerk looked up kindly at him. "Oh, my. Not in this bad storm, dear."

Then from behind him a familiar voice spoke. "I'll take you anywhere you want to go, Chip."

Carolyn . . . He turned, disbelieving. But there she stood, her long dark hair wet and windblown, her slender figure wrapped in a navy peacoat of his, miles too big for her.

In the next moment, she was in his arms. "Carolyn . . ." Her hair smelled of chamomile, her skin of some exotically scented lotion or other. He held her away from him, scrutinizing her.

Thin, pale . . . but all right. Not sick, or wasted away from a diet of whatever it was she ate—or didn't eat—when he wasn't around. "But . . . how did you get here? How did you even . . . ?"

Her huge blue eyes, heavily outlined and lash-thickened, regarded him gravely. And—were those tears sparkling in them?

"I'm a neurotic, Chip, not an invalid. And when you stopped calling me every twenty minutes to check up on me—"

He bowed his head, embarrassed. She was right.

"—I got worried, and called Jake Tiptree's house. And her housekeeper told me about you. So—"

She smiled winsomely. "I got in the car, and here I am."

He couldn't speak, only smile. Over Carolyn's shoulder, the clerk smiled, too.

The lights in the courtroom offices began to go out. There had been some kind of commotion outside earlier, but he didn't know what. And at the moment, he didn't care.

She was parked just across the street; they ran through a downpour to get to her car.

"Why'd they let you go, anyway?" she wanted to know as, still wondering if he should pinch himself, he settled behind the wheel; she'd been driving long enough.

"I'm not sure. Maybe someone else confessed? They said some other suspect was in custody, but I don't know any more about it than that, only that they dropped me like a hot rock."

The storm was slacking off, but the streets were full of debris: branches, shingles, strips of vinyl and aluminum siding, God knew what else. He steered carefully around the stuff.

"Really." She turned eagerly to him, her huge blue eyes full of speculative interest. "Someone confessed, huh? So d'you think there's a book in it?"

He laughed in spite of himself, thinking of the long, dark road between here and Eastport. "If there is, somebody else will have to write it. Living it's been enough."

She sat back. "Huh. You're no fun at all." But her voice was affectionate; if he hadn't been driving, he'd have hugged her again. Then: "Chip?"

"Yeah." Across Route 1 was a pleasant-looking motel with a parking lot in front of it. The motel's Vacancy sign was lit, and so were the lights in Helen's Restaurant, right next door.

"I'm glad you're okay," said Carolyn. "I missed you. Truth is, I just don't do very well without you," she said.

"Me either. Without you, I mean." Thinking, *I'm never going to tell her what I did. Not her or anyone else.*

"You ever call Maury Cahill?" The lawyer she'd told him she wanted to talk to, he meant; though the conversation was only forty-eight hours ago, it felt like years.

Carolyn nodded. "Yes. A friend of Siobhan's needed him."

Of her editor's, she meant. She turned to him. "I called him again just before I left the city, too, to tell him about what was going on and that we might be needing him."

"Uh-huh," he said, thinking. *She'd cared!* And not only that, he realized, but she had *done something useful about it!* Maybe she wasn't as helpless as he'd thought she was.

Or maybe not helpless at all. "Funny thing was, he already knew, and he was getting ready to come up here himself. Because he tried calling you back, but of course you weren't there and instead he talked to the same housekeeper I did."

Good old Bella, thought Chip affectionately, imagining what the proper old Manhattan attorney Maury Cahill and Bella Diamond must've sounded like, having a conversation. He hoped Maury was not still trying to make it here through the storm.

But no; if he knew Maury, the lawyer was tucked up in a good hotel in Boston or Providence, having a martini and a good steak very rare, while he waited out the weather.

"We'll call him again, then," Chip said. "And the Tiptrees in Eastport, too. We'll tell them all everything's all right."

Which it was; completely all right, he thought with an inward sigh so deep, he thought briefly that he might just burst into tears. But then the traffic cleared and he crossed Route 1, instead, into the parking lot that served the motel and eatery.

When she realized his intention, Carolyn nodded approval and angled her head toward the back seat. "I brought clothes for you. Shaving stuff and so on. Just in case. I mean, I didn't know what might be happening, so—"

Which to him was the most unexpected thing, that she had thought so much ahead about all of it. She wasn't very much of a planner, and not for other people, especially.

But maybe she still had surprises for him, he thought, just as he'd had in the last few days for himself. Through the car's barely open window, a whiff of some delicious cooking aroma from the restaurant reached him. He was starving, he realized.

A decent meal, a hot shower, and a soft, warm bed—he could call Eastport from there, he thought, let them know he was all right. And he could find out tomorrow just what all had gone on to get him un-accused, freed from the charge of bloody murder.

Tomorrow. It would be okay—even more than okay, now that Carolyn was here—and it would be soon enough.

"Come on," he told her, noticing her sniffing with interest at the good smells now, too. "Come on, let's go in."

First Carol emerged, and then Sam's wet head popped up out of the flooded cavern. In the next instant, he was slogging across the rocks toward us, his face slack with shock, a tail of orange buoy-line trailing from his right wrist.

When he reached us, he dropped to a patch of sand and lay there, gasping and gagging, trying to get his breath.

"Ellie!" I yelled, but she was already on it, sprinting away toward where there would be a phone, people, some kind of . . .

"Help," Carol whispered, looking back fearfully. "Someone, somebody's got to help her, she's—"

From the water there, a hand thrust up. Red-tipped nails, fingers clutching . . . reaching.

Then the hand went limp, falling back. "Stuck," Carol wept, "the rope was all tangled in there, I think she might be—"

"Stay here." I sprinted to the cavern's submerged opening, reached in, and found Lizzie Snow's hand. It clamped hard around mine, but I could feel it spasming. Weakening . . .

Sam was already crawling to me. On all fours, his head with its dark curly hair moving slowly from side to side like a sick animal's. When he got to me, Lizzie's hand had begun loosening.

"Get away." He shoved me aside, his face twisted with fury. Whatever had happened, he was not going to let it end like this.

He just wasn't. "When I kick, you're going to pull me. You got that?"

He snarled it at me, and the next thing I knew, the whole top half of his body was underwater again. His right leg kicked a demand at me; I seized his foot, and then the other one, braced my feet on a granite outcropping and pulled. With the effort a yell burst out of me, a shriek.

A *howl*. But nothing happened. He kicked again: no result, though I hauled on him with every muscle I had. Then suddenly he was flying out of there, hurtling backwards at me, Lizzie's hands clutched in his own.

I flew backwards, too, hit my head on something hard, and saw high above me in the clouds and rain a whole skyful of whirling stars, plus one red one winking steadily from what looked like, but of course could not possibly be, the lofty tip of the arrow-shaped weathervane atop the All Faith Chapel, all the way across town on Two Church Lane.

It took me a week to get out of the hospital; turns out a granite boulder is even harder than my head. By that time, Chip and Carolyn had gone home to Manhattan. Carol Stedman, too, had packed up her belongings and lit out for parts unknown, driving a new car that nobody around here knew how she'd managed to buy.

But then, no one really knew much about Carol. "So, just let me get this straight," said my husband, Wade Sorenson.

We sat outside on the porch swing; it was a freakishly warm evening, for late November.

"This girl, Karen Hansen, was down on the breakwater with Harvey Spratt, trying to get money from him. And while she was with him, she found out he'd been selling—"

"Right. Heroin. Like downeast Maine needs more hard drugs," I said in disgust. "And for Harvey that'd be a big deal."

Because he'd already been through drug court once, it turned out. And now that he wasn't a juvenile anymore, a big-boy-sized prison term for selling hard drugs was almost a certainty for him if he got caught.

"So he made a bet with her, that she couldn't go up into the belfry and shine a light out of it. If she did, she'd get cash."

"Right again," I replied. "That's what he told her, that he would finance her getaway out of Eastport."

"But what Spratt really wanted was to get her alone in a place where he thought her body wouldn't be found?" Wade asked. "Or not for a long time, anyway?"

With us on the porch was Lizzie Snow, looking chipper after recovering from her near drowning. "Um, not exactly," she said. "He sent Bogie to find him a knife, one that no one would connect with him or any of his gang."

Wade had been working at the freight terminal nearly nonstop for the past two weeks, helping to clean up after the havoc the storm had wreaked on shipping all along the eastern seaboard.

So he needed updating. "Meanwhile, Bogie's dad—"

Wade nodded. "Was in my shop that day," he finished for her. Up in the ell of our old house, he meant, where he repaired guns, including the one Bogie's dad used for deer hunting.

"Where he must've seen my big knife," Wade added. "And said something about it to Bogie?"

"More like threatened him with it," Lizzie said. "I gather Mr. Kopmeir was big on threatening his son."

She sipped her coffee. Bella had cooked an amazing dinner of fried bay shrimp, fish chowder, and a salad of mixed greens out of Ellie's cold frame.

"Bogie says his dad told him he knew just where to get a great big one to use on him if Bogie screwed up again. And to make the threat believable, he said where the knife was."

"So that's how Bogie knew. But . . . he broke into my shop? And I didn't realize it?" Wade sounded skeptical.

"Yeah. Turns out he can pick locks, among his other stellar talents. Kid's got a great future," Lizzie said. "If by 'future' you mean in a federal prison."

Bogie, it turned out after Bob Arnold had questioned him thoroughly, was behind a string of burglaries so expert, most of the victims didn't even know they'd been hit until Bob told them, while he was in the process returning whatever stolen goods Bogie hadn't already ruined or sold.

"The thing is," Lizzie added, "there's been a twist in the tale. Because Harvey confessed to the murder, but . . ."

"Uh-huh." Wade nodded again, slowly. "But Bogie would do anything for him. And I'll bet the twist is that Bogie did it, isn't it?" He looked at Lizzie for confirmation of his hunch. "Got the knife for Harvey, but when the time came, Harvey sent Bogie to do the chore, instead. To . . . what? Scare her with it?"

"Um. Not exactly." Lizzie said it quietly. "Harvey sent Bogie to scare Karen, that's for sure. And told him to take the knife. But it was never in Harvey's plan that Bogie would kill her."

"Then why did he?" Wade wanted to know. "If he didn't have to, why do something so over-the-top that it would be sure to—"

"Get him in terrible trouble if he was caught?" Lizzie nodded. "When he could've just threatened her, waved the knife at her and told her to keep her mouth shut, knowing that with a young girl like her it would be enough?"

"Right," Wade responded, "and it seems as if she was getting out of town soon anyway, so she wouldn't even be around to—"

"Right, to tattle on Harvey. But once he got up in that belfry with her, Bogie wasn't thinking about that. Or thinking at all, really. Because—"

"She did something to him," I guessed aloud. "Scratched him, bit him . . . something that made him mad. And . . ."

"Bingo." Lizzie turned to me. "She had a lighter, a little plastic cigarette lighter with her. And even after he had her tied and blindfolded, she managed to burn him with it. Which made him lose his temper, and . . . well. We know what happens when Bogie loses his temper. Or we do now, anyway."

She sighed, looking sad. "She had nerve, that girl. I'll bet she'd have made it to New York, maybe even have survived there."

Yeah. But instead, she hadn't survived Eastport. And in a way, Bogie Kopmeir hadn't, either.

"But," Wade objected, "then why did Harvey confess?"

Lizzie made a soft noise of disgust. "Yeah. Well, it

turns out there was a problem with that confession," she replied, and was about to say more but just then Sam came out onto the porch.

He'd told us about Bogie's beating of David Thompson, the kid he'd pounded to within an inch of his life down on the beach when David tried to stop the attack on Sam and Carol.

Sam hadn't seen the other kid from Harvey's gang intervening in the fight, or witnessed Bogie cutting the other kid's throat, again in a frenzy of temper. Like David, at the last minute the other kid had objected, too, it seemed, to the notion of leaving Carol and Sam in the cave to drown.

David would survive, but the other kid had gotten killed for his trouble. "Hey, you guys, come and see," Sam told us now, "Harvey Spratt's on the evening news."

"Uh-uh. You go watch with Maggie," I said. I'd had enough of Harvey for a while; possibly forever.

"They're back together?" Wade asked when Sam went in again.

Maggie hadn't been here for dinner, and when she arrived Wade had been showing Lizzie how to load and fire a black-powder rifle, whatever that was; I'd long since given up trying to stay current with Wade's firearms expertise.

"Mm-hmm. Don't ask me why," I told him, "but she's decided to give Sam another chance." The boatyard had, too, for which I was deeply grateful.

Wade nodded bemusedly, then went back to questioning Lizzie. "So when Sam got to the beach, Harvey thought Sam knew Bogie had killed the girl? But why—?"

"Why go to such lengths to protect Bogie?" Lizzie asked. "A good question. But think: if Bogie's in trouble, whose drug deeds does he talk about to try getting leniency for himself?"

"Oh, I get it," replied Wade, satisfied. "So now Harvey had to protect Bogie to keep himself out of trouble. Or that's what he believed, anyway."

"Yep. Don't worry, it wasn't a case of honor among thieves or any nonsense like that." Lizzie got up.

"Hey, thanks for dinner. But I've go to go now. I want to get on the road before it gets too awfully late."

I got up, too, in surprise. Inside, Bella was doing dishes; after that she'd said she meant to head on up to bed. But I knew she just wanted to sit with my father, who wasn't feeling well.

Soon, I realized with a hard pulse of sorrow. *Soon he'll be gone. We all will be, and other people will live in our houses.*

I looked at Lizzie. "You're leaving? But I thought—"

She laughed, running a red-tipped hand over her spiky hair. "That I was going to be the police chief here? Yeah, Paulie Waters told me about that rumor going around. Maybe," she added, "because he felt bad about being the one who started it. But it's just a rumor; Bob's not quitting. Not that I know of, anyway."

She followed me inside to the dining room, where I handed her an envelope. "Well, whatever your plans are, Ellie's been doing some detective work for you."

In the envelope were slips of paper with names and addresses on them, and some with phone numbers.

"These are folks who might know something about your niece now," I said.

The addresses were in a town called Allagash, way up north in Aroostook County. From what Ellie had been able to glean, the baby might've been taken there—by whom, nobody recalled for sure—after Lizzie's sister died.

Lizzie stared at the papers. "How did you know?"

On the hearth, the fire hit a pocket of pine sap and blazed up, sending sparks flying. "Know?" I asked, puzzled. "Know what?"

She tucked the papers into her purse. "When I said I wasn't taking Bob Arnold's job . . . well. I didn't say where I *am* going."

I walked with her to the back door.

"There's some personnel problem in Aroostook County, in the sheriff's department," she said. "They'll be needing a deputy."

"So you're—?"

She nodded. "Bob Arnold told me about it and I had my résumé and records faxed up, and I guess they're desperate, because . . ."

"Wow." Not so much desperate, maybe, as wanting someone who wasn't already a part of whatever problem they were having.

"Yeah," she said. "Pending an interview, I'm in. Pretty sudden, but I'll give it a try, I guess. We'll see how it goes."

For them, and for her, because if she thought Eastport was the back of beyond, she'd think the County was the far side of the moon, and the tiny town of Allagash itself was just a little crossroads plus a couple of houses and more trees than you could shake a stick at.

We stepped out onto the porch. The night was clear, the air scented with salt and woodsmoke. She sniffed appreciatively.

"Guess I'd better get used to peace and quiet," she admitted. "Listen, about Chip Hahn—"

I glanced back into the house; Sam and Maggie were in the front parlor, where she was teaching him to play the spoons, or trying. As a musician, he made a very capable audience member.

But Maggie had a big heart, fortunately. "What about him?" I asked, but I knew.

Of course Lizzie Snow would've thought of it; why hadn't Chip just said where he was the night of the murder, instead of lying about it?

"He was sleeping with her, wasn't he?" Lizzie asked. "Chip was, I mean, with that other girl. The one who took off, Carol with the red car? Or . . . maybe he was only with her just the once, the night of the murder?"

Carol Stedman, Lizzie meant, and it was what I thought, too. He could have run into her while he was out walking that night; it was why he might've wanted to hide where he'd been, and if anyone could lure someone into a car and seduce them, it was that little . . .

Well. She was an attractive young woman, is all I'm saying.

"Yeah. I think so, too," I told Lizzie. "But if he'd said so . . ."

I tipped my head toward the parlor. "Chip and Sam have been friends for a long time," I finished.

She nodded, understanding. "Right. Well, wish me luck."

With that, she went down the front steps, hopped into her car, and drove away, and it wasn't until her CRV's taillights disappeared that I realized: I'd forgotten to thank her.

But then, she probably wouldn't have wanted me to.

I went inside and turned out the porch light.

Lizzie saw the blinking red light on the top of the church tower as she bundled her bags into her car. The motel's parking lot was dark; she didn't notice Dylan until she'd reached the car again.

"Hey." She hadn't spoken with him since the night he'd nearly shot Hank Hansen across from the courthouse in Machias, just before Bob Arnold ran his squad car into Hansen's vehicle.

Now she stopped at the driver's-side door of her CRV, key in hand. "Hey, yourself. What're you doing here?"

He shrugged. "I'd stopped in to see Bob Arnold. He said you were leaving town. Just wanted to say so long."

"Oh. Well, so long, then." It looked like his shoulder was healed, or at least he wasn't wearing a sling anymore. She got in and settled behind the wheel.

What she'd felt for him was like another country, too far off now to visit casually. He crouched at the car window. "Funny about that other kid."

"Who, David Thompson?" The kid in the athletic jacket, Dylan meant, that Bogie Kopmeir had nearly beaten to death.

The kid was still recovering in the hospital. "I get why the kid hung out with Bogie," Dylan went on.

When he woke up, the victim had explained about the bullying he'd endured, and that Bogie Kopmeir had protected him. "But why would Bogie do anything to help a kid like David?"

"Isn't it obvious?" Lizzie answered. "Bogie wanted to be like Harvey Spratt, and Harvey had followers. I'm guessing that Bogie was starting to put together a crew of his own."

Dylan nodded thoughtfully. "Yeah, you could be right." Then: "Long drive tonight."

His turn to be right. "Five hours, maybe." To Fort Kent, up in what Mainers called the state's rooftop, nearly in Canada. She wondered what the hell she would do when she got there.

Because hiring a stranger who didn't know the territory for deputy work just didn't make sense. The sheriff up there had some other plan he wanted her to be a part of, she felt certain; he just hadn't told anyone what it was yet.

Not even Lizzie. But she supposed she'd find out, and Nicki might be there, so—

Oh, the hell with it. She wanted an answer: "How'd you get that kid's confession so messed up, Dylan?"

Because after she'd left them at the accident scene, Dylan had somehow gotten Harvey Spratt to say he'd killed the girl, that he had slit her poor throat with a hunting knife that Bogie Kopmeir stole. But the confession Harvey Spratt had made wasn't true, and what Lizzie wanted to know was . . .

Dylan shrugged again. "Told him he was dying. That I'd seen it dozens of times, guy walks away from an accident, feels okay, then he checks out from internal bleeding."

Ohh, she thought, understanding washing over her.

"Kid had a Saint Christopher medal on a chain, I figured maybe his family was religious and he might have remnants of it, too, in that hideous little psyche of his," he said.

"Uh-huh." You could lie to them while questioning them, she knew. She'd never done it, but it was legal.

Harsh, though. Risky, too, as they'd found out. "And?"

"And after I told him his nosebleed was the first sign of a ruptured heart artery, and did he want to die with the girl's death on his conscience, he started blubbering, begging for a doctor and a priest in that order, the chickenshit little prick."

"I see." She kept her voice neutral; hey, it could've worked and it might have, if Harvey had been guilty. Instead he'd broken down and said whatever his questioner wanted to hear, because as it turned out Harvey Spratt hadn't been exactly psychologically sturdy: surprise, surprise.

"So sue me," Dylan finished unworriedly. "Truth came out in the wash anyway, once he really started talking."

Confessions convinced people, but they weren't always true. Hard to believe, especially for juries, but there it was.

"And then you hopped in a car, drove to Machias because—"

Dylan made a face, as if this part must be obvious. "All the comms were out, remember? No phones, no radio, so I grabbed the keys to one of the squad cars from a desk drawer at the police station—"

Where Bob Arnold's office was, he meant, and God, were there really still places where the motor pool keys weren't all locked up and you had to practically sign your life away to get hold of them?

Apparently there were. "—so I could tell 'em that Hahn kid didn't do it. Or that peeping thing, either, by the way; turns out the charge on that got dismissed. Bogus accusation. This guy Hahn was writing a crime book about got ticked off; Hahn wasn't even in New Hampshire when it supposedly happened, which in court the guy finally admitted that it didn't. Happen, I mean."

Sheesh, thought Lizzie; for something that was supposed to help people, the system sure had plenty of ways to screw you.

"I mean, what the hell, no sense him getting jammed up even more, right?" Dylan finished.

Yeah, right. Besides, getting Chip Hahn off the hook might earn him a few brownie points with her, Lizzie thought acutely. Still, Dylan had done it: a certifiable good deed.

"And therein," he frowned, "lies another tale."

"No kidding." Because if Bob Arnold hadn't shown up when *he* did, Dylan would have blown Hank Hansen's fool head off; that, or the other way around. After that, Hansen might have shot the Hahn kid, maybe other people, too.

But instead none of that had occurred. And, luckily, Bob hadn't suffered any injuries in the car crash he'd had to have in order to prevent it. Lucky for everyone, but . . .

A new thought struck her. "What made the church bell ring? Jake Tiptree told me it did, back when this all started. But does anyone know why?"

Dylan laughed without humor. "Tower was collapsing, is why. Bob Arnold says now that it's stabilized they've found so much rot and insect damage it's a wonder it didn't fall years ago."

"So . . . you mean it shifted? Like, enough to—"

He nodded, gazing uphill to where the crane's red light blinked rhythmically. "Can't see it with the naked eye, but one whole side of that belfry is nearly a foot lower than the other. When it sank, it put the bell off-balance, started it ringing."

He leaned down to the window opening. "Guy who finally got the crane hooked to it's got a hell of a story to tell down at the diner, though, I'll say that much. I heard his foot slipped while he was up there that night and he nearly . . ."

A new thought appeared to strike him. "Have you had dinner?"

"Yes. And anyway I wouldn't be having it with—"

He tipped his head persuasively, his smile so charming and guile-free, she could almost believe he was harmless.

Almost. "Listen, if it weren't for me, you wouldn't be hot on the trail again after all this time, and I can still help you find Nicki, you know."

She hesitated. He was right: he had gotten her here. And he could help; for one thing, knowing someone with the state cops wouldn't hurt her a bit, she guessed, once she got all the way up to Allagash, where she knew no one.

Besides, she'd skipped dessert. And the truth was . . .

The truth was that she didn't really know what the truth was now. A place like this, all water and sky with the island a small hard rock in the middle of it, could make you wonder which of the things you'd thought you knew were really true, and which were just the ones other people had told you.

And right this minute might be as good a time as any to start finding out. The red light atop the distant church spire pulsed on-off-on again, regular as a heartbeat.

"Get in," she said.

If you enjoyed *A Bat in the Belfry*,
read on for a preview of

Winter at the Door

the first in a thrilling new mystery series
by Sarah Graves!

Carl Bogart's old Fleetwood double-wide mobile home stood on a cleared half acre surrounded by a forest of mixed hardwoods, spruce, and hackmatack trees shedding their dark-gold needles onto the unpaved driveway.

It was late October. From the black rubberized roof at the mobile home's kitchen end protruded a sheet metal stovepipe topped by a screened metal spark guard and a cone-shaped sheet metal rain cap.

No smoke came from the stovepipe. Cody Chevrier pulled the white Blazer with the Aroostook County Sheriff's Department decal stenciled on its door up alongside the double-wide and parked. Bogart's truck, an old green Ford F-150 pickup, was backed halfway into the lean-to shed that stood at right angles to the trailer.

A day's worth of fallen hackmatack needles veiled the truck's windshield. Cody got out, his door-slam loud in the clearing's silence.

"Hey, Carl?" Half a cord of white maple logs chain-sawed to stove length lay in a mess of wood chips with Carl's splitting axe stuck in the chopping block at the center of them, as if he'd just gone inside for a drink of water or something.

"Carl?" At midmorning, frost still glazed the fallen leaves lying in coppery drifts in the trailer's shade, the day clear and cold now after a night that had gotten down into the twenties. There were no marks in the rime under the trailer's windows that Cody could see.

Besides the pickup truck, Carl's shed held a shotgun-shell reloading press bolted to a massively overbuilt wooden workbench, the bench's legs fastened through big galvanized angle irons to a pair of old railroad ties set parallel into the shed's poured concrete floor. Seeing this reminded Cody that it was about time for him and Carl to start thinking about lugging the shell press indoors for winter. Turning slowly, he regarded the double-wide again.

Around it, long grass lay flattened by the deer who used the clearing as a sleeping yard; Carl didn't hunt anymore himself, just reloaded the shotgun shells for others. No tire tracks were on the grass, and the hackmatack needles on the driveway had already been disturbed by Cody's own vehicle, as well as by the breeze that had sprung up at dawn.

So: no sign that anyone else had been here recently, Cody thought, unable to keep his mind from running that way even with no real evidence yet of anything amiss.

A red squirrel scampered up the steps to the double-wide's screened porch—from May through September, the mosquitoes here could stand flat-footed and look right over the house at you, and the blackflies were worse—then reversed itself in mid-leap and ran back down them again, hot-footing it across the yard into the woods.

"Carl, you old son of a bitch, get your ragged ass out here," Cody yelled, because Carl was scaring him now. This was not like the old retired ex-cop.

It was not like him at all. A low howl rose from the back seat of Cody's vehicle, where Carl's black and tan hound, Rascal, had been confined for nearly an hour already. The dog had been found way over on the old White Oak Station Road, nobody with him, and calls to Carl to come down and get the animal hadn't been answered.

Which was also not like him. Cody mounted the steps, shading his eyes with his hands to peer into the screened enclosure. As he did so, memories from years past assailed him, from back when a much younger Cody Chevrier was the newest, greenest Aroostook County sheriff's deputy imaginable, and Carl was his boss.

Back then, by this time of the morning Carl's wife Audrey would've had her day's laundry out drying already, Carl's flannel shirts and tomato-red long johns flapping from a line strung on pulleys between the porch and the shed. She'd have had strong coffee burbling in a percolator and fresh-baked coffee cake laid out on a white paper doily, sweet smelling in the warm, bright kitchen.

Broiled brown-sugar topping on the coffee cake, she'd have had; Cody could almost taste it. But Audrey had been gone all of ten years now, and from the porch's far corner the old clothesline hung slack on bent wheels, a few blackened wooden clothespins still clipped to it.

Cody called through the screen, heard Carl's radio playing tinnily inside. No other sound, though. And Carl wouldn't ever have left his axe out that way.

Or his dog roaming. Rascal howled dismally again from the rear of the Blazer, the sound raising the hairs on Cody's neck. The breeze kicked up another notch, chilling his armpits inside his jacket and giving him gooseflesh.

Oh, he didn't like this. He didn't like it a bit.

With a feeling of deep reluctance, he pulled open the screen door and crossed the porch he and Carl had built together one fine autumn weekend all those years ago. Rascal's predecessor, Rowdy, was just a pup at the time, Cody recalled, the young dog nosing around and getting in their way, while inside, Audrey fried ham-and-egg sandwiches for lunch.

The eggs were from her own hens, the crisp homemade pickles preserved from cukes grown in her garden. She'd raised prize dahlias, too, back then, or was it roses? Cody couldn't recall.

No matter, though; once she died, Carl had quit mowing so much and let the raised beds and the cold frame go to ruin. Now in the screened porch a rickety wooden card table heaped with old copies of *Field & Stream* and *Sports Illustrated* stood beside a bent-ash rocker with a striped blanket for a cushion, a reading lamp with a blue plaid shade on a tripod stand, and a trash-bag-lined barrel half full of empty Budweiser cans.

No ashtray. Carl never smoked. He always said a

cop couldn't afford to mess up his sense of smell. From inside the trailer, Cody sniffed scorched baked beans and a rank whiff of something else.

"Oh, man," he said softly.

Carl Bogart's body lay sprawled on the linoleum just inside the double-wide's entry. Cody stepped over it into the familiar kitchen, then turned and crouched to feel for a pulse in his old friend's whiskery neck.

He'd known there wouldn't be one, though. Blood stained the cabinet fronts in the kitchen and a dark pool had begun drying under Carl's head near the weapon, a .45 revolver that Chevrier recognized, fallen by Carl's hand.

"Oh, buddy," Chevrier said sadly. "I'm so sorry."

Then he went back outside to call dispatch.

1

"This is not what I signed up for," Lizzie Snow said. "And you know it."

She gazed around in dismay at the small, dusty office whose plate-glass front window looked out at the remote northern town of Bearkill, Maine. The office walls were covered with fake wood paneling, the ceiling was stained 1960s-era acoustical tiles, and the ratty beige carpet was worn through to the backing in the traffic areas.

"You said I'd be . . ." The furnishings consisted of a beat-up metal desk, an office chair with one of its cheap plastic wheels missing, and a metal shelf rack of the kind used to store car parts in an auto supply store, plus one old phone book.

Not that sticking her in a *better* office would've helped. ". . . on patrol," she finished, trying to control her temper.

Squinting out across Main Street, she told herself that the town, at least, wasn't so bad. Two rows of small businesses and shops, a luncheonette, and a corner bar called Area 51 whose sign featured a big-eyed alien with a cocktail in its hand made up the downtown district. There was a laundromat, a flower shop, a supermarket, and an office supply place called The Paper Chase.

All were apparently doing business, though not exactly thriving; years ago in the post-WWII housing boom and for decades after, timber harvesting had supported this community and many others like it. But with the lumber industry sadly diminished, the area's agriculture—potatoes, oats, broccoli—couldn't take up the slack, and there wasn't much else here to work at.

Or so she'd read. Bearkill was one of many Maine towns she'd Googled before coming here, but this was her first visit.

Too bad it's not my last . . .

She supposed she should've liked the little town's air of brave defiance, stuck way out here in the woods with not even a movie theater or a Whole Foods, much less a museum or jazz club.

But dear God, there wasn't even a Starbucks, the only hair salon was called The Cut-n-Run, and if you could buy any makeup but Maybelline in this town, she'd eat her hat.

"Yeah, I know the job's not like I described," Aroostook County sheriff Cody Chevrier admitted.

Six-two and one-eighty or so with close-clipped silver hair and the perma-tanned skin of a guy who spent a lot of his time outdoors, summer and winter, Chevrier was in his late fifties but still trimly athletic looking in his tan uniform.

"Since you and I talked last, though, there've been a few developments."

"Yeah? Like what, a crime wave?" she asked skeptically. On the sixty-mile drive north up Route 1 from the Aroostook County seat of Houlton this morning, she'd seen little evidence of that.

Farms, forest land, widely spaced homes and small roadside businesses were the norm here, she'd seen after filling out the stacks of pre-employment paperwork Chevrier had put before her. Around the courthouse and the sheriff's office, men and women in business garb carried briefcases and drove late-model sedans, but once she'd left Houlton it was good old boys in gimme caps and women in pastel sweatshirts all the way. Nobody looked as if they had a whole lot to steal, or the inclination to steal anything, either.

"You might be surprised at what goes on in this area," said Chevrier.

"Uh-huh." She eyed him sideways. "Maybe."

And moonbeams might fly out of her ass the next time she passed gas, too. But she'd been a cop for a dozen years now, and she wasn't betting on it; crime-wise—*and otherwise,* she thought bleakly— this place was deader than Elvis.

"You said I'd be on the road," she reminded Chevrier again. "First with a partner, and then . . ."

According to the Aroostook County Sheriff's Department's website, there were 2,500 miles of public roadway in "the County" (locals always used the capital C), which spread across half of northern Maine. Eight thousand miles more of privately maintained roads belonged to major landowners, primarily lumber companies. In area the County was larger than Rhode Island and Connecticut combined; its 71,000-plus residents generated approximately 600 criminal complaints and 400 traffic incidents each quarter.

In addition, the sheriff's department served court orders and warrants, moved prisoners and psych patients, worked with the Maine DEA, the warden service, Border Patrol, and Homeland Security, and staffed a seventy-two-bed county jail; the transport detail alone logged 160,000 miles per year.

And none of it could afford to get screwed up just because she was a new deputy. She'd need an experienced partner for a while before working a patrol assignment on her own; that much she'd understood.

Eventually, though, she'd be out there solo: keeping her eyes and ears open, asking polite questions and maybe a few not-so-polite ones. Searching—

And sooner or later finding. If, that is, it turned out that there was really anything—any*one*—up here to find . . .

Out of the blue, Chevrier asked the question she'd seen on his face when he'd first met her in person the day before.

"So, you will pass the physical, right?"

The Aroostook County Sheriff's Department's mandatory pre-employment fitness test, he meant. Sit-ups, push-ups, a mile-and-a-half run . . . all required in order to finalize her hiring.

"Yeah," she replied, controlling her impatience. Back in Boston, where she'd been a homicide detective until a few weeks ago—*dear God, was it only that long?*—she'd done those things religiously at the police academy gym on Williams Avenue. Six days a week, sometimes seven . . .

Usually seven. It was among the joys of being a

woman cop: to the dirtbags—and to some of your coworkers, too, though they'd deny it—you were a pushover until proven otherwise. So there was no sense allowing for even the slightest chance of it being true; on a good day, she bench-pressed 220. She just didn't look like she could, or at any rate not at first glance.

Short, spiky black hair expertly cut, blood-red nails matching her lipstick, and smoky-dark eye makeup meticulously applied took care of that, as did her scent, which was Guerlain's Rose Barbare, and her high-heeled black boots rising to the tops of her tightly muscled calves, snug as a second skin.

She had no uniforms here yet, so today she wore black jeans, a white silk T-shirt and navy hoodie, and a butter-soft leather jacket. The look wasn't fancy, but perhaps partly as a result of all those gym hours it was effective; exiting Chevrier's vehicle, she'd attracted second glances from several of Bearkill's passing citizens, some even approving.

Some not so much. Hey, screw them. "I'll do just fine," she repeated evenly, "on the fitness tests."

"Okay," Chevrier replied. *If you say so,* his face added, but not as doubtfully this time; whether it was the confidence in her voice, a closer appraisal of her gym-toned form, or a combination of the two that convinced him, she didn't know.

Or care. "In that case, you're the new community liaison officer here in Bearkill," he said. "First one we've ever had."

Gesturing at the dingy room, "I'll set you up with account numbers for furniture and supplies, and we've got people on contract to get the place cleaned and painted for you," he added.

On the way here, he'd explained that her assignment had changed because a federal grant he'd been expecting to lose had come through after all. So he had funding for this new position.

But he hadn't described her duties, an omission she thought odd. Could it be he believed that being from a big city meant she already knew the usual activities and objectives of such a job? Or . . . was she supposed to invent them herself?

Her hiring had been fast-tracked, too: a mere two weeks between the time he'd learned that she was in the coastal Maine town of Eastport—her first stop after leaving Boston—and this morning's paperwork.

It was another thing she felt curious about: why he'd been so interested in her, and in her homicide experience especially. She made a mental note to ask him about all of it if he didn't volunteer the information soon, just as a husky teenager on an old balloon-tired Schwinn bike pedaled by the big front window.

Sporting a nose stud and a silvery lip ring and with his pale hair twisted into utterly improbable-looking dreadlocks, the kid wore faded jeans and a drab T-shirt and was tattooed on all visible parts of his body except his face.

Really? she thought in surprise. So apparently not every young male in Aroostook County was a good old boy; she wondered if Tattoo Kid here was a skilled fighter, or if he survived looking the way he did by trading something other than punches.

". . . department credit card for gas, but we do repairs back at the house," Chevrier was saying, meaning that vehicles were taken care of in Houlton, she thought, likely through a local car dealer's service department.

Which as news was not earthshaking, nor was the rest of the procedural stuff he was reciting. Lizzie slipped a hand into her jacket pocket and withdrew a creased photograph of a little girl who was about nine years old.

The child had straight, shoulder-length blond hair and blue eyes, and wore a red, white, and blue striped cape of some shiny material; she held a small banner that read HAPPY 4TH OF JULY!

I'm coming, honey, Lizzie thought at the photograph, worn from frequent handling. *I'll find you. And when I do . . .*

She tucked the picture away again. It was why she had left Boston, why she was here in Maine at all: an anonymous tip, her first hint in years that she had living family after all. But she still didn't know the end of that last sentence.

When I do . . . then what?

". . . get yourself a PO box right away so we can send you your paychecks," Chevrier was saying.

She wasn't even sure that the child in the photograph was the one she sought. Her younger sister Cecily's infant daughter, Nicolette, had gone missing from Eastport eight years earlier, right after Cecily's own mysterious death.

If she wasn't a sad little pile of bones in an unmarked grave somewhere, Nicki was Lizzie's only living kin, and after a long time of believing the child was dead there'd been other hints recently, too, that instead she was somewhere in northern Maine.

But Lizzie wasn't sure of that, either, and anyway, northern Maine was a big place. There was, she realized for the thousandth time, so much she didn't know.

I should have done more, started sooner.

I shouldn't have just let it go.

But she had; for one thing, she'd needed to earn a living, and there was no undoing any of it now. Tattoo Kid pedaled by the front windows a second time, his eyes meeting hers briefly and then looking quickly away again as Chevrier went on:

"I'll get a requisition going for your computer stuff, have a carpet crew come up from Bangor . . ."

She turned to him. "No."

His brow furrowed. "So . . . what, you mean you've decided that you don't want the spot?"

For a moment she was tempted; she'd have loved telling him to take his job and stick it. After all, who offered somebody one position, then waited until they showed up before informing them that it had turned into something entirely different? But . . .

"Oh, I'm taking it." She crossed to the desk, grabbed the phone book, and threw it into a corner. Who used a phone book anymore, either? "But only on two conditions. First . . ."

She aimed a finger at the front window. "You want me to build friendly relationships with the people here in Bearkill? I mean, that's what a liaison officer does, right?"

She had the funniest feeling that Chevrier might not know quite what one of those did, himself. But never mind:

"There's only one way I can quick-start relationships with these folks—"

At the far end of the downtown block, the office supply store was somehow still alive, while at the other end a run-down gas station survived, as did the tiny convenience store attached.

"—and that's for me to buy stuff from them."

Which was also true in Boston, and anywhere else there were cops: coffee and a lottery ticket at the bodega, an apple at the fruit stand, sandwiches at the luncheonette—you bought a little of this or that anywhere you thought you might get the chance to talk to people, hear things.

"Supplies, cleaning, painting, new tires for the squad car whether it needs 'em or not," she went on. "All of it has to get done locally. And as for computer equipment?"

She turned to face him. "Look, Sheriff, I've got my own reasons for wanting the job you're trying to foist on me, okay? So I'm not walking away even though you know damned well you absolutely deserve it."

He shrugged again, acknowledging this. "But," she went on, "as far as computers and printer paper and everything else this place needs?"

She waved a hand around the bleak little storefront. "Either that office supply joint down the street is about to hit a big payday, *and* my car gets serviced here in town, or you can forget you met me."

She expected pushback about the car, at least; regulations, routine. But instead he kept nodding at her demands, which among other things gave her an even stronger sense of how very much he wanted her here.

Curiouser and curiouser. "Okay," he said. "That

makes sense. Do it however you want. You'll need purchase orders, but . . ."

"Not so fast. You haven't heard the other condition."

Chevrier looked wary—"What's that?"—as the tattooed kid on the bike rolled by yet a third time.

Briskly she zipped her jacket, settled her black leather satchel on her shoulder, and pulled the creaky front door open, waving him out ahead of her.

"Come on," she told him.

The kid with the piercings, body art, and blond dreadlocks was now halfway down the street, looking back at them. She yanked the balky door shut, then jiggled the key in the lock until the tumblers fell sluggishly.

"I'm hungry. We'll talk over lunch. You're buying."

There he is! Sighing in relief, Margaret Brantwell hurried down the canned goods aisle of the Food King in Bearkill. She'd looked away for only a moment, she was certain, and when she looked back her year-old grandson's stroller wasn't where she'd left it, parked by the frozen foods case.

Oh, if Missy knew that I'd lost track of him even for an instant, she'd—

Well, she wouldn't let Margaret take care of him anymore if that happened. But Margaret adored her daughter's baby boy, she'd be desolate if she couldn't—

"Mrs. Brantwell?" The store manager stood by the stroller. A clerk was there, too, looking worried. Both frowned accusingly at Margaret.

"Mrs. Brantwell, we were just about to call the police. The baby's been here all alone for ten minutes, we didn't know—"

"Ten minutes?" Margaret glanced around. Everyone was looking at her. And the baby was crying; she crouched hurriedly by him.

"Oh, no, I've been right here, I was—"

But then she stopped as it hit her with a horrible internal lurch that she didn't remember where she'd been, didn't recall the moment when she'd walked away from the baby in his stroller.

That she didn't know how long she'd been gone. Defensively she grabbed up the baby, cradling him against her chest.

"I was just down the aisle, I can't imagine how you missed seeing me. You must not have been trying very hard."

There, turn it around on them, see how *they* liked it. Poor little Jeffrey wailed fiercely, his face squinched and reddened.

"There, there," she soothed him. "Did all these strangers scare you, baby? There, it's okay, Grandma's got you now."

A red-aproned clerk hurried up pushing a grocery cart. "Oh, Mrs. Brantwell, there you are, you left your—"

Margaret drew back. "*That's* not mine!" She hugged Jeffrey closer. His cries grew louder. She felt like crying now, too, surrounded by these unpleasant strangers all trying to tell her things that weren't true.

The items in the cart—milk, lettuce, coffee beans—*might* be hers. But where did that huge chocolate bar come from, and the cheap wine? And the jug of motor oil wasn't even from this store.

They were trying to trick her, that's what it was. But it wouldn't work, because she was too smart for them. *Can't pull one over on Margaret,* her father used to say, and it was still . . .

Grabbing the stroller's handle, she whirled and stalked away from them, all the foolish people with the unfriendly looks on their faces. Outside the store, she carried Jeffrey to the car and put him in his car seat, buckling him in carefully the way she had promised Missy she would always do.

Then she settled behind the wheel and sat there for a moment to gather her thoughts, get over the awful fright she'd had.

There, that's better, she thought as her heart slowed. Even Jeffrey calmed down, sucking energetically on his pacifier, his sweet little face relaxing, so cute in his blue knitted hat.

She'd made him that hat. If she could find where she'd put the yarn, she might make mittens. Meanwhile . . .

She looked around at the busy parking lot outside the Food King, people bustling back and forth with their carts in the cold November sunshine. It was a lovely day.

Just lovely, and the drive down here to the store had been so easy and uneventful, she didn't even remember it.

She turned to the baby. "Jeffrey, we're here! We're at the store, and now we're going to go in. Are you ready?"

He grinned, waving his pacifier in his chubby fist. She got out and found his stroller waiting by the passenger-side door as if someone had put it there for her. She looked around mystified, then decided that it was too nice a day to worry about it.

Blue sky, crisp air . . . now, what exactly had she come to the store for, again? She'd made a list but she must have left it at home. She was always doing that. *Silly. Getting so forgetful.*

"Never mind," she told Jeffrey as she pushed him across the parking lot in the stroller. Such a beautiful baby, she simply adored him, and felt so grateful that Missy allowed her to take care of him the way she did. *My grandson . . .*

At the entrance she slowed uncertainly; the store looked so unfamiliar all of a sudden. But how could it? She'd been here—*surely she had*—a thousand times before. Only—

"Never mind," she repeated, as much for herself this time as for the baby. "We'll figure it all out when we get inside."

It was the biggest slab of meat loaf Lizzie had ever seen, flanked by a mound of gravy-drenched mashed potatoes the size of a softball and a fluted paper cup of celery-seed-flecked coleslaw, the shredded orange carrot and purple cabbage drenched in enough dressing to float a barge.

"What's so funny?" she demanded at Chevrier's smile when the waitress delivered their food. He'd ordered a chef's salad, which was also enormous but not quite as artery-clogging as her own meal.

"You ever heard the old saying 'Never eat anything bigger than your head'?" he replied with a chuckle.

Lizzie dug in. She hadn't eaten since the night before, and the meat loaf was as delicious as it looked. "You ever heard the old saying 'Don't criticize what other people are eating'?"

He nodded, chewing. "Good one."

The Coca-Cola was so cold that it made her head hurt, and the gravy on the potatoes hadn't come out of a jar or a can. They ate in silence for a few minutes.

"So," he said around a mouthful of dinner roll.

Driving out of Bearkill, he'd sped them down a rural highway between fenced fields green with what he said was winter wheat. Huge outbuildings dug into the sides of hills were, he informed her, for potato storage; yards full of machinery, from familiar-looking tractors to massive contraptions resembling some science-fiction variety of praying mantis, flanked pretty, old-fashioned farmhouses whose long, low ells linked them to massive, gambrel-roofed barns.

"That way, Farmer John doesn't have to go outside so much in winter, when he needs to do chores," Chevrier had explained about the house-barn connections.

"In the blizzards we get here, you could get lost ten feet off the porch," he'd added, while she'd stared out the car window at a little girl in denim overalls riding a bike in a farmyard driveway, pigtails flying.

It wasn't Nicki, of course. For one thing, the pigtails were red. And the child looked a bit too old, maybe ten or eleven. *But what if it was her?* she'd thought. *Would you take her away from . . .*

But it wasn't, she told herself again now. "Which reminds me," said Chevrier, "you got any survival gear? Winter stuff or wilderness stuff? Or to have in your vehicle?"

In Boston she'd thought of the wilderness as anything past Route 128; at her headshake he went on:

"Okay, got some items kicking around at home, I'll bring 'em in for you. Flares, emergency blanket . . ."

He shrugged. "Can't be too careful." Then: "Anyway, I guess you think I've got some explaining to do."

That, of course, had been the other condition: that he level with her.

"Yeah," she agreed, eating another forkful of coleslaw. The cabbage was peppery-fresh, the sweet dressing full of celery seed so delicious she was tempted to sip the remaining puddles with a spoon. "You could put it that way."

Coming into the restaurant, he'd been greeted by everyone they passed, and when he stopped at booths and tables to chat, he knew their names, and their kids' and grandkids' names. In Maine, she recalled, county sheriffs were elected officials.

"The thing is," he went on, washing the last bit of roll down with a sip of coffee. "The thing is, I've got ex-cops dying on me. When they shouldn't be. And I've got questions about it."

He'd chosen a booth farthest from the rest of the room, a noisy spot near the cash register. She stopped chewing.

"Really." In her experience, when somebody started talking like this, you just tried not to get in the way.

You just let them know you were listening. Chevrier took a slow, casual look around the room to make sure no one else was, then went on.

"Yeah. Last year or so, four of 'em. All on the up-and-up, says the medical examiner."

"But you don't think so." Obviously, or he wouldn't be talking to her about it. "So they were all unwitnessed deaths?"

Because otherwise the medical examiner probably wouldn't have been called at all. Chevrier nodded, speared half a hard-boiled egg, and ate it.

"First one, Dillard Sprague, last December," he recited. "He was a boozer, lost his job with the Buckthorn PD over it a few months before."

He washed the egg down with some coffee. "Supposedly he slipped on an icy step coming out of his back door, late. Got knocked out, lay there and froze to death. His wife Althea found him when she got home the next morning from her night shift at the hospital."

Lizzie winced. "Not a fun discovery, huh? But if that's all there was, couldn't it have been accidental, just the way it seemed?"

Chevrier looked sour. "Right. Could've. If he was the only one. Next guy, Cliff Arbogast, a few months later. He lives right up next to the Canadian border, got let go off the Caribou force when it turned out he'd been running the family car with his department gas card."

He ate more salad. "Which," he went on around it, "wouldn't have been so bad, but his wife was an Avon lady, drove all over taking orders and making deliveries."

Lizzie loaded mashed potatoes and gravy onto her fork. From outside, Grammy's Restaurant had looked like any other roadside joint: red and white sign, aluminum siding, twenty feet of gravel parking lot separating it from the highway it sat beside.

Inside, though, it was clean as a whistle and smelled like a place where somebody really knew how to cook.

Which somebody did. She ate some more meat loaf. Then: "What happened?" she asked. "To the Avon lady's ex-cop husband?"

Chevrier dragged a chunk of iceberg lettuce through a dollop of Russian dressing and chomped it. "Electrocuted."

"Excuse me?" She'd heard him, all right. But modern building codes and wiring regulations made such accidents rare. The only fatal power mishap she'd ever seen, in fact, wasn't a household event at all.

It was after a big storm, back when she was a rookie street patrol cop on the Boston PD: downed trees, live wires, standing water. Add a bunch of pain-in-the-butt looky-loos out gawking at the damage and presto, one dead civilian.

But cops knew better. Some she'd worked with wouldn't go near a live-wire situation until the power company was on scene.

Chevrier seemed skeptical, too. "Yeah. Spring evening, Cliff's taking a bath, listening to the Red Sox on the radio," he said.

"Radio's on the sink, it's plugged into the outlet by the mirror, you know? So he reached for his razor and shaving cream and somehow he knocked the radio into the tub with him."

He grimaced. "Or that's how the story goes," he added.

"Huh." She ate the last bite of her mashed potato,

drank some Coke, meanwhile trying to picture all this. Just pulling a radio into the tub with you was a pretty good trick, and . . .

"Breaker didn't trip?"

Because even though it was not a good idea, in a properly wired house you ought to be able to float a radio in the bathtub like a rubber duckie, the power cutting off microseconds after the overload hit the circuit breaker.

You wouldn't like it much, but you wouldn't necessarily die, either. Chevrier looked across the room to where a big man in a denim barn coat and rubber boots was just getting up from his table.

"Place didn't have circuit breakers," Chevrier said while watching the man approach.

"Old house, still had fuses. One of 'em had burned out some time earlier—he'd stuck a bent nail in there."

He sighed, remembering. "So the wires melted, started a fire, and that's how it got called in, originally. Dwelling fire."

"I see. So that makes two of them so far? Sprague, Clifford Arbogast . . ."

"Yeah, and two more. Michael Fontine, ex–state cop, he lived way over by the border crossing in Van Buren. And . . ."

But just then the big man in the barn coat arrived at their booth. "Hey, Cody."

The new arrival had ruddy cheeks, thinning blond hair, and a linebacker's meaty build. Twenty or thirty pounds more than he needed packed his tall, powerful frame, but on him it didn't look too bad, maybe because it was distributed evenly instead of all hanging around his waist.

Or maybe it was because he had the brightest, bluest, and possibly the smartest-looking eyes she'd ever seen, pleasantly crinkled at the corners.

"And whom do we have here?" The little ironic stress he put on *whom* was just audible enough to be charming.

She stuck out her hand. "Lizzie Snow." With a nod across the table, she added, "I'm Sheriff Chevrier's newest deputy."